# MOTET

Also by Keith Maillard:

*Two Strand River*
*Alex Driving South*
*The Knife in My Hands*
*Cutting Through*

# MOTET

KEITH MAILLARD

Random House
*Toronto*

Published in Canada in 1989 by Random House of Canada Limited.


**Canadian Cataloguing in Publication Data**
Maillard, Keith, 1942-
    Motet

ISBN 0-394-22028-5 (HC)
I. Title.

PS8576.A34M67 1988   C813'.54   C88-093363-1
PR9199.3.M32M67   1988




Jacket Design: Brant Cowie/ArtPlus
Jacket Illustration: Ken Suzana
Author Photograph: Sara Woodwark




Printed and bound in Canada by
T.H. Best Printing Company Ltd.

...Since it [the motet] underwent numerous changes during the more than five centuries of its existence..., it is impossible to formulate a general definition that covers all the phases of its development. As a rule, a motet is an unaccompanied choral composition based on a Latin sacred text and designed to be performed in the Roman Catholic service, chiefly at Vespers.

— *Harvard Dictionary of Music*

...If we survey the centuries, we find that a motet may have one text, or two or more simultaneously sung texts; the words may be in Latin or in a vernacular tongue, or two different languages may be sung at the same time...

— Gustave Reese, *Music in the Renaissance*

# Acknowledgements and notes

I would like to thank the Canada Council and the Ontario Arts Council who assisted me while I was writing early drafts of this book.

Short selections from this book first appeared, in a somewhat different form, in: *The New Quarterly*; Volume V, Number 1; Kenyon, Linda, ed.; Spring, 1985; Waterloo, Ontario, Canada. *Vancouver Fiction*; Watmough, David, ed.; Polestar Press, Winlaw, B.C., 1985. *Magic Realism and Canadian Literature: Essays and Stories, Proceedings of the Conference on Magic Realist Writing in Canada, University of Waterloo/ Wilfred Laurier University, May, 1985*; Hinchcliffe, Peter and Ed Jewinski, eds.; University of Waterloo Press; Waterloo, Ontario, Canada, 1986.

Except for musicologists, musicians, and historical figures mentioned in passing, all the characters in this book are purely fictitious.

Of the real people mentioned, the foremost is the great German musicologist, Edward E. Lowinsky, who discovered the secret chromaticism and published his findings in *Secret Chromatic Art in the Netherlands Motet* (Columbia University Press, New York, 1946). As a novelist, I was attracted to the secret chromaticism on the level of metaphor; the musicological stratum of this novel was inspired by the beauty, complexity, and daring of Lowinsky's pioneering work.

In Chapter 2, Paul gives Kathy a good general introduction to Lowinsky and his work, and I need add little here other than to say that, after the initial storm of controversy died down, his theories have been gradually accepted by his colleagues. Paul's reading of the (fictitious) van Dorestad motet in Chapter 1 is, of course, suggested by Lowinsky's reading of secret chromatic material. Van der Geest's arguments in Chapter 5 that van Dorestad was an Anabaptist were suggested by arguments used by Lowinsky. The line Paul finds in Chapter 1 — *Dat woordt Gotz is al duyster ende onbegrypeliijk even als God selve isz.* —

is from the Dutch mystic Henrick Rol and is quoted by Low-insky.

The linking of the secret chromaticism through Bosch back to the Adamite tradition, based as it is upon no historical evidence whatsoever, exists only in Paul's (and my) fantasy.

The careers and martyrdom of Jan and Michael van Dorestad and "Katrei the Silent" are fictitious. Details of their trial and death, however, have been borrowed from genuine accounts of the period, particularly from the deaths of Mantz, Sattler, Hubmaier, and Hutter. I cannot emphasize too strongly that this book is fiction (something made) not fact (something found); I have freely borrowed, paraphrased, and altered doctrines, myths and texts to suit the story.

Whatever inaccuracies, errors, and solecisms occur are un-doubtedly mine, but what is accurate — *im echten Stil* — can undoubtedly be attributed to the considerable guidance and advice I received. It would require several pages to list everyone who contributed to this book, so let me simply say, "thank you." There are those, however, whose contributions were so large that I must mention them. Gordon Callon helped me plan the musicological underlay; Susie Napper and Carlo Novi patiently answered all my questions about playing Baroque music (Susie, with Bruce Haines, also graciously hosted me in the Nether-lands, and Carlo assisted me with German matters); Geordie McDonald and Glen Hendrickson told me about drummers and drumming; Joan Robertson showed me where Paul grew up. I hope that my experience of *playing* music shows in the text; if it does, it wouldn't be there without Ferron and Steve Nikleva, the group at Rose's, my old recorder pals, and every other musician who has ever put up with me pretending that I was a musician too.

Bob Harlow, Bonnelle Strickling, and Felicia Eth read early drafts and offered invaluable comment. Rick Archbold sent me the best rejection letter I've ever received. Ed Carson heard me read from the first draft, came up to me afterward and said he wanted to publish *Motet*; he's helped me out a dozen times in a dozen ways since, has stuck with the book (and me) through thick and thin, and now finally *is* publishing it. Judi Saltman shared this work with me for more than ten years; whenever I needed an opinion I could believe, or simply a belief in the work, she was always there. Joyce Frazee was the right person at the right time. And, finally, without the love I shared with the dear hearts who lived with me while I wrote this book, I might well not have finished it.

*Perfectum non alteratur, sed corrumpitur. Sed imperfectum bene alteratur, ergo curruptio unius est generatio alterius.*

K. M.
Vancouver
October, 1988

... tibi
non ante verso lene merum cado
jamdudum apud me est; eripe te morae.

I

"When the bass descends by stepwise motion," Paul said, beginning the ancient ritual formula he'd been repeating for years in music theory classes.

"All other parts must rise," the boy said dutifully, finishing the sentence. His eyes met Paul's a moment, then skittered away; his face contracted into worried lines as though he were trying to illustrate, by mugging the effort, just how difficult all this was for him.

Paul forced a tone of avuncular good humour into his voice: "Right you are." With red pen slashes, he marked the parallel fifths in the boy's work.

"Doctor Crane, I just can't take a P in theory. I just can't afford that."

"Stop worrying about the grade. Hand in all the assignments, and you've got a C." The boy's face broke into a smile of relief; this, after all, was what he had come for, not for any help with his homework.

Paul watched the boy recede down the long, beige hall that always looked to him like a line drawing from the early Renaissance when perspective had just been discovered. No matter how many colourful posters he and his colleagues pinned to the walls, nothing could disguise the fact that the hallway was designed to be nothing more than two straight lines stretching away to the distant vanishing point of the stairwell. He'd liked the old music building better; it had been wooden, live enough for the quietest chamber music, full of Victorian curlicues, thoroughly in bad taste, but warm and human as a concerto by some deservedly minor eighteenth-century composer. Now the department was stuck up here in this modern concrete erection, this wretchedly contemporary Tower of Babel.

Paul did not appreciate all this passion for change, all this striving for efficiency, for the modern. Even the students had changed over the years. They'd lost their sense of humour; one could no longer tease them. These days they scurried through university with obsessive spectres of grades and requirements floating about their ears like clouds of fat and unpleasant pink *putti*.

And they were calling him *doctor* now. Only he and Hanna Rossenmüller who was German and seventy years old got called doctor, and what had he ever done to deserve that? Perhaps one could tell them, "Take two aspirin and see me in the morning." But no, they wouldn't get the joke; they'd just smile obligingly and continue to pile up outside his office with their theory assignments in their hands. He might as well *be* a medical doctor; he felt just as much on call. He knew what they called him among themselves. (He'd walked quietly into 507 through the rear door and heard them.) They called him *the* doctor. That was worse; that was positively mediaeval, made him sound like some Faustian cleric, *Doctor Mirabilis et Diabolis.*

Here, approaching from the vanishing point, was the departmental secretary. Was she looking for him? She most certainly was. "Excuse me, Doctor Crane." She was bearing a thick file folder in her hand. Oh, Jesus, what now? "I've finally got your microfilm Xeroxes."

What microfilm Xeroxes? He took the folder, opened it, and read: *Bibliotheek der Vereeniging voor Nederlandshe Muziekgeschiedenis.* Oh, that's right, the van Dorestad motet. He'd completely forgotten about it.

"Your wife called. Twice."

"If she calls again, tell her I've gone home... No, don't do that. I'll call back."

"And Mark Perry called. He said he'd stop by your office."

That does it, Paul thought. Perry will want to sit and chat for hours. "Please take my calls. I'll see Perry, but for the rest of the world, I'm not here."

She nodded and walked away. The motion of her gentle green skirt from behind was nearly enough to break one's heart. Oh, ridiculous, he thought, ridiculous and predictable. One's wife leaves in the summer, and by fall the departmental secretary has begun to assume all the virtues of womanhood, become a veritable subject for a courtly motet: *Trop plus est belle que biauté.* All right, Doctor Crane, he told himself, and *you* are being ridiculous. If you don't watch yourself, you will become a silly old man chasing women who are too young for you — secretaries and graduate students — all over the campus. You are, as either of your daughters would have put it, freaking out.

From 507, he heard the muffled sound of a string ensemble. Hanna Rossenmüller had somehow managed to get them in tune, which was more than he'd ever done. It had begun to rain, was beating against the windows in his office behind him. The sound of rain and distant strings — he felt suddenly vacated and empty. Like a mediaeval cadence, just as bare, just as resonant.

Paul closed himself away behind his office door, stuffed his pipe with the good Dutch tobacco he'd brought back from Amsterdam; it was the last tin of it. From his vantage point in his severe tower of music, he could look out across the rain-swept campus. Never before had he found himself staring out his office window at the passing girls.

It had been stupidly easy to manage sixteen years of marriage without having been, even once, unfaithful to Evelyn; now he wouldn't know how to go about having an affair if he wanted one, and he didn't approve of professors who had affairs. (And this, he saw, was a perfect day for indulging in such Wagnerian emotions: sky clumped up into dark, threatening knots — timpani and horns. A girl surely not more than a few years older than his daughter Wendy was racing across the parking lot for her car; in her curiously graceful blue jeans, she looked lithe as a wind-blown willow branch. And if one should desire an affair, should desire it — absurdity of absurdities — with the departmental secretary, just what could one say? "Would you care to have dinner with me? Could I drive you home?" It was unthinkable.) It hadn't come as any great shock when Evelyn had moved out the week after they'd returned from Europe. The shock had been that she'd taken both Cindy and Wendy with her.

"The pattern is broken." Those words appeared suddenly from nowhere in his mind. He pondered them. What on earth was he thinking about? Of course it disrupts everything when one's wife and daughters move out of the house one has bought for them (*is buying*, he corrected himself, with a mortgage as big as the Colossus at Rhodes). It's disturbing; yes, of course it is. But there seemed to be more to it than that. Always before he'd felt as though he were writing his life like Palestrina counterpoint. He'd written the first notes in his teens, and those choices had conditioned everything that had come after, strictly and severely. Now the long, flowing lines were broken (that must be what it had meant); inside him was where it had stopped making sense. The university went on, his students went on, the Vancouver Pro Musica (of which he was, at least nominally, the musical director) went on. But he suspected that he could just as easily be doing anything else, and *that* was a totally new thought. It could be his age, that he'd climbed over the hill of the middle of his life and was now on his way down the far side. But still — something more. Goddamn it, he told himself, if one is feeling something new, one has to have enough time to know what it is one is feeling. He didn't have any time at all.

The window opened exactly two inches. It wasn't worth the effort; there was no way he could get close to the weather. He returned to his desk, sat down, put fire to his pipe. Written out on his memo pad was the list of things he had to get done. It now covered two pages. He picked up the pad deliberately and turned it face down. He blew a cloud of blue pipe smoke and watched it rise until it was caught by the air-conditioning and drawn away. The file folder with the van Dorestad motet was lying directly in front of him. He opened it, saw the imprint of the National Musicological Library in Amsterdam.

It had been Evelyn's idea to go to Europe last spring as soon as school was out. "All right, Paul," she'd said, "it's been years since we've taken a holiday, all of us together. *You've* always been too busy. Well, this summer you'd better get yourself *unbusy* for a change, because if things go on like this, there isn't going to be any of our marriage left to salvage."

The moment the four of them had stepped off the plane into the gleaming, plastic, and depressingly modern Schiphol airport, they had divided into two camps that, if they had not exactly been at war, had at least been suffering a strained and profoundly uneasy peace. Evelyn and Cindy had drawn together into a mother-and-daughter team, boisterous, exuberant, and out for a good time in the most boorish tourist tradition, zipping about Amsterdam on rented bicycles, chugging along the ring canals in those hideous tourist boats with their crackling metallic speakers that pointed out the sights in half a dozen languages. But he and Wendy seemed to have been caught up in an identical mood of sadness and introspection (perhaps they'd both known full well that it was the last time they would all be together as one family), had walked for miles in the old districts, not saying much, hurting their feet on the cobblestones. It seemed appropriate that Evelyn and Cindy had preferred Italy, he and Wendy the Low Countries. They'd followed the route of the Netherlandish composers (as he'd carefully explained to Wendy, if not to his wife) from the rainy north down into the dazzling sun of the south; the movement had been from the High Renaissance to the Baroque. In Rome, he and Evelyn had staged that series of *Opera Buffa* scenes that had culminated in their mutual decision to separate as soon as they got back to Canada.

By now (only three months later), that Italian drama had receded into a flat, bloodless memory as though it had been a movie Paul had seen — great wordy speeches and arioso posturings filmed with Roman pigeons and priests as a backdrop, starring actors who looked remarkably like himself and his wife. But the ambience of Holland had not faded, was still as pungently real for him as the Dutch tobacco he was smoking.

Wendy had taken a morning-long gamba lesson with Klaas Achterberg in his home a few miles outside Amsterdam; the land there had been flatter than even the most fervent expectation of flatness would have allowed for, flat as if it had been planed down to the rigid standard of a spirit-level. And it had been cultivated to the last inch (flowers everywhere); overhead, that enormous, lowering sky had been like the Jan van Goyen paintings they'd just seen in the Rijksmuseum. "I love the way it feels here," Wendy had said. "You can tell that the people really care about things, about their gardens and houses... I could live here. I could even learn Dutch. It sounds all round and friendly and funny. Do you suppose it's ever possible to say anything nasty in Dutch?" Even with her hair in braids and wearing one of her pleated grey school skirts with knee socks, she'd seemed nearly adult to him then; he'd forgotten that she was only fifteen.

Back in town, Wendy had asked to see the red-light district, and he hadn't been able to think of any reason she shouldn't be allowed to (except for Evelyn, and they hadn't bothered to tell her). The prostitutes had been arranged on display in the windows of their houses; many had been exotic to say the least, painted butterflies in provocative lingerie, but others had looked like matronly housewives resting in their armchairs for a quiet evening at home, some even knitting. Wendy had taken it all in stride, except for the empty windows. No, she'd said, it hadn't been the fact that the woman had gone inside with a man that had bothered her; it had been something else; she hadn't been able to explain it. "There's the chair where she was sitting... and it's empty. Don't you see how sad it is... how sad and mysterious?" Wendy, too, had seemed sad and mysterious; she'd had tears in her eyes. They'd walked back to the safer streets and sat outside at a corner cafe; he'd drunk beer and she chocolate. He hadn't felt like a father with his daughter, certainly not like an older man with a young sweetheart, either, but, in retrospect, those few days in Amsterdam had acquired all the keen, intense nostalgia of a sweet, brief, and unconsummated love affair.

He didn't believe in the Freudian view of the world. It might be easier, he thought, if he did; then he'd have a safe and conventional formula to explain the convoluted emotions he felt toward his elder daughter. They'd become too close in Amsterdam; he'd felt it happening and done nothing to stop it. By the time they'd reached Florence, something had gone noticeably wrong between them, and under the summer sun in Rome, Wendy had pulled back into herself, become a remote, childish, ill-tempered stranger. Now, back in Vancouver, she seemed to have retreated even further, had become completely inaccessible behind a formal, daughterly mask.

He had been smoking and staring down at the van Dorestad motet without seeing it. The neat stack of Xerox paper resonated with the bitter-sweet memory of Amsterdam and drew him toward the work of transcribing the notes into modern notation. But there was no possible way he could allow himself the time for that until next summer, no way at all. But damn it, one had to leave something for oneself out of all this rat-like, maze-running activity. One could at least spare an hour to form some impression of the work.

Even twice removed from the original, the Xerox was beautifully clear, nearly as dense and black as the Kuiper Manuscript must have been. It was a delight just to see that crabbed and stylized High Renaissance script laid out on one's desk. It looked just the way Professor van der Geest had described it: the notes careful and precise, lovingly hand-written. Van der Geest had guessed it to be a student's copy. Well, if that were the case, then they must have produced better students in the sixteenth century than one was getting these days. Paul turned the pages, spread them out in front of him. The motet was a long work for six voices, one flat in the signature of the upper four parts, two flats in the lower two — nothing unusual about that. It began in the Lydian mode. He puzzled out the Latin underlay. *"Tunc Jesus ductus est in desertum a Spiritu, ut rentarentur a diabolo..."* That was interesting. Christ's temptation by the devil. *"Iterum assumpsit eum diabolus in montem excelsum valde; et ostendit ei omnia regna mundi, et gloriam eorum..."* Which should translate something like, "And again the devil took him up onto a very high mountain and showed him all the kingdoms of the world and the glories of them." Oh, he thought, this is going to be great fun. He knew suddenly that he was going to transcribe the motet over the next few days, and everything else could just go hang.

Ah, what was this? A whole cluster of flats. What were they doing? Every single one of them was obvious, either in the key signature or clearly required by the rules of *ficta*. He followed the lines onto the next page. Right, so this had to be an E flat. He wrote the flat in lightly with a lead pencil over the note. But then an A flat was required to avoid the tritone. He skimmed quickly along the notes. And the A flat would require a D flat over here, so that couldn't be right. He backtracked to the E. It had to be read as E natural: cross-relation of E flat major to C major, a perfectly acceptable interpretation. But wait a minute; what would happen if he did read it as flat? He looked ahead again. The D would would probably require — yes, here it was, right over here — a G flat. Of course; the flat syndrome had begun. The thing was going around the cycle of fifths. It was modulating! A thrill vivid as an electric charge passed through his entire body. He had to stand up.

And Paul was lost in a most peculiar illusion: every object in his office seemed to be glowing with a preternatural brilliance. It was as though he were being bathed in dazzling white light. He stepped to the window to see if the sun had suddenly come out from behind the dense clouds and saw at once that the sky was still grey, overcast, and raining. He turned back. The light was not coming through the window at all; it was so bright now that he could scarcely see. He couldn't trust himself to stand; the floor under his feet seemed to be floating. He sank into the leather chair he kept for visitors. He was afraid that he was going to faint. He closed his eyes, forced himself to breathe deeply, bent forward to lower his head to the level of his knees. Later, when he would try to remember what had happened, all he would be able to say about it would be: "I suppose I must have blacked out for a few seconds."

Paul had somehow managed to relight his pipe. He stopped in the middle of the carpeted floor and tried to shake off this strange experience bodily, like a dog shaking off water. He was actually shivering with excitement. He found that he had been pacing back and forth across the small space of his office; the memory of walking was left behind like a drifting bit of an elusive melody. He had no idea how much time had passed.

Gradually the colours in the room were falling back into their original tones; he became aware again of the sound of rain on the window. That will teach you to miss lunch, he told himself. One works too hard, doesn't get enough sleep, and then doesn't eat. Low blood sugar. And, of course, one doesn't find something as monumental as this little gem lying casually on one's desk every day of the week. He spread the pages of the Xerox out in front of him, turned each carefully. And he saw that at the very end of the motet someone had scrawled a line of Dutch onto the original. The words were very faint; he could barely make them out. *"Dat woordt Gotz is al duyster ende onbegrypeliijk even als God selve isz."*

Kathy had stopped walking. It was not something she'd consciously planned to do, but for the last few blocks she'd felt her body slowing down, her boot heels dragging reluctantly on the sidewalk, and now — here at the corner where she would have to turn down to the school — she'd apparently been brought to a complete standstill. Below her, in the parking lot at the bottom of the hill, her students were clustered. Even at the distance of three blocks, Kathy could see the gleam of Wendy Crane's impossibly blond hair. The prissy little bitch was, as usual, standing off to one side not talking to anyone. And Kathy still couldn't shake off the weight of the nightmare that had damned near strangled her at dawn. Wendy Crane had starred in it.

Kathy had never learned to feel at home in Vancouver, but after seven years she did know what to expect. Every fall the insistent rain would gradually return until a familiar nostalgic aquarium haze would take over everything and blot out the sky. Her basement apartment would turn dank and bleak; in the evenings the walls would sweat and the windows steam up. By mid-January she'd have her winter cough again, but it wouldn't stop her from smoking. She'd get out her Selmer, hold it carefully between her hands as though it were the relic of a saint, but, as usual, she wouldn't be able to blow a note on it. She'd sit wrapped up in bed night after night, going through all the rituals that kept her from having asthma — breathing slowly, not thinking about anything serious, rationing her cigarettes, listening to jazz on Co-op Radio. And drinking Southern Comfort because it reminded her of Steve. He'd drunk it by the tumblerful, on ice, had always called it "Sudden Discomfort," and had never bought a bottle without saying, "If it's good enough to fuck up Janis, it's good enough to fuck up me."

Kathy gave up. She turned away from the school, walked on up the hill and into the small park. It was overgrown with immense trees — thick, hoary trunks and deeply green smears trailing down — an effect like walking into a period movie. Hundreds of tiny black birds were chattering madly to each other; they exploded into flight as Kathy approached.

She lowered herself into one of the swings in the miniature playground and began to roll a cigarette. The birds resettled themselves around her. They hopped stiffly and complained. In her mind a dry, bitter voice, sang, "I thought I heard Buddy Bolden say, 'You nasty buncha dirty, take it away. You're terrible. You're awful. Take it away. And let Mister Bolden play.'"

And then it came back to her unexpectedly — that somber, bleak, and *satisfying* detachment. It was the way she'd felt as a teenager when she'd wandered alone around Harvard Square or walked the streets of Boston, in the rain, wearing boots and black leather pants, pretending she was a boy — or at least that she was as cold, aloof, self-controlled, and savage as a boy — but what she'd wanted, or thought she'd wanted, had been a companion, a real boy to be as cold, aloof, self-controlled, and savage as she, to be her lover and sweep away the prim curtain that seemed to hang over her, deadening her, that she blamed for everything. "You're awful. You're terrible. Take it away." The voice was no longer Jelly Roll Morton's. It was Steve's. *You bastard*, she addressed her absent husband, *you lame son of a bitch, you left me nothing. And that's exactly what I deserve for thinking that a man could be the solution to anything.*

The nightmare had arrived at dawn and sat on her just like the one in the Fuselli print Steve used to have tacked to their wall in Boston. When she'd fought clear, she'd found herself already out of bed reaching for the Ventolin, her lungs wheezing like old bellows. Then she'd run out into the back lane where the cold sky looked heartbreaking behind the crisscrossed power lines. She'd paced, slowly, a step at a time, welcoming the bite of the gravel under her bare feet. She'd found herself praying like a terrified child, "Oh, please. I'll stop smoking. I really will this time. I'll do anything. But please, dear God, just let me breathe."

In the dream Kathy has a seat at ringside. She knows she doesn't belong there. She's dressed wrong — in spike heels, evening gloves, and a tight, black sheath dress; she's holding a patent-leather purse on her lap. She's painfully embarrassed.

She looks around and sees that she's the only woman in a roped-off section full of men. They have press cards stuck into the bands of their Humphrey Bogart hats. They're all banging away on antique typewriters held on their laps. Maybe she's a reporter too. She looks inside her purse and finds a stenographer's notebook and a fountain pen.

This place is an arena. But no, it's bigger than that. A coliseum. Thousands of people are jammed in — middle-aged fat men with bleach-blond wives, boys who look like burnt-out junkies, trashy girls with vicious, hungry eyes. And everyone looks sick. Kathy sees running sores, poxlike skin diseases, coarse tremors, huge dangling goiters, pulpy, cancerous growths. Everyone is smoking and drinking, eating things out of cellophane bags. And the din is tremendous. The people are howling, shrieking. Someone is shouting, "Kill her! Kill her!"

"And so the spirit of Altamont has taken over everything," Kathy writes in the stenographer's notebook, "and our glorious beginnings come down in the end to nothing but..." She doesn't know how to finish the sentence. A band has set up on the stage. Everyone in the band is black. And Kathy realizes that everyone in the audience is white. She writes "white."

The band begins to play. It's New Orleans jazz. The lead singer is a white man wearing blackface like a sad clown in a minstrel show. He steps up to the mike, winks directly at Kathy. Now she knows why she's wearing this sleazy outfit — she's supposed to play with them. She sees the gleaming alto sax waiting for her at the side of the stage. But she can't play anymore. Sorrow wells up in her. She writes, "alto sax."

The clown is singing, "I thought I heard Buddy Bolden say, 'You nasty buncha dirty, take it away. You're awful. You're terrible. Take it away. And let Mister Bolden play.'" And the show has begun. She looks up and sees, thousands of feet in the air, a set of parallel bars suspended from the ceiling. The audience begins to chant, "Die, die, die." And the performer is walking out on a tiny catwalk. She's a girl, an exquisite girl. She has a lean, trained body like an Olympic gymnast's, and she's in perfect health. But her face is painted like a doll's. She's wearing ribbons in her hair, and she's carrying something in her arms that looks like a life-size doll. It's a mannequin, a shiny, humanoid form. The performer, in pink tights and pink ballet shoes, balances on the parallel bars, holds the huge silver doll in her arms, and smiles down at the howling crowd. The performer is Wendy Crane.

Wendy throws the doll up and leaps after it, spinning in a

cartwheel. Wendy and the doll revolve around each other a moment, high in the air above the parallel bars. Then she catches the doll and lands perfectly. And Kathy understands now that the doll is meant to represent a corpse. That's to show that if she makes one slip, she'll fall and die. Wendy throws up the corpse, pirouettes and leaps, catching it. She swings the corpse over her head. She slides under it and over it. With each movement she comes close to falling, and people spring to their feet, begin to shout. They want her blood. How marvelous, Kathy is thinking. How beautifully Wendy dances with death.

But suddenly it's Kathy who is up there dancing, Kathy who is balanced thousands of feet in the air. But no, she's not dancing with the corpse, she's making love to it. She's impaled herself on the huge, gleaming, silver penis. She's bearing down with her hips frantically, thrusting herself onto the cold, dead body, the body that isn't even a real corpse but a model of a corpse. She begins to weep with rage and frustration. She won't be able to come unless she can wake up the corpse, but the corpse is still and cold and silver. It was never alive to begin with. The corpse is Steve.

Kathy stared at the sky. Fragments of cloud were blowing by like strips of torn banners. She was glad she was outside, able to feel the wind and rain on her face. Then, surprising herself, she took off running down the hill. The wind at her back, she ran away from the children's swings and the ancient trees, down the tipped street of stucco houses, past the gray high-rises, and into the parking lot behind the school. She stopped, out of breath, at the foot of the stairs. Smoking too much, she thought. Then she took the stairs two at a time. It had been too fast; she wasn't ready yet to be inside. Somewhere in the building a male teenage voice was intoning, "Tell me about it, man. Why don't you just tell me about it?"

Kathy walked on down the hall. Her group was waiting for her in the music room. Wendy Crane was sitting on a straight-backed chair as though she were waiting for something specific to happen — discreetly out of the way, arranged in her prim, finishing-school manner, back as upright as a maiden aunt's, her hands folded in her lap, her knees pressed together even though she was wearing jeans. Seeing the girl closed the circle perfectly, and, with an uncanny surge of the world slanting sideways, back into dream, Kathy, from a remote vantage point, watched herself struggle at first to control, then to hide the chill of repulsion and shock — like touching a lizard unexpectedly — as the girl stood up and walked toward her. Wendy's jeans were so new they made tiny crackling sounds when she moved. She was wearing her brown, round-toed shoes and one of her standard, totally unadorned white blouses. She handed Kathy several pieces of manuscript paper. Her fingers were long and as beautifully delicate as an insect's antennae. The nails were cut painfully short.

Kathy was suffering inside a curious mental tunnel vision; the other kids, the objects around her — chairs and pillows and overloaded ashtrays — all seemed far away, dim and unsubstantial. Wendy, by contrast, was positively luminous. Kathy looked down at the paper. A week ago she'd assigned the kids a Leonard Cohen song, told them to transcribe it from the record and then figure out the chords that went with it. It took Kathy a long time to understand what she was seeing in those handsomely drawn black ink notes of Wendy's. There was the song, but the slow-moving melody had been divided into running eighth notes, had been harmonized in Bach keyboard style complete with figured bass. Digging back years for memories of her not wholly successful encounter with legit theory, Kathy managed to make out secondary dominants, modulations through other keys and back again. Wendy had turned the damn silly little tune into a solo keyboard piece. It was something a fourth-year conservatory student would have handed in.

Kathy looked up from the notes. She had to admit that the girl was beautiful if you liked porcelain children — the pale skin, tiny pointed chin, valentine oval face, blond hair brushed back Alice-style, revealing a high, white, unmarked forehead. Kathy saw those cold china-blue eyes staring at her. They were unreadable. Under the steady, expressionless gaze she felt herself shrinking up, withering into a tiny, useless point that was nothing at all.


The hall outside was suddenly filled with the warm, friendly clatter of students pouring out of the classrooms, and then Paul heard Doctor Hanna Rossenmüller's stolid, old woman's walk approaching his office. It had taken him four years of bureaucratic finagling to get her over from Switzerland, but all the effort had been worth it. And here she was, entering like a shark, with Mark Perry floating at her elbow like one of those little fish who hang around to pick up the pieces. "Like a dream," he was saying, "like an angel!" Hanna's eyes, amused, met Paul's.

The woman had such age and dignity that her mere presence seemed to be turning the moment into something of a solemn ritual. She intensified this effect by placing, with studied deliberation, a bottle of cognac and three crystal glasses on Paul's desk. She slowly twisted the cork from the bottle; the squeak of cork on glass entered perfectly above the ostinato hiss of the rain. The movement was marked *grave*. "Gentlemen," she said.

"L'Chai'im," Perry said.

"Just so." She was not smiling at all. "To life."

Paul, who was not a drinker, sipped out of politeness. In his empty stomach the cognac was a finger of fire. It was painful to continue sitting upright behind his desk; the day had somehow grown fantastically long beneath him. He looked at Hanna. She wore a drab, shapeless dress with the air of someone who has to wear something, after all, but can't be bothered beyond establishing that it's *correct*. There was still black in the steel-grey hair wound around her head in an uncompromising bun, and her eyes were still black and intense, but the face behind them was sagging and deeply lined; the bone of her skull stood out. She's only got a few years left, Paul thought. What a wonderful gift for the students to have her here.

Oh, but she made them work. She was ferocious and intimidating in the venerable tradition of the European music masters. One of her lines, delivered during her first week at the university, had already become a legend around the department. To a string ensemble so terrified of her that they had been incapable of playing at all, she had said — and at this point, the teller of the anecdote always exaggerated her thick German accent — "Vot is ze problem? Ze black vons are ze notes."

"And now," she said, "you must tell me about your daughter... about whom Mark has already told me so much."

I'll bet he has, Paul thought. "She's promising," he said. "She's hardly ready to play with the Pro Musica."

"For Christ's sake," Perry said, "she's more than *promising*. I didn't think it was possible for a student to make the progress she's made in the last year. Christ, Hanna, you should hear her play the second Bach. She can take that first allegro like a presto... no fumble, no scramble, right there, bang on."

"It's not meant to go that fast," Paul said.

"I know it's not meant to go that fast. I'm just trying to tell you what she can do. Good God! I'm running out of things to teach her..."

"Well, for starters, teach her not to take that bloody allegro too fast."

Hanna laughed; it was a deep laugh all the way up from the belly. "She has studied with Klaas Achterberg, ya?"

"I wouldn't say she's *studied* with him. She had one lesson with him. When we were in Amsterdam last spring."

Paul saw that Hanna wanted more. "She was with him all morning. When she came out, she looked pale as death... as though he'd had her on the rack for hours. Apparently he didn't talk much. Just had her play, and then he'd play, and then he'd have her play again."

"Ach, that's it," Hanna said. "Klaas plays. It is the best way. I myself talk too much when I teach. It is vice, ya? It is good for me to teach in English. I cannot then indulge myself with this vice... What does Klaas say about her, then?"

"Well, if he has a reputation for reticence, he certainly stayed in character. All he said was that if we ever cared to send Wendy to Amsterdam, he'd be delighted to have her for a student."

"That is very high praise he has given your daughter," Hanna said. "The very highest. I have known Klaas now many years. Many times he has said to me, 'Hanna, God preserve me from the...'" She frowned. "I do not know the word in English. 'From the ordinary ones,' he meant. He is not a rich man, but he does not take students he does not wish to take."

"See!" Perry said triumphantly. "And all I want is one piece. Continuo. One bloody piece. If I don't use Wendy, who the hell else am I going to use?"

"Use anybody you damn well please," Paul heard himself saying, unrehearsed; he was surprised at his own anger. "Get some cello player."

"Paul, that's beneath you." Perry actually sounded hurt. "What is it? Is it because she's your daughter? What exactly is going on here?"

"My God, Mark, she's only fifteen."

"When's the last time you heard her play?"

That was a damned good question. What had happened to the little girl who used to come around in the evenings to ask, "Dad, do you have time to listen to something?" Maybe she was ready. He felt baffled. He looked at Hanna for direction.

"We play at your house, ya?" she said. "It is simple, then. Your daughter plays. We listen. It is friendly. We do not..." She hesitated, searching for words. "We are most kind to her. But later, when we are among ourselves, we talk. It will be clear then, will it not?"

"All right," Paul said.

"One must not promise in these things," Hanna said, raising

a warning finger. "A young girl's heart is a very..." She shook her head. "Like a teacup," she said firmly. "A very fine teacup. One must not promise, ya?"

"No, I won't promise her anything."

"And now I am tired. I must go home. You see how it is, gentlemen? You wish to do this and that, but your body says, 'You are old, Hanna.'"

Paul began gathering his things together. He picked up the file folder with the van Dorestad motet. "Can you read Dutch, Hanna?" he said. "Didn't you live in Holland for a while?"

"Many years ago. My Dutch is not good."

"Can you remember anything? Can you read this?" He drew out the last page of the motet and handed it to her. "It's just one sentence. That faint writing there at the bottom of the page."

She took the Xerox paper reluctantly and stared at it. Her thick brows contracted into a single shaggy line. "Ya, ya, I can read it," she said after a few seconds. "It is old Dutch. It is strange... It says: 'The word of God is... all dark and ...' I do not know what... I do not remember. Oh, ya, I remember. It says, 'The word of God is all dark and incomprehensible even as God himself is.'"


As soon as Paul closed his front door behind him, he knew that he should have gone to dinner with Mark Perry. Standing in the dark hallway, he felt the penetrating chill of the house. And this is the time of day, he thought, that one dreads now more than any other. One returns to find — not Evelyn busy in the kitchen, ready with a day's worth of stored-up complaints; not the girls squabbling over Cindy's right to play her rock records versus Wendy's right to practice; not warmth, light, the smell of cooking — but cold and silence. Perhaps he should take to eating at the Faculty Club.

He could turn a plastic knob on the wall and the forced-air heating would warm every corner of the house in a matter of minutes, but he wanted to see genuine flame. Cindy, a great splitter of kindling, had left him a nearly full box; he built a fire, threw himself into the reclining chair to watch it. He was filled with a grim and meagre satisfaction. Firelight always did wonderful things for the carefully antiqued green finish on the Flemish harpsichord, a superb instrument, with a dense tone rich as good, strong coffee.

The fire was doing quite nicely now; despite his hunger, he was reluctant to do anything but continue to recline in front of that life-giving warmth. He'd never learned to cook; in another month he wouldn't be able to look an egg in its white, bland, ovular face. But now he should eat something. Christ, it had been hours. He wandered into Evelyn's gleaming, chrome and plastic kitchen, poured himself a glass of milk. The fluorescent lights hummed waspishly; they were worse than silence. He climbed the stairs to the bedroom.

Perhaps one should begin to accept the invitations one had been receiving from one's solicitous colleagues to attend parties where, it was always promised, there would be unattached women. He found himself standing flaccidly in the corner of the bedroom with the milk, still undrunk, clutched in his hand. He couldn't imagine anything more ghastly, however, than leaning about — exactly like this, as a matter of fact, uneasily with-drawn into a corner, not with milk but with a glass of ginger-ale to disguise the fact that he did not drink — talking to some overly eager lady with two children who was looking for a new husband. She would be bright, attentive, and smiling (this hypothetical divorcée), would try to thaw him out, get him to talk about his work, but she would not really want to hear about Johannes Ockeghem. After he had departed at ten-thirty, she would gossip with the hostess. "What a strange, stiff, formal man. *A real professor*, eh? I can't imagine why you thought I'd like him."

He turned on the lamp, the pink monstrosity like a tomato with a hat on it that rested on Evelyn's kidney-shaped dressing table. He'd come to think of the bedroom, with its attendant bathroom, en suite, as "Evelyn's revenge." The double-sized brass bed was an authentic art deco period piece; the dusty-rose spread matched the drapes. The only chair was black for accent, black continued in the woodwork; the walls were creamy off-white. The effect had always struck him as one of monumental hideousness. So why didn't he take to sleeping in the downstairs guest room? But even there, one could not escape from evidence of Evelyn; she had used it as a study and jammed it end to end with her art history books.

He had touched nothing since she'd left, hadn't even opened the drapes. The sun rose and set, but the bedroom remained continually occluded under the same artificial, rose-coloured gloom. He fell into exhausted sleep there, furtively crept away like a leper who had clandestinely been using the queen's chambers. Evelyn's musky perfume was everywhere. Yes, she wanted her things, she'd said, but she never came to get them. She had not set foot in the house since her definitive exit in July.

She had packed a couple of suitcases, taken her painting gear and canvasses (and his two daughters), and left the rest behind.

In Cindy's room he turned on the overhead light. He felt like the curator of a sad museum dedicated to nostalgia for the recent past. The room smelled sour and unused; a fine layer of dust had settled over everything. On the wall was an immense poster of some cross-sexed rock-and-roll counter-tenor, a modern troubadour of anxiety and ambiguity, a boy as pretty as a thirties actress, made up like a woman, with a cigarette in his hand, staring out with disturbing, sultry provocativeness. What could such people possibly mean to pre-pubescent girls? The popular culture eluded one, as always. He read the caption — DAVID BOWIE. It meant nothing to him.

He walked on down the hall, arrived in Wendy's room. She had stripped it bare. Little to see but the ballet barre he'd built, and the wooden bracket he'd mounted for her to hang the Tielke. And so vividly in his memory that it could still be going on, that old, daily routine — waking in the rainy dark to hear the etched line of Wendy's gamba, the click of her metronome. What a curious girl she is, he thought. She seemed to have no social life. Once or twice a year she was invited to a party and dutifully went. If asked about it afterward, said, "Oh, it was all right," with a shrug. She had none of her younger sister's fascination with styles and make-up, remained uninfluenced by teen-age fads. She had yet to have her first date.

Both he and Wendy were early risers. Already dressed in her school uniform, she'd be in the kitchen ahead of him. She would have made a pot of coffee for him. And they would sit alone together, across the small table in the nook, eating, not saying much of anything. He turned abruptly away from her room and walked out, down the stairs. His briefcase was waiting for him at the bottom.

In the guest room he opened his briefcase and drew out the copy of the van Dorestad motet and the notes he'd taken in Amsterdam. He opened the folder with the summary of his talk with Doctor van der Geest and read what he had written.

## CONVERSATION WITH DOCTOR WILLEM VAN DER GEEST AT THE DEPARTMENT OF MUSIC, UNIVERSITY OF AMSTERDAM
June, 1977

### THE MANUSCRIPT (KUIPER 526)

Family of wealthy merchants named Kuiper, four generations of collectors of rare books. In 1975, old Piet Kuiper died and left the entire collection to the National Museum. The task of cataloguing the books was enormous; they seemed to have been kept in no particular order. Early in 1977, Professor van der Geest's attention was called to the collection of motets known now as Kuiper 526. This book was a bound volume of seven motets from the Netherlandish school of the generation after Josquin and contained works of Gombert, Clemens non Papa, Willaert, Waelrant, as well as one previously unknown motet, "Tunc Jesus Ductus Est," by a certain "Jan van Dorestad." No record has yet been found among the extensive Kuiper papers concerning the purchase of Kuiper 526, so it remains impossible, so far, to trace the origin of the manuscript.

Kuiper 526 is a hand-written manuscript in the score form. Preliminary investigation indicates that it may date as late as 1650 and is certainly no earlier than 1590. Van der Geest thinks that it may be a collection compiled by a student.

### JAN VAN DORESTAD

Catalogues of the publishing house of Hubert Waelrant in Antwerp show that his edition of Liber Primus Sacrarum Cantionum, No. 7, contained a motet by a "Johannes van Dorestad." All copies of this book have vanished. There was thought to be no other record of a composer of that time called van Dorestad. From the catalogues, we know that the van Dorestad motet was for six voices; the motet found in Kuiper 526 is for six voices. It is possible that Kuiper 526 contains the lost motet.

Looking for any further record of the composer, Professor van der Geest checked the archives of the Cathedral of Antwerp. He discovered that between the years of 1544-46 a "Jennyn de Bois-le-duc called van Dorestad" was consulted concerning the tuning of the church bells. Bois-le-duc is the French name for the small Dutch town of 'sHertogenbosch, which is about sixty miles from Antwerp.

Professor van der Geest then checked the archives of the Lieve Vrouwe Broederschap — the Brotherhood of Our Lady —

in 'sHertogenbosch. The records show that in 1506 a "Janus Willemssoen van Dorestad" was admitted to membership in the Brotherhood. In 1514, Jan van Dorestad was married to Maria Bueken, age nineteen. The account books of the Brotherhood show that van Dorestad was paid for singing, choir leading, and composing between the years 1528 and 1534.

Beyond these "meagre scraps of information" as van der Geest put it, he has been able to learn nothing about van Dorestad. In the archives at 'sHertogenbosch there is no record of van Dorestad's death. "It is curious," van der Geest said, "that this man left behind only one surviving motet and such little record of himself."

Paul closed his notes from Amsterdam back into their folder. He was remembering how Doctor van der Geest, after their talk, had presented him with the microfilm. "Here's a copy for you, Professor Crane. Yes, yes, of course you can take it back to Canada with you. I'm very curious to know your opinion. *Very curious.* I'm sure you'll find it...interesting." Said with an enigmatic smile.

Oh, Willem van der Geest, Paul thought, I can well believe that you were curious to know my opinion. For surely you must have already prepared an edition of the van Dorestad motet for your own journal. If you hadn't, you would never have given the microfilm to another musicologist.

Paul spread out the pages of the motet on Evelyn's desk. And the phone began to ring.

"Goddamn it!" he said. He continued to sit, his annoyance growing, and counted the rings — four, five, six. He walked into the kitchen and grabbed up the phone. It was Evelyn saying, "Thanks for calling me back, Paul."

"Oh, sorry, Ev. I was just on the point of doing it."

"I'll bet you were."

"What do you expect me to say to that?"

"Nothing. But it's so goddamned boring. Call you at your office and get your secretary because you won't take your own calls. Leave a message and wait. And you don't call back. This isn't the first time, you know."

"I always return your calls."

"The hell you do. Last week I left a message three days running. Wednesday, Thursday, Friday. I'm still waiting."

Had she really done that? Yes, he supposed she had. "It's better to try me at home in the evenings," he said.

"Sure. And then if you're rehearsing, you take the phone off the hook."

"I don't rehearse every night of the week, Evelyn."

"So it seems. I'm talking to you *now.*"

"Right you are. Here I am. You're talking to me now. *What the hell do you want?*"

"Goddamn you, Paul Crane, if you forget to pick up Cindy tomorrow, you're going to have one furious child on your hands."

"Good God, Evelyn, it's on my calendar."

"All right. All right. If I could have got you, it would have been simple. But you sit up in your goddamned ivory tower..."

"It's concrete."

"What?"

"My tower. It's concrete."

"Oh, Christ, Crane," she said, laughing grudgingly as though she would have preferred not to.

When he'd been courting her, she'd frequently called him by his last name; it had seemed charming then. Now she only called him "Crane" when she was feeling affectionate or furious — at the moment probably some combination of both those emotions. Oh yes, one comes to know one's wife, all the twists and turns of her; one wonders how the new lover is getting on, having to learn so much so quickly.

"One does not intentionally place a thorn hedge around one," he said, pressing his advantage by giving her an opportunity to laugh at him.

"Oh, *one* does not?" she said, taking him up on it.

"How *are* you, Evelyn?"

She paused, and, in the delay, he could hear sounds of her busy household behind her — children's voices, one of them undoubtedly Cindy's. "Fuck off!" one of the kids was yelling. Was *that* Cindy? Ah, he thought, the liberated household. And very far away, muffled by distance and closed doors, was the pure line of the Tielke — Wendy playing Bach. He strained to hear, but Evelyn said, "I'm doing just fine, Crane. How are you?" They were talking in shorthand now; every inflection was shaded with nuance.

"Tired, but otherwise managing." He could see, as clearly as if she were sitting in the kitchen in front of him, Wendy's serious, pale face behind the gamba, her fluid bow strokes. "Evelyn," he said, "have you had dinner yet?"

"No, not yet. We're eating late tonight... Why? Do you want to come over?" Her voice was wary now; she was expecting a trap.

"No. Thank you anyway. I'd like to take Wendy out if she wants to go."

"Just like that? Out of the blue? That's not like you."

"One can surely be allowed one's moments of impulse."

"Oh, *one* can indeed... Oh, hell, why not? I don't know what the girls had planned."

"Not Cindy. Just Wendy."

"Do you think that's a good idea?"

"I don't know whether it's a good idea or not, but they're not indissolubly joined like Siamese twins."

"I don't know, Paul."

"Tomorrow Cindy will have me from ten-thirty in the morning until God knows when at night. It seems only fair, doesn't it?"

"Yes, I suppose it does. Oh, Christ, yes, get Wendy out of here for the night. I've about had it with her."


Paul floated the Volvo up to the curb behind his wife's lover's pick-up truck. Whenever he came to visit Evelyn and the children, he always felt an irresistible impulse to do everything in his power to emphasize the difference between himself and Davey Cavanaugh — between their "lifestyles" as the current jargon had it — so he'd changed into one of his Harris tweed suits. He turned off the ignition and sat listening to the rain and looking up at the old east end house where Evelyn was now managing to live, however improbably, as something of an earth mother in a communal setting. Davey, that handy young man, had set stained glass into the front windows. The brilliant colours were shining cheerfully out into the night.

Ah, the stained glass. And Paul had been as thick as a post, a fit model of a husband in the frothiest of librettos. In the first act he's sitting with Mark Perry in the Faculty Club. "Is there another man?" Perry asks. Good heavens, of course not. Another man? What nonsense! But by the second act (same setting), the plot has evolved sufficiently for Perry to be able to ask the next inevitable question: "How long has it been going on?" Not for very long, surely. Must be a fairly recent thing. One would have noticed, after all. Leading to the point at which the bemused husband, in an aria both poignant and droll, remembers that his wife had been quite excited by a workshop in stained glass taken at the art school nearly two years before.

The rain was coming down in torrents now; Paul slid out of the car and made a run for the porch. It was not a house where one had to knock, but he knocked anyway. Formal — yes, Evelyn — absolutely correct. I am arriving as discreetly as a Papal Nuncio.

Cindy jerked open the door. "Hi, Paul." Calling adults, even one's father, by their Christian names seemed to be one of the traditions of that household. But then she struck him in the stomach. He hadn't been even remotely prepared for anything like that, and she had hurt him. For an instant he and his younger daughter were the same age; he couldn't believe how angry he was. "Pull your punches, Cynthia."

"Or you'll do what?" Her eyes were glittering with a look that was just like one of her mother's. She was daring him. She had hair like her mother's, too, curly and ash-blonde, but cut short. She shook her head, and her curls bounced; she was breathing hard. "You're on my shit list."

Nonetheless, he thought, one does not punch one's father in the stomach by way of greeting. "I know that self-expression is all the rage around here," he said, "but don't push your luck."

"How does Wendy rate?" she yelled at him.

About Cindy, there was no indirection. "You're not being reasonable," he said.

"I don't give a shit if I'm reasonable." But she was already grinning ear to ear.

"I'm taking you in search of your bloody elusive shoes tomorrow," he said, "and I'll take you to dinner, too."

"Well, you'd better."

He followed her into the kitchen. Evelyn rose to give him a perfunctory kiss on the cheek. "It's the professor himself."

The entire household (he'd never figured out how many people actually lived there) was gathered around in the midst of dinner. Steaming woks of vegetables, curries, and grains were set about the table. Everyone was talking at once — a domestic little allegro full of warmth and good cheer. He felt the bile of envy rising into his throat. (And where was Wendy?)

"Where are you taking her, Crane," Evelyn said, "to the Faculty Club?"

"You can take *me* to the Faculty Club," Cindy yelled.

"Cynthia," Evelyn said in an absent-minded undertone, "you're being a bitch."

"I'll be a bitch if I want."

"Hey, Paul, how are you keeping?" Davey Cavanaugh finally managed to say. And he rose awkwardly to take Paul's hand with the effusive, guilty friendliness of the cuckolder to the cuckoldee. Not an unpleasant person, Paul thought. A young man who seemed to be good at a myriad of things — stained glass, carpentry, gardening, home auto repairs, wine making, who knows what else. The only thing Davey seemed to have trouble doing was supporting himself.

"And after we go the the Faculty Club," Cindy said, "you're going to take me to a movie."

"Stop blackmailing your father," Evelyn said. Chameleon of a woman, she was wearing a man's shirt and blue jeans; there seemed nothing left of the handsome matron in nylons and conservative skirts she'd been only a few months before. And he saw that her wonderful head of hair was now being encouraged to turn back to the ash-blonde it had been when he'd met her. Yes, Evelyn, he thought, if one is nearly ten years older than one's lover, one has to watch little things like that.

The youngest children were in the midst of shrieking at each other; the other father was waving chopsticks in Paul's direction, a gesture Paul supposed was meant to be a greeting, and Cindy, kicking her clogs on the floor, was saying, "I don't intend to forgive you, you know," with a sideways smile that told him she'd forgiven him already. The noise and steam had driven Paul back into himself; he felt at bay. "Where *is* Wendy?" he said.

"I don't know," Evelyn said, yelled, "Gwendolyn! Your fa- ther's here." And, under her breath so Cindy wouldn't hear, "She's been impossible lately."

He had been so taken up with Evelyn that he had failed to see Wendy entering; the first he knew of it was by the silence that fell over the table. Everyone — all the way down to eight-year- old Dawn — stopped talking at once. Paul turned away from his wife and saw that his elder daughter was standing directly next to him. His first impression (indeed the first impression that must have struck everyone to render them all so instantly dumb) was that there was something disturbing about Wendy, something distressingly wrong. It was as though time had been dislocated and she were eleven again and not fifteen. Then he saw that the effect was created by the old dress she was wearing, a grey jumper. It fit her too tightly across the chest; the skirt was too short. It effectively transformed her from a young woman into a little girl. She wore white knee socks with it. Her hair, blonde as a Flemish angel's, was brushed straight back from her high forehead and hung down her back nearly to her waist. She was looking at Paul with eyes that gave away nothing. "Jesus," her sister said in the assertive voice of one newly permitted to say every forbidden word she's ever heard in her life, "you looking fucking ridiculous!"

Cindy's voice had cut the silence and broken it; nervous laughter rose up. "No, she doesn't," Davey said, his voice greasy with embarrassment. "She looks quite... nice."

And Wendy had brought with her the scent of roses — cloying, overpowering, a thousand flowers compressed to the size of a teardrop.

"What did you do, Wendy," Evelyn said, "take a bath in that perfume?"

Wendy said nothing. She walked away.

"Christ, Paul," Evelyn said, hissing, "you certainly bring out the worst in her."

Wendy was waiting for him just inside the front door. She was wearing black kid gloves and her best dress coat. As soon as she saw him, she walked out; he followed her down the stairs. He got into the car, said automatically, "Fasten your seatbelt."

"I did."

"It certainly is raining," he said awkwardly.

"I like it."

"I like it, too. But I don't like driving in it."

Enclosed with her in the small space of the automobile, he began to feel nauseated by the scent of roses. His heart felt like a slab of stone. He rolled down the window an inch. "I think you did overdo the perfume a bit."

"The bottle broke." Her voice was expressionless. "It fell off the dresser and broke. It splashed all over me. I'm soaked with it."

"We could go back so you could change."

"No." After a moment, she added, "You know I don't wear perfume."

"I didn't think you did."

"It was Dawn's. Janet gave it to her to play with. It was just cheap perfume... Dad?... How can a bottle break like that?"

"Like what?"

"On the carpet. It fell on the carpet. And it was like... It just exploded. It's even in my *hair*."

"Was it one of those spray cans?"

"No, just an ordinary glass bottle. And of course Mother thinks I did it on purpose."

"Why would she think that?"

"Because that's what she thinks," annoyed. "Doesn't she?"

"Yes."

He looked at her and saw that she was looking at him. "All right then," she said.

He drove without speaking, winding the car toward Main. "Where do you want to go?" he said.

"The Lohan?" It was a vegetarian restaurant run by one of those imported Hindu sects.

"All right."

"Is it really?"

"Of course it is." He looked again at her milk-white profile. "Wendy... How are you?"

"I'm miserable."


As they were settling in the booth in the restaurant, Paul reached for Wendy's coat, but she shook her head, pulled back — a slight but unmistakable gesture. Hurt, he sat down, watched her work her hands free of her gloves. Wendy's hands seemed to be her only vanity. She collected gloves the way her mother collected shoes. It was the sort of detail one absorbed without conscious effort over the years, but now, he thought, in a mere three months, one's daughter had become something of a stranger.

They hadn't planned on Wendy. He'd still been working on his PhD, and they'd agreed that it was too soon to think of children, but the treacherous diaphragm had malfunctioned. Evelyn had gone into false labour in the small hours of the morning four nights running, on the fifth into genuine labour, had continued in it for nearly twenty-four hours until she'd been exhausted and hysterical, screaming, "I want to get it over with, for Christ's sake! *I can't stand it!*" Their doctor had taken him aside to say, "I'm going to do a C-section. I just can't let it go on." Paul, who did not cry from one year to the next, had collapsed into the corner of the waiting room and wept. But the doctor had walked into the delivery room to find that Wendy was in the process of being born. The first Paul had seen of her had been through the glass window, lined up with the other newborns. She had been the only one of them not crying. He'd known perfectly well that she couldn't have been focusing on anything yet, but she'd seemed to be staring gravely straight at him with enormous, milky-blue eyes. She'd been born with a full head of hair.

"I'll just have a salad," Wendy said.

"Don't you think you need some protein?"

She glanced up quickly, then away. "All right," she said in her most monotonal voice, "a glass of milk."

What a curiously strange daughter one has. What could she have been thinking, squeezing herself into that child's jumper? "Do you remember the German shepherd?" he said.

"Of course I don't." She was obviously annoyed. "I was too young."

She *should* remember, he thought. She'd been nearly five. They hadn't bought the house in Kerrisdale yet, had still been living in that nice old place on Sasamat. The neighbour two houses down owned a wolfish German shepherd kept locked away behind a high fence. If one came too near, the dog exploded into a rage, leaping for the top of the fence, the hair on its thick neck standing straight up like a ruff. The dog's bad temper was not sham; it had seriously bitten two people already and would eventually bite a B.C. Hydro man so badly that it would have to be put away at the pound. And one afternoon (one never understood quite how), Evelyn misplaced Wendy. The gate in the fence should have been child-proof, but obviously had not been. Evelyn, after a frantic search of the neighbourhood, found Wendy inside with the dog. "That goddamned dog was grinning, Paul. You know how dogs can grin? And wagging his tail. And there was Wendy hugging him as though he were a great big teddy bear."

Evelyn ran through the gate. The dog snarled and went for her. She ran out and slammed the gate just in time. The dog walked back to Wendy and sat down. The sight of Wendy plunked on her bottom with her fresh, clean skirt puffed up around her waist and her bare legs sticking out in the mud infuriated Evelyn, but she managed to control herself and called in her sweetest voice, "Come to Mummy." Wendy, however, was not going to come to Mummy. Wendy was not going anywhere. She remained with the dog all afternoon until his owner came home and led her away by the hand. Paul returned from the university to find Cindy asleep in her crib, Wendy (bathed and changed) playing quietly, and Evelyn stretched out on their bed. Her first words to him were in that hissing, between-the-teeth voice she reserved for special moments. "That goddamned little bitch!"

"Well," Paul said to break the silence, "if Cindy were with us, we'd be at McDonald's."

Wendy awarded him with a brief smile. "We would be, wouldn't we?"

"Now tell me," he said in his most firm and fatherly of sonorities, "what are you so miserable about?"

After a moment, she said, "Nothing's going right for me. I'm not in the room with Cindy anymore. I traded with Kelly. Now I'm in with Dawn."

He turned that piece of information over in his mind: She was sharing a room with an eight-year-old. "Isn't Dawn a bit of a distraction?"

"She's better than Cindy." Nothing more seemed to be forthcoming.

"You're not getting on with Cindy?"

"That's putting it mildly."

"That happens quite a bit with sisters in their teens. It's not uncommon."

"Isn't it?"

"You could stay out of her way for a while."

"That's hard. She takes up too much space."

"That's an interesting way of putting it."

"Oh, that's the way they talk," she said with a dismissive gesture. "One gets in the habit of doing it too. We have meetings, you know, once a week, and talk about things like that... how much space people are taking up. And it doesn't seem to matter what I say. I always lose. If I say, 'People won't leave me alone to practice,' they say, 'But you don't interact with the household.' And Cindy says, 'Wendy thinks she doesn't have to. Wendy thinks she's special.' But if I say, 'Cindy plays her rock records so loud that there's nowhere I can go to get away from it, and I can't practice,' they say, 'Don't you think Cindy has a right to *her thing*, too?' But if I get up before school to practice, that's not practicing, that's me *acting out my resentments* because I wake people up."

She had delivered this staring down; now she looked directly at him. "That sounds fairly dreadful," he said.

And there he was, of course, living alone in his enormous house. It would be a simple enough thing to ask her if she wanted to move back into it, but he didn't know if he wanted her to. He didn't know if she would want to. He had a strong suspicion that the two of them might be acutely uncomfortable alone there together. But he ought to try. "Do you want to come home?"

"I don't know. I've thought about it."

"You could, you know. Oh, your mother would raise bloody hell, but she'd give in eventually."

"I don't know, Dad. I'll think about it. Thanks for asking me. I'm glad somebody's started asking me what I want."

"Oh?"

"I didn't want to leave Stafford House, but... I don't know. Mummy seemed..." Oh, he thought, she *is* feeling young tonight. But she caught herself. "*Mother* seemed so determined."

"Oh, indeed she was."

"Oh, God, Dad, it's awful. They put me in Kathy's group, and she doesn't like me at all. And on top of everything else, I have to go see her tomorrow."

"On Saturday? Why?"

"Oh, it's one of these personal conferences they have all the time."

Damn Evelyn, Paul thought. And damn her screwy notions

about progressive schools. "Oh, Dad, I'm so sick of it," Wendy
was saying. "She gave us this silly Leonard Cohen song and told
us to figure out the chords to it, so I wrote it out like a keyboard
piece. In Bach harmony."

"Oh, you did, did you?"

"It was dumb of me. I just wanted to *show* her, but it..."
Wendy stopped suddenly. Paul followed her gaze and saw an
intrusive flurry of movement. It took him a moment to make
sense of it.

A pale, bearded youth, a boy surely no more than a teenager,
had materialized out of nowhere to drop a mimeographed sheet
of paper onto the table. Bird-like, the boy bobbed up and down.
Looking at the paper, Paul read: JESUS CHRIST IS COMING
AGAIN IN ALL HIS GLORY! WILL YOU BE READY? Beneath
appeared to be a listing of disasters — war in the Middle East,
oil tanker spills, unemployment, ecological catastrophes —
worked into an elaborate Biblical exegesis.

"Could you spare something for our work, brother?" the boy
said.

Paul extracted his wallet and handed over a two-dollar bill.
The boy bowed first to Wendy and then to Paul, shouted out,
"God bless you! The Lord be praised!" and, backing up the whole
way, vanished.

Paul felt unaccountably disoriented. "Poor, bloody, pathetic
fool," he said.

Wendy sat absolutely still. "Why did you say that, Dad?"

"All those poor kids and their sects. They're obviously so
sincere, and so profoundly silly. It just seems sad, that's all."

"Maybe we're the ones who are sad," Wendy said. "Maybe it
makes them happy."

He was astonished at her remark. "Perhaps you're right."
And what, he wondered, characterizes that "we" under which
she included both herself and him? "You're a very strange girl."
It was the most personal thing he'd said to her since they'd been
in Amsterdam together.

"Oh, I certainly know *that*." She smiled slightly. "I always
have been, you know, but nobody's noticed before. Now everybody seems to notice. I want to go back to being..." She frowned.
"I want to be invisible again."

"Do you?" Now was the time, he supposed; he wasn't going to
find a better one. "It's curious that you should say that just
now... about being invisible. Perry wants you to play in the next
Pro Musica concert."

She looked, for a moment, as though he had slapped her. "I

told him you weren't quite ready for that," he blundered on,
embarrassed and fumbling. "I told him it wasn't quite the..."
Good Christ, she had tears in her eyes. "Wendy? I'm sorry.
What's the matter?"

"You didn't just say no just like that?"

"Of course I didn't. I thought I'd ask you first."

"I thought he was kidding," she said. "You know how he is,
how he's always kidding?" She was weeping openly. "I'm sorry.
Excuse me, Dad. Please." She fled.

He saw that all the other young people in the restaurant were
staring at him accusingly: *What have you done to her?* Nothing,
you bloody twits, he told them silently and stared them down.
I've done nothing to her.

But when Wendy came back from the washroom, she seemed
to have regained her self-control absolutely. She sat down at the
table and asked in a matter-of-fact tone, "What did he want me
to play?"

"Marais. I don't know which one. Continuo."

"Would I have to audition?"

"Something like that. We thought we'd just have you over to
a rehearsal, completely informal, you know. Do you mean that
you'd want to do it?"

"Of course I want to do it."

"Are you all right? I'm sorry if..."

She made a chopping gesture with one of her thin, white
hands, cutting him off. "It's all right, Dad. I'm sorry. It's just
that... I've always wanted to play with the Pro Musica as long as
I can remember. It's what I used to dream about when I was
little... I guess the way some girls want to be ballerinas. I never
thought I'd be good enough."

She was suddenly no longer a grave, strange girl he didn't
quite know. Her face was gleaming; he hadn't seen her so happy
in months. But one doesn't *know* how she's playing these days,
he thought. If she weren't up to scratch, it could be dreadful.
"Can you assess yourself?" he asked her. "Can you do it? I don't
mean just deliver the notes. I mean get up on a stage with
professional musicians and make *music* of it?"

She did not hesitate; her eyes were shining. "It's not as though
*I'd* be playing the Marais solo. Of course I can do it."

Kathy was getting drunk. Like much of what seemed to be
happening to her lately, it was not something she had consciously planned to do, but since she'd got home from school,
she'd found herself pacing the few feet from one end of her

basement apartment to the other, listening to the rain pounding on the pavement, listening to Coltrane over it, coming to rest in front of the tiny slit window where the glass and the bottle waited for her. (Sticky, sweet Southern Comfort — she didn't even like it. And a frozen pizza passed through the microwave. And the screwy notion that she would, somehow, get drunk enough to figure everything out, get some mystical insight that would make it all make sense.) There was never anything to see through that window except occasional feet passing by on the sidewalk — tonight not even that, just the rain. But the ledge was a good place for an ashtray, a good place to rest her elbows, a good place to stop. And yes, she should have moved. Of course she should have. But it wasn't as though she'd spent all of the seven years like this, night after night getting loaded. She had plenty of friends — well, at least friendly people. When anybody invited her to anything, she always went, didn't she? And — what else? Well, she'd always been physically active, and that hadn't changed. In the summer she rode her ten-speed for miles, went for long walks, played volleyball and softball with the kids. And she hadn't turned into a nun either, had slept with (count them) four men, and one of those affairs had even managed to last nearly five months. But now she was feeling it clearly, unmistakably — what she'd known in her heart all along — that no matter what she'd done with them, those seven years were empty, insubstantial, compared to the luminous intensity of Steve.

When they'd fled the States, running, for once, from something more menacing than Steve's internal voices — from the FBI — he had wanted to get as far away as geography would allow. Interrupted by the sea, they'd walked up and down the beach at Tofino, British Columbia, under a gun-metal sky full of screaming gulls. Kathy looked back at the track her exhausted feet had dragged through the sand. Their passage through the world felt endless, pointless. They'd made the run from downtown Boston in four days; she didn't have the remotest idea where they'd arrived, but she didn't think it very likely that they could find work there. "Let's go back to Vancouver," she said. But he was in one of his high-flying, eye-popped, manic states. "Look, Kath. It's fucking great. *There's nothing here!*"

They slept on the beach, woke and counted their money, discovered that they were damned near broke, took the ferry back to the mainland, and then it was the Hotel Cecil, Kathy collapsed on the bed, unable to do anything at all, saying to herself over and over like a mantra, "I'm in a foreign country, and I'm married to a madman." But they still had their old dynamic going — when she went down, he went up. He turned into a driven, speeding dervish of energy, applied for every conceivable job, laughing and lying to interviewers, contradicting himself, leaning over their desks to wave his long fingers in their amazed faces, yelling, "It's your last chance, man. You better grab me now or I'm walking out the door." Within a week he'd landed two jobs, driving a delivery truck in the daytime, working as a janitor on the graveyard shift. He ran on coffee and cigarettes, lost so much weight he began to look like a survivor from Auschwitz. He found them a cheap apartment in Kits (this apartment).

Kathy pulled herself together, put on the only dress she owned — prim navy blue with a white Peter Pan collar (she'd been married in it, had crossed the border in it) — and began to look for a job. Taking her cue from Steve, she learned to lie too, found herself working as a secretary, higher paid than she'd ever been in her life. Then the seesaw tilted; Steve lost both his jobs. When she came home, she began to find him staring out the tiny slit window (where she was standing now). She never knew exactly how he got fired; every time he told the stories, the details changed. If she'd say, "Hey, that isn't what you told me before," he'd grin and answer, "Shit, Kath, can't you allow a man a little poetic license?"

In the evenings they'd drive. They logged hundreds of miles, must have ridden over every road and highway on the lower mainland. He didn't have much to say. He sat hunched over the wheel, smoothly guiding the van along, not speeding particularly, but always five or ten miles over the limit. She sat uneasily next to him and lit his cigarettes. At midnight or so, she'd always have to say, "Hey, man, I've got to work tomorrow."

Whenever she came home, she'd find him at the window. Every day he worked on the apartment. He repainted the walls and even the ceiling. He laid down wiring everywhere. He bought old furniture and refinished it. He put up posters. (They, at least, had been easy to tear town — his black leather motorcycle girls, his Hieronymus Bosch prints.) He slapped up a shelf in every corner, a peg-board in the kitchen. He made lamp shades out of balsa wood and rice paper. He bought an ancient wringer washer and cycled their laundry through it. And when he finally ran out of projects, he spent his time cleaning. He made the bed, washed the dishes, swept up, scrubbed the floors — and the bathtub, and the toilet. And Kathy would walk through the door a little after six, smell the cleanser, smell the coffee. (He would always have just made a fresh pot of coffee.) He would have given out by then, and she'd find him standing in front of the window, looking out. The apartment would be gleaming like something from a TV ad, but he would never have planned anything for dinner. "Fuck it, let's order a pizza." His communications had deteriorated into cryptic fragments, and she never knew what he was thinking. The first two fingers of his right hand were stained brown as nuts by Player's plain. "Jesus Christ, Kathy, this place is dull!"

"Get yourself a gig in a club, man. It's the only thing you can stand to do. Go down and join the union. Or put your name up in all the music stores. Do *something*."

"Fuck it, Kath. I'm done with music."

Then she said back to him just the sort of thing she'd been hearing from him for years. "Yeah, but is music done with you?"

He stood, leaning against the wall next to the window, a cup of freshly brewed mocha java in his hand, and looked at her as though he'd just rediscovered her existence. She had to admit, uncomfortably, that she found him sexiest when he was unhealthy — gaunt, with cheeks sunken in, the bones showing under stretched skin, his lank black hair, uncut for months, falling over his forehead, covering his eyebrows, and his eyes gone huge and secret. He had black eyelashes — as long, thick, and dark as if he'd curled and coated them with mascara. He stared at her with those immense liquid eyes disquietingly placed above the twist at the bridge of his nose where it had been broken and said, slowly, "Hey, that's good. It really is. *Is music done with me?* That's really a good one, Kath."


Kathy had come home from work one night (exactly a month after Janis Joplin had died; this seemingly unrelated fact had become stuck in her mind and nagged at her) and found that Steve was gone. He'd taken his drum set, his van, most of his clothes, and left her a note on the side of a brown paper bag. She hadn't been able to cry that day or the next, or ever. She'd settled into a routine, expecting nothing, just as Steve had left her nothing, not even enough information to begin to figure out what had been going on during their years together.

(And it wasn't fair that she was feeling it now so intensely all over again. She'd thought she was done with it; she'd thought she was getting better.) A few weeks after he'd left, she'd been on her way out to teach, had met the postman at the door, grabbed the letter, read it on the bus, hadn't been able to teach.

She hadn't wanted to read the letter again after that first time; she'd shoved it into the back of a drawer. She got it out now, unfolded the paper on the kitchen table, and saw with surprisingly fresh anguish his hurried black scrawl.


Kathy, my love, what the fuck can I say? Here I am in Toronto, which aint how the people say it. They slur it, Eastern style. Written down it would probably look like TRANNA. Here I am in Tranna, Canada. The weather's beautiful if you like it cold, clear, and snowing in November. People tell me the winters are harsh and I can believe it what with the little I've already seen. Don't know if I'll stay around to see the snow piled up to my asshole, not sure I could hack that. Maybe I'll be back in Vancouver by then, who knows? And all this is just beating around the bush because really what the fuck can I say? This makes the second time I've run out on you, and what with your only one time running out on me, that puts me one up. That's supposed to be a joke, but it does limp a bit.

I've been taking in the sights just like any other tourist. Kensington Market which is kind of cute, and Rochdale, of course, a legend in its own time. Oh, you'd love Rochdale, Kath. Druggies, flamed out, burnt out, screwed up, lowest common denominator druggies, crammed in with the few poor idealistic kids who still seem to be left, all of them in this big gray concrete building that looks like the headquarters for the Bureau of Statistics for the People's Republic of Bulgaria. I just couldn't believe it. Something like that wouldn't last in the States five minutes, wouldn't even have been conceived of in the States, but there it is, live and in full grisly color, with high windows for bad trippers to leap out of in full flame, and the local park which is called Dogshit Park because that's where all the heavy dealers walk their dogs. Well, maybe "dogs" isn't descriptive enough. Baskerville hounds, nine foot tall Tibetan mastiffs, German Wehrmacht shepherds with their fangs filed down, wolves crossed with panthers, various other great hulking brutes with studded collars, and all led around on good thick leashes by The Dealers. And The Dealers are your standard issue subhuman robotized rip-off machines with their blood replaced by various chemicals, can tell which particular chemicals by the standardized features just like you can tell a Ford from a Chevy, the electro-speed model motormouthing away to nobody in particular like a talking doll, the vapo-grass model trailing peace signs like the Buddha trailed lotus petals. It's quite a show, everybody paranoid and full of 1970 uptight vibrations, the hounds snarling and attacking each other, ripping off hunks of flesh, the park piled up with little mounds of shit, and inside that monstrous gray building the poor dumb kids stoned and sitting around talking about changing the world while the vultures rip them off, and they rip each other off, everybody screwing everybody else and a kind of weary cynicism settling over it all. And we were supposed to be the love generation? But I don't suppose you want to hear about Rochdale. You probably want to hear why I took off. I don't know why I took off. I don't know why the fuck I do anything I do. I don't even know why I left Georgia.

Now there's a good alternative question — should I ever have left Georgia? I could have run to seed so beautifully down there, oh yeah, I could have become so dilapidated. The South, having been defeated as a whole, understands about people who are defeated as individuals and treasures them in a curious way. (Now isn't that a wonderful sentence, worthy of Humanities I at Harvard?) But anyhow I could have been — "You know, that's Jimmy Beuhl's boy, Steven. He never was much use, but he sure is a nice feller. He'll always stand you a drink or two and I never seen him fall down in the street once." Could have lived at home, drunk sour mash whiskey and played poker with the old man, mosed around town in an ice-cream-colored suit, maybe picked up a little honey here and there just to pass the time.

Oh, it's so fucking hot in the South. And it's wonderful how nothing has to make any sense. I remember one of the first civil rights things, and a bunch of the boys went down to give the people sitting-in a hard time, waving Confederate flags and doing it up right, you know, and this dude come out in the paper, wrote an editorial, allowed as how it pained him to see "a bunch of redneck yahoos carrying the banner from the last war fought by gentlemen." Oh, I love it, I love it, I love it. And the honeys are just too much. You'd really dig them, Kath. You just wouldn't believe how trashy they can be, little tarty waitresses with their dresses two sizes too small and their mouths dripping with that molasses bullshit. There's one I remember. We boys, having that highly developed sense of wit and fun for which the Southern male is noted, called her Charlotte the Harlot. She had a taste for sucking dick that was unbelievable. I mean it was like sticking it in a Hoover. And she had a cunt — well shit, she could tighten up on a rat tail. See, I'm getting more Southern by the minute.

But I'm getting off the track. What I really should have done was let you alone, right? I mean with my head I should have run an ad in the *Weasel* — CRAZED YOUNG MAN CAPABLE OF OCCASIONAL MOMENTS OF COMPATIBILITY SEEKS PSYCHOTIC YOUNG WOMAN OF WHATEVER DELUSIONS, OBJECT; MUTUAL SELF-DESTRUCTION. I mean you probably would have done just fine if you'd never met me, right? I'll flatter myself and say that there was probably a cheap thrill or two you would have missed out on, but I think you could have made it OK without any of that shit. The problem is, Kath, you saved my life. It's not a metaphor or anything like that, it's the literal honest to God truth. You came in and took over and I just gave up and said, OK man, ride it, see what route Kathy wants to go, and that's how we'll go. And then pretty soon we were a young married couple working for a living in the dullest fucking city I ever saw in my life. I thought, well, shit, if that's what's happening, that's what's happening. Now we're going to be normal. We'll work like normal people, and eat like normal people, and live in a normal apartment (and they all lived together in a crooked little house), and, of course, fuck like normal people, right? And Kathy can go and pretend she's a secretary and wear straight little dresses and pink lipstick.

See, that's finally what did it to me. It was getting up in the morning and being ordinary. And I kept remembering how the music used to be, you know, when it still meant something. And also, Kath, remember the nights we spent chasing after sweet death? And for what? To watch the time dribble by? And I just got up one of those mornings and couldn't hack it anymore. It's that simple. And so I packed it up and put it on the road.

Really got the insomniac curse tonight. Despite the rather vast quantity of grass, not to mention the port wine (praeteritio, as I pointlessly remember all the way back to high school), sleep aint in sight, stranded on my feet, etc., to quote Saint Robert. Lying in bed and continuing to compose this letter to you in my mind, great long Ciceronian sentences of it, endless unwritable paragraphs of self-justification. But I've go to try, just for once, to get it straight. All the stuff I've written so far is crap. It really is. Pure bullshit. The inside of my head looks like a series of closed rooms with the doors locked going back in an infinite regress. I'm so good at hiding the truth from myself that it's no wonder I had a hard time being straight with you. OK, so first of all, don't listen to any of that "it was the ordinariness that did it" crap, that's a con job. Kathy, I just can't stop thinking of you. Jesus Christ, you were something else! I loved you naked and I loved you with clothes on and I loved you in those weirdo outfits I got for you. I mean I just thought you were great. That first year we were together I was just like a pig in shit walking around grinning ear to ear. I thought I'd pulled off the crime of the century, picking you up, or letting you pick me up, however the fuck it happened. I loved the way you could get wet so fast. Can see you above me, riding me, your hair hanging down like Sloopy, old rock-and-roll sweetheart, and me trying to shove my cock up through you to the ceiling. I liked to slow down at the end and keep you right at the edge as long as I could, liked the madness in it, the sounds you'd make. Jesus, we were something else then, you know that, don't you? "All right, you bastard," you're probably saying, "how come you're telling me all this from three thousand miles away?" The answer is — I don't know.

But no, that's not true at all. All right, let me try it again, same song, second verse. Remember how bad I was in Boston? Well, I'm worse now. Does that give you some idea? I mean it's never been this bad before, ever. And I didn't want to lay it on you again, I can be the corpse in the corner in somebody else's corner, but I didn't want to be the corpse in your corner, not again. But goddamn it, it was coming down or in or however the fuck it comes, I could feel it sneaking up to me on tiptoes...tap on the shoulder. Surprise! You're nuts again.

Sorry, what I've just written is a bit of a con job too — I'm not that fucking altruistic. But maybe if you could take this letter, cut it apart and paste it back together at random the way Burroughs wrote his books, there'd be just a hair of truth somewhere between the edges. Because — yes, it was the ordinariness. And yes, I was going crazy again. But there's something else. Kathy, I am scared, I am fucking scared. I sit here and play with my little deck of metaphysical cards, keep trying to see how I managed to deal myself this bum hand. It's murderous and just — but I can't get out of it, any way you cut it. Got to bluff on a pair again, and the dude on the other side of the table, pleasant enough fellow except for his funny feet and a bit of a sulphur smell about him, well, he aint giving away a thing. Remember how you used to say, "But what if they're right? What if they are right and we're just fucked up kids?" And I could never admit that possibility. I think you were the stronger of us to admit that possibility. I think maybe you can save yourself with it. Kathy, for God's sake, forget you ever knew me. I'm sorry I made you quit your job. (Yeah, I knew I was doing it.) Go get it back, or another one just like it. Go buy some dresses at Eaton's and some more lipstick. Have an affair with the boss, or marry him, for Christ's sake. And just get out of it. Because I've said to myself too long that this world will end, will crash,

bang, smash, burn, will go up in fucking flames before I can
make it. The old argument about burning down Weidner Library. Yes, I'd still burn the library. I'd burn all the libraries. I
still want to make people listen. Come on, you motherfuckers,
wake up! Ravachol lives! (A stoned hippy voice says, "Who the
fuck's Ravachol, man?") Oh God, I used to have, still have, as far
back as Georgia I used to have the fantasy that I'd cut myself all
over, cut after bloody cut, until I was dripping from head to foot,
and then walk out onto the street and yell, LOOK AT ME! THIS
IS HOW BAD IT IS! ("The lad needs extensive psychiatric care,"
somebody says. Right man. Of course. Anything you say, man.
I was just taking a leak on the side of this building here, don't
mean no harm. I never heard of the cat you're talking about.
Now will you please go shut up that fucking rooster.) Or maybe
cut off my balls right there on the sidewalk and fling them
through the open window of the police car like a priest of Cybele
onto the lap of his lady.

A couple hours later. Still can't sleep. Will try again. Please
disregard all of the above. It's not that bad. I have a great talent
for self-dramatization, as you, of all people, should know. And
maybe that's how I can try to say — forgive me. I'm still trying
to break through that dreadful passivity, and sometimes I'm
megalomaniac enough to think that I'm still trying to break
through for the whole world. You do remember all the nights we
chased death? You do, don't you, Kathy? If I could do anything
else, I'd do it.

Next day. I'm sorry about the tone of all of the above. I was
pretty fucking weirded out when I wrote it, so please disregard
my usual excesses. I'm crashing with some nice people. Aint in
no danger of being busted or starving to death or any of the other
ills the flesh is heir to in the Kali Yuga. Even got a gig lined up
in a country band. I don't know where I'll be, so don't write. I'll
call you. If everything works out, maybe I won't have to be gone
very long. In so far as love is possible, I love you (and I think
you'd be perfectly justified for kicking my teeth in for that one).

Steve

Kathy folded away the letter, shoved it back inside the drawer.
She'd taken the hints he'd dropped, written to him at General
Delivery, Toronto, and at Rochdale. The general delivery letter
had returned, the one to Rochdale hadn't. She'd never heard
from him again. (And now she was so drunk she was stumbling,
had to steady herself against the wall. And now she was so

drunk, maybe could sleep. And hope to God she wouldn't throw up. And hope to God she wouldn't dream.)


Wendy was late. Outside in the parking lot, a few of the kids from the school were playing a half-assed game of soccer. Kathy leaned out the window to let the cold wind wash over her face — an ineffective hangover cure. Thud of the soccer ball, throb on the back of her neck. Her headache was beating her damned near blind. The afternoon was turning dark and cold as winter, but even now, late on a Saturday, there was always this handful of kids still hanging around the school — because they didn't have anywhere else to go. The poor bastards.

Maybe Wendy chickened out, Kathy thought, or worse, maybe she'd planned it — the perfect passive-aggressive strategy — agree to a meeting and then don't show up. Beautiful. Then Kathy heard the precise footsteps — not silent runners, the Van Free uniform — but hard leather heels. Forty minutes late. Kathy turned toward the door. The girl pushed through the batik curtain, paused, grasping the fabric, parting the space. In dress gloves, her fingers looked impossibly delicate — a fine drawing in black ink. "Hello?" she said tentatively, blond hair swinging along the oval line of her cheekbone. "I wasn't sure you were here."

"Yeah, I'm here." Kathy had tried to sound neutral, but it had come out snappish and hard.

"I'm sorry I'm late. My lesson kept going on and on. I finally just had to tell him I had to go." Precise voice with that slight British coloring that drove Kathy mad.

Wendy stepped definitively into the room. She set her instrument case down by the wall, stood a moment, her face alert but expressionless. Then she shed her coat, looked around for a place to hang it, found nothing, so laid it carefully onto the floor. She obeyed the SHOES OFF! sign, unbuckled her mary janes. Ordinarily Wendy wore jeans to school, but now she was dressed in stockings and a skirt. Kathy felt a rattling apprehension; her mind had gone out of tune. Wendy had come to rest directly in front of the portable blackboard. She finally took her gloves off.

Kathy was suddenly so angry she felt her heartbeat slamming her throat. "You're all fancy today," she managed to say.

Wendy said nothing.

"Had a cello lesson?"

"It's not a cello."

"It's not?"

"No. It's a viola da gamba."

"I don't even know what a viola da gamba is." Kathy's hands were automatically rolling a cigarette she didn't want.

"I'll show you if you like."

The damned thing *looked* like a cello (except that it had too many strings) — an exquisitely curved instrument of ancient dark brown wood, the body intricately carved, a woman's head with flowing hair sculpted above the peg box. It was fretted, not like a guitar, but with gut strings tied around the neck. "It's a cello with frets?" Kathy said.

"It's not a cello *at all*. It's not even in the same family." Wendy lifted the instrument out of the case and offered it to Kathy.

"It's certainly beautiful," Kathy said, took the instrument reluctantly. "Is it old?"

"It's an eighteenth-century original. A Tielke."

"Must be valuable."

"It is. Although gambas haven't appreciated as much as violins and cellos. My father bought it years ago in England." She smiled slightly. "He gave it to me."

"Will you play something?"

Wendy looked around. The lights were turned off, and the room was falling into a murky twilight. "There's nothing to sit on." She laid the instrument in its case and locked it away. Then, giving Kathy an Alice-at-the-tea-party expression, she said, "Do you play anything?"

You goddamned little bitch, Kathy thought. What a wonderful question for the music teacher. "Just keyboard and guitar a bit now. I used to play alto sax. I was good."

And why "used to"? Why had she stopped? And why, after all these years, hadn't she figured out why?

Wendy sat down on the floor, tucking her skirt under her. Her oval face looked as white as a Japanese doll's "What did you want to see me about?" She was as blond as Rapunzel. *She's not like me*, Kathy thought. *She can't possibly be like me.*

"You don't seem very happy here," Kathy said.

"I'm not."

"Maybe you should go somewhere else."

After a silence so long that Kathy was beginning to make out intelligible phrases in the voices of the kids in the parking lot, Wendy said, "Do you think so?"

For Christ's sake, Kathy thought. *That's* what she made me wait for? "I don't seem to be able to do much for you," she said, "or *we* don't. Maybe the school isn't the right place for you." Kathy felt helpless, bogged down. "I'm having a lot of trouble with you," she said. "Do you know that?"

"Well, I'm having a lot of trouble with *you*."

Kathy laughed. "I'm really glad to hear you say that. All right, that's a good place to start. Why is it happening?"

Wendy said nothing.

"I'm supposed to be the bloody adult, eh? I should go first? OK, you remind me of myself at your age, and it bothers me."

Whatever Wendy had been expecting, that obviously had not been it. She blinked rapidly several times. For the first time, Kathy thought that she might be able to control the situation. "I imagine you have a lot going on inside you that you don't show anyone," she said, "because I did when I was fifteen. Do you? Or is that just *my* fantasy?"

Wendy looked away. "I don't understand."

"Forget it then... But look, we've been at war, haven't we? That hasn't just been my imagination."

Wendy looked back into her eyes; it was as though she were searching for a clue as to how to proceed. "That's right," she said, "I *have* been giving you a hard time. But you've been giving *me* a hard time too."

"Why?"

"It's the music class."

"I shouldn't be teaching it? I don't know enough?"

Wendy shrugged.

"Not enough for you, but enough for most of the kids. Jazz is what I know about, but that's not what you're interested in. I don't know why you've kept coming to the class."

Wendy smiled. "I just wanted to see what you'd do."

"Thanks a lot!" But Kathy was laughing.

"All right, I won't come to it any more. I knew it bothered you, Mrs. Beuhl."

"For Christ's sake, don't do that to me. Nobody around here calls anybody by their last name. It's just another jerk off!"

"A what?"

"A way of getting at me."

Wendy said nothing.

"Well, isn't it?" Kathy said.

"Yes." Flash of anger. "I don't think you'll have to put up with me very much longer, *Kathy*. I don't think I'll be here next term."

*Am I disappointed*? Kathy thought. *Incredible*. "Oh?"

"I think I'll go back to Stafford House."

"You liked it there?"

"Yes."

"What did you like about it?"

"I liked not having boys around. I liked wearing a uniform."

"You did? Why?"

Wendy shrugged. "Because you don't have to think about it."

Kathy thought she understood. "There's a uniform here too, you know, but I don't suppose it's a uniform you're comfortable with."

"No, I suppose it isn't."

"You like it when things are clear, stated. You don't like it when they're unstated, when you have to figure them out?"

"I suppose so."

"I can sympathize with that. This place does have a lot of rules, but nobody wrote them down. No matter what the hell the staff might say about freedom, we don't tolerate differences very much." Kathy thought she'd finally caught something inside the girl. "You probably weren't very involved at Stafford House, were you?"

"I don't know what you mean."

"You probably just showed up and put in your time and went home, eh? And there wasn't anybody telling you that you had to be involved. But around here, if you're not involved, you get shit all the time."

Wendy nodded.

"What you want is to be left alone? Is that right?" Wendy took a deep breath but didn't speak. "Left alone to do what?" Kathy said. But she already knew the answer. She reached out and grabbed Wendy's left hand. She had to force herself to touch the girl.

The hand was just as small, soft, and delicate as she'd thought it would be, but it was also moist and icy cold. Kathy felt the thick disk of callus on the tip of each narrow finger. She let the hand go, and Wendy jerked it away, scooted backward on the floor. The girl's eyes were shocked — outraged. "How much do you practice?"

Wendy said nothing, continued to stare at her with angry eyes.

"Yeah, damn it," Kathy said, "I know you don't like to be touched. That's not important. How much do you practice a day? A couple hours?"

"Four hours at the minimum. Six if I can get it in. More on weekends."

"So did I." Kathy knew now that there was nothing she could say that would be the least bit of help — except the one thing that really mattered. "Do it," she said. "Don't let anybody stop you."

Wendy's eyes widened, filled with moisture. But the tears

didn't spill over; they remained trapped by the lower eyelids. And the words came out of Kathy before she could think about them, or stop them, or understand where they'd come from: "It's crazy, but it's not just that you remind me of myself. I feel like I've known you before."

The blackboard was struck once, from behind, by an immense, invisible sledgehammer. The blow was so loud that Kathy was sure the slate must have been split end to end. She saw at once that it was still intact, although it had begun to fall in slow motion — in a series of horrible, undulating wobbles, it was beginning to topple down. She and Wendy were both on their feet, grabbing for it. Kathy caught the left side and Wendy the right. Together they set it back onto its rollers. Looking at both sides of the board, Kathy couldn't see a single mark. "What happened?" Wendy said. "What made it do that? What was it?"

"I don't know." Kathy's heart was racing. She had no control over what she was doing. She caught the girl in her arms and held her. Wendy clung to her. Kathy couldn't tell one heartbeat from the other.

**II**

"I'm running out of money."

How wonderfully direct she has become, how to the point. No dilly-dallying about with it, just presented to one scarcely through the door — simple as handing over the coffee he was now sipping. She must have formulated this notion of herself as early as she'd been able to formulate anything at all: that she was owed, not for anything that she might do, but merely for being.

"People have been known to take jobs," he said. "I've heard that it is done from time to time."

"Paul. My God. Please spare me."

Evelyn had opened the curtains, turned off the slide projector. Her painting was nearly finished: the Bank of Nova Scotia, a dentist's office above, the clock in the bank informing the viewer that it was six-ten, presumably in the morning (grey Vancouver overcast, street wet with rain). There was not a human being to be seen on the canvas. What could it mean, this careful copying of a photograph that had taken her since July? One supposed that it was meant to be nothing more than it appeared to be, the corner of Broadway and Macdonald painted so realistically that it could have been a colour print of the slide upon which the work was based. Why then was it not a photographic print? "Does one sell these things?" he asked her.

"I've heard that it is done from time to time."

He met her eyes, saw in them something unaltered of the clever young woman he'd married. The ideal type for girls at the time when he'd met her had been artificial, sentimental, and highly mannered — a veritable *style galant*. Against it she had stood out: as beautiful as any of them, certainly as well put together, but that tongue of hers had frightened men away. Not him. Curious what had aroused him then — the need to cohabit with her perpetually sophomoric wit.

"Will you sell it?" he asked her.

She shrugged. "Who buys paintings?"

Having been a child dancer (good enough to have auditioned for the New York City Ballet School), a graduate student pianist (her Chopin, he remembered, had been remarkable for its delicacy) who also won awards for poetry (crystalline little things in the style of Emily Dickinson), a young-mother writer (she'd sold three of her pieces to *Chatelaine*), could she now be — if, indeed, that word were not too strong to describe the activity involved in copying a Kodachrome slide — a painter?

"What are you thinking, Crane?"

"Thinking?" That he would always remember her the way she had been on a night that had smelled of burning wood in nineteen sixty-two when he had first made love to her. "How you were when I met you."

"And how I've changed for the worse?"

"Of course not."

"Polite to the end. How was I?"

"I've told you, surely."

"Tell me again."

It will accomplish nothing, he thought, to indulge in sentimentality. "That you seemed to be one of those pampered American girls whose family spent too much money on them."

"Right. 'A very nearly perfect example of type.' Isn't that the next line?"

He laughed. "I suppose it is."

"One of the things I've always liked about you, Crane, and I'm not being catty, I mean it, is how everything remains so constant for you. Not only do you remember things in exactly the same way, but you use exactly the same words. Let's see, what comes next? 'But then when I came to know you, Ev, I saw how you were always undercutting it.' And that, I suppose, was meant to be a compliment."

"Oh, indeed it was."

She looked away. "But let's not get side-tracked into a nostalgia number, okay? That woman from the school will be here any minute, and I want to deal with this. I really do need money."

He was hurt. He'd enjoyed being with her for most of those sixteen years, and, for a few seconds, he'd enjoyed being with her again.

"Look," she said, "why don't we settle it? Legally, half's mine. You know that as well as I do. I hate to keep coming to you like a beggar. It makes me feel tacky."

"The last I heard from you... through your lawyer — which, if you remember, is how you've been communicating with me on this topic — is that you wanted a cash settlement. How do you expect me to generate that kind of cash?"

"Sell some of your bloody instruments."

"I have no intention of selling any of my bloody instruments."

"Sell the Tielke."

"Evelyn, you're not going to get a rise out of me that easily."

"Quite an extravagant present for a fifteen-year-old to carry around on the bus in the rain."

"She plays it. Every day."

"Oh, you don't have to tell me that. What's it worth now?"

"I haven't any idea."

"Of course you have some idea. All right, I know how peculiar you are about money. We won't mention figures. Is it worth the price of a car?"

"Possibly."

"A big one?"

"No, a modest one. But what the hell's the point of this?"

"I'm just curious how much money Wendy carts around on the bus in the rain, that's all."

"No, it's more than that. You still resent it that I gave it to her."

"Well, I would have thought the Tielke *copy* would have been more appropriate, but it's done, right? So what about the cello? She doesn't play that anymore."

"Jesus, Ev! Look, if you can't get this straight, we can't get anywhere. The instruments are personal property, not family property."

"Right. Sure. Like my piano that turned into Wendy's harpsichord."

Here we go again, he thought. Back into the wasp's nest. "I don't want to be doing this. I really don't. That bloody woman from that bloody school is going to show up and... All right, what do you want? The bonds? Fine. The house? You can have it. I don't give a damn. It just doesn't make any sense to liquidate everything."

He saw the surprise on her face. "The house," she said slowly, "I don't want it... Paul? Why the hell are we going to court?"

"You know perfectly well why."

"What do you think she is, one of your show pieces? Why don't you offer me the cello for her? Throw in the crumhorns?"

"Do we have to be so unpleasant? Isn't there some... I don't know, plain, decent friendliness left between us?"

"Oh, hell, Paul, I don't want to fight, either. All we're doing is making our lawyers rich."

Next move? One must step carefully. "I've given up on Cindy," he said.

He saw her assessing him. "Everything's tied up, and I need cash," she said. "And the last *I* heard from *you* was how you'd be damned if you were going to support my lover."

"I was playing the injured husband. It's your money, Ev."

"Well, that's a change. Okay, but no court is going to put a fifteen-year-old where she doesn't want to go, and I'm not convinced that Wendy wants to live with you."

He, unfortunately, was not convinced of it, either. "She's not saying anything, is she? She's getting even with us."

Evelyn nodded. And he knew how much restraint they were both exercising to arrive at this point. He had not said: "Wendy's getting even with *you*, my dear." He had not said a word about the amiable young man who was screwing his wife. She, in turn, had not trotted out her set speech about how no daughter of hers was going to grow up to be some tight-assed little WASP debutante. Perhaps they might be unraveling it. And he was tired. "Thank you, Evelyn," he said.


"I don't get it," Kathy said. "How can she be planning to go back to Stafford House if she hasn't talked to you about it?"

"She hasn't said a word to me," Wendy's mother said. Her face had gone white and then, in a matter of seconds, flushed with blood. "It seems just a shade too unilateral for a fifte-year-old."

Paul Crane smiled and turned to hide his reaction from his wife. *Oh yeah?* Kathy thought.

Kathy had seen Paul Crane studying her from the moment she'd walked through the door. His eyes had a sad, bearlike complexity to them, and Kathy had liked him at once. To her surprise, she even found him sexy. He had a magnificent head of thick, brown hair, much more of it than most men his age would have worn, and his high dome of a forehead — prototype for Wendy's — was creased with dignified lines, and she didn't know why, but she liked that. And liked his size. She did not meet many men who were much taller than she was, and he was not only taller, he was something on the order of six-feet four and big along with it, not fat but muscular, built like a boxer.

Fantastically large and powerful hands. She kept looking at them.

"She actually likes that damned place," Wendy's mother said and gave Kathy a look that expected an automatic ally.

"You thought it exactly the right place for her when she was ten," Paul said. And Kathy was sure that he'd just tried to catch her eye—although when she turned to look at him, his face was giving nothing away. God help me, Kathy thought. I do not want to get caught in the middle between these two.

"I don't think we should just go along automatically," Evelyn said. "She's already too much like a... Well, she has no notion of cooperation, of give and take. And she *knows* she doesn't, and she doesn't care. What do *you* think?"

"I don't know Wendy all that well," Kathy said, sidestepping.

"You must have some opinion."

Wendy's mother was dressed to create an effect—something like hip elegance. But the wire-thin bracelets were a little too *Vogue*, her jeans (an expensive designer brand) a little too sleek, her makeup, even though there wasn't much of it, a little too carefully done, and under her blue work shirt she wore one of those old-fashioned push-me-up bras. Evelyn Crane was exactly the sort of woman who brought out in Kathy a stereotypical female cattiness she despised but couldn't suppress, so she was working hard to try to like the woman. She wasn't succeeding.

"Wendy's about five years too late for Van Free," Kathy said. "She might have enjoyed it back in the old days when we were still very experimental, but now we're getting... well, the bottom of the barrel. Broken homes. Foster homes. Drug problems. Children's Aid. Reading difficulties. And some real bad asses."

Neither Paul nor Evelyn said a word; they were both looking at her. "Wendy doesn't need us," she said. "She's not in any real trouble... And she's a distraction. I've got half a dozen kids who can't read or write well enough to fill out a job application, and I just can't spend much energy on her." That had a good ring to it, but it wasn't true at all. Kathy knew by now that she was so interested in Wendy that it bordered on obsession.

Evelyn was giving her a betrayed stare. "I think it's good for Wendy to see the kinds of kids you're talking about."

"You want to rub her nose in it?" Kathy said before she could stop herself.

Evelyn inhaled sharply. After a moment she said, "OK, let her go back to Stafford House. She can grow up as... a pampered little aesthete. Fine. Great. Just the way her daddy likes his girls. Beautiful and useless." Paul turned away. His body had become absolutely motionless.

Evelyn began to gather up coffee cups and spoons. She was spinning out words in a tinkling, inconsequential voice. "Thank you so much for your time, Kathy. We shouldn't be keeping you any longer on such a beautiful morning."

Paul Crane stood up slowly. Then he gave Kathy a single, astonishing look — one of amusement and complicity, his eyes focused precisely on hers. Kathy felt herself freeze, her skin goosebump. She turned away in confusion, saw Evelyn's eyes. The woman's expression was tight and malicious.

"How's Cindy doing then?" Evelyn said. "We haven't even mentioned her."

"Oh, Cindy's doing just fine," Kathy heard herself, from some impossible distance, answering. "She fits right in."

"Can I drop you somewhere... Kathy?" Paul said. He wasn't comfortable with her first name. And she should have guessed it before — he didn't live there.

She couldn't look at him. "I'm going back to Kits."

"That's on my way."

"Well, Cindy *should* be doing fine," Evelyn was saying. "She doesn't have a personality conflict with her group leader." Kathy saw the woman looking at her with a glittering smile. You fucking bitch, she thought.

Then they were outside in the sunlight and seemed to have come to rest in front of a blue Volvo. Paul Crane was lighting his pipe. "Ev's lover's an antitobacco man," he said, grinning around the pipe stem. (She wouldn't have thought him capable of a grin, but here he was doing it.) "Takes it all quite seriously. Stern as Cromwell about it, actually. Can't smoke a puff in that damned house."

"I noticed," Kathy said. "Not an ashtray in sight." And he'd just sounded like something off a BBC manners comedy — probably because he'd been working hard at every word he'd said. He's as nervous as I am, she thought.

"How long have you been separated?" she asked him.

"Since July."

"Divorce?"

"In the wings." He still hadn't unlocked his car; he stood leaning against it. "Are you, ah... I don't know exactly how people your age put it... in a relationship?"

She laughed. "No." Their eyes met. "People my age," she said. "Good God."

And he obviously couldn't find the next line. "Why don't you take me to lunch?" she said to help him. "Or... It's a little early for lunch. Or something." Her mouth had gone dry.

He looked away. "I'm not good at this," he said without looking at her. "I'd be delighted to do *something*. Would you care to walk around Little Mountain with the Japanese tourists?"

How odd, Paul thought. Here he was with this strange, beautiful woman enjoying the autumn sun, scuffing through fallen leaves, feeling the wind on his face — it was enough to make him feel young and distinctly giddy. "What a glorious day," he said.

It had begun, he knew perfectly well, because she was so totally unlike Evelyn. And then, curiously enough, he'd even been pleased that she and Eveleyn had detested each other. But the longer Paul studied Kathy, the more certain he was that he liked everything about her — her directness, her height, her angular body, her white skin and black hair, even her American accent, and he didn't usually like American accents. And since it was patently impossible for anything much to happen between them, one could, he thought, enjoy flirting without having to take any of it seriously.

"Are you English?" she asked him.

It took him a moment to make sense of the question. What was happening to him? It was a perfectly straightforward question. "Oh, good Christ, no. I'm from Toronto. Do I seem English?"

"If I'd met you in the States before I came to Canada, I would have thought you were English. But you're ah, what's called English-Canadian?"

"With all the pejoratives?"

"I didn't intend any."

"Well, implied or not, I'll own up to them all... and I think I must also have been stamped with a certain Englishness from having lived there so long, and... Well, I suppose I could say I came into my own in London."

He watched her take a bar of rest before she delivered the line. "You got laid there, eh?"

He could fall in love with a woman who could make him laugh like that. "Yes," he said. "I did."

Oh, God, he thought. Now what am I supposed to say? His mouth had dried up. He felt like a teenager.

"What were you doing in England?" she asked him.

He had trouble speaking. "Oh, I studied a bit at the Guild Hall and did a lot of accompanying. Got involved in early music."

She was looking down over the park with veiled and thoughtful eyes. She kept her smoking gear in the pockets of her jeans; she brought it out now. They'd stopped on the bridge to lean on the railing and look down into the clipped hollow of the park. She finished rolling her cigarette, and her tongue slid along the crisp edge of the paper, and yes, that's the way tongues are, he told himself, annoyed — pink and wet and, in all probability, quite warm. There's no reason to regard this particular woman's tongue as a revelation. "Let's walk back up," she said.

She turned to him and smiled; her black hair spun in the bright light. "I should have stayed at BU and got my degree," she said. "But I wanted to play jazz, and the classical bullshit busted my ass."

"Unfortunately it does that to a lot of students," he said. "I know. I teach that classical bullshit."

They were walking toward the dome of the Bloedel Conservatory, which always looked to him like a landed spaceship. And his prediction had been accurate: there were tourists on every side of them. The day was too fine, and wherever they went, they would be moving through crowds. "Surely you must be hungry by now?" he said.

"Why don't you take me home?" she said.

"Oh?" He was absurdly disappointed. "Of course."

"No. Not to my home. To yours."

Damn it, now what could she mean by that? One felt totally out of one's depth.

"Do you have anything to eat at home?" she said. He heard a tiny buzz in her voice.

Without warning, she walked away toward the parking lot. It took him a moment to catch up. He thought he must have angered her in some unaccountable way. But then he saw that she was smiling.

"When did you start playing music?" she asked him, making conversation again.

"They tell me that as soon as I could walk, I used to climb up onto the piano bench and sit there by the hour pushing the keys down."

"Happy childhood?"

"Oh, yes."

"Prep school, I bet?"

"Upper Canada College."

She laughed. "Are you serious? I thought it was a Canadian myth. I wasn't sure it really existed."

"Oh, it exists. Quite formidably, I can assure you."

"Did you like it there?"

"Absolutely."

"Did you really?"

"Oh, yes. What's so strange about that?"

"So you're really one of the élite?" she said. He could hear the lightness in her tone; she was teasing him.

"Yes, I suppose I am."

"Did you know it?"

"I suppose we all knew it, that we'd been singled out by birth. And we felt—I don't expect you to believe this, even though it's perfectly true — a kind of humility. We wanted to be of some use."

They had reached the car and stopped alongside it. "This is amazing," she said.

"Amazing?"

"Yeah, if I'd read a report on you, just a simple listing of the facts of your life, I would have been prepared to hate your guts. And instead... Well, I like you." And one couldn't say it any more simply than that, he thought.

He drove down the circular road away from the height. Now he was afraid of silences between them. She'd been smoking incessantly. "The next, most obvious, conversational gambit," he said, "is for me to ask you about your life."

She hesitated before she answered. "Certain similarities to yours. Old New England family. Money. Weird combination of old-fashioned Boston stuffiness along with the wildest screwball liberal Unitarianism. Never felt any sense of limits. It was always, 'Anything you want, Kathy.' Even when what I wanted turned out to be jazz."

"You didn't get your degree?" he said, leading her.

"Oh, hell, no. That would have been too safe and normal. Dropped out. Played every kind of gig under the sun. Took some courses at Berklee." He waited, knowing there was more. "I found out that it was easier to screw a musician than to be one."

She'd managed to shock him again, but he was almost getting used to it, had almost come to like it. He risked a look at her. She'd rolled down the window and was staring out. All he could see was the back of her head.

"I auditioned for a band once," she said. Her voice had changed. "Mixed. One white guy, two black guys. And they just couldn't believe I was for real... 'Jesus, man, can you believe the nerve of this chick? She thinks she can play the saxophone.' The piano player was a kind of imitation Monk, pretty good, but not good enough. He said, 'Let's do "Round Midnight",' and I said, 'Sure.' And then they went through their number. 'Hey, Joe, you got a lead sheet for that?... 'Shit, man, I think I left the fucker at home.' So no music, eh?

"I said, 'That's OK, I know the tune.' They're all grinning at me. They just couldn't believe it, right? But I knew every fucking note. I'd worn the grooves off the record.

"All right, here we go. Unison at the head. Everybody solos. With a tune like that, you can memorize the head, but when it comes time to solo, the changes will cut you to pieces. Well, I blew those guys out the door. I had them fighting for their lives. And do you think they'd hire me?"

She seemed to expect an answer. "What happened?" he said.

"Of course they didn't hire me. I'd just cut their balls off. And I was so dumb I didn't even know it. I just thought we'd been playing music."

He was astonished at the transformation in her; he couldn't define it. "Paul?" He looked and saw that her eyes had a kind of wintry desolation to them. "Do you mind if we stop by my place a minute?"

"No, of course not."

Now it was exactly what he had been fearing — the conversation had dried up. She didn't speak other than to guide him to her apartment, a basement suite below one of Vancouver's standard stucco houses. She didn't invite him in, jumped out of the car, left behind the ambience of a theme broken in the middle. What could she have been thinking? Missed opportunities? A lost career? He left the engine running, took the empty moment to light his pipe. Eastern trees lined both sides of the street; the colours were dazzling. And sad. And he, too, had lost his original purpose somewhere along the way. The live music vibrating in the air had always been what had fired him.

Then she was back. She threw a brown purse into the back seat with a dismissive toss as though it were a football.

Knowing that he would need to take her home again, he parked in the front rather than in the garage. She followed him into the house. He turned back at the end of the hall, saw that she'd come to rest just inside the door to the living room; she was staring in. "Holy shit!" she said.

"You don't need to take your boots off," he said. "Rugs are meant to be walked on."

But she took them off anyway, and, in her white cotton socks, padded silently across Evelyn's Oriental rug to the harpsichord. She turned slowly and stared at the room. "Good Christ! It's unbelievable. It's like a museum."

He was embarrassed, fully aware of how much money was hanging about on the walls. "One's hobbies do rather take over one's life."

"Do they all play?"

"Not by themselves."

She laughed. "Oh, come on, Paul. Are they playable?"

"Oh, yes. They're all working instruments. I wouldn't own anything that couldn't be played."

"I don't know what to say. I'm just... blown away. It's beautiful."

"Thank you," he said uneasily.

She dropped her long white fingers onto the keys of the harpsichord; the strings were plucked. She held the keys down. Her eyes in the dim light (the draperies were closed) seemed green as jade. He saw her for the first time, he thought, as fully herself — a magnificent, unique woman. The chord hung uneasily in the air, the tritone obvious in it — *diabolus in musica* — and in the restless beating of the upper partials he heard the sound of his own desire.

"This little gem rose to light rather unexpectedly," Paul was saying, "surfaced in a private collection. An unknown composer called Jan van Dorestad. The first of his work that's ever been discovered."

Kathy had as much as told this man outright that she wanted to sleep with him. What did she have to do, write a sign and hang it on the wall? But now he seemed to want her to look at the music, so she did. It was written in a precise black hand wholly unlike anything she'd ever seen before. The notes were shaped like diamonds. She could make out six staves, one over the other, like a score, but the clefs were unintelligible.

"There were rules in the Renaissance," he went on, sounding exactly like what he was — a university professor. "The rules of *musica ficta*. They were absolutely ground into a musician's bones until they were automatic... in the way, I suppose, that you don't have to tell a jazz musician to swing the eighth notes. Are you with me?"

"Sure." Maybe she'd read all the signals wrong. Maybe all he'd wanted had been an afternoon spent in the company of a woman who was not his bitter, beautiful wife.

"And there was an interval that was forbidden. The tritone. 'The devil in music,' they called it. Balance and repose were the ideals of the Renaissance, and they didn't like that restless, ambiguous sound. A flat five, I believe you'd call it in jazz."

"Yeah, I know what a tritone is."

"Right. Of course you do... Well, it was so automatic to avoid the tritone that they didn't bother to write in the accidentals because any bloody fool would do it without thinking, all right?"

"I'm following you so far."

Kathy hadn't gone to bed with a man the first day she'd met him since Steve. Today she'd not only been willing to do it, but it had felt inevitable. She'd even made him stop at her place so she could picked up her goddamned stupid diaphragm. And so far the only move he'd made of intimacy had been to take off his suit jacket.

"But in this particular work the problem is more complex than merely finding the right *ficta* notes," he said. "This piece is *intentionally* ambiguous." He stuffed tobacco into his pipe but didn't light it.

Good God, now what? He was handing her a book. She automatically read the title — E. E. Lowinsky, *Secret Chromatic Art in the Netherlands Motet*.

"This man proposed a theory that set off a storm of controversy among musicologists back in the forties. He claimed to have discovered in the work of several Netherlandish composers what he called a secret procedure. He claimed that they wrote works that had two possible ways of reading them, one for the uninitiated and one for those who were in on the secret. There were hints, clues in the music. At a crucial point, one could go one of two ways, ignore the hints and keep on going in an ordinary fashion, or see the possibility of something else and introduce a flat. Once you introduced the flat, you were caught in what's sometimes called 'the flat syndrome.' You make something flat to avoid the tritone, and then you've got to make something else flat farther along to avoid another tritone, and before you know it, you're off around the cycle of fifths.

"Now what Lowinsky claimed was that those points of modulation occurred at highly charged and emotional moments in the text... that the composers who used the secret chromaticism were associated with heretical movements, that the texts they chose were critical of the established church, dangerous... that the whole technique had to be kept secret to avoid confrontation with the Inquisition."

"That's interesting," she said. The autumnal sun was setting — nostalgic lemonish glow through the white curtains. Soon they'd need to turn on the lights. And she was getting a headache from the tension.

"Look here." He spread out sheets of manuscript paper on the desk. "I've transcribed most of the van Dorestad motet, and there's no doubt in my mind that it's an example of secret chromaticism. To start with, it's a highly charged text. 'Then was Jesus led out by the Spirit into the wilderness.' That first line is repeated several times in imitative counterpart... *Tunc Jesus ductus est in desertum a Spiritu*... and so far everything is clear-cut, no funny business. But here," he pointed, "are the hints. These flats written in. Because they're not necessary. Everybody would have known that those notes were to be flattened. It's a hint to the initiated. Watch out, there's something coming.

"And then van Dorestad skips a large part of the story. Nothing about Christ fasting forty days or forty nights, not the famous part about man not living by bread alone... No, he picks up the story here. *Iterum assumpsit eum diabolus in montem excelsum valde.* 'Again the devil took him up onto a very high mountain and showed all the kingdoms of the world and the glory of them. And said to him, all these things will I give thee, if thou wilt fall down and worship me. And Jesus said to him, "Get thee behind me, Satan, for it is written: Thou shalt worship the Lord thy God and him only shalt thou serve.' " That's the entire text that Van Dorestad uses.

"The ambiguous point occurs at the second appearance of the word 'devil.' See, right here, that's the crucial note, that E. If you read it as E natural — which is perfectly legitimate, by the way — from there on you get a square, clumsy, somewhat dull work of music. But if you flatten that note, you begin to modulate, and suddenly you have a vividly exciting passage. The modulation continues for quite some time, but when Jesus speaks, 'Get thee behind me, Satan,' we return to our original key through an empty fifth. It's a moment of absolute power and drama. And then, as Jesus continues to speak, we have a long, sinuous, winding melody that drifts away until there's nothing left but the bass voices, and the piece ends with a dark, melancholy, brooding effect. It's one of the most dramatic examples of word painting I've seen from the period."

He smiled at her, his eyes bright with excitement, lifted his pipe, drew out a match, but again didn't light the tobacco. "All the kingdoms of the world," he said. "Well, at the time when this motet was composed, Luther was just getting underway in Germany, and all the kingdoms of the world were still Catholic. The Low Countries were under the control of Spain, were *particularly* Catholic. So the message of the motet seems to be this... If you go along with the established church, play ball with the devil, then you can have every good thing in life. Material success, safety, security, ordinary happiness. But, 'Thou shalt worship the Lord thy God,' Christ says. And if you worship Christ in a way the church thinks is heretical, you might enter the Kingdom of Heaven in the next life, but you might also get yourself burned at the stake in this one."

Finally he lit his pipe; the room was filled at once with the smell of burning tobacco.

"You must be a hell of a good teacher," Kathy said.

He said nothing. Religious music written in the sixteenth century, she thought. What a bizarre thing to be talking about. And the prospect of going on with this — whatever it was they were doing — made her tired before she began. She was tired of games. Her headache was killing her. And she was just plain tired.

"Listen," he said. "It's starting to rain."

He was right. She heard them first, then looked through the window, saw fat, widely spaced drops begin to spatter on the sidewalk. The sun had set; the yellowish light of only a few minutes before had vanished, and the afterglow was painfully cool and gray. With no warning at all, she felt alone and lost. Not a polite ritual left, scarcely even a social role. She no longer knew in any substantial or useful way who or where she was. "Paul," she said to this stranger, "do you want to sleep with me?"

He tapped out his pipe in the ashtray before he answered. Then, with a smile shy and sweet as a young boy's, he said, "Of course I do."

A production out of *Vogue* via the psycho ward, Kathy thought, and turned slowly, looking at the black-and-gold bathroom. This can't be Paul's taste, must have been done by his screwy wife. The upper portion of the wall above the wainscoting was divided into panels, alternating: a plate — yes, goddamned dinner plates painted with pictures from an Egyptian tomb — and then a mirror. There wasn't anywhere she could go to escape her reflection. And *here*, not the bedroom, is where Steve would have wanted to make love, right on the cold tile, watching himself doing it from as many angles as possible. He'd loved conceptual turn-ons.

Like that hot summer's night at Peter's in Philadelphia. The parents safely away on vacation, Peter and one of his giggly girlfriends downstairs eating pizza in front of the TV, and she and Steve upstairs playing. He'd found not only a whole wall of smoked mirror in the master bedroom, but also, stored in the attic, party clothes that must have belonged to Peter's older sisters. And so Kathy had been transformed into a life-size doll, nothing required of her beyond passive cooperation. Fine with her — she'd been so stoned she could hardly move.

He'd arranged her in various poses as though, instead of making love to her, he were going to photograph her for a sleazy men's magazine. He'd saved long gloves, stockings, and a fifties cocktail dress for last. He bent her over a fake Louis Quatorze chair, and she stared over her shoulder at her own smoky reflection as Steve, grinning like a demented idiot, lifted her skirt, lifted the layers of frothy petticoats, thrust into her from behind, hard and greedy, and pumped away. Guided by his skillful fingers, she had a painful orgasm and passed straight out. Woke up an hour later right on the floor where he'd dumped her. Still fully dressed, sweating and itchy, and everything too small. Still stoned, still — God knows why — turned on. Lay there listening to his laugh drifting up from below. Knew he was totally out of control. Fantasized, quite vividly, of cutting his throat.

Jesus, she was as bad as Steve, couldn't stop her mind from rattling away, talking to itself. And that night in Philadelphia seemed now as innocent as a child's romp. What she was about to do felt truly dangerous. Always paranoid since she'd gone off the pill, she used too much jelly. It made her feel squishy inside, full of some nasty glue. She walked quickly across the hall to the bedroom where Paul was waiting. He'd left a light burning.

He seemed to be undressed already, although she couldn't be sure. He was sitting in bed, bare-chested, with the covers drawn up to his waist. "No fair," she said.

"What's that?"

"You're hiding. Christ, I always hate the first few minutes."

"Come under the covers then."

"Sure. Then we can both hide." She slipped in quickly and pulled the sheet up to her chin. She finally let herself know how scared she was.

He looked into her eyes — a long, searching appraisal — not yet sexual interest, but, *How are you? How are you feeling?* "It has sometimes seemed to me," he said, "that this is the most curiously ineffectual way to get to know another human being that's ever been discovered."

She laughed. "Come on, let's look at each other and get it over with." I am *not* going to apologize for the hair on my legs, she thought.

"Is that how you approach most things?" he said, "Cut the Gordian knot?"

She heard herself laugh again — nervous reflex. "That's funny. That was the name of one of Steve's bands... Yeah, that is my style. Or if it isn't, I try to make it my style. Don't screw around. Get right down to it." She pulled the covers back.

"Am I supposed to comment?" he said after a moment, "You look impossibly fit."

"You make me sound like a racehorse. You're not in such bad shape yourself. The hair on your chest's going gray." She touched it gingerly. "I like it. I was hoping you wouldn't have a middle-aged belly on you, and you don't."

He smiled, but his expression was still remote, even melancholy. "I seem to be losing weight now. Can't bear my own cooking. This mutual assessment of our physical attributes seems somewhat brutal to me, Kathy... Katherine... Is your name Katherine?"

"Yeah, that's my name."

"I'm glad. I was afraid that you might be a Kathleen."

"God forbid I should be a Kathleen. I'm sorry about the hair on my legs." Shit!

"Did you think I would mind?"

"Do you mind?"

"It seems absolutely trivial."

Kathy looked away. She wanted to see where she'd arrived, size up the space around her. And this goddamned bedroom was *hers*, of course. "Hey, is there somewhere we can go to get away from your wife?"

"I'm afraid not. Even the guest room is full of her things."

"It's the first time in my life I've ever felt like an adulteress."

"There's always the living-room floor."

"Really, Doctor Crane?"

They both laughed. He opened his arms to her, and she slipped quickly into them. Jesus, she thought, he's big. Bigger than any man I've ever been with. "It seems chicken to turn out the light, but maybe we should. Damn, she left all her stuff behind, didn't she?"

"She certainly did. Part of her plan for a new life, I suppose. New beginnings."

"They never have the common courtesy to clean up after themselves, do they? The bastards. I lived for months with Steve's shit everywhere. Always seemed one of the cruelest things he ever did to me."

"Perhaps we could try one of the girls' rooms."

"That'd be worse. No, let's stay here. I'll get used to it. Goddamn, Paul, but you're big."

"Indeed. All the Cranes are large. Luckily the girls are like their mother..." She heard him stop himself from talking. It was consoling, she supposed — he was frightened too. "I'll get the light," he said.

He slid out of bed and crossed the room, turned to look at her, gave her a concerned, shy smile. He was a huge, massive weight of a man, the shape of his muscles clearly defined, his shoulders broad and slightly stooped. A lot of curly hair on his body. Physically just about as different from Steve as she could imagine — which, she thought, is probably one of the reasons I'm here with him. He hesitated, hand on the light switch, a puzzled look on his face, and then said, "I've never been with another woman the entire time Evelyn and I were married." The room went dark.

She felt his weight settle onto the bed next to her. Her eyes began to adjust, and she could see him in silhouette, a black, looming form, and she felt a moment of panic. She'd never realized before just how carefully she must have been avoiding, all her life, sex with men bigger than she was. "Maybe we should keep the light on," she said.

"Whatever you want."

"It doesn't matter. Come on, Paul, hold me. I'm scared." Her teeth were chattering.

He was nothing like Steve whose angular shoulder had never made much of a pillow. Paul was obviously used to holding women. "Katherine," he said, "forgive me if this sounds... I don't know what, actually... if it sounds absurd of me to have to say it. I haven't had much experience with this sort of thing, and I don't know quite how people your age go about it, but... Well, I think you're a magnificent woman."

She was far more touched than she would have thought possible. "Thank you," she said, hearing the smallness of her voice.

She wanted to get the energy going. Slid her hand down to find his prick. It came alive at once — thick and blunt, circumsised. Not, thank God, the least bit like Steve's long slippery eel. She heard him draw in his breath sharply. He touched her breasts with light fingertips. His huge hands were gentle. A musician. "You don't have to be shy with me," she said.

"I'm somewhat in awe of you, actually. I can't quite believe that this is happening."

"Awe isn't good for sex." Although Steve had thought it was. She tried to laugh. "You're right, what you said, 'curiously ineffectual.' Well, let's be a couple of happy animals then, and we'll get to know each other afterward."

She kissed him, felt the tickle of his beard and mustache. She was turning it into her most provocative, teasing kiss, executed with a certain cold-blooded deliberateness. She was feeling the full force of what Steve used to say: "Kathy, I want my mind to turn off."

His reaction was explosive. Surprised, curiously pleased, she found herself rolled, not gently, onto her back. Her hands found him fully erect. He was kissing her the way a thirsty man would go for a pail of water. It was all too fast, and she felt fear like ice down her spine — a hint of what could turn into a black panic if she let it — but she was afraid of doing anything that might break the current. Feeling alone and desperate, she kissed him back. She wasn't the least bit turned on, her body wasn't the least bit ready, but she seemed to be going through the motions of an instant passion — quite convincingly — and she didn't know why.

She'd never liked the feeling of being pinned down by a man, but she seemed to have evoked from him the need to use the full force of his size to squash her to the bed, and some demon in her was continuing to come up with every trick in the book to make sure he kept on doing it — writhing, panting, raking his back and ass with her fingernails. And her damnable mind wouldn't stop chattering. *Maybe it's because you're so big*, she thought, *maybe he needs to show you just how much bigger he is. And maybe that's exactly why you picked him.* But no juices flowing, no charge.

Now he was already trying to come into her, and she must be still dry as a bone. But no, enough vaginal jelly in there to do the trick. Artificial juices, more simulated sex. Then her body decided not to cooperate. He could have forced her, but didn't, drew back at once. But he'd hurt her, and he knew it. She felt the force go out of him at once, and he hovered uncertainly above, a big animal baffled at the gate. And, as absolutely bizarre as it might be, the last thing she wanted was for him to turn back into that polite, careful university professor. She kissed him, a quick, reassuring nibble, then filled up her hands with her own spit, reached down to massage it into his penis. He sprang erect again as soon as she touched him. What am I trying to do? she thought. Get it over with as fast as I can? Yeah. Right. But why? *So I don't end up here flat on my back screaming my head off in the dark with this huge stranger on top of me, that's why.*

She arched her pelvis and guided him in with her hands. She still wasn't ready, felt a contracted, sullen resistance, but gritted her teeth until he pushed through it. Now she was totally flattened, her thighs scissored apart. Suddenly she began to struggle to get out from under, to force herself a little clear breathing space, but she knew (and that's what set the full panic off in her at last, exploding like a flashbulb at the back of her head) that he was too far gone, that it'd seem to him like increasing passion. *Just don't scream*, she told herself. And suddenly no air and the giveaway wheeze at the bottom of her lungs.

She was gone, blown out on fear. Green lake water, silt soft under her toes near the shore, but too far out, diving like a fool. Then her opened eyes saw light the wrong side up. Just float to the top, but couldn't remember. Panic. Kicked, clawed. Green lake water pouring into her open mouth. Bobbed free to scream. *I can't breathe.* Horrible pressing weight. *Kathy, you went out too far.*

For the first time, terrified and mindless, she felt something ignite in her, and she rose to meet him (bobbed up, broke clear). Still pinned down but her breath was coming, shallow and quick. (Daddy had squashed her onto the dock on her back. Breathed air into her mouth. She'd turned away her head and vomited green lake water.) And she was turned on, pretty damned late in the game, but finally turned on. "Oh Jesus!" she heard her own angry cry, and kissed this man to keep herself from screaming.

She couldn't think any more. She arched up, guided his motion against hers. Caught his ass with both hands and pulled him into her. But too late. (Damn it, she was thinking again!) He was coming. She felt the kick in his penis — delicious but too soon. He'd been making sounds back in his throat. It could have been sobbing.

She lay there squashed, her thighs forced apart. Her left leg was cramping. He was still inside but useless now, and she was, damn it, fully charged and humming like an engine. Her mind slowly reconstructed itself. Dark expanse of ceiling above, rain coming down out in the world, round orange face of the clock radio on the bed table, reflected light from the hall. She'd never been more amazed at anything she'd ever done before in her life. "Get off me," she said.

"Oh. Sorry."

"Shut up. *Don't say you're sorry.*" She kissed his nose. His beard was wet. "Here," she said, "put your head on me."

He settled into her. Her nipples were burning. "Katherine," he said, and then, in a few minutes, fell asleep.

You son of a bitch, she thought. Well, at least you know my

name. She badly needed a cigarette, but she let him rest on her. She felt profoundly confused — and curiously pleased with herself. God, but men were crazy. Something weirdly mutable about them. This huge man was now sleeping on her breasts like a two-year-old.

Sound was transformed immediately into notation, appeared in a rapid, spidery hand, the notes black as liquid soot, written out on a milky, unrolling paper. It was absolutely singular. Surely he couldn't have worked with music his entire life and never before noticed a secret as simple as this one. Staring, bending closer, he saw the notes themselves as sound. The breves and minims and semiminims sang themselves under his eyes. He must make a record of it; this discovery would revolutionize the teaching of music. And then, compressed and distorted as though through the speaker of a cheap car radio, some wretched popular song came squawking from somewhere in the high, stone building, echoing off the walls. He was frightened and knew that he had to try to wake up.

It was night. There were candles burning in the cathedral, but they gave nowhere near enough light to enable him to see where he was going. He hurried back to the nave, afraid of losing his way, and heard that somewhere out of sight, hidden in a dark recess, six singers were performing the van Dorestad motet. They were nearing the end of the composition; he knew it by the deep tessitura, the slow, winding, infinitely sad drift to cadence. He began to run. He'd never get another chance to hear it sung in the sixteenth century.

He pushed through a massive wooden door and found himself in the Pacific Centre Mall. Why do they have to do these things? he thought. Don't they know what they're doing? Children the age of his daughters hurried by and ignored him as he stood and wept. Outside, under the open sky, it was raining. He had to get to the rain before they closed off the sky. With a tremendous tightening, effort of the will, he reached for the rain. The rain itself was made of black minims; it drew him. His eyes felt as heavy as if there were a penny on each lid, but he forced them open, saw the familiar shapes of his own bedroom. Outside the partially opened window, the rain fell.

And he saw, against the cold street light coming in, the silhouette of a naked woman sitting on a chair. She inhaled on a cigarette, and her face was illuminated for a brief moment; she was watching him. "Paul," she said, and her voice brought him fully awake.

"How long have I been asleep?"

"I don't know. An hour." He heard something withdrawn and sullen, a tone like Cindy's when she was having a sulk.

"Kathy?" he said.

"Yeah, it's me."

"Are you all right?"

"Of course I'm all right."

"You've opened the window, opened Ev's bloody drapes," he said.

"Do you mind?"

"No. In fact I'm delighted... I'm sorry I fell asleep. You must feel deserted."

She shrugged.

Something was wrong — elusive but nasty like the most minute of intonation problems. "Are you really all right?"

"Yes, damn it, I'm all right. Let's make a deal, okay? Let's not talk about it after we do it... For Christ's sake, stop looking so worried. You didn't damage me."

He didn't know how to break the silence. Having tried out and discarded a number of opening lines, he said, "What have you been thinking sitting there all this time?"

"I haven't just been sitting here. Treated myself to a tour of the mansion."

"Like that."

"Of course like this. I hate getting dressed after, and... What the fuck was I supposed to wear?"

It didn't quite make sense. What on earth was going on? "My bathrobe's on the other chair." And he found the thought of her walking naked around his house ridiculously erotic, felt the stir of blood in his penis.

"Your bathrobe. Right. Thanks for telling me."

"Kathy?"

"Oh, shit. I feel really bitchy. Sorry. Yes, I have been think-ing. Not exactly cheery thoughts. Or new ones. I envy you your home, Doctor Crane. And your security. And your goddamned fucking harpsichord."

"And my wife who took off with my children?"

"Yeah, but you did have it for a while, what everybody's supposed to have. Just a plain old-fashioned, decent life, a family. And I've been thinking, *what if they were right?* All the smug assholes who told me how to live. Get married, Kathy. Settle down, Kathy. Girls don't play saxophones in jazz bands... Shit. If I were one of my own students, I'd write in my file, 'Problems with authority.'"

He heard so much anger in her voice he knew he had to be

careful. "The greener grass, eh? I took it all quite for granted until it came collapsing down around my ears. I used to wander around here after everyone had gone to sleep and feel an emptiness... a dissatisfaction. I'd never thought I'd end up as an academic with a wife and children and a mortgage. And then when Ev left... Oh, looking back, it feels inevitable now. She and I had been growing apart for years. But I miss the girls terribly."

She didn't reply. She lit another cigarette. He waited.

"You may have got your relief," she said, "but I'm strung out like a wire."

*Oh!* he thought. One's stupidity is, at times, monumental. "Come back to bed, Katherine."

He'd thought that she might hesitate, but she didn't. Within a matter of minutes she'd seized his hand and pressed it between her legs. He loved her for it. Evelyn had never been that direct in the entire time they'd been married. And so quickly it took him by surprise, her body arched, contracted. She gasped. She fell limply onto him but said, "More. Can you?"

"Yes."

"No, lie still. Let me get on top."

This was certainly new to him: the man so totally passive, but he was perfectly content to lie beneath her, letting her move, letting his muscles relax into the mattress. The furnace had been blowing dry, hot air through the grate; now it fell silent, and he heard the house settle and groan to itself. He felt a sense of timelessness he'd never known before in sex, as though his usual heavy self had departed and left behind only a light spray of consciousness.

She was working; her sweat poured over him. She was panting like an athlete; he felt the rise and fall of her ribs. She began to moan, a long, drawn-out resonance — string tone. She arched onto him, locked him down. Awestruck, he could only hold her. But she caught her breath, was moving again. Good Christ, was she going to go on forever?

Her eyes seemed to have gone quite crazy, showing whites. It was taking so long, so very long. Chain of suspended sevenths, *Duo Seraphim*. She was leading them both up to an astonishingly refined elevation. Then she abandoned herself and departed, her trust in him total. Tears that weren't the least bit sad stung his eyes. He stopped up her screaming mouth with his, felt her body go rigid, every fibre of it. "Jesus!" she yelled and pulled her face away. She was bent like a bow. Her stare was blind as stone.

She fell away. He took her into his arms. She'd also been

brought to tears; they streaked her cheeks. "Thank you," she said.

"Thank you, too. How inadequate. Sweet Katherine."

Gradually she fell asleep. Her open mouth laid warm spittle on his shoulder. But he was far from sleep now; energy stirred in all his limbs. He gently untwined himself, swung his feet over the edge of the bed, sat up. Still sleeping, she reached for him. "Steve?" she said.

"No, it's me."

And then he understood that neither she sleeping, nor he awake, could possibly know what that statement had meant. He walked to the window. The rain falling in the street light was as insubstantial as a dream.


One of the last records he made before he died. The one where he was begging for sanctuary. Goddamn strange choice to pull out of the stack and play at a party in a loft on Queen Street in 1977, not any of the famous tunes, but this late weird record that nobody remembers. Maybe it's supposed to be cute – the voice of a dead man. And Steve let himself sag back, dumped sack of potatoes, and listened to the voice of the dead man.

The girl was still a tense spring jamming up the far wall, alone, still giving Steve the eye. And so outrageous that for a while he'd thought she was a boy in drag. Hair chopped off to a couple of inches, dyed day-glo orange and greased up into pointed tufts. Earlobes hung with five-and-dime rhinestone pendants. Stubby nails painted black. An honest-to-God dog collar at the throat, straight from the pet store, silver studs and all. Black shirt, too big, ripped in half a dozen places and held together with safety pins. Baggy plastic knee pants the nasty green of a garbage bag. Tight lizard-skin boots with whorish heels, run-down and scuffed. God, no way the kid could mean to be sexy. She's a walking insult. Absurd, exaggerated, campy, kinky, a stone mess. And frightening. Of course.

She must have stripped her face bare as an egg and recreated it from zero. Eyebrows shaved clean away and redrawn. Skin pancaked gray-white, cheekbones smeared fever red. False lashes thick as feather dusters, moth wings. Eyes lined with stripes, black lids, cartoon Bambi. But looking out a pinched and bleak stare. (Listening to the voice of the dead man?) Can see the bitter mouth, indented, perfectly well under the waxed purple pout painted on. And exploding from the stereo, trump of the Judgment card, the dead man's voice – echoing in the mind, closed tape loop. The girl saw Steve looking. She didn't smile. She contracted, arching. A spasm, brief and electric, moved down her body and ended in a forward thrust of her hips. The fear felt like iron. Steve walked.

"If the doors of perception were cleansed," Steve heard himself absurdly saying.

The girl looked up, a moth on the wall. Eventually she said, "We could see everything as it is — infinite."

Singed and dizzy, Steve dug the Player's out of his jacket. "No," she said. Then with a twisted smile, "Did I pass?"

"None of us passed. What the fuck you want, kid?"

"I want a drummer."

Steve closed his eyes and slid to the floor. When he looked again, the girl was sitting next to him. "They say on my good nights you can't tell the difference between me and a drummer. You ever heard me play?"

"Yeah. Caught you at the Brunswick."

"What? With that bunch of clowns?"

"I could tell you were good by what you *weren't* playing."

Steve shrugged. "You got a name?"

"Annie Epoxy."

"Oh, for fuck's sake. Look, Annie Epoxy, find a kid your own age. That's where you'll get the sound you want."

"How do you know what sound I want?"

"Just by looking at you." Steve jerked his head toward the speakers. "So what do you think of him?"

"He was the best there was."

"Yeah. Right. *Well, listen to him then.* You were just a baby when that record came out, but shit, my whole history's right there. I'm tired. You don't need me. I've been running too long... And it's horrible to play that record now at this fucking sick party. He was telling us he was on the way out. Every fucking line he was telling us. It's obscene that we're still around to hear it."

What happened to him? To the leather queen, the beautiful boy, the prophet and madman, the singer and seer — the saint. Jim Morrison. "He made it," Steve said. "He died." And: "There's no way for us to be successful now. None."

"It's fucked," the girl said. "Fucked. It's all fucked."

"That's right. So find yourself another drummer."

Their eyes met. The whites of the kid's eyes were perfectly clear, the corneas were hazel. It was a street-corner tomboy face, late teens, a sandlot softball face painted like a fool's.

"I'll take you home," the girl said.

Out on the street the girl's wrapped in a black vinyl raincoat straight out of that time, the end of the sixties. At her age it's probably as lost as Paris between the wars, nostalgia bought off the rack at the Sally Ann, but you remember that black vinyl raincoat, don't you, Steven? You bet your sweet ass you do. "Men ever hassle you on the street?"

"What do you think?"

"I think: Yes."

"You're right then."

Toronto's a crueler city than Boston because sometimes in the winter the sun shines brilliantly in a postcard-blue sky and the white clouds are like banners, because there are trees, because the subways are clean. What the fuck's a poor Georgia boy doing up here? October, by God, and only a few weeks left. Then winter. The cold wind is blowing and freezing to rain, but there's hot blood still running in these rebel veins. Shee-it, at one in the morning. Did his songs in Harvard Yard for the strike. Walked through the occupied buildings and saw nothing but heavies, PL heavies, SDS heavies, talk talk talk, no joy at all. "All right, let's go show them what it's about!" Set up in the Yard, ran the power out of one of those official ivy buildings, cranked it up, could hear us in fucking Central Square. Had them dancing, the dope going around, peace and love, vision and drugs, and shit, you believed it all. You and Kathy were still like Romeo and Juliet then, so of course you believed it all. SDS dude came out and asked you to stop. You asked him if he wanted to have your ride cymbal shoved up his ass. Sang, "Break On Through," and "Light My Fire," and "Five to One," but you never tried to sing "The End," because you can cover a tune, but you can't cover Morrison. Oh, the old Lizard King, owing him a death. "You've got a real name, don't you?" Steve said.

The girl in her sleazy boots was like a child on stilts, not a tease but a balancing act. "Forgot it."

Oh, baby, you're too young to take that tone, but me — I remember it all. Wisteria and lilacs smelling like a goddamn funeral, a lawn party for Christ's sake, and my God, in Georgia the summer nights are so close they hang around your neck like drunken little girls. Listen to the whisper telling you there's something incredible just a step away, maybe over there in the shadow under the tree, maybe around the corner at the end of the street. You're the whiz kid drummer with every lick stolen from Gene Krupa or Max Roach, sweat like a fucking pig just to make those crinolines move, just to see those hot shiny eyes looking, telling you what's waiting, maybe tomorrow night. So you beat your way across twenty years just to see that evening sun go down.

Swear to God, you almost broke through when Kathy was still wearing miniskirts and you had a little help from sweet acid. All the girls were your marionettes then, asses jerking to your beat, and one night you got each of your limbs going in a different time, sure you'd split at the seams right then and there to depart in four dwarflike directions having achieved immortality in your own lifetime. But it's been the rocky road to nowhere ever since, now it's "Proud Mary" in the Legion for Christ's sake, even disco in the singles meat markets where all you are is a metronome, so is this the last act? Dumb ass punk with a kid who was probably born the same year you got your first paying gig, some little alien calling herself Annie Epoxy? "Oh, great God, I'm coming down!" Steve said.

Lowered himself to the floor, leaned against the wall, looked at the poster of Patti Smith. The room was a hole on Parliament Street just as he'd known it would be, a flight above the bakery, but not all grunge and sleaze, curiously neat, the double bed made up, even with a reasonably clean blanket. "Your name's Steven Beuhl," she said.

"You got it, babe. Same name I've always had."

Deliberately the girl began to undress. Threw the coat into a chair, threw the leather shirt and plastic pants into a corner. Naked now except for boots and a few sex-boutique items — garter belt and stockings, red lace panties — and what the hell was going on here anyway?

Steve looked around. Tiny room, sloping ceiling. Hot plate with a jar of silverware. Stereo, records, a Mann guitar with a pig's nose amp, half a dozen cardboard cartons, stack of paper and a box of sharpened pencils. Nail polish, makeup, bottle of Jordan wine with an inch or two at the bottom. A few books. The only title he could see was the one on top, *Lies*. Perfect, he thought. And then, letting his eyes drift, Steve saw in a corner, not on display at all, discreetly out of the way — leather straps and buckles, chains, a bit and a bridle, a riding crop.

Too fast, Steve said, "Try a little hard core, why don't you?" And was on his feet too fast.

The girl jumped back. "Hey," she said, "let's get one thing straight. I'm in charge here. You want anything else, forget it."

"Not in charge of *me* you're not."

"Yeah I am." And drew up from the inside of one boot a long narrow object, held it a moment, then made it suddenly jump open, light on the bright edge reflecting back like oil slick — a switchblade. "Any asshole who tries to hurt me is going to take his balls home in his pocket."

"Where the hell'd you get that thing?" Steve said. He heard the sound of his own voice — suddenly very southern.

"Haven't seen a switchblade in years," Steve said. "Kids used to carry them down home. Saw a fight once. Shit, you can sure make a mess out of somebody with a knife like that. But the only problem with knives — you know, things with sharp edges on them — is that they can cut you the same as they can cut somebody else."

The girl sat down slowly on the chair.

"Yeah," Steve went on, "the problem with things with sharp edges is that you've got to be an artist with them, and if you're not, you're just asking to get your own throat cut. I saw a kid peeled back to the tune of twenty stitches because he pulled a knife out and flicked it open on the wrong dude, if you know what I mean.

"Now I'm not saying that you can't be an artist with a knife. I'm sure there are dudes who can carve you like a chicken before you can cluck. But it takes practice, right? Now for my money, give me a ball bat. Or any kind of club for that matter — walking stick, ax handle — even this wine bottle here." He tapped it with his knuckle. "Thing is you can move in with a club and take the sharp edge on it, don't cut like flesh, and any idiot can swing a club. Talked with a karate man once, and he told me he'd take on a man with a knife any day, even a man with a gun if he was up close, but no way he'd take on a man with a club, just walk away from that if he could.

"But the best thing you can do with something with a sharp edge, a knife — seeing as that's what we seem to be talking about — is just show it to somebody. Are you with me? And usually that's enough because people get to thinking about how soft they are and how wet they are inside with all that blood that's waiting to come out. So you just flick open your switchblade and say, 'Look at this,' and that will do it. But unless you're an artist, it's just a bluff.

"Now being an old poker player from way back, I know a thing or two about bluffs. I've pulled in more pots on a lousy pair than I had any right to, and I didn't think of it before now, but I suppose one of the reasons I was able to do it was because I left my clothes on. You see, one of the problems with sporting around in nothing but red panties and a pair of high-heeled boots is that the dude you're playing against can see your legs shaking."

Steve lit a cigarette. His hands were quite steady. "Now that we've scared the bat piss out of each other," he said, "why don't you put that knife away and let's forget we ever mentioned it."

The girl smiled slightly. "There's something else you can do with a knife, you know."

"Oh yeah?"

"You can cut a man's throat while he's asleep."

"Man would be a fool to go to sleep then, wouldn't he?" Steve felt the flesh on his face drawing back into something like a grin. "Come on, give it up and we'll call it a draw." The girl didn't speak. "Look," Steve said, "all I'm trying to tell you in my half-assed way is to be careful who you show that thing to. You go around picking up men at parties and eventually you'll hit some psychotic who hates women and you'll bring him up here and show him that damned thing and he'll end up carving you for dinner."

The girl was sitting stiffly with the knife cradled in the palm of her hand. "How about you?" she said. "Do you hate women?"

Steve stood. The girl was already on her feet, fast, despite the heels, uncoiling, crouched, the knife tense and ready. Steve pushed his hands into the air, palms out. "Look," he said, "I'm going to walk very slowly around the far side of the room, as far away from you as I can get, and when I get to the door I'm going to walk right through it and down to the street and that's the last you'll see of me. All right?"

The girl's mouth was drawn back, open, showing teeth. "Oh shit!" she said, "this is really fucked. How the hell do we stop it?"

"You tell me."

"Look, I'm not a psychotic either. I'm not a psychotic who hates men. I didn't invite you up here to cut your throat."

No games in that voice now, Steve. Maybe. But then again she could be as crazy as one of Charlie Manson's girls. "Anything we're saying now could be more bluff," he said. "You know that. So somebody's got to give up. I guess it's got to be me, right?... I'll do it. Just tell me how."

The girl thought about it. "Take off your clothes," she said.

So here it is, right? Getting down to it. Sweat pouring out of your hairy armpits like acid. If you do it fast, maybe you can make it down to the bare skin without shaking like a branch in a gale. Strip off the coat and toss it across the room, toss the shirt on top of it. Odds are good but not perfect. What you've got riding for you is what you heard in her voice, but still she could cut you twenty times before you could take that damn thing away from her, and when you've got two strangers standing there assuring each other with sincerity dripping off the edges "I'm not psychotic," chances are at least one of them's flaming nuts. Pull off your boots and expose your squashable feet. And pull off your socks next because they don't count. But you love a good disaster, man, it's the only time you can function. Step out of the jeans and throw them away. Don't hedge. You couldn't get the belt out of the loops fast enough. If she's coming in, it'll be when you've got the T-shirt over your head. Fast. Cut deep into your stomach. But no, she hasn't moved, still just watching. Throw away the shorts and it's done, ready to make your exit taking nothing more than you came with, what they read at Peter's funeral. And you can't stop shaking.

The girl closed the space between them, walking slowly, her eyes fixed on Steve's face.

So slowly that it's like a ritual, something out of a sick Leonard Cohen song. But she'll telegraph it sure as shit. You'll have to jump left fast, out of the way, pivot and back in, knock those pin heels out from under her. Easy. Then go for the chair and you're home free.

The girl had stopped just a few inches away. Steve forced himself to continue staring into the ringed, fixed eyes where he knew the tip-off would come. The fear felt like iron. The girl folded up the knife, hiding away the cutting edge, and pressed it into the palm of Steve's ready hand. Steve threw the knife away, heard it arrive, sharp, on the linoleum.

The easiest thing to do, the only thing to do, was take her into his arms and feel the narrow chest, ribs and backbone hard as glass beads just under the thin sheath of skin. They were both shaking, they both stank of fear. Steve felt lips, tongue, teeth pressed into his shoulder, stopping up sound. A hurried knocking where their chests were pressed together. "Look," Steve said, "if you cut my throat while I'm asleep, do it fast and deep, OK?"

She pulled back from Steve's shoulder, said, "I'm not going to cut your throat," her fingers just like a woman's, like Kathy's, cupping the back of his neck.

Steve stripped away the hands. "I'm freezing," he said. "Can you make coffee or something? Is there any way to turn up the heat in here?"

"Close the window. It'll get hot really fast. The Greek keeps the heat up high all winter."

Window goes down—plonk—and outside it's not Georgia or Massachusetts but Toronto, Canada. Why are you still here, man? Looking for the ghosts of Dylan and The Band, waltzing up and down Yonge Street like a trapped mouse? Kid's bending over the hot plate, tight little ass in shiny panties. There's not a single fucking day of the world that you don't think about Kathy at least once, and you don't even know if she's still in Vancouver. What the fuck you doing playing country and western in Riverdale bars, for shit, for less than shit? What the fuck you doing *here*? Fear usually turns you on, but now it's just cold. It's cold. It's fucking cold.

"You were right, eh?" the girl said. "I don't know what to do with it. Just a bluff."

"It's all right to bluff, just save it till you need it." Steve clamped his jaws tight to keep his teeth from chattering. He stripped a blanket from the bed and wrapped it around himself. "What the hell were you thinking?" he said.

She didn't answer. The water had come to a boil. "Do you want anything in this?" Like a sullen waitress.

"No, black's all right." Steve reached out from under the blanket and took the cup. His hand was shaking. "Jesus, I'm cold." The instant coffee tasted like tin.

"You'll get warm... It's for real, eh? I want you to play in my band."

Steve laughed. "Baby you can drive my car." But he couldn't help asking, "What do you do? What kind of material?"

"Mine."

"What's that like?"

"Like what they're doing in England now. X-Ray Spex, the Sex Pistols, the Clash."

"I'm not really up on that shit. But if I had a dollar for every time some asshole has said to me, 'Jesus, Steve, got some dynamite material here. Get us a band together and we'll make a fortune,' I'd own the biggest hotel this side of Babylon."

"I don't give a good fuck about money."

"What do you want then?"

"To tell the truth."

"Oh, for Christ's sake. I've been *there* too. We could enlighten the world, right? Oh, it's a bad joke."

"Why'd you come back with me then?"

"For the twist, you should know that. Isn't that what we're all looking for these days, the last fucking kink? Making love to the space girl? How the hell old are you anyway?"

"What difference does it make?"

"I just want to know."

"Nineteen."

"Is that straight?"

"Yeah, that's straight."

Well, Stevo, want to play punk rock at thirty-five years old? For no money at all? You're tempted, aren't you, dumb fuck? Jesus, the sky full of falling hatchets and you'd have to be the one to stick your head out the window to count them coming down. "All right," he said. "Sure. Music. Band. All that bullshit. *But why did you take your clothes off?*"

She was sitting next to him on the bed, legs spread open, feet pushed up to the limit by the lizard-skin heels, garters pulling stockings tight. The paint on her face, color of bread mold, stopped dead in a line under her jaws, left the skin beneath soft and alive. A girl, small breasts, tender as new grass. "I asked all over town about drummers," she said. "Your name kept coming up."

"Yeah?"

"Heard you were good. Maybe the best. And heard you were crazy. I thought, that's what I need. Crazy."

"Yeah?"

"Caught you at the Brunswick. Jesus, what a lame band. But you were exactly what I wanted to hear. Thought, this guy's bored, he's cynical and bitter and bored. And fucked up or he wouldn't be playing this shit. Maybe he'd want to do something new, something real, something where he could really play again."

"Yeah. Go on."

"I knew I'd run into you sometime. Wasn't in any hurry. Just waited. Then there you were at that party. I wanted you to come to me, kept sending you a signal. I saw you pick it up. Somebody put on that old Doors record. It was perfect, a perfect connection. I wanted you to want something from me, and you did. I could feel the rush, eh? Like speed. And then I wanted something from you... and not just a drummer. Shit, so I took my clothes off. All right?"

Her eyes were focused on the wall, blank, words coming out mechanical as ticker tape. Then, in a voice so low he almost didn't hear it, "I'm tired of this shit."

"Then something happened," she said, looking at him. "He's scared, I thought, or... I don't know what. He's an old burnt-out hippy. He could go rank on you in two seconds flat, beat the piss out of you, or..."

"Old burnt-out hippy," Steve said. "Sure. Yeah."

Ten years down the rocky road since you walked into the jazz club and there was Kathy waiting on tables. Five-feet ten of hard-ass woman wired on methamphetamine, wearing boots over the knee and a black leather miniskirt, dead white skin, same skin as yours, Stevo, and for the same reason. Had long black hair swinging, green gypsy eyes and a hard full mouth. Looked *dangerous*, and you were on a bizzarro trip, candy man, your mind fucked once by the South and then fucked again by Owsley Stanley, but Jesus, Kathy was something else. Only a half inch shorter than you, like looking in a mirror, could wear each other's clothes, and did, had people actually ask if she was your sister. Got into each other's heads so tight it was like the old marriage vow — one flesh — and those nights curled by like a dream, and ended, and it's a wonder you've got a functioning brain cell left what with all the chemicals and the running, and you know that the golden kingdom you kept seeing right around the corner was what you had with Kathy all the time. So what do you have to do to let yourself go back?

Steve ran it by again, like cutting himself with that switch-blade. "Old. Burnt-out. Hippy."

"Yeah, and I'm a young, crazy, fucked-up kid. What did you mean, the last kink? How do you want to make love to the space girl?"

Their eyes met. "I can feel it again," she said. "You're scared. Well, stop it, OK? *It's all right*. You guys are all so fucking predictable. I broke one of my own rules with you, you know that? I never bring a man up here I don't know. Never. But I guessed right with you, didn't I?"

"What the fuck you talking about?"

"You know what I'm talking about. What turns you on? What's your fantasy? I bet it's not simple, bet it's not just a one-act play. You're a lot more complicated than that, aren't you? But it does have to happen in your head or it won't happen at all. That's right, isn't it?"

"You're good," Steve said.

"Yeah, I know... First band I sang with, I was doing a Suzi Quatro sort of thing. Wore a black leather jumpsuit, skin tight. So tight every move I made I could feel it here." She stroked herself between the legs. "You like that, don't you?" Reached under the blanket, let her fingers rest lightly on Steve's prick. "See, I'm turning you on just by talking about it... So anyhow, this guy kept following me around town like a dog. Middle-aged, nice looking. Polite, pleasant, kind of shy. Poor bastard was married, had a couple of kids, worked for Air Canada. Every time I'd sing somewhere, I'd look out and see him. My number-one fan. He sent me flowers, took me to dinner. Finally figured him out, thought, hey, sick and weird. But he left me a hundred bucks under the pillow and I didn't even have to fuck him.

"I don't think it's sick and weird anymore. Back at that party, I passed your test, eh? So now you pass mine. Tell me the one about unacted desires."

Steve heard his own voice distanced, harsh static through an old crapped-out monitor. "Who the hell are you?" the man said. "Dumb ass street kids don't read Blake."

"Doesn't matter who I am."

"Listen. I'm broke."

"I don't fuck for money. I only fuck my friends. I'll fuck you if you want."

"If I want... If *I* want... What do *you* want? You don't have to fuck for a drummer either."

"Cut that bullshit, will you? If I can feel what's happening between us, so can you."

The man closed his eyes. Control, control, control.

Still want to ride that bicycle on the tight wire, candy man, stretched across the crack between the worlds? Still think you'll make it? Well shit, you're just a baby crawling in a box of razor blades, wish to God you were back in Georgia with nothing to do but drink sour mash whiskey on the back porch and kick the dog now and again just to hear him bark.

"I understand everything you're saying." Steve said. "You picked right."

"Yeah, I knew I did. Look at me."

Easy as whipped cream, the girl drew her legs together and rolled onto her belly, onto all fours, then arched into a yoga posture, stretching like a cat, deep ballerina curve in the lower back. A couple of vertebrae snapped, falling dominoes. She glanced at Steve over one shoulder, arched again to intensify the current that was already running clear along smooth muscles. She rose, walked across the room, taking a multitude of tiny steps to get there, knees pressed tightly together and all the forward motion in the gliding feet, all the electricity pulsing in the fluid metronome of her ass. She looked back, posing, then bent at the waist, straight-legged, to caress her thighs — down the garters, down the stockings, down the alien lizard skin, down the spike heels — film of red panties drawing taut.

"You really are good," Steve said. He watched her walk toward him, watched her place one foot in the center of his bare stomach. She pushed him over. He could feel the care, control — enough to hurt, not too much.

"Slow down," Steve said. "Come here." She lay down next to him. "Listen," he said. "There's a thing in T. E. Lawrence about getting up so early you leave your mind asleep. That's my fantasy if you want to know it. I keep looking for the mind to go out like a candle when you blow on it, right? A place where it just fucking well stops."

"I'll make it stop." She took Steve's prick in her hands.

"Not yet," he said. "Listen. Now I'm thinking about how all this stuff you're doing is for a man, for a man's fantasy. I'm thinking about how you must have learned it. And that's just it. *I'm thinking about it.* My mind never turns off."

"No. Listen to *me*." She was speaking with her lips resting against his. "It's the timing. You're a drummer, you know that. It's got to go on and on until you don't think you can stand it, and then it's got to keep on going even longer than that."

"Yeah."

Magicianlike, the girl had obscurely produced a black scarf. She trailed it back and forth between Steve's legs. "It's got to be slow slow slow. That's right, isn't it? Tell me a story then. Tell it to me slow."

A story? All right. Out of that first year with Kathy when your band was called Gordian Knot and you played that good old mindfuck, endless tunes on one chord so Ned could hack his way through them when his brains were shorted out. Sang words out of personal acid puzzles, your own went, "lilacs in the ditch with the hound and his bitch" over and over for damned near an hour. The audience seemed to get off on it. They were stoned too.

And it was all part of one big thing — the music, the drugs, the running, the flicker around the bend. The last thing you wanted from sex was *just fun.*

"I just want to get to the place where it stops," you said. "It goes on and on like movies playing over and over, saying the same thing. But back in there somewhere is something else, so far back you never get to the point where you can really see it. And to see it, all the other stuff has got to stop, just fucking well *turn off.*"

"You think you can do it with sex?" Her voice says she doesn't believe it for a minute.

"That's just one of the doors, right? If the doors of perception were cleansed..."

"Yeah, I know. Everything as it is. Infinite. What do you want me to do, man?"

"Just what I tell you for as long as it lasts, that's all."

Generated tremendous current because she was doing something she didn't want to do and *it turned her on*. You shaved every inch of her body. Massaged her with baby oil until she shone like a white angel. Put a ton of mascara on her. Painted her lips and nails bright fire-truck red. The white mini dress clung to every line of her. The skirt didn't even reach to midthigh. And nothing underneath. "Hey, Steven, this is obscene. At least let me wear a slip."

"No. Got to be able to see your nipples get hard." And just saying it made her nipples hard.

You both got stoned. Took her to a dark restaurant in the dangerous Italian North end where they hated hippies and beat them up on the street. Ordered dinner. The place was full of big middle-aged men in suits. And their women. And Kathy was like a little kid, silent and frightened, hands folded on the table in front of her, the only time you remember when she couldn't come up with a single smartass line.

And when she wasn't expecting it, you pushed a finger into her, not hard but insistent. Her breath jerked in, her eyes flickered shut, then open, her face went blank. Played with her under the table until her hands were shaking, her face trembling, her nipples hard. A long hour. She couldn't eat, pushed the pasta around her plate, drank wine as fast as soda pop. She was flowing beautifully, a sea between her thighs. "For God's sake, I can't stand it. I'm not kidding. Let's get out of here."

"Not yet. Walk over to the ladies' room. Do it slow. Turn on every man in the place. I want to see them all looking at you."

That was when you saw the hatred in her eyes, the sullen crackle like feedback noise. *But she was so turned on she was already forgetting how to want to stop it.* "You bastard."

She took a deep breath, then smiled and stood up. And walked. Don't know how far down into herself she had to reach to know how to do it—that teasing, promising, fuck-me walk—and so slowly you were sweating like a pig waiting for her to come back. You thought you'd pushed it too far. Felt like a wolf pack in there. You got her out fast.

In the van she said, "Enough's enough!" But not yet. As soon as you got to the party, you took her straight into the bathroom and locked the door. Bent her over the tub, played with her until her hips were jerking. Teeth clenched, she wouldn't make a sound. "OK, Kath, tell me when you're going to come so I can stop in time."

And by God, she did *that* too. "*Now*, Steven. Jesus, I'm going to die!" Pulled down her skirt, kept tugging at it like she was trying to make it longer.

"All right, babe, go dance with the men in the living room. Tease them. Turn them on. *Turn them all on.*"

Some of the parties were pretty fucking weird even back then, all the girls trying to outflash each other, sex fantasies everywhere, in the air just like the dope and the music, anything goes and if you're shocked, well then you're hopeless, that's all. But Kathy was one step farther than even that bunch of freaks had seen yet. You stood back in a corner, rolled a joint, and watched.

Dancing, she had a charge to her nobody could miss, beautiful, Christ. All wild-eyed like a running mare, dangerous. Starting to sweat, her hair came tumbling down, she was so tall and her skin was so goddamned white and shining. Worked her hips to the music, swung her arms high into the air so her skirt rode up, showed the hard cheeks of her ass in the back, in the front her shaved pussy. That was what really did it, that shaved pussy, hit the men like a thousand volts, and she wasn't caring anymore who saw it, wasn't caring anymore about anything, eyes like black fire.

That's right. It *does* start to sing. Sex is everywhere like a drug. You haven't taken the drug, the drug's taken you, you're inside it and all you can do is ride it out to the end. The guys in the band thought you'd brought her to gang fuck, and they would have done it too. Ned had her dragged halfway into the bedroom. She was like an angry sleepwalker, but still together enough to hang onto the doorjamb. You said, "Hold it, Nedward, not tonight."

She was all over you in the van so you nearly ran it onto the sidewalk. Back at the apartment, pinned her to the wall just inside the door. She came before you got the door shut. Dumped her down on the floor and fucked her. Hating you, she bit, clawed your back until you bled. She screamed and came over and over again. Afterward she was taffy limp and you had to carry her to bed. "Did your mind stop, Kath?"

"Oh, Jesus, man. I was gone. But I don't want to do that again, Steve. *Not ever.*"

*But your mind never stopped.*

"Listen. I want you to understand. My mind never stopped. I want to get there. To that shearing point. *I want to turn it off.*"

After the sound of his own voice there was silence. He knew he couldn't speak again, and the girl was saying nothing. But the black silk continued to circle with infuriating elusiveness around the head of his prick. And suddenly he realized how thoroughly, immaculately turned on he was, took a moment to savor it, like crushing a grape on his tongue. Then, abruptly, the guy wires that hold the world together came loose, were shifting. With a movement in the mind that was nearly physical, definite as a leap across a ditch, he uncoiled and grabbed for an edge on where he'd arrived — a state suspended and breathless — as he and the girl stared into each other's faces. She raised one finger to round 0 of lips, made the sound, "Shh." The gesture fell into place with an appalling inevitability, for Steve must surely have seen her doing it before she'd done it. Thrill of the old teaser's veil blown back again so unexpectedly was translated immediately into more fire up the prick and his hips jerked. His ability to continue to suffer the growing tension was immediately pinched down to zero, like a sob breaking through clenched jaws, and he had to drain off current so turned his mind loose to begin another transmission of weary chattering. *But now all bets are off, gentlemen, and where was Don Juan when you needed him? Should have been around years earlier to tell you that the drugs were absolutely incidental.*

He hadn't seen it before. Back of the makeup, the girl's eyes were genuinely beautiful, half a dozen colors, greens and grays, mixing into a darkly seductive gaze. But the moment for staring at each other seemed to be over, the girl was tugging at Steve's hips. Passive, Steve allowed himself to be dragged halfway down the bed, positioned. Raised his head and shoulders for all three pillows. The lovely eyes drifted away, rising above his head, replaced by hips and thighs. Steve knew that the message was — Look. And sight had never been so icy and definite. Clear lines of veins and tendons in the backs of the girl's hands. Short blunt nails with reflective jackets of black paint catching straight edges of sheer light. The fingers were pushing the panties down. Slithered with a scratched lizard voice, folded up into discarded insect wings, and were thrown away. Mad black rush — *the girl's pubic hair had been shaved off.* For a moment Steve was sure he'd shaved her merely by talking about shaving Kathy. His mind was a thin tenuous thread leading nowhere.

Twin points of bone at the hips connected by the black strip of the garter belt, gentle human rise and the center, smooth. Then his mouth is filled with her, flowing beautifully, and he meets her motion with his tongue, his lips, hears her groan aloud. The sound burns him. Thoughts peeled and useless. Fingers clutching his neck, pulling his mouth tight into her. His own hips jerking in sympathy, but his need is lost somewhere below, thrusting into empty air. "Oh God." she says. "Daddy."

And his mouth is suddenly empty. Neatly as a gymnast, she swings a leg over, she's mounted him, taken him into her.

"Hey," she says, "tell me when you're going to come so I can stop in time."

Can't possibly do that, it's too close, too goddamned painfully close, but he hears the man say, "Now," and she's gone.

Takes his prick in her hand, holds it hard, motionless. "My name's Kathy. That's what you call me now, OK? *Answer me.*"

"Yeah. OK."

"Say it."

"Kathy."

"You know what you deserve. Beg for it."

"Kathy. Please."

"All right then. Turn over. Get on your knees."

He's already forgotten now to want to stop it. He waits for her, holds himself motionless, makes himself helpless by his own will. Then she makes him truly helpless, and he can turn his will loose. That he can feel terror, and awe, and even something like love — that he can feel *anything* — is such a relief his eyes fill. Love is pain is the whistling edge of thin black wind. Hears sound beginning to unwind from himself, up deep from the belly. "If you scream," she says, "I'll have to fix it so you can't." Like pushing against a high wide door. Extremes of twisting effort move it only a quarter inch at a time. Door is iron is fear. Then with a slam he's through and stretched out across a bleak plain where the wind pours forever in an endless dark light.


Waking, hears someone say, "I left the water running for you." Doesn't know where he is, even his name. Lips brushing his ear, "Do you want me to turn it off?" Rolls over, works his way out from under the covers, sits up. Doesn't know who this person is looking at him. Seems he's supposed to do something. Slowly the room assembles itself.

"How long I been asleep?" Steve says.

"About an hour."

He pushes to his feet and shuffles into the tiny bathroom where the water is pouring down in the shower stall. Jungle steam. Sees a hazed image of himself in the mirror, wipes the mist away, sees his face smeared with purple lipstick — kid in a jam jar. Items around him simply state themselves, add up to nothing. Towel on a nail, line of rust running down from the base of the nail, can of shaving gel with the top left off, tube of toothpaste squeezed from the middle. He divides the plastic curtains, steps into the falling water. It's beautifully hot. His muscles are flaccid and aching, ass throbs like a bad sunburn.

Corners of his mouth are sore. Inside himself nobody's home.

Turns off the taps, dries himself. And the girl is sitting naked on the bed, reading. Washed hair lying flat to her head like an orange cap. Nail polish gone, makeup gone, but shaved all over, gives her a sleek prepubescent look. Steve can't connect this smooth white child with anything at all, certainly not with smoky memories of sex that now seem melodramatic and thoroughly silly. The face is a sympathetic schoolgirl's — intelligent and not particularly pretty. Should be homework she's doing, but she's reading that book called *Lies*. Steve files these pictures away inside himself. Right now nothing adds up to nothing. Steve falls onto the bed, crawls under the covers, jerks them up to his chin.

"You all right?" she says.

"Yeah. Sure. But Christ, I've got to sleep." The light goes out. He feels lips brush his shoulder.

Steve awoke with a crash, his body rigid as a spike. He knew immediately where he was, opened his eyes and the room came swimming up out of a blue-gray murk just before dawn. The girl was breathing in a slow deep rhythm; he felt the moist breath on the back of his neck. Steve edged quietly out of the bed. The room was an icebox. His clothes were scattered all over the place. Stiff as a cold snake, he gathered them up. He put his boots on last. He stood a moment looking down at the sleeping girl, then knelt on the floor to write with one of the sharpened pencils on one of the pieces of lined paper stacked against the cardboard carton. He hesitated. There were all these goddamned books of poetry, some twenty or more, and half a dozen music books — guitar studies, chord books, harmony texts. And what appeared to be hundreds of sheets of lined paper covered with a small rapid handwriting. "Shit," Steve said half aloud. His surprise was profound and chilling. He wrote, "Infinite. Of course. As it is."

The streetlights were still on. No cars. Steve walked. The phone booth stood out like a lighthouse. Dime down the slot, and the buzz of the dial tone. Only a thousand times he'd gone this far before, maybe this time he'd actually do it. Dawn in Toronto meant the middle of the night in Vancouver, but was she still going to be there after seven years? Lyons' voice said. "Well, Stevo, are you quick enough?" Steve hung up and hit the side of the booth. Dull slam and rebound. He sucked his knuckles. On the empty street the wind was blowing newspapers into tiny mad circles of whirlwind like dust devils.

The fog had sat on Vancouver for several days now, piling up the air with pollutants — and no wind to move it away. This evening was the worst yet; nearly as thick as anything Paul remembered from London, it was fog with a substance, like cold, wet breath, and he was walking quickly to keep warm. The trees of the park were invisible at twenty feet, dim silhouettes at ten; if he stood directly beneath them and looked up, he could see autumnal branches forming a complex, abstract design of uniform grey. The fog had left nothing, he thought, but a figured bass, a branch-stark structure from which the decoration had been sponged away. He heard voices of children calling to each other, a sound that struck him as immeasurably melancholy and old.

His feet felt the difference between soft earth and concrete; he'd reached the edge of the park by the school. A car passed on his right: shimmer in the cloud, rattle of metal, swish of tires, and a vague apprehension left behind like a sympathetic resonance. The school beyond was lost, and he had never seen the iron web of the fence like this before, so perfectly isolated from the playground. He could hear the muted voices of the children, the repeated tapping of a ball on asphalt, but he couldn't see a single human form. Good Christ, he thought, they're shooting baskets!

A small, energetic figure, long-haired, wrapped in a thick coat, appeared suddenly, passed in front of him, called back in a treble voice to invisible playmates, "See you tomorrow, eh?" and was swallowed up immediately, sweeping through fallen leaves, away into the milky blank. Paul turned and began walking purposefully homeward. If he hadn't known this neighbourhood perfectly, he would have been afraid of losing his way.

How simple things are for children, he thought. The fog must be a grand adventure for them, a chance to play safely at being lost, but to him it was like a nasty objectification of his own tenuous inner state: that all the known and planned paths had recently become obscured. He was on his own street now — that is, he surely had to be so long as he could trust his body's memory of the hundreds of times he'd walked this route before. And suddenly he heard rapid, running footsteps, claws on pavement, and a black dog, a full-sized poodle rendered flat as paper by the fog, whisked by him and was gone. It didn't help that he knew the dog, knew where it lived and who owned it; he was deeply frightened. He felt his pulse race to match the receding clicks of the claws. The hair on the back of his neck was actually standing straight up. He wanted to be inside his own home surrounded by familiar things. He ran up the steps and pushed through his own front door.

He was dazzled by the light. An old record (crackle of surface noise) was playing in the living room: long, breathy, fluid saxophone lines delivered with assured virtuosity. Jazz. And in the kitchen Kathy was sitting at the table reading the paper.

She'd cleaned up after dinner; water was pouring into the dishwasher. This unfamiliar music (unfamiliar woman), light and warmth, steam on the windows — and it was as though he'd been preparing deep inside himself for precisely this moment. She looked up and smiled, and his certainty of her struck him speechless.

"Paul? What's the matter?"

"Nothing. The fog... Oh, and you've made a new pot of coffee. How nice."

"My parting gift."

"Don't go."

"Come on. You know damned well Wendy's coming over."

She didn't need to remind him of that. He had been thinking about it all day. "I don't like this secretiveness," he said. "She has to know sometime."

"Sure. But don't you think it'd be a bit of a shock if she just... well, walked in and found me?"

"Perhaps you're right... You should put something on your feet. You'll catch cold."

"I've got socks on. Lay off, Paul. You've got two daughters. You don't need another one."

"My feelings aren't exactly paternal at the moment. I don't want you to go."

"I could hide out upstairs," she said doubtfully.

"Just be here. Naturally. Easily. That's the best way for her to find out about it."

"You're out of your mind."

"Perhaps we could be having a conference. Isn't that one of the hallmarks of your damnable school? Frequent, interminable conferences?"

"You're really reaching for that one. She'd take one look at us and know immediately."

"Come back?"

"What do you think?"

"I'll pick you up. It'll be late. After eleven." *And how*, he thought, *can one be so sure so quickly?* He wanted to walk into his home and find her in it every time. He wanted to sleep in the same bed with her every night. He thought about what he was going to say before he said it: "Damn it, I'm running out of patience with this... arrangement. I want you to live with me."

She looked at him quickly, then away. "You don't know how much a part of me would like to do just that. Unfortunately it's a part of me I don't trust. Yet. Maybe it's a bit too soon."

"It doesn't feel too soon for me. It feels..."

The front door opened and closed. "Shit!" she said.

"It feels right," he said quickly, "absolutely right. And believe me, I didn't expect her this early."

"Oh, I believe you. Jesus fucking Christ." They listened to the sound of Wendy's footsteps approaching down the hall.

"Dad?"

"In the kitchen, Wendy."

The jazz record was still playing, and Wendy must find it absolutely singular, he thought, to walk in to this music. He looked directly to Kathy, saw that her face had gone blank. Extraordinary. Two adults afraid of a fifteen-year-old — and a fifteen-year-old who also happens to be one's daughter.

Wendy stepped through the door to the kitchen, set the Tielke in its case down at her feet. Her face looked fantastically pale, but she wasn't showing the least sign of surprise. "Hello, Kathy," she said.

"Hello, Wendy."

His daughter was looking at him. "I know I wasn't supposed to come this early," she said — polite, distant, formal. "But I have to warm up. I need at least an hour."

"It's all right," he said.

She picked up the gamba and walked out — up the stairs to her old room. "Are you going to let her go?" Kathy said.

"It seems best."

"The Crane method." She sounded angry. "The two of you are exactly alike."

"Bloody balls! All right, I'll go talk to her."

She caught his hand, stopping him. "No, I think *I* should."

He sat staring at the emptiness she'd left behind. The fluorescent lights were buzzing in their usual raspy, unpleasant voices. The fog seemed to have got into everything; he felt chilled and apprehensive.

Kathy hesitated a moment outside the closed door, listened for movement on the other side but heard nothing. She knocked. Wendy opened the door with such immediacy that she must have been standing just inside, immobilized and waiting. "Can I talk to you?" Kathy said, trying to sound like a calm adult.

Wendy was dressed too young for her age. In sweater and tights, mary janes, and a brown corduroy jumper with a skirt above her knees, she looked like a picture-perfect twelve-year-old on her way to church. She couldn't have grown much in the last few years; except for the tension over her small breasts, the dress fit her. She stood, unmoving, and regarded Kathy with her white absence of any interpretable expression.

"Look," Kathy said, "I know this isn't the best way for you to find out, but..."

Wendy shook her head, produced a thin smile, then held out her hands, open, palms up, offering them — a solemnly ritualized gesture — and Kathy felt that they were involved in a conspiracy that no one had bothered to explain to her. She took the girl's hands into her own; they were cold and damp.

"That's where I am," Wendy said flatly. She withdrew, sat down on the edge of her bed, and nodded toward the music on the stand. "Marin Marais. Right now I hate him more than I've ever hated anybody in my life."

"Oh?"

"Kathy, please don't say anything that's going to distract me. *Do you understand?*"

"Yes, I do." With a nasty intuition of everything going wrong, Kathy realized that Wendy was sitting on her own bed, that this was Wendy's room, that they were in Wendy's house. Kathy's own position there seemed immediately problematical — as though *she* were the one who might require explanations and reassurances. But the girl closed her eyes and covered them with the tips of her slender fingers. Her body was shaking just enough to be noticeable.

"How long have you been doing this?" Kathy said.

"What?"

"Working yourself up to this."

"Since yesterday. I couldn't sleep last night."

"That's why you didn't come to school today?"

"Yes."

"Practicing all day?"

"Yes."

"Rough, eh?"

"I think I'm going to throw up."

"Maybe you should."

"But there isn't anything in there to come up."

"Nothing at all?"

"Toast and tea at noon. That's all."

"Wendy, you're crazy. Your blood sugar's low."

"Is it?"

"Look, do you like cocoa? I'll make you some. You need the protein and the hit of sugar and the caffeine. It'll help."

Wendy lowered her hands, opened her eyes. "Thank you. Oh, I hate that goddamned woman, and I've never even met her." The inflection had sound just like her father's.

"Who?"

"Hanna Rossenmüller. I dressed for her. Do you think she'll like me?" Bitter, self-mocking.

"Oh, so that's what you're doing?"

"I changed my clothes four times. Isn't it ridiculous? And finally I thought maybe I should look like a little kid. Maybe she'll feel sorry for me. Now I wish I'd worn something else. Pants."

"I think you're all right. A seventy-year-old German spinster lady should approve. Wendy, I know it's easy enough for me to stand here and say it, but... Well, what I used to do was try to find so many things to concentrate on in the music that I didn't have any room left for thinking about myself."

"I know. I can do that too, but I have to work at it. Yes, I'll drink some cocoa. But please leave me alone now." She managed a small, tight smile. "I want to be alone with Marin Marais," she said in a surprisingly accurate parody of a femme fatal from a thirties movie.

Paul was sitting in the kitchen exactly where he had been; he didn't look as though he'd moved a muscle. "Well?"

"She's not to be distracted. She's preparing for her audition."

"What about us?"

"Not a word. She's scared shitless."

"Is she? Poor kid. I'll go talk to her."

"You won't do anything of the kind. Right now what she needs from you is distance."

"That's going to be a difficult stance to maintain when we start playing together."

Kathy hadn't understood before. "You're afraid too," she said.


"Ach, there is no part for you," Hanna said to Perry. "We need only one gamba. But of course you do not mind?"

He looked stunned, hands fluttering in the air. "No, of course not. Whenever you play, I'll always listen. Gladly. But Hanna," his rising pitch giving him away, "Wendy and I have been working up some Marais."

The old lady's smile was about as reassuring as a crocodile's. "Ya, ya, but too much work is not good. The spirit dries up. Telemann he knows how to make happy music. We will play first some happy music."

"I've never seen this before," Wendy said in an expressionless voice.

"But my dear, you will see it again," Hanna said. "This you will play many times in your life."

Damn, Paul thought, that was neatly done. The redoubtable Doctor Rossenmüller has turned the tables on us. And she was handing him his music. "I must apologize. The realization is..." She couldn't find the word, shook her head and made a sour mouth.

He saw that the page was black with notes. "Right," he said, "some editor's idiocy. Don't worry, I never pay any attention." He sat down at the harpsichord.

The *Tafelmusik*, absolutely standard to the Baroque repertoire, so why the devil had Wendy never played it before? Because he'd been neglecting her, that's why. But no, that was too simple. There was more to it than that.

The two musicians who perform the single function called "continuo" are like Siamese twins; they have to be close, have to phrase together, think together, practically breathe together. When it worked, it might be the closest one ever came to another human being (short of making love with them — and, at rare times, it was even closer than that). So could he allow himself, even in the abstract manner demanded by the music, to get that close to his own daughter? Now she sat down next to him, drew up her short skirt, and settled the Tielke between her legs. She looked directly at him.

He couldn't smile, but he gave her a deliberate nod. And Hanna was setting the tempo, languidly counting it out in the air with her bow — relaxed *andante*. The old woman drew in her breath, let her shoulders fall, and Paul felt his fingers fall automatically onto the first chord. The scope of his hearing seemed to have expanded to the size of a cathedral — listening for Wendy's bow stroke. She was there, right where she should be, but he heard her hesitancy like a thin shadow. "Damn it," he wanted to yell at her, "it's not enough to deliver the notes. And sight reading's no excuse. Lift it. Be there. Believe it." He moved his head with the phrasing, breathed with it, exaggerating the motions for her to see. He tried to push her by sheer will, heard it in the pluck of the strings. He saw her eyes on him a moment. She was badly frightened.

Hanna lifted her bow and brought them to a halt. "Ya, ya," she said, "it is good. But we must leave here and there a space, I think. An openness. Round like a stone. Not a big stone. Just a small stone. Placed."

"Rubato," Paul said to Wendy. He was sweating, took the opportunity to wipe his hands on his pants.

"Forgive me, Paul," Hanna said, "Ya, rubato, but no. That is an idea. Too much in the mind. Just a space, ya? Just a silence. Small and round, so," she drew a circle in the air, "but not too much." She made a slight preparatory motion, a lifting of the shoulders, and they began again.

Paul had memorized the harmonies. He was playing with his eyes on his daughter, trying to help her, show it to her. He inhaled; *now!* And the space Hanna wanted was audible, barely the length of a heartbeat. Paul's eyes were locked to Wendy's. He let his head fall, and she moved with him, perfectly timed. Wendy was relaxing, sinking into the music, and, out of the corner of his eye, he saw that Hanna had smiled for the first time.

It wasn't right yet, but it was going to be right; he felt it growing. He was beginning to know what Wendy was going to do, and he could sense that she was moving toward him, no longer merely allowing herself to be guided but taking up a slack between them. It was as though they'd played together before hundreds of times and were now remembering and adjusting to an old familiarity. An inevitable motion was pushing them; he heard it blend, lift. Hanna heard it; he felt the old woman's violin riding on it. More than surprising, he thought, it's terrifying — how absolutely easy it seems to be.

Kathy didn't know exactly what she'd been expecting, but it certainly wasn't the music she was hearing now. She was sitting on the couch sipping her coffee, keeping out of the way, pretending to be — what, she thought, *inconspicuous*? All goddamned five feet ten of me? And she must have been expecting a sound that would match what she'd learned of the Cranes by now — their reserve, their formality—but the tone from the two string instruments was rich and engaging, the harpsichord not a sewing-machine tinkle but a full multicolored resonance. It was a friendly music, even jolly, like a high-class Dixieland. Now she understood what Paul must have been talking about. This must be the first time she'd ever heard Baroque music played *right*.

Hanna Rossenmüller hadn't reacted at all — not even a twitch of her thick brows at finding Kathy there unexplained and unexplainable — but Mark Perry, Wendy's teacher, had stared at her openly, avidly inquisitive. A stuffed partridge of a man with a foxy mustache. A chatterer. "Oh yes, Paul and I are quite old friends. Goes back years and years, actually. Without Paul, we'd still be pumping out Beethoven string quartets by the yard and convinced that we were doing our duty to the dead... Have you known him long?" The question a throwaway effect — Oh, please don't notice that I'm burning up with curiosity.

It was the first time Kathy had felt herself being assessed as "Paul's new girlfriend," and she didn't like it one bit, but then Wendy had taken up everyone's attention simply by walking into the room. Except for the sickly color of her face, she'd managed to hide most of her nervousness. And then the old lady had thrown them all for a loss with her unexpected music. Now Perry was sitting on the couch next to Kathy. He was so obviously miserable — smoking furiously — that she almost liked him. "How's she doing?" she whispered.

He made a gesture as though flipping a pancake. "So-so. She's sight reading, you know. She's not quite firm enough." Wendy was concentrating so hard she looked pop-eyed, and Paul was pressing out the chords discreetly, a lovely filigreed spray of notes, a shifting statement of the changes that tied the gamba and violin together. Comping, Kathy thought, amazed. That's what he's doing. By God, in a crazy way, it *is* something like jazz.

"Listen to the old gal's fiddle," Perry said. The old woman was playing with a suave assurance so ancient it seemed years beyond mere virtuosity. Kathy was reminded, oddly enough, of Parker, of his absolute sureness.

The movement ended. Hanna turned directly to Wendy, said, "So. How long have you been playing the gamba?" Her tone couldn't have been friendlier.

"Five years," Wendy answered without looking up.

"Since you were ten. Very good. It was not too big for you when you started?"

"She got her growth quickly," Paul said. "She was a big girl when she was ten."

"And then I stopped growing when I was twelve," Wendy said.

"The stretch wasn't too big for her," Paul said.

"My left hand ached every night for months," Wendy said, staring at the floor, and left behind a small, round silence like the one Hanna had asked for in the music.

"So?" Hanna said after a moment, "and how long before that the cello?"

Paul answered. "We started her when she was four."

"Four?" The black eyebrows rose. "So young then? And you still play the cello also?"

"No, Daddy says the techniques of the two instruments are incompatible."

Daddy, is it? Kathy thought. She *is* laying it on a bit thick.

"Ya, it is musically correct. But one must be..." The old woman made an angry gesture in the air with her bow. "If one wishes to work, one must be... *vielseitig.*" She appealed to Paul.

"Versatile?" he said.

"Just so. Now why can I not remember that? Perhaps one day you will come back to the cello?"

"Maybe I will."

"The cello, it is good for the ear, ya? But now we play for fun. Is that not what you say? For fun? And Telemann, he knows how to make happy music. He also is versatile. He himself the harpsichord played, the *Blockflöte* and the violin. Also with oboe, flute, gamba and even trombone he has studied. Some are more deep, but no one understands better how each must speak with the other. But I talk too much, and you already these things know.

"And now the *vivace.* In the Baroque that means not tempo, but feeling. So it must be fast enough to *springen*, but not in a hurry. Like this." She made a few passes in the air to indicate the speed, inhaled, let her shoulders fall, and they were off. Hanna whipped out a wonderfully rapid handful of notes, lovely as light on fountain water, just as she'd said it — not in a hurry at all. Then she stopped. "I feel... *Ach! Ich muss Dich ja wie einen Anker schleppen!*... Ach, where has my English gone?"

"Bounce off the beat, Wendy," Paul said.

"Just so. Thank you, Paul."

Wendy nodded.

The music suddenly fell into place for Kathy. Paul and Wendy were the rhythm section — bass and keyboard. Hanna was the soloist floating along on their life and drive. Wendy was now pushing the beat, moving it ahead in exactly the firmly assured way any horn player would want to hear beneath, and Paul was swinging with her, comping. It wasn't just a crazy metaphor; the damned stuff *was* jazz. Wendy seemed to have completely forgotten her own nervousness; she looked up, across the music stand at her father, a broad smile on her face. He gave her back a slightly askew grin. They're starting to cook, Kathy thought. My God, it's wonderful!

Hanna let the movement run to its end. She bobbed jerkily, a kind of a bow, first to Paul, then to Wendy; she looked like some large bird pleased with itself. "Now we are playing *music*," she said. "Many of my colleagues say, 'Hanna she is old. She plays in the old way. She is romantic, ya?' But they are wrong, I think, those who say the Baroque has no feeling."

She lifted her bow as though to play but lowered it immediately. "They say, 'Hanna she is schmaltzy.' It is my weakness, but it is also my right, I think. What I feel. It does not need to be Wagner, so? But it must not be dry, so very dry as many try to make it. So let me have my feeling." The birdlike expression, brittle and amused, fell away. "Expressivo," she said. Paul pressed out a broken chord, and Wendy entered with a single deeply sweet note.

For the first time Kathy felt about the music that it was more than merely lovely. The tempo was what she would have called "dead slow"; the violin and gamba were engaged in a tender, melancholy conversation. Oh, she thought, the motions of making music are always beautiful — the graceful sweep of Wendy's bow hand, the fluid turn of her wrist at the ends of the strokes. And Hanna was breathing into her playing, swaying with the motion of the introspective, lyrical phrases.

Kathy closed her eyes and went back to Boston. Smoke in her lungs, her breath against the reed. Smoke curling into her mind — just on the edge of revelation. Everything that could be said about the possibility of night was being said. It was amazing how vividly she could remember the feel of the reed in her mouth. Under closed lids, her eyes burned.

And Kathy, in her white athletic socks, would pad silently through the safe Beacon Hill apartment where her parents were asleep, let herself out the kitchen door, stand for a moment in the cobblestone alley, and then pull on her boy's boots and begin to walk — in the rain, down the hill, into the dangerous streets, into the night that always sounded like fifties jazz. *Thelonious Monk, Milt Jackson, Gerry Mulligan, Art Blakey, Sonny Rollins, John Coltrane. Mingus. Parker.* And she'd stand for hours in the corner of her room, focus herself into the wedge where the walls came together, and push her breath against the reed of her alto, searching for that final, high, and ultimately impossible sweep of notes, beyond any mere conception of melody or changes, beyond any memories of Parker (and later of Eric Dolphy), that would let her say, definitively so no one could miss it — *streets, rain, night, and myself alone.*

She knew now that she'd been complete and awake her last few years as a teenager. When she'd been alone and untouched. Damned uncomfortable word. *Untouched.* But that was it, that said it. But then at nineteen she'd allowed herself to be spread all over the back seat of a Chevy convertible by a huge, inarticulate lout of a bass player from Berklee. The only action required of her had been that of taking off her pants. She lay there — was laid there — and tried to keep her left thigh from cramping while she wondered if he'd get finished before the car she heard turning around in the parking lot would come by and rake them with its headlights. And the horrible thing was that once laid, even as ridiculous as it had been, she kept coming back for more. Four years of her life lost to the absurd search — overheated, itchy, time-wasting, obsessive, and mindless — for the next guy who was going to lay her. It had all led to Steve.

Hanging onto the back of his bike, wired, screaming deep inside with a new sound, not jazz but a simple-minded murderous drive, embryo of what would later grow into a style called "heavy metal." His bands with the mind-fucked names that changed every few months as the personnel changed — "Gordian Knot," "Deadlock," "Aground," and finally "Trackless Waste." To burn around some hairpin curve at four in the morning at a hundred and thirty miles an hour, to fuck all night on crystal ice, to sweep the mind clean as an eggshell, to push beyond limits — still searching for that final scream of notes that would change everything. But *she* hadn't been playing any longer, and Steve's music was sex and sex was everything, and now she thought it would have been better if she'd passed it all up, had become instead some madly chaste nun of the alto saxophone, as saintly as Sonny Rollins who quit performing to work on his chops, who practiced at night alone in the middle of a bridge.

The movement ended. Left behind was a rich tangle of connections leading off into hidden corners — the dominant hanging in the air, begging for resolution. Kathy opened her eyes. Hanna was standing poised, bow lifted; Wendy and Paul were waiting, tense and ready. That must be the only time they let their hearts show, she thought — the reticent Cranes — when they're playing. Hanna's shoulders rose and fell, and they were off and running. The old woman's face broke open into an unexpectedly sunny smile.

The music leapt, propelled forward, sank as they inhaled (they were breathing together now, timed perfectly), then rose again, pushing. Hanna left her music stand behind, walked to the side of the harpsichord, and began to play directly to Paul and Wendy; she was conducting with her body, and they were moving with her. "Jesus Christ!" Kathy heard Mark Perry whisper. And then again, "Jesus Christ." Whipping out a series of fiery trills, Hanna began a jerky dance. Her plain black shoes were doing a little jig on the carpet. Back around to the head, Kathy thought, to begin it again. The old woman was dancing for joy. Kathy felt her own loss of music then. It was unbearable.

The piece was over. Wendy swept across a broken chord, ringing out notes fat as milk chocolate, carried the bow away into the air, held it there. She shook back her hair, grinning like a cat, and laughed — a light, silvery sound that floated above the resolution and completed it. Hanna stepped over to Wendy and bent awkwardly to give her something like a hug.

"You will play with us," Hanna said.

"Will I?"

"Oh, ya ya. You will play with us."

"You mean I'm in?"

Hanna looked over to Paul, puzzled. "Looks like you're in, yes," he said to his daughter.

"I can't believe it," Wendy said.

"You will believe it when you see how much you now must practice," Hanna said, jabbing toward Wendy with her bow.

And Kathy couldn't stand to be there any longer. She hurried out, hoping that no one would notice her, climbed the stairs to Paul's bedroom (Evelyn's bedroom, damn it!). After a moment, she heard Wendy trotting up the stairs. The girl didn't even have time to get the bathroom door shut — splash of falling liquid. Kathy rose into a flattened-out dream, on into the hallway and down to the bathroom. The walls were moving by on their own. Wendy was on her knees in front of the toilet bowl; despite the vomited cocoa that was running down her chin, she managed a smile. "I made it."

Kathy wet a washcloth and wiped the girl's face. "Christ, you're good."

"Thanks," Wendy said, jumped to her feet and took off at a run, skipping. Kathy stared a moment at the washcloth in her hand, then threw it into the sink, followed. Wendy was bouncing up and down on her own bed as though it were a trampoline. After a dozen leaps she fell flat on her back, panting for breath. She kicked off her shoes. "I feel as though I'm going to float away," she said. Her normal color had returned — inwardly lit alabaster.

"But you must have known you were good enough."

"In my mind, but I still had to *do* it. I get so nervous, it's awful. But she wasn't so scary. She liked me. And my God, can she play!" It was one of Wendy's beautiful moments — radiant eyes.

"You're sleeping with Dad, aren't you?"

"Yeah."

"I should be surprised, but I don't think I am. Do you like him?"

"I like him a lot."

"Well, I'm glad then. Mummy doesn't know about it yet. She'll have a fit." Wendy turned her head away; Kathy was freed from the compelling blue eyes. "I should go back to Stafford House soon. If I stay at Van Free it'll get too... complicated."

"It's too complicated already."

"Yes, it is, isn't it?... I didn't think I'd ever like you, but I do. Are you going to live with him?"

"I don't know. I might."

"It's all right with me."

From a long way away, Kathy heard herself laugh. Wendy's just given me permission, she thought. "I didn't think I'd ever like you either," she said, "but I do."

Wendy extended a hand. Kathy took it. "See, I'm warm now. I'm only cold when I'm scared."


Time collapsed, Kathy walked downstairs before she was aware of what she was doing. She came to rest in the archway to the living room. The musicians were so absorbed they didn't notice her, and she couldn't stop asking herself the same irritating question — when had she stopped playing, *exactly when*? She'd always thought it had been when she'd moved in with Steve, but she'd just remembered practicing in the bedroom of his tiny apartment in downtown Boston, the first place she'd lived with him. Everyone in the band had lived in the same building. And then, suddenly, she remembered standing on a little balcony practicing. Looking out over a street in Cambridge. Right, that little balcony Steve always called a porch. Where had that been?

Must have been in one of their apartments, but which one? How strange. She hadn't thought of that odd little balcony in years. She turned and drifted away with Hanna's lovely violin tone pushing her. The door to the guest room at the end of the hall was closed.

Paul did most of his regular work at the university, but during the time she'd been getting to know him, he'd been using this room at the end of the hall to work on the van Dorestad motet. And something was falling into place — a tiny, perhaps unimportant, but disturbing fact — the door to that room had always been open; in the last few days Paul had begun to keep it closed.

Kathy felt a wave of anger. *Come on*, she thought, *no secrets.* But standing in front of the closed door, she felt like Bluebeard's wife. A twinge of asthma at the base of her lungs. *Damn it, move!* she told herself, and pushed through the door.

At first she didn't notice much of anything different, but then she saw that there were new books, dozens of them, and file folders, and large note cards covered with writing. She picked up the books randomly; they all seemed to be about history and religion. *The Radical Reformation, The Low Countries in the Sixteenth Century, Hieronymus Bosch.* She opened a file folder labeled "heresy" and read what Paul had written on the top card:

Innocent VIII — *Summis desiderantes affectibus* (1484) — issued to stop the growing spread of black magic

Heinrich Kramer and James Sprenger — *Malleus Maleficarum* (1487) — used by the Inquisition as a guide for witchcraft trials

From the *Maleus Maleficarum*: And when she is being questioned about each several point, let her be often and frequently exposed to torture, beginning with the more gentle of them, for the Judge should not be too hasty to proceed to the graver kind. And while this is being done, let the Notary write all down, how she is tortured and what questions are asked and how she answers. The next step of the Judge should be that, if after being fittingly tortured she refuses to confess the truth, he should have other engines of torture brought before her, and tell her that she will have to endure these if she does not confess. If then she is not induced by terror to confess, the torture must be continued on the second or third day.

Kathy closed the file folder. She felt sick, dizzy. Her lungs were wheezing. What's the matter with me? she thought. Everybody knows they tortured people in those days. It's not exactly news. But she wouldn't have been more shocked if she'd found some volume of nasty pornography hidden in Paul's study. Why couldn't she ever find a man who was direct, honest, and open? What did they want, these secretive men? What had *Steve* wanted? "Come on, Kath, play with us. Why won't you, for fuck's sake?"

Steve had actually got her to bring her saxophone the night they were opening at the Circle of Fire, their first concert in a couple months, Peter just back from Philadelphia where he'd been hiding out from something Steve wouldn't tell her about. Yeah, she'd thought, amazed, I'm really going to do it. Why not? And then had worried for hours, not about her playing, but about *what she was going to wear.* As bad as Wendy getting ready for Hanna Rossenmüller, she'd changed her clothes half a dozen times, stuck in front of the mirror, her door closed so that Steve wouldn't see how close she was running toward hysteria. Not her ordinary jeans and boots and baggy sweater. Not the leather mini-skirt she'd been wearing to waitress at Arturo's the night Steve had first picked her up. And certainly not the shining black vinyl outfit he'd given her to wear to bed (although she'd tried it on). Staring into the mirror thinking, why doesn't he *tell* me? It'd be so much simpler then.

But all his crazy words reverberating in her mind. "Lead the children out into the wilderness... stars falling like manna... Kath, I want my mind to stop." Too much acid, too much running. Even Steve, who'd always been the coolest head in the band, was breaking down. Ned, the lead guitarist, lead singer, was long gone into outer space. Ned had started to come apart right after the FBI had turned up, making noises about "conspiracy to obstruct the Selective Service Act" and dropping dark hints about ten-year jail terms, and he brought to their concerts now an explosively dangerous quality, might stay on the stage forever, lost in a solo that no one, not even Steve, could follow, or walk off in a paranoid sweat.

Astarte, Hecate, Ishtar, Cybele, what does Steve want? (He's called her all of those names.) And where's the introspective purity of the jazz she's been learning so long to play, the complex changes, elusive rhythms? She finally decides to put on no makeup at all, knowing she'll look dead white under the lights and not caring, chooses, not sure why, her tightest jeans, worn before only as a sex game with Steve, black knee-high boots over them, and a gray metallic blouse so at least some of her will shine. She checks her case for the magical number of reeds — four. But at the club everything's fucking up, Steve as frazzled as she's ever seen him, jiggling, twitching, muttering to himself, and he doesn't even notice what she looks like. "What the hell's the matter with you, man?"

"Ned's fucking out to lunch. Keeps talking about the agents in the audience. The *agents*, for Christ's sake! And Peter's not here. Where the fuck is he? He's never late."

Ten minutes away from show time, Jerry lighting the candles and incense that always decorate their stages, and still no Peter. Steve's face is gray and pinched; his eyes are elusive. He can't stand still, bounces on the balls of his feet, already drumming, dancing in the air like a hanged man. "Kathy, can you run the board?"

"Are you out of your fucking mind? There's a million knobs on there, and Peter hasn't labeled one of them."

"Shit, maybe the manager can do it. Fuck, Kath, it's cracking. It's coming apart."

"What's coming apart?" He doesn't answer, bounces up and down, his face inhuman, savage with craziness and despair — lank, black hair falling over his forehead, his beautiful dark eyes staring and dead, pockets of tiredness under them like bruise. She doesn't know if he can see her at all.

She yells at him, "Steven, what's going on? What's the big secret? Tell me, for God's sake."

He falls back against the wall. He seems to think about it. Then starts handing her keys. "The van," he says, "and these are for Lyons' place. The big one's the front door, the medium one's the apartment door, and the little one's the garage."

The keys are flat and cold in her hand. "Steven, what are you asking me to do? Goddamn it, talk to me." They're staring at each other. Lyons? Good fucking Christ! "What are you and Lyons up to? Answer me."

More Zen. "Look, just get your ass over there fast. Go right in and see if Peter's there, all right? If he is, bring him back here, all right?"

"This isn't making any sense, no sense at all."

He's yelling. "I'll get Peter, and you play the drums. How's that one, Kathy? Do you like that one? Besides, *you* can push Lyons, and I can't."

"Push him to do what?"

He stares at her, his face twisting. He looks damaged. "Please,

Kathy. We're in it together, babe, all right?"

"If we're in it together, then tell me what's happening."

"There's no time, Kath!" His voice is rising, a hysteria worse than anything of hers. "We've run out of time."

No answer to the buzzer downstairs. She lets herself into the building, takes the elevator up. Hating herself for the triviality of it, thinking, *Why do I have to be dressed like this?* Knowing that Lyons will focus on her ass in the tight jeans, say something like, "Hey, all right!"

But no answer at the door of the apartment. She unlocks it, walks in. She doesn't have a clue why Steve has the keys to Lyons' apartment, doesn't know what she's been sent to do, and there's no one there. She walks back to the kitchenette. People have been drinking beer and cocoa. Then in Lyons' bedroom, sees herself lean and tall in the mirror, mad eyes, hair swinging, turns away at once. Lyons' clothes thrown everywhere, mixed with stuff from whatever little girlfriend he has at the moment — miniskirts and underwear.

In the living room Kathy comes to rest in front of the stereo. She doesn't know what she's supposed to be looking for. The place reeks of dope. And something else, a sickroom smell.

The place stinks of shit. She walks into the bathroom. The smell's very strong there, like somebody took a crap all over the floor. Walks back to the living room, sees a puddle soaked into the carpet at her feet. Bends over it. Smells like piss. She slowly straightens up. Dizzy, wondering if she's going to throw up.

She moves out of Lyons' apartment fast, takes off running between the buildings to the alley, unlocks the garage door and shoves it up with a crash. Empty. Lyons' Alfa Romeo is gone. Dry mouth, heart pounding, she jumps into the van and drives back to the club, runs half a dozen red lights to get there, finds that everything's totally fucked up. Ned's walked off the stage, and the manager's making a mess of the board. No lead guitar, no lead singer. Ned's long gone and nobody knows where. The audience feels ripped off, noisy and stoned, throwing ice cubes at the stage. There's talk about refunding the money. At the break, Steve says, "For Christ's sake, Kath, you've got to play that god-damned saxophone. No more bullshit, all right? *This is it*. We've got to have somebody playing lead." But she can't do it. She's frozen.

I let him down, she thought. She'd watched, paralyzed, the end of Trackless Waste. On its good nights it might well have been what Steve had always called it — the best goddamned rock band in the country. She might have saved it if she'd played; to that audience her image would have been damned near as good as her sax on lead, probably better, and it had been that fucking triviality that had stopped her — and all Steve's lies and evasions — but now her guilt felt like death in her stomach.

And then it had been in the papers the next morning. Peter had been killed. Shot in an alley. The headline, jumping up at her off the page — GANGLAND STYLE SLAYING IN ROXBURY. Steve had thrown the paper at her face and turned away to pound his forehead into the wall, to crack the plaster and bloody himself. She'd had to slap him to stop it. He'd sunk to the floor sobbing, and she hadn't been able to ask him then, or ever, to explain to her just what the fuck had been going on.

And the worst thing was that now, years later, she'd forgotten all of it so completely that until a few minutes ago there hadn't been even a trace of it in her memory.


Paul found Kathy in the guest room, back against the wall, smoking, her face a few inches from the closed window. "What's the matter?" he asked her and sat down at the desk.

"Oh, hell, I don't know." She looked at him with sombre eyes. "Well, for one thing I'm not sure who I am here. It took other people coming in to make me realize it. How did they see me? As your lover? Your mistress?"

*No*, he thought, *that's not it*. He said nothing.

"I hate categories like that," she said, inhaling smoke, "but the social web closes in, eh?"

"It's clear to me who you are."

"Oh, is it? Do you want to tell *me*?"

"You're my dear friend who sleeps with me... not quite often enough." He tried to speak lightly.

"No," she said.

He could feel her confusion. It was like the fog outside: what meetings there might be would be fortuitous only; one could become lost as easily as not.

"Is what you played tonight," she said, her voice tentative, nearly parenthetical, "what that motet sounds like?" She gestured toward the desk where the van Dorestad material in all its forms — Xerox of the original, rough working copy, and his final edition with the *ficta* notes indicated — lay in piles behind all that other nonsense he had been accumulating.

"Oh, heavens, no," he said. "We were playing Telemann and Bach tonight."

"So there's a difference, eh?"

"Between the the Renaissance and the Baroque? Yes."

"Don't patronize me. Please."

"I'm sorry. I didn't mean to."

"Look, you, ah... I don't know what I want... You don't perform *that* music." She gestured toward the desk.

What the devil could she be after? "Of course I do. In the field of early music one becomes rather a jack-of-all-trades. I'm not sure what it is that you're asking me. The Pro Musica is doing all Baroque music this season because Hanna's here and she's a Baroque specialist, but we've done earlier music before, and we will again."

"Are you going to perform *that*?" She gestured again toward the desk.

"Not immediately."

"Could you?"

"Are you asking if I'm sure enough of my reading to risk a public performance? The answer to that is yes. Do we have the forces? Yes, again, but... Kathy what's the matter? What has upset you?"

"Damn it, I don't know." She pushed herself up, walked the length of the small room, and turned to face him. "Damn it, Paul, what the hell have you been doing in here?"

The chilly apprehension he had been hearing as a secondary theme leapt suddenly into prominence. "What do you mean?"

"Living with Steve as long as I did made me extremely sensitive to picking up clues from a man... Which I didn't think I'd ever have to do with you, thank God, but... shit, you've been keeping the door shut. That might seem like a tiny thing to you, but..."

She made an exasperated gesture. "I stood outside that door like I expected to find ten dead women hanging in a row in here, but all I found were books on history and religion. And your field's not history and religion. Is it? I don't know, Paul. Something just feels screwy, wrong, fucked up... You never seemed like a secretive man to me."

Oh, hell, he thought, the closed door, is it? "I'm not exactly secretive, but... You're right. History and religion aren't my fields."

It was exactly what he had been telling himself: musicology was his field, and perhaps he should stick to it. When it came to history, he was as well — or as badly — educated as anybody else. What he was, of course, was a bloody specialist, so much so that if every extant copy of Ockeghem's *Missa Mi Mi* were to vanish suddenly in the night, he probably could reconstruct it from memory. But as to what was going on in the world at the time Ockeghem wrote it, Paul knew that he knew surprisingly little. "There's this maddening thing about contemporary scholarship," he said. "We should stay closed away inside our own little specialities, and God help us if we try to get out... Well, I seem to want more than that."

"And *I* just want to know what you're doing," she said. "That's all. I suppose I'm taking it far too personally, eh?"

"That seems to be my problem, too. Taking it far too personally. Jan van Dorestad, I mean. I want to know who he was, why he wrote that extraordinary piece of music. If he held heretical opinions, I want to know what they were. I want to know what happened to him. And I suppose it's become so personal, so involving, that I'm ashamed of it."

"Ashamed?" she said. He could see her puzzlement.

He used the motions of filling his pipe to give himself a bit more time. "Let me tell you a story," he said. "The Pro Musica had been rehearsing here, and Evelyn had most emphatically stopped playing hostess by then. When everyone left, I went upstairs and found her in bed. She was always taking a course in this or that, and right then it was art history. There were books and notes piled all around her. She said, 'It's just dawned on me after all these years what you are, Crane. You're a bloody Pre-Raphaelite.'

"She lay there on all those decorative pillows of hers and told me exactly *how* I was a Pre-Raphaelite. Like them, I had a distaste for everything modern, a nostalgia for the long-dead past. I saw women not as people but as muses, Beatrices, works of art. I refused absolutely to become involved on any level whatsoever with real life... which is why it was a damn good thing I was an academic. It was the only area of modern life that would have me.

"Oh, I can't begin to tell you how good it was... her performance. She delivered it like a parody of a university lecture, so that both the content and the style of it were an attack on me. And all the time smiling as though it weren't an attack at all. It was both terribly funny and terribly painful. I laughed, of course. What else could I do?"

"Wait," Kathy said. "I'm having trouble with this. Did Evelyn make you ashamed? Ashamed of what? Reading history books?"

He was finding all this damnably difficult. "She never let up on me. It became a kind of *cantus firmus* for her. I wanted to crush out her creativity, turn her into a beautiful object... just the way the Pre-Raphaelites had done to their models. I was trying

to do it to the girls. Which was ridiculous, of course. Evelyn was
the one who started putting Wendy in designer dresses and..."

"Hey, stop," Kathy said. "Listen. *I'm not Evelyn.* OK?... I think
it's neat that you're a professor. I like that in you."

Silenced, his mind was racing. "And the corollary," he said, "is
that I'm not Steve."

"Right."

"Tell me about him."

He saw her step back from him, wrap her arms around herself.
"Haven't I told you about him?"

"Not very much. He had a lot of closed doors, I gather?"

"Oh, doors and doors. He talked in code. I was supposed to pick
up the clues. Everything was music, and the music was about the
clues." She looked away. "He didn't just want to be an enter-
tainer, a pop musician. He wanted to — I don't know — enlighten
the audience. It was... religious. The people he admired were
saints. Saint Dylan, Saint Morrison. That's actually how he
talked about them. And he was going to be Saint Steven. Does
that make any sense to you? Can you understand it at all?"

"Yes, strangely enough, I think I can." He didn't know whether
he should tell her what he was thinking. Then, on the premise
that she was not like Evelyn, would not give him a mocking smile
because he was lecturing, he told her: "All the way back to Plato,
the theorists have always known how powerful music is, how
directly it moves on the spirit. It has only been in the twentieth
century that they've begun to say that it is merely sound —
vibrating air."

No, she didn't smile. She looked directly into his eyes. He
didn't know what she was thinking.

She looked down. Her voice sounded dim. "I don't trust Steve's
way anymore. I don't know, but... Paul? I think you and I might
want the same thing. A kind of order. A kind of sanity. And the
music will grow out of that. The music *has* to grow out of that."


*Do I love him?* Kathy thought. *Could I be in love with him?* Those
ancient questions, just like in some creepy romance, but even
after you thought you'd tossed them on the historical scrap heap,
there they were turning up again. She and Paul were climbing
the stairs hand in hand, and she was thinking of Steve. *He* had
never offered love, at least not the good old-fashioned kind. Oh,
he'd said the words — "I love you" — but he'd meant something
else, something brand new. Breakthrough. A fat, insane, generational love, all of us, the children, a great inter-fucking tribe of

mind-damaged astronauts on the way out, western civilization itself blowing apart like the puffball on a dandelion gone to seed.

Steve's problem had been that he'd mixed up sex with speed, just as he'd mixed up sex with everything else. And with that odd twist to him — something almost maidenly — his love of deadly black motorcycles must have arisen from the same ambiguous longing that makes girls fall in love with horses. But a horse is alive, at least points back to human flesh; the mistake he'd made had been to get machinery involved. The hot thunder between his thighs had been an engine. Steel and chrome and shiny black paint had worked for him just like the electronically amplified and distorted music, just like the gleaming black vinyl outfits he'd bought for her. In that complex field of vision and feedback noise, transmissions from outer space, *anything* could turn him on. Motorcycles were sex, drugs were sex, music was sex, and sex — well, then, sex had to be deadly, shining, intoxicating, and played for a crowd, screwing not just for pleasure but to redeem an entire generation, Wilhelm Reich applauding in the wings.

And she'd believed it all, or at least had convinced herself she did, but now she was talking about order and sanity, and meaning it. Or was she meaning it? And (yes, put the question just the way it would appear in any romance) did she *really* love Paul? Or was she just looking for a place to be safe? But safety wasn't such a bad thing, was it? Maybe she did love Paul. But something still wasn't right. What about the longing in the night so fierce it felt like dying?

Paul was tapping lightly on Wendy's closed door. "Come on, Gwendolyn," he said. There was no answer. He gave Kathy a puzzled look and pushed the door open.

The overhead light was still on — harsh, bare bulb in the center of the ceiling — and Wendy lay sound asleep on her bed where she had fallen. Her face was turned to the side, and her hair, usually so carefully brushed, was spread around her on the pillow. The lashes of her closed eyes, the curve of her cheek, the spray of blond hair — she was, Kathy thought, exquisite.

Wendy's skirt had ridden halfway up her thighs, and her long legs in pragmatic white knee socks were stretched out at ease, open, with a bit of plain cotton underpants showing. The damned kid who'd never before seemed the least bit sexy was now, asleep and unaware of it, one of the most beautifully seductive female images Kathy had ever seen. She glanced quickly at Paul, saw a kind of rarefied shock on his face. "Wendy," he said.

The girl rolled onto her back, looked up at him with her eyes half opened, still smoky with sleep. Kathy was growing more uncomfortable by the moment. She stepped back to leave. "Oh, hi," Wendy said in a silly child's voice.

"Come on, baby," Paul said, "I'll take you home."

Wendy sat up, yawned, drew her knees together and her skirt down. Then, with a quick flash of smile, she seemed to wake up, remember herself, recognize the two adults who were staring at her. "I made it," she said, "didn't I? Was I all right?"

"Oh, you were a marvel," Paul said. "Some things we've got to clean up, but for sight reading you did just fine. Come on, we'll talk about it in the car. I've got to get you home."

"I *am* home," she said.

They waited inside a fat and unpleasant silence. Kathy knew that the time was long past for her to walk away and keep on walking, on down the hall to escape into Paul's bedroom. It really was none of her business, but her curiosity kept her stuck to the spot — and something more than curiosity. Paul was recovering himself; he'd already drawn his expression back into place. "What do you mean?" he said.

"I want to live here now." She couldn't have said it any more simply than that, Kathy thought.

"Good Christ, Gwendolyn," Paul said, "don't you think we ought at least talk to your mother?"

"I already did. I called her while you were playing."

"You astonish me," Paul said. "Of course you can stay, but... What did she say?"

"Oh, she was glad enough to get rid of me."

Paul hesitated, then said, "You've made sure of that, haven't you?"

Wendy's face closed into a reflexive white mask, then something unpleasant flashed for only a moment in her eyes — adamantine, blue steel. "Yes," she said, "I certainly have made sure of that."

Kathy was horrified. Behind the poses — Kathy knew now that they *were* poses — behind the disturbed child, the withdrawn little girl, the sullen teenage bitch, the musical prodigy, even behind the budding performer so highly strung she'd lost her cookies in the toilet bowl, Kathy was sure she'd seen an edge of naked, powerful, self-assured will. Jesus, Wendy, she thought, remind me not to turn my back on you.

# IV

*Why the fuck can't I sleep?*

And Steve finally admitted to himself how bad it was. But when he opened his eyes, all he saw was his place in Toronto just as goofy as he'd left it with a month's worth of dirty clothes, and old greasy fast-food cartons, and a million empty beer bottles, and a dozen records with their jackets off. And a set of gongs and tuned bells and tubular chimes and, good God, ratchets and claves, bongos, tablas, maracas, and cow bells in three different sizes, and even a set of Tibetan temple stones. Jesus, he thought, if you didn't know better, you'd think a percussionist lived here. And threw back the sleeping bag, grabbed dirty jockey shorts out of a boot. Pulled on jeans, found the crumpled pack of Player's in the side pocket, inhaled smoke, felt the familiar vice tightening up at the base of his skull. And he knew perfectly well why he couldn't sleep — it was because that evil no-name kid had fucked his head.

He stepped out onto his porch, felt the cold wind cut at his bare chest, felt the flames of the glorious autumn trees cut at his heart. Goddamn, but a man would have to be a fool to live like this, he thought. You need a woman to wash out the taste of that sicko orange-haired girl, he thought. *You need, you need, you need,* he thought. Shit, stop talking to yourself, you crazy fool. Strange as it might seem, there really *is* only one of you living in here.

All right, *I* do not have to go through this horror show again. *I* can short-circuit it. *I* will make a plan. *I* will walk over to the beer store fast to work off some energy, buy a case of beer and a sub sandwich and a copy of *Glamour*. Run back, hop in bed, jerk off, eat, listen to *Astral Weeks* twenty times. Drink all the fucking beer and pass out cold.

*And what happens if you don't?* He didn't even want to think about that one.

What the fuck day is it anyway? It's Saturday, you lame bastard, and one of the main problems is you haven't got a gig for tonight, and you aint going to get one because every musician in Toronto knows you by now and remembers some night when you blew it. The fifteen-minute solo you decided to take right in the middle of some ordinary country set. All the times you got so sick of hearing some lame son of a bitch trying to play lead that something snapped and you rode him to death. Or your brilliant breaks that telescope the form, two bars into eight, three against four, off into deep space, and nobody knows when to come in, all the dudes standing there with their axes in their hands staring at you like you're jerking off in public. Not to mention all the times you just stood up and walked off the stage. Like you did last night.

And Steve looked out across at the flaming October trees and knew that he remembered every twist and turn of every tune from Trackless Waste when it had been the best goddamned rock band in the country. He could pick up his sticks then and there and play every one of those tunes. But where's Jerry now with his vintage Fender bass? Jesus, he could punch in ahead of you like an ice pick or honker down on your beat like a mad king shitting gold turds. And where's Dave the rhythm king with his years of bluegrass to give him all that corn-fed drive? Oh, sweet Jesus, the three of you were like a single instrument, didn't have to look, didn't have to think, tuned into each other, lightning tying it all together like science fiction. The beat's as wide as a barn door, which it takes years of playing to know, aint no clock it's more like fucking, if you've got to talk about it, you're already too slow. And Ned on lead, riding on top like the star chaser. Whiz kid Peter on the board, his mind full of fiery electronics like hieroglyphs on the wall of a tomb, mixing it all together, making it work.

Oh sweet acid. You knew Jerry was going to go with you when you opened up "The Hounds" after the second verse — not a question, not a problem, not even something to think about. Bit of Alla Rakha cycling in the back of your brain, probably what started it, but the acid pulled us in so tight it could have been in Jerry's head and you caught it from him, and all of a sudden cabam-a-diddle chink pop, passing around the toms, and we're gone out of four like a shot without even a cloud of smoke to show for it. Jerry's moving right with you, Fender cranked up to a dragon's scream. Aint in Western music no more, no chords, which Dave knows right away because he's inside our heads, and he's finger picking high on the fret board, punching little spikes through the triads like bursting balloons. And Ned with his eyes shut, snarling in, old hound himself.

We're talking about how the stiff old blocks of the world are going to fall down because they're so gray and dumb. We're saying, here's music that don't sound like the FBI. We're talking about flying saucers and the end of the world. And the kids are pushing up on the stage, all breathless and their faces shining like lights in a fog. Which is what *far out* meant when it still meant something. Exactly. We're gathering it all up, taking home our children like the Dead said it, Uncle John's band, going to lead them out of this sick time and place, going to take them onto the dark planes where we're going to eat manna that's falling like fiery comets pouring off Ned's guitar. And the sweat's running down as we're talking about truth. Oh sweet acid, how long can we ring it around the sun without bursting open like seed pods and scattering ourselves out to the world?

But we know when we've got to bring it back. It's all one when we're coming down on it, saying, yeah, but *this* is where we got to live. Coming back to the U.S.A., to Vietnam, but we're bringing back the fire that's going to change everything. And the beat is an avalanche coming back, old four four, old split eight, stiff and pushing. Ned howls like he's been disemboweled, his blind face turned up to the lights, sweat streaming like blood. And the kids are insane. Leaping screaming. Hundreds of people, and we're all coming at once. We're all cock and cunt, all male and female, all coming home. We're supernova. We're stars across the night blazing together. And we're all one. Sun.

But how were you supposed to know that night was as good as it was ever going to get? How were you supposed to know that's when he comes to you — when it's as good as it's ever going to get? You didn't have a clue who he was when you met him, bobbing and jerking his head like a clown, just another one of all the people who'd come pouring onto the stage, pushing in where he's not wanted, but so mad, so into it, you couldn't turn away. "Far out, man. So far fucking out. You guys was really doing it, no fucking lie, man," giggling and jerking, shoving his little girlfriend forward to show her off to you. "This is sweet Cindy Sue, Mary Lou, hee hee hee... No, man, seriously, her name's Alice, isn't it, baby?"

And out of nowhere he's got a joint the size of a Havana

Corona. You take a drag, and you're looking around for Kathy, but she's way off somewhere, hundreds of people in between. And this tall skinny guy with his mustache and big cowboy hat has reached up under the girlfriend's white vinyl miniskirt, absentmindedly like he'd reached for a cigarette, hand between her legs in the crack of her ass. Lips parted and eyes focused down to BBs, she shoves her cheeks back to squeeze that casual hand. She's about sixteen, little mod outfit all made of shining white plastic, boots and dress and cap, all very English and out of place in this denim and work-shirt crowd. "Hey," the dude's saying in his silly high-pitched voice, "well, hey there. Hey hey hey. I dig your sound, man. Incredible. Hey, all right. My name's Bobby Lyons, and I want to show you guys a good time."

And you're staring at the honey, Steven, bud breasts and pert little ass shining away in her white plastic like an illustration from *Galaxy* Magazine. Hanging on a chain around her neck is a hunk of machinery, a small chrome doo-dad, bit of bracket with threads in it, could be part of a carburetor or some damn thing, and you never knew why she was wearing it, that open-threaded hole where the pipe would go in, and you never heard her say one single word, not there, not in the van, and not back at Lyons' apartment, jammed up with people, the boys in the band, lots of hippy girls, GIs and ex-GIs. Needle freak Ned and Lyons shooting up crystal in the can, don't even bother to shut the door. You're exhausted from the set, but still up and running with Frodo through Acidland. Every drug anybody could ever want is there like an exotic garden, the Stones Jack-flashing it away on the stereo, and Lyons takes your hand just like he's your playmate in the school yard, takes silent Alice in the other, and leads you into the bedroom.

"This is Alice, hee hee hee. And this is Steven Beuhl, the drummer. Now isn't he far out?" And he raises her skirt in the front, jerks it right up like a little kid showing off his sister's anatomy to a crew of dirty six-year-old boys. She's wearing tight silver panties, bikini briefs, and he holds up her skirt with one hand while he shoves his other between her legs and starts massaging her pussy, working his fingers in the crack until she slides her white boots on the carpet, opens her thighs, until her hips start to move. She's got no expression at all, just blank and turned on, her mouth open and breathing hard, and she never takes her eyes off your face. "Say hello to each other now, children," Lyons says and laughs. Then he jerks her panties down. She helps him by stepping out of them. And those panties aren't anything at all, so tiny, just a little bit of silver. He closes his hand over them and shoves them in his jeans. He bobs and giggles. He walks out and shuts the door.

I mean, Steven, just how fucking inadequate to say you shouldn't have done it? But no way you could have passed, which is more than likely why you're in Toronto, Canada, to this day and can't get a gig. Her arms are around your neck and her tongue down your throat. You've got your jeans off and she's cupped your cock and balls with her little white fingers. Then you've tumbled her down onto the bed and you're screwing away for dear life. It's all part of the trip, and even as you're shoving it in her, you're wondering what in God's name it could all mean. Know it's got to fit in with all the other things, Kathy drinking beer in the kitchen not thirty feet away. And this little kid hanging onto you is wet like the sea, probably been wet since the middle of the concert. Yeah, man, sure, that's what rock and roll's all about. *You've already been fucking her all night.*

She doesn't make a sound, space girl Alice (if that was her name), just eats your mouth, moves her hips smooth as syrup, and swear to God you come in a minute and a half. Then with your sperm oozing out between her legs, she's back in the living room on her knees between the stereo speakers rolling a joint, and you're wandering around, stunned, looking for the next clue. Lyons is sitting haunch to haunch with Peter whose eyes have gone gooey with stone. Lyons is saying, "Chemistry? You're working on a degree in chemistry? Now isn't that interesting." And you walk on down the hall and into the kitchen. The acid's boosted you up to the point where something as simple as exchanging a look is heavy as *The Book of the Dead.* Stare into Kathy's witchy green eyes, and you can't understand how she did it, but *you just know she knows.*


His plan abandoned, feeling as though he'd just jumped the fence and taken off into forbidden pastures, Steve was charging down Howland toward Bloor, his spirits whirligigging around his head. "Manic, manic, manic, manic," he was singing to himself. Sign by the church flashed by — ST. ALBAN THE MARTYR WELCOMES YOU. No thanks, St. Alban, appreciate the offer, but not today. Wonder how they did it to him? Tossed him down a well? Ran him into the ground with a juggernaut? Roasted him over a slow fire? Oh, those dudes were so fucking imaginative, couldn't just beat a man's brains out, had to come up with something that would stick to the ribs, the Quaker Oats of pain. But not today, not with all the girls, all the women, on the street.

Follow that honey down the subway stairs, sweet Lord, how'd she manage to get those jeans over her ass and the zipper pulled up? Voice from nowhere, Roxbury hip, popping absurdly out of Steven's mouth, "Say, baby, what's happening?"

She scoots away down the subway car, strike one. Come on, plan what you're going to do, asshole, don't just bubble over like an unwatched pot. But get out anywhere at all, Yonge and Bloor, who gives a shit, anywhere there are girls on the street, and *everywhere* there are girls on the street. The store windows are a turn-on, the billboards are a turn-on — LIVING FOR THE CITY — and just the way it should be, the girl on the billboard's in focus but the city's blurred. Red lips, sooty eyelashes, painted face says, "Power to the hard young miss." The city lies behind, night lit, a smear of desire, promises every detail you ever dreamed up in a third-time jerk-off fantasy at four in the morning and gives you nothing but hazy tease of false clues, boot heels on the pavement down the Yonge Streets of the mind. "Hi, honey, where you going?"

Neat little frosted blond, jeans rolled to the knee, marching along like a little soldier. Come on, baby, you know me, I've just stepped off the record jacket. Which one? Any one. I'm Jumping Jack Flash himself. But Steve saw the panic in her eyes. "Have a good day," he told her with a wave. Strike two, Steven, and next time pick them a little older, OK?

But hey, what's this? Another young miss stepping off the curb, and no bullshit about this one being old enough. "Mind if I step off the curb with you?"

Well-kept, sleek, and just a few extra pounds to make her look pampered as a cream-fed cat. Sling-back heels, gray nylons, painted lips heavy as ripe plums. Her expression said, "This has only happened to me a hundred million times before."

"Mind if I cross the street with you?" See what an amiable goof I am, and lots of laughs in bed too. Swear to God, you won't be able to tell the difference between me and a human being.

"It's a public street." Not the least bit ruffled.

"Now I'm glad to hear you say that," he heard himself rattling away. "There's many a young lady would not take that point of view. Now me, I've always been big on the notion that the streets are public, but there are those who figure that we all carry around with us small bubbles of space, force fields like alien visitors, and woe unto you should you push too far into somebody else's space. One of the problems in North American cities is that the space is being used up, like Toronto, for instance. You can't go anywhere without being continually assaulted."

"You seem to be proving that," she said with a hint of a smile. Her tiny heels were nibbling at the sidewalk so slowly that Steve couldn't force himself down to her tempo. He bounded around her like a big dog.

"Ah," he said, "but *you* assaulted me first. The Chinese have the right notion. If you're going to jam a trillion people into a space the size of a barnyard, you'd damn well better put all the girls into baggy pants, but we, however, do not follow that persuasion. We are big on the notion of continuous excitation with no release, as I believe Wilhelm Reich pointed out. Here on Yonge Street, for instance, we cannot walk two blocks without being assaulted. All I have done is retaliate in kind, thinking in my own somewhat distraught manner that if you did not want me talking to you, you would not look like that. 'Me' used in the generic sense."

She laughed openly.

"Of course," he said, "when you've got continuous excitation and no release, you sell more cosmetics, *Playboy* magazines, vibrators, high heels, and tranquilizers, and thus maintain the gross national product, so my actions, of course, can be seen to have a distinctly subversive element, shall we say. You are quite expensive as any fool can plainly see. I don't mean this in a crass or vulgar manner, but in the most refined capitalist terms. And if I walk directly up to you and begin speaking, and if you should respond in kind, we will have between us subverted the entire system, because we shall be enjoying each other's company without spending a cent."

She stopped walking, turned to him, grinning. "You've got an incredible line of bullshit, and at some other time I might just want to hear more of it. But in a minute you're going to get to meet my husband, and I don't think that's what you've got in mind."

Strike three and you're out. And looking around for some place to regroup, Steve saw a sign promising TOPLESS BUSI-NESSMEN'S LUNCHEON — cartoon-simple female outline in blue paint, huge torpedo breasts, nipped waist, tiptoe heels, presenting a drink on a tray. He plunged immediately in, stopped at the closing off of light, the door swinging shut behind him. The most banal of disco rock was pounding out from ceiling speakers, the only thing to see a small square stage, translucent plastic lit from beneath, now perfectly empty. As he paused and waited, his pupils swelled and he began to make out the dim lumpish forms of men hunched at tables, sitting motionless around the stage. If any of them were bothering to talk, their voices were lost completely under that wall of sound. An enormous familiarity to the place, its gloom and seediness, and having jumped into it out of the wine-crisp day, Steve was brought down immediately, felt his charge give out. Sank into a padded chair. And a young woman, her painted face as remote as the sign on the wall outside, was paddling toward him in Fredericks of Hollywood bedroom wear. "You got Southern Comfort?" he said, southernly.

"Yeah, I think so."

"Want to bring me a double? Throw a couple ice cubes in it?"

"You want a menu?"

"Naw." Come in here and eat? Are you out of your mind? And he knew why the place looked so familiar. He'd played in here a few years back when they'd still hired live bands. Oh, you pricks, he thought, so now you've put in disco, have you? Plastique bombs to your fat asses, that's what you need. And his drink arrived at his wrist, ice cubes tinkling like stones, along with a machine-printed bar bill for eight bucks.

With a change of tune, a skinny young girl came bobbing and shuffling through a curtain and out onto the glowing plastic stage. The slickness of the surface under her feet and the height of her silver heels reduced her motion to an Oriental ticky-tack. Dimpled knees pressed together, perversely short stockings stretched bright as glass, worked her hips to the music, rotating slowly to the left. The bones in her silver corset were outlined in black, the oversize garters trimmed in silver lace, she'd painted her nipples with lipstick, and she didn't bother to smile at all. "Here's to you, baby," Steve said, toasting her, knowing that she couldn't possibly hear him, "we're in the same business," and drank off half the cloyingly sweet fluid.

Steve closed his eyes and saw, eerie as an unwinding wisp of ectoplasm, memory of Lyons' little girlfriend, the first of them, Alice (if that was her name) in white plastic. Fucked her more than once. If you're going to addict someone you've got to keep giving them a hit. Fucked her in the bathroom, bent over the tub. Stoned on acid, fucked her again with Lyons watching. Was *his* acid. Oh, shit. And then Alice went the way they all went, replaced by the next one, Sheri or Sandy or Sally or Susie. Lyons gave everybody what they wanted. Ned and Jerry and Dave got to eat and shoot, pig pleased, drug city. And Peter got a nice new chemistry set over in Brooklyn. And you got to play with his dolls.

Baby on the stage stripped off one long silver glove, looped it between her legs, and worked it, timed to the computerized beat, body collecting wages but her face still on a coffee break. Steve tipped back the last of the sticky South across his tongue, knife tingle of ice cubes, and tasted the memory of his own blood. He was up and running.

LIVING FOR THE CITY. The girl's in focus but the city's blurred. A hundred million people on the street, light searing eyeballs, flaying knives. Push through bodies, move them out of the way, careful elbow here, quick pass there through an open space there, and he's already two blocks away, congratulating himself. *You can function, man.* And laughing out loud because he didn't pay the bar bill.

Jesus, Steve, don't lose the day. Stay out of the fucking bars, keep moving it along. Get out of the downtown, grab the ferry to the islands, because somewhere there are trees turning gold-red and fire-hot, and the air is swift current to the blood. Oh sweet October, redeem me yet! Stunned on the street corner, and breathless, the jam of people pouring around him, some with quick curious glances. No food, alcohol dancing across the brain pan, far too bright after the pit, dig out rock-and-roller shades to hide the spouting tears. Come on, man, you *can* function, you were doing it just a minute ago. But what the hell is it, God knows? Do you want to fuck every woman on the street, every sassy long-legged blue jean teenager, every lip-gloss panty hose Perma-press matron? Even that wouldn't be enough. Jesus, man, you're dealing with a condition that's got no relief.

"Now listen to me," Kathy said.

You tilted your head so you could see her better, and the whole room, the whole world, tilted. "You've always told me that when it comes down to the crunch, you can function. All right, Steven, *the crunch is here.* Now I'm going to untie you, and you're going to get up, and take a bath, and shave, and get dressed. And then we're going to get it together and leave."

"What are we going to do?"

"You don't have to think about that. *You're* going to do what *I* tell you." You were coming a fuck of a long way to be able to see those hard bitch eyes of hers, and you thought, yeah, she finally understands.

She'd scored a bottle of Valium, fed you a couple, and you walked on your hind legs again, sat on a stool in a restaurant and ate a cheeseburger just like a human being. Then she led you back to the apartment. She'd bought a plastic bucket, a box of Spic and Span, and two pairs of rubber gloves. She was talking to you steady, feeding out a constant transmission that was just as important as the Valium — reality reference. "I don't want a single fingerprint left in here, Steven. Not one. Not anywhere." It took hours.

It was beginning to make sense, and around noon you went down into the garage where she gave you the new clothes that turned you into Steven, the used-car dealer. She changed her image too — navy blue dress with a white collar and a pair of Bonwit Teller pumps brand new out of the box. Fed you more Valium, took one herself, got into the driver's side. Bad fucking day, you thought, when you can't do your own driving, but Cambridge drifted by the window, everything floaty and strange, and the soft-focus movie turned into Boston. You stood up with her, straight as a Confederate ramrod, and said the words. "Steven Beuhl, do you take this woman?" Oh yeah, no problem. I do. Of course I do. What else could I do? Be a goddamned fool not to, wouldn't I?

Then it was Beacon Hill, and it jolted you when you saw how close they lived to the Kennedy place. She was saying, "Mom. Dad. This is my husband." She didn't even give them a decent chance to get their act together. "We need money."

The old guy was beautiful with it. "Can't get to the bank today, Katherine. Will tomorrow morning do?"

So you ate dinner and the Valium was holding you down, but the apartment was full of so many strange things that your mind kept getting drawn away like the newborn into Maya. Easy to hallucinate on the patterns in the Oriental rugs, to wonder how the old man came by the camel saddle he used for a footrest or the Chinese gong you almost hit before Kathy stopped you with her eyes. Picture of him in his World War Two uniform, British Air Force, because, he said, he'd been so young and stupid he hadn't been able to wait for the States to get in. Huge chess set with carved pieces lined up and ready to go. And you kept thinking, shit, this is where she grew up. *Right here.*

You could see that it hurt her to sleep in her old bedroom, and it hurt you to see it. Showed you the corner where she used to stand to play her saxophone, that angle of the walls she'd used to drive her own sound back at her, and through the window saw what she must have seen — other houses and the cobblestone street below — when she'd been trapped there, tall crazy kid with energy driving her too fast to handle, sex juices and menstrual blood and everything turning into music that'd always be one jump ahead, yeah, even if she was dressed like a boy and running, Jill Flash in her black leather pants. It was all

just too fucking much, swear to God, and then the old man had
to come in and give us the formal speech he'd prepared for the
occasion: "I just wanted to say that I genuinely respect what
you're doing."

"Thanks, Dad," she said with nothing on her face, but after he
left, she lay down on her old bed and cried. It was the only time
you ever saw her cry.

Ate Valium for breakfast and drove north with the old man's
beautiful U.S. greenback dollars in your wallet. "Where we
going, babe?"

"Canada."

"So you think that'll do it, huh?"

"Well, Steven, I figured it'd take too long to drive to Brazil."
Looked into her eyes and finally saw everything she'd been
dealing with and no help from you — terrible fear and her steel
control holding it down — and then it came back hammering in
a rush, too fast to handle but you had to handle it anyway.

"I'd better drive," you said.

"We can't afford to get stopped," she said, "not even for a
routine check. Not for anything."

"You don't have to tell me *that*, for fuck's sake. Is there a
warrant out for me?"

"You know there is. Been one out for months." Meaning the
FBI, so you let it go, let her go on thinking that.

Stopped at a motel in a little town in New Hampshire just an
hour south of the Canadian border. No more Valium to keep
down the buzz because you had to have all the sharpness you
could get.

"What did you do with the goddamned gun, Kath?"


*Why does the sky feel like it's going to come cracking down?* Steve
had walked for hours along the curving edge of the Toronto
Islands with the sun, burning quarter, falling down the horizon,
but had found no relief. He stopped now to light a cigarette, boots
in the sand and Lake Ontario laid out before him sullen as
mucilage. He looked up to the industrial skudge on the skyline,
then farther up for that elusive blue where doom would come,
falling down like iron. The pressure of the sky seemed direct and
immediate as if cinder blocks were piled on his head. No doubt
about it, he said to himself, offered it as some perverse reassur-
ance —you're nuts again. As bad as it was when you left Kathy.
As bad as it was any of the times before that.

Just as he'd wanted, the trees *had* been flaming out, last brilliant scream of color before snuffed for winter. The wind *had* been blowing sideways, linking one crisp October to another, jerking memories along the sand like crumpled newspapers. New school clothes, football games, drinking black coffee from a paper cup, the same brilliant light in the stadium, girls in cashmere sweaters, girls in plaid wool skirts, and you were moving easily across the bleachers, through kids and class-mates, talking your trash, a wink here and a smile there, to come to a stop with the afternoon sun full on your face, some good buddy at your elbow, and count a dozen girls you'd made out with and a couple more you'd actually screwed. You were the candy man then, best kid drummer in the whole state of Georgia, and you didn't think it could ever get any better than that. But then it's another October and you're walking along the Charles with Kathy, stop to snake a frisbee out of the sky, fire it back, and she leans into your arm, smiles into your eyes, perfect in her leather miniskirt, and your heart feels like it's going to break you're so fucking happy. Why wasn't it enough?

The temperature was sinking fast and Steve was beginning to shake, teeth rattling in his head, hands and feet bloodless as suet. Over a day since he'd eaten a damn thing and now a glittering jet trail sliced above his head like an incision. He took off jerkily, gathering twigs for kindling, thicker debris for cross members, and built a small scaffold at the edge of the lake, the crumpled ferry schedule dead at the center. Flat on his belly, shoved in a careful match and fanned until it caught. The flame shot up, spraying sparks against the failing light. He crouched and warmed his hands, then stood and looked out across to the buildings of Toronto. LIVING FOR THE CITY. And you came over here to get away from it, didn't you, asshole? But brought every bit of it with you. At least here, you're harmless, but Christ, the sun's going to lose again, and night gobble up the sky like a cancer.

Don Juan was right the way he always is, smug little Indian prick. You do have to erase your personal history, but how, man, how? If you knew, you'd do it, start all over here and now with your Boy Scout fire going up and Toronto sinking into dark like a magician's illusion, lights in high-rises winking on, bead game in the sky. You'd leave it all behind in Lake Ontario, every memory, and come bouncing back, fresh and pink as a new baby boy. But no, you've got to carry the weight, got to ask her, "What did you do with the goddamned gun, Kath?"

"You know that high-rise they were slapping up about six blocks over?"

"Yeah."

"Well, I pushed it into the wet concrete and covered it up."

"Jesus Christ, how'd you get up there?"

"How the fuck do you think I got up there? I climbed up there."

"And you're sure they didn't find it?"

"Steve, I shoved that gun down really deep into the wet concrete and covered up the marks, and that building's kept right on going. That gun's buried so deep by now that the only way anybody'd ever find it is if the whole fucking building cracked."

You stared at her then because you didn't know who the hell she was anymore. She'd climbed up forty or fifty feet in the air, on narrow scaffolding with that nasty blue thirty-eight in the pocket of her jacket, alone with no light at all except whatever moon might have been hanging up there. Yeah, cat-padding it along in her sneakers, summer camp tomboy finally having some use for her old skills. She couldn't have known anything about that gun, just that it had to go, and she didn't even tell you about it. She'd been alone as it's possible to get.

Playing Bonnie to your Clyde, the gun taken care of, the apartment left clean as a whistle, and you were married, by Jesus, and she couldn't testify against you. Said to her, "Do they know about you?"

She looked back with a face like nothing at all. "Dad told me that the FBI had been to see him."

"Oh fucking shit."

"He loved it. He's always had that bomber pilot in him, never lost it. Told me that for the first time since the Vietnam war started, he felt like he was doing something real." Right, his beautiful thousand bills to make the run.

Drove north. Stopped and stripped off the phony plates, buried them in the woods with the phony registration. Put the real plates back on, making yourself vulnerable again. Not much Valium left, but enough to do the job. You each ate two caps, climbed back in, looked at each other, and drove across the border into Canada.

Sweet Quebec. Yes, the nice old man with the French accent said, they would certainly permit us to go through the immigration process at the border, but please couldn't we come back after one? Seemed the fellows in the office hadn't had lunch yet. And when you did come back and he started filling out the forms, he had to ball them up and throw them away because they were a year out of date. Mr. and Mrs. Steven Beuhl. Yeah, that's us. Destination? "Montreal," you said automatically because it was the only place in Canada you'd ever been. He seemed to like that.

"Oh, and do you speak French?"

"Two years in high school and two more in university."

*Belle journée pour venir visiter le Canada, n'est-ce pas, monsieur Beuhl?"* he said without any warning at all.

You managed, God knows how. *"Oui. Cela est une belle journée,"* and that was your French test. He gave you full points for it.

Maybe it was Kathy. He kept looking at her. She sat there like a sweet little wife not saying a word, showing some leg but not too much, knees crossed, smiling like Miss America. "Welcome to Canada, Mr. and Mrs. Beuhl," he said, rose with formal Quebecois gallantry and took your hand across the desk. That gesture stung your eyes.

All those drums and toys turned into "settler's effects." The customs man was delighted. Thought he was going to spend the whole afternoon playing Gene Krupa, but you didn't care how long he took because you were through the border and clear, gentle maple leaf flying over your head instead of that mean coiled-up snake saying, "Don't tread on me." After an hour they stamped all your papers and there was the beautiful road, big and straight as the yellow-bricker to Oz, and you were moving again.

"All right, Kath," you said, "let's see how far this country runs."

In the line you took it, runs all the way to Tofino, British Columbia.

Night had completed itself all along the edge. Steve had stopped feeding his fire, and it was burning out now, leaving a smoldering bed of coals. He began to kick it, wood and hot sand, hissing into the lake. Can understand how everybody wants a guru these days, how sweet it would be to say, "OK, daddy, here's my karma, now *you* take it on." Except that it's your karma and you've got to run it out, play with what's dealt you. And nothing for you here, got to go back to the city because that's where you live, so stomp your fire into the lake and keep on running. And nothing left now but cold and the aftermath of the sun sunk over the edge of the world, blowing out the west with blue breath. Steve began to jog back toward the ferry slip.

What he feared most was the loss of control, that moment when something else came and took over and ran him. He feared the giveaway signs, the voices in his mind that wouldn't stop, the sickness that hit like rotten meat boiling in the gut, sweating and dizzy as a poisoned dog, then he'd see the solid objects of the world moving, squirming and swirling away like worms. And then the voices in his head would start coming out his mouth. He'd be launched and running, no way to stop it. And he was running now because he could see that the ferry was about to close up her mouth and leave. He slap-dashed it down the concrete in his cowboy boots and leaped on board at the last possible moment, voice in his ear that proved to be a real person, an old man on deck who said, "Good going, son," with an Ottawa Valley chuckle.

And sick, leaning over the railing as the water moved around and under him, afraid to look up, afraid that the flesh on the faces would be rippling like leaves in a wind. Heard guys with their girls, bright good-time voices. Kept himself bent double, pressure pounding at his temples. Got to eat, got to get back somehow, got to try to sleep. But the girl on the billboard would tell him the truth — LIVING FOR THE CITY — that she'd always be in focus, but the city would melt, dissolve, and he'd jump along fast on the alien pavements to keep pace with the night, dancing to music that couldn't be written down. Dark flare at the back of the eyeballs, saw a face painted the color of bread mold. And what mask would the no-name kid be wearing tonight? The bright-lit hard-edged girl who could stop it, maybe could stop it, a few steps short of hacked-up human meat in a clear plastic body bag. But Jesus, *it can't be that bad, can it*?

"Can I get anything to eat in here?"

"No, I'm sorry. The grill's shut down."

Steve had a flash of himself as an old black derelict shuffling at the back door, the last of the white cotton hair puffed around the edge of his bald pate, slouch hat in hand, mumbling, "Scuse me, Missus, you got any leftover grits?" Goofy, old, broken down, and useless, his hip joints full of sand, his feet burning and swollen, the pressure on his head so persistent that he was reduced, bowed and shambling, just barely making out the nearest chair to stick his ass in just before the crack at the end. But what the hell, it was only another dark bar, just the same Saturday night crowd, escorted candy floss, and the young waiter in the cute little outfit the manager laid out — straw hat and bow tie — following, worried. "About the most I've got is potato chips."

"Sure. Just dandy. Wonderful wonderful. Bag of potato chips and a couple of beers...Yeah, two... Oh fuck, I don't care. Any kind."

You've been cranked up too long for any relief as simple as

mere lust, can't even see whole girls anymore, nothing left but neon fragments. Curve of ass under polyester skirt, Kodachrome light reflecting off heels, lips slick as the finest polyvinyl chloride. You're a cartoon slave in a plastic harem designed by Eaton's, got nothing to do but trot around all night with silver trays of honey sherbet, only the tray aint silver, it's Mylar, and the sherbet aint honey, it's a coal tar derivative, and you can't tell anymore if the sultan pumping away between the thighs of that lovely simulated teenage doll is really the sultan or only some guy left over from a TV ad. Yeah, you haven't eaten the drug, the drug's eaten you, and it didn't grow on its own in sunny Mexico but came from somebody's shiny white lab, so don't sit here too long, asshole, just move it along and then maybe later you can scrape away your mind with that double-edged, bonded and coated, molybdenum stainless steel for a sleep so smooth you'll think you're back in the womb.

First cold beer down in ten seconds flat, but go easy on the second. Light a smoke. And oh shit, the problem with Lyons was that you knew what he was like. The night he fucked one of them, whichever one it was, Sally or Susie, up the ass even though she begged him not to, and hurt her so she cried, and you were watching as usual, waiting for *your* turn, of course. She kept clenching her hands, and unclenching them, fingers spread out, then white fists again, still with her dress on, naturally, for the kink, and even with her mouth pressed into the pillow, she couldn't stop up the sounds. What were you thinking about, Steven, to get turned on by the salty taste of her tears under your tongue? That you could be gentle after that, the one to bring her comfort? What a fucking joke. Oh, it's perfectly clear how Charlie Manson brought it off.

He drank the second beer, all of it. Dry throat, empty guts, the alcohol jumped him in a rush. "You're too sick to live," a voice said, which, after a moment's reflection, proved to be one of his own. And all around him was a hivelike buzzing — boys and girls, girls and boys. Anything was possible. He could throw these two empty bottles across the room, he could scream and overturn the table, he could get up and run out silently without paying, he could continue to sit and do nothing at all, he could walk into the men's room and punch out the first man he saw. He couldn't understand how he had ever thought he could possibly eat potato chips.

And, unfortunately, there is a rather exquisite blond at the next table, and you seem to have been staring at her for the last ten minutes. Her gentleman friend has begun to send the darts back — Screw off, buddy! I'm the one who paid for the tight dress with the slit skirt, for the whisper-sheer stockings by Hanes, so you can just shove those gooey eyes back into their sockets and eat your potato chips and clear out. *Oh yeah!* Steve thought, four million volts catching sight of a polished copper post marked GROUND. Fuck you, he said with his grin, you're big enough. And raised a hand in a V for victory sign for the waiter.

Beer like cream down the cat, and Steve no longer felt old or tired, the current clean and useful in every muscle. Oh, it's a shame almost, the poor fucker doesn't know who he's dealing with, and no way he can get out of it, not being fifty years old and having to prove it for Miss Lovely. But hope to God he can still come up with something, don't want to just knock him down and stomp on him. Now that's not too much to ask, is it? Just to see his eyes when it dawns on him that you just might be crazy enough to kill him.

*Oh Christ help me!* Steve closed his eyes. Behind the lids, lights exploded at great depth, one after the other, like huge luminous fish giving up the ghost. He was turned on. *I don't want to be like this,* he thought. *Why can't I ever help somebody, do some good for somebody?* Yeah, another voice kicked in and said, you were the one, big daddy, who was going to redeem an entire generation, right? You were going to take it farther than Saint Morrison or Saint Dylan, stick your neck out like Jesus, come back and pour down love like stars, take all your children home, and now look how far you've sunk.

Steve opened his eyes and the man was leaning over his table. Saw at once the scared shifty eyes. He knew the man was leaning on the table so his hands wouldn't shake. "You want something?" the man said.

"Naw," Steve said. "Don't want nothing." He handed over the potato chips, which the man, his face suddenly slack and stupid, took.

A loose door banging in the wind, Steve was already two blocks up the street. The bar bill unpaid, leather jacket flapping, LIVING FOR THE CITY. Once it was a joy to rattle down the streets, drummer, pulse of the world, something great just around every corner, just beyond reach. But stopped, struck by an oblique gust against cheek, raised one hand to wipe it away. *Christ,* he thought, *snow.* The sky had done it, broken, and cut by another gust, wiped it away, saw solid flakes on the hand a moment before, quick as illusion, they fell back to water. Won't last, gone by morning, but a reminder of what's coming. Loss of light, holed up again, and the end of your mind contracted, frozen, Georgia boy. He felt the other world that runs parallel to this one, so close now that if he jumped he might make it, the tall buildings gone leaving bare planes across which cold wind drives continually from a black center. And stepping off the curb, waved down a cab. You've known since morning, haven't you, where you were going?

Yeah, I know where I'm going.


Leaning against the wall in the dark at the top of the stairs. Lock on the door to the street gives with a boot heel, but lock on the door to the apartment is solid, so wait. Don't smoke, don't think, just wait. Night's closing down the city, rain mixed with snow rattling on the roof. Listen to the traffic on Parliament Street, inhale the nasty odors of the hallway, and wait. Time's folded up, don't mean a thing as long as you keep your place. Pulse goes on in absolute silence, and the drummer's counting bars of rests. You're the drummer even with your eyes shut, and you know all there is to know about waiting. No way the girl's going to see you until she's unlocked her door and pushed it open.

No way in hell she's going to know you're there at all, right behind her, arm bar across her throat to choke off sound. *But why?* Don't ask why, just wait. And down on the street a car pulls up. Tinny rattle, doors slam. Small car, foreign. You're a German shepherd in the dark, ears pricked. Footsteps on pavement, a man's heavy shuffle, a girl's staccato heels, and a key in the lock at the foot of the stairs. Door swings open and the voices are suddenly clear, perfectly audible. The man's laughing, the sound of spring-loaded nerves. The girl's saying, "I told you what happens to naughty boys. Have you been a naughty boy?"

Two bodies scraping along the wall, harsh breathing. Can tell the girl's breath from the man's perfectly. She's faking it for effect, but the man aint faking a thing, thick rattle in the throat. Must be big, can hear the weight of him. They've stopped to kiss, shift of balance against the wall, creaking wood underfoot. The door swings shut behind them, rattle of loosened lock. Again the man's difficult laugh full of raw fear. "Christ, it's black as a fucking coal bin in here." No answer but the dry insect crackling of some stiff fabric.

They're climbing the stairs now. Slowly, leaning into each other. But they've stopped. "Wait," the girl says.

"What?"

"There's somebody up there."

"Oh, for Christ's sake!"

"There is."

"It's black as pitch up there."

"Hey," she calls out, "who's there?"

Steve doesn't answer, stands motionless, controlling his breath.

"Hey!" again. "Who is it?"

"There's nobody there." The man's voice says he could flip either way at a moment's notice — anger or panic.

"You got a match?" Her voice is frightened.

"Oh, fuck." Scrape, sulphur, and flame goes up. Two faces staring at you. Middle-aged man with glasses, caught, startled, holding the match high like a candle. Painted young woman with orange hair. Just that much, that quick, and then gone, leaving behind flare-trace yellow in the eyeballs, illusion floating on the new thick dark. "Jesus!" the man yells. Bull clumsy, he's scrambling, rattling the door, then through it and running, feet flat and slapping the sidewalk. So eager to get away, damn sure he'll flood his engine, sputtering. But no, it's caught, it's in gear, and tires scream halfway up the block. Can hear him accelerating for a long time, minutes, and then no sounds left but rain on the roof, creak of settling wood in the old building. Eventually another car drifts by on Parliament Street, not in a hurry, easy-going hiss of tires on wet pavement.

"Hello, Steven." Her voice quiet.

"Hello, kid."

"I'm not coming up, you know."

"Yeah, I know."

"It's when you didn't answer me."

"Yeah." Steve let his muscles sag back into the wall. He lit a cigarette, glad for the smoke in his lungs after the long wait. "How'd you know I was here?"

"I don't know. I just knew. It felt... I don't know. Wrong."

"You're good."

"Sometimes."

Steve smoked the cigarette down to the filter. He couldn't hear any motion from the girl below on the stairs, but he could feel her tense presence just inside the door, ready to jump.

"What do you want?" she said.

"You know what I want."

"Yeah. But why?"

"Christ, I don't know."

"I'm not going to come up."

"You said that. I know you're not going to come up. You're not crazy, are you?"

"What do you think?"

Steve said nothing.

"Was it what I did to you the other night? The game?"

"I don't know," Steve said. "Maybe."

"I've got to watch shit like that. I get into it and then I forget."

Steve said nothing.

"I didn't figure you right," she said. "That's all. I made a mistake. I thought you were into it."

"Yeah, and maybe I was. Look, why don't you take a walk around the block, and when you get back, I'll be gone. All right?"

Hesitation. "All right."

"And look. Something else. Why don't you move? Do you understand? I don't want to know where you're living."

"All right. It was about time anyway."

"I'm going to leave you some money up here on the floor. Maybe that will help."

"Don't do that." After a moment, "Hey, I'm sorry, OK? All that stuff about the band was for real."

"Was it?" Steve's body had begun to shake. "Oh fuck, just get the hell out of here, will you."

But the girl didn't move. "I didn't understand what I was doing," she said. And then, deliberately, began to climb the stairs.

The sound of the high heels was maddening.

She unlocked the door, pushed it open and lit the light. "See, I'm crazy after all. Come on." And again, "Come on." She held out her hand.

She was wearing black kid gloves. Steve didn't take the hand, but he stepped through the door. He felt as detached from his body as if he were floating a foot in the air above it, watching. Loose sprung hip joints, marionette legs. "Christ, you take chances," he heard himself saying, the sound of it harsh and strange. He watched himself squeeze his arms tightly around his chest so the shaking couldn't rip him apart.

The man needed to get his back up against something, found the nearest wall. The yellow overhead bulb hurt the man's eyeballs just under the ridge of skull, thumb on bruise. The pressure on the man's head was enormous.

The girl pushed the door shut. The lock fell into place. The girl was black and shining. Long black raincoat, belted at the waist, shining. Droplets of white light beading down, shining. Black patent heels, black gloves, black scarf at the throat, and all that was not black was pale as moon, mask of face, shining. Damp

orange hair, shining. Painted face, ringed eyes, lips red and
shining. The city's blurred, but the girl's in focus, shining. "You
just blew a hundred bucks for me." The man could hear the
tremendous effort in her flat voice, the forced control. She peeled
off the gloves, tossed them onto a chair, movement to fill up time,
create a space so she could go on living in it. "At least a hundred."
She dropped the purse onto the floor. Her shoes were open at the
toe, red nails showing through nylon, slender ankles bound with
thin straps, shining.

The man felt the linoleum under his feet begin to move like
ripples in a water bed. He squeezed his elbows into his chest
until he was compressed, compacted, a pinched iron pipe. Then
he exploded.

It doesn't scream, but twists and fights, biting, punching.
Black, slick, impossible to hold. If the man could think, he'd jab
and fake, he'd roll block, he'd chop at the throat with stiff hands.
But can't think, so grabs. Grabs and hangs on. Hardly feels the
fists and elbows battering his face and chest. It gets away. Man
hurls himself and grabs. It's just beyond reach. Grabs again,
he's got it in his arms, he's lifted it clear of the ground. But it
twists and arches, kicks back, black and slippery. It twists away.
Raw sounds are coming out of the man. He grabs again and
breaks apart. Pain. Kicked in the balls, goes down on his knees.
The switchblade is still lying in the corner where it's been since
the last time.

The man's got the switchblade. He's got it open. He's slashing
himself with it. He's flailing the blade into his chest and left arm.
The man can't tell if he's cutting through jacket and shirt to bare
flesh. The man can't feel anything.

"Like this," he's yelling to the girl, the woman, his wife, the
angel. "You do it like this. Like this. Like this. Like this." He's
slashing at himself with the sharp bare blade.

"Stop it."

"Like this. Like this. Like this."

"Stop it, for Christ's sake. Stop it."

"Like this. Like this. Like this."

"*Stop it!*" The girl strikes the man on the face with her open
hand. The man's head jerks away to one side, then rolls back,
hanging. His mouth is hanging open. A thin whining sound is
unwinding out of the man. He lifts the knife. The girl slaps him
again. The man's head is slammed to one side and then rolls
back. "Give it to me."

The girl jerks the knife out of the man's slack fingers. The
man is laughing and crying, shaking and howling, rocking back

and forth on his knees. Deliberately the girl winds up and swings her entire arm, her hip and twisting body behind it. The sound is sharp as a rifle shot.

Steve tasted tears and blood, raised his hand to his face. Cut lip, blood streaming out of his nose. "Oh, fuck," he said. Cupping his balls, he fell over slowly onto the floor. Stake of pain shoved up his ass. Fire on his chest and shoulder. "Oh fuck. Sick. Sick as a yellow dog." Stomach contracted and squirted out acid. Rolled over to get away from it. "Christ, Kath," he said, "I've really done it this time."

He could see her toes only a few feet away from his face. Red nails, the precise straps of her shoes. "I don't care where you've been," he said. "I don't care. Don't even tell me, all right?"

A deep coil of pain spun up from his balls. Rolled himself tighter, squeezing. "Jesus," he said through clenched teeth, "when does it stop? Oh fuck. Oh Christ. Why the fuck don't you go ahead and do it? Just be another fucking hippy body. Just like Peter. You could be in California a month before they found me."

She knelt and rolled him onto his side. "Can you sit up?"

"I don't know. Yeah. Oh fuck, it hurts." He allowed his jacket and shirt to be peeled away. The jacket was cut to ribbons.

"It's a good thing you're into leather," she said in a flat voice. Steve saw two long incisions on the deltoid of his left arm, several shorter ones over the pectoral muscle. "They're not that deep," she said. "They're really not that deep."

"I'm chopped up." His voice sounded so bleak and funereal and full of self-pity he had to laugh at it. But the laughter turned into sobbing.

"Come on. Lie down on the bed."

"You know, that old fucker Van Gogh botched his suicide. Couldn't even do that right, the poor prick. You know what his last words were? 'The misery will never end.' Now isn't that a wonderful exit line?"

"Will you just shut the fuck up."

She pulled off his boots and socks, his jeans and shorts. She wrapped a blanket around him.

"Here, take these."

"What? What?"

"Sit up. Come on." Five small round pills lay in the palm of her hand. Steve licked them into his mouth, drank water. "Kath," he said, "I'm sick of it."

He lay for long vacant minutes listening to the sounds she made moving around the apartment. Always what she has to do with you, isn't it, asshole? — clean up the mess. Then he felt his muscles begin to unknot. Something like sleep.

"Better?" she said.

"Kathy?"

"Hey. Look at me. I'm not Kathy, all right?"

Saw the tough tomboy face under the paint. "Shit. Yeah. You're not, are you?" The room came into focus a moment and he knew where he was before another wave of darkness sucked at him. "Jesus. What did you give me?"

"Mellaril. And if you don't clean up your act, you're getting five more."

Steve laughed. "Beautiful." As good as if she'd tied him to the bed. He couldn't even sit up. But screwing his back tight into the mattress, managed to open his eyes, managed to form a thought, a question. "What are you doing with Mellaril?"

He saw the girl unbuckle her shoes, kick them off. "I know about bad nights." She raised her skirt, unfastened nylons. They were slashed with long runs all the way to the toe. "You owe me a pair of stockings."

"Shit. More than that. Hey, what's your name? Tell me your real name."

"What do you want to know for?"

Steve couldn't answer.

"Alison," the girl said. "My name's Alison."

"Oh fuck." It was almost funny.

She looked down at him. Her face blurred. "Shut up," she said and pressed gentle fingers over his eyelids, closing them down.

Rain. And then out of the six o'clock darkness a single note held for eight beats of the clicking metronome. Kathy, floating unattached, loose cradle on a pond, was awakened immediately by the first bite of the bow into the string — the deeply melancholy gamba sound, no vibrato yet but each note shaped and sustained.

When Wendy first begins, her hands cold, you can hear the bow change direction. (She's always complaining about how her hands are cold.) But after she's warmed up, you can't hear the shift anymore, just continuous tone with no giveaway jerk at the center. Slow eight beats (Kathy listened, counting), and then Wendy moved up to the next note of the scale. Kathy knew her routine by now. All the way to the top of the instrument beyond the frets, then back down, half a dozen keys. Then she'll start over and play whole notes, half notes, quarter notes, eighth notes. And finally, after forty minutes of that infinitely patient warming up, she'll begin to work for speed, moving the metronome down a notch at a time until she's at the edge of her technique.

When she doesn't have to stop for school, she tortures herself with two empty shoe boxes, one placed on either side of her, five pennies in the left box. Each time she completes a passage without a mistake, she bends and transfers one penny from the left box to the right. "The motion of bending over keeps my back from getting stiff," she says. When she's managed to move all the pennies, she pushes the metronome a notch faster and begins again, trying to move them back. When she's reached the speed at which she can't move the pennies, she stops for breakfast. But that won't be all. She'll sight read most of the morning, getting herself in shape, as she says, "to be able to play what's placed in front of me." In the afternoon, finally, she'll get to the Marais she's memorizing for her debut as a soloist. And every time I stay here, Kathy thought, she wakes me up.

It was still night, but Kathy could see a hint of blue dawn at the crack below the window blind. Paul was sleeping deeply as he always did, the covers pulled up to his nose, hibernating bear. Why didn't Wendy wake *him* up, the peaceful son of a bitch? Probably because he'd been hearing her practice every morning for years. It was wet and cold — damp nibbled at Kathy's bare shoulder above the covers. End of January. Strange how it was happening. Kathy's things kept trickling over bit by bit, and soon she'd cross some crucial balance point and then there would be more of her life here in this house than at her apartment. And then she would have done it without ever having made a conscious decision — moved in with him. And with Wendy. By God, it was strange. She burrowed under the covers and pressed against Paul's broad back for warmth.

The bowed notes stopped, and Kathy was suddenly aware of herself again. Paul was gone. Already up and out without her noticing. Nine o'clock. She'd been asleep for another three hours, and this time what had awakened her had been the *silence* Wendy had left when she'd stopped. Amazing, Kathy thought, I'm learning how to live here. She got up, opened the drapes — Evelyn's drapes. She hated them. Then she opened the door to the walk-in closet. That damned woman must have kept every article of clothing she'd ever bought in her adult life. OK, Kathy thought, even though I'm not exactly a resident, I'm no longer a guest either, and one of these days that closet's going to be empty.

She wrapped herself in Paul's bathrobe, started downstairs. Heard Wendy following like a sleepwalker. The girl floated into the kitchen behind her. "Good morning," Kathy said.

Wendy didn't speak but drifted across the linoleum, rose on tiptoe, and deposited a small, dry kiss on Kathy's cheek, continued to the sink where she began to run hot water onto her hands. Those quick, brushing kisses were so extraordinary that Kathy had counted them. The first had been shortly after Wendy had moved back into the house with her father, the second on Christmas day, and this was the third. Kathy's cheek tingled where the girl's lips had brushed her.

Wendy bent over the sink, rubbed her hands together, stared into the steaming water with single-minded concentration. What the hell is it with Wendy and her hands? Kathy thought.

If you had beautiful hands and wanted to show them off, you'd paint your nails, wouldn't you, or wear rings or bracelets? And Wendy did none of those things. But vanity must play some part in it; whenever Wendy went out, even on warm days, she always wore gloves. She owned at least twenty pairs of them — expensive kid leather dress gloves. Kathy had seen them neatly arranged on the top of Wendy's bookshelf.

"What would you live on if you were alone," Kathy said, "mandarin oranges and toast and tea?"

"Probably," Wendy said without looking up.

"No wonder your circulation's lousy. Well, today you're going to eat a serious breakfast."

"Sure."

"If I fix it, right? Jesus, kid, you need a maid."

Wendy glanced back, smiling faintly. The girl always looked young and a bit silly in the morning — flannelette pajamas and threadbare terry-cloth bathrobe, everything too small. Her blue eyes seemed distant and abstracted, in the flat morning light milky, nearly opaque. Her hands had turned pink under the hot water. She dried them on a tea towel. "Yes, it'd help, wouldn't it?" She sat down on the very edge of a chair, arched herself like a cat, stretching her lower back muscles. "I'll be human again after the concert."

"Oh, you mean you're human sometimes?"

"Of course I'm human." The girl rubbed her hands together and blew on them. Then she said, "You hurt my feelings, you know."

"Oh? Did I?"

"I know I'm not easy to live with. Especially not right now. But you *did* hurt my feelings."

"Hey look, I'm sorry, OK? Sometimes I see a chance for a good line and I can't resist."

Wendy didn't answer. She turned away to stare out the window, leaving nothing of herself to be seen but a mass of tangled hair. To hell with you, child genius, Kathy thought and began to crack eggs into a bowl. Sometimes she felt that everything Evelyn said about Wendy was true — pampered, spoiled, inconsiderate, selfish. Right, kid gloves suited her. The perfect accessory to a personality like that.

Kathy heard her father's voice. "What the hell's the matter with you, Katherine?"

She's still wearing bangs. She's deliberately let them get too long, ragged; they're hanging over her eyes. Whenever her mother says, "Kathy, you look like a sheepdog," she's pleased — scored again! — but would never show it. Says nothing, turns away icily. Now she tilts her head forward so her hair swings over her face, covering it, looks out through that protective screen at her father across the dining-room table. She's really got to him. He's furious. Can see it in the white tension at the corners of his mouth. Careful to keep her face expressionless, she pushes back her chair and stands up. "Where the hell are you going?" he yells at her. "Katherine, come back here and eat your dinner!"

She doesn't answer. Walks away slowly. On the stairs, bangs the hard leather heels of her loafers down savagely with each step. In her own room, takes the door in both hands, winds up, grits her teeth, and then throws it away. The release is wonderful, the entire apartment reverberating for minutes with the enormous slam. She locks herself in. She hasn't bought the first Selmer yet (it's the second Conn); she picks it up off her bed, which hasn't been made in months, attaches the mouthpiece, shoves the mouthpiece between her lips, and blows — top-of-the-register high screaming wail — pushes it on and on, howling against the walls of her room until she runs out of breath.

"There are people harder than you to live with," Kathy said to Wendy and beat the eggs with a fork.

Still facing the window, Wendy said, "Mother called me a monster once. Maybe I am."

Kathy laughed. "What were you doing to get her that mad at you?"

"Not answering her."

"You're really good at that."

"I just wanted *out* of that damned house."

"You got what you wanted."

"Yes, I know."

"You don't sound very pleased with it."

"Oh, I'm glad to be here. It's just that..."

"What?"

"Well, I can't blame everything on other people anymore."

"That's insightful of you. Blame what?"

Wendy didn't answer, but just about the time Kathy decided that the conversation must have ended, Wendy said, "When I played with the Pro Musica, it felt as though someone else were playing, as though there were a *me* floating along, watching. Oh, so one walks out on stage. One sits down, takes the gamba between the legs, waits for the signal, and then one plays. It just passed by and was over. Everyone said I played very well. I knew it. But I didn't *feel* anything... just that strange distance. And I thought, why? What is it for?"

"Did you come up with an answer?"

"Just that if I weren't doing that, I wouldn't be doing anything... It's the strangest thing, Kathy, my earliest memory is of a cello. Isn't that odd? It didn't seem like a tiny cello then. It was just the right size for me. Dad would say, 'Wendy, can you play me a D major scale?'... or an E minor, or whatever... and I'd play it. It seemed so easy, a game. I was just four, you know.

"I had some dolls, but I didn't play with them. I didn't have any friends either. I just played with my cello. It was a person to me, a friend, and... Mummy was always dressing me up and taking me to concerts. I used to hate it when she'd brush my hair because she hurt me, but I never said anything. That's how I learned to count. I'd count up to a hundred because I knew that when she got to a hundred, she'd stop. No one ever asked me what I wanted. Never. Not once."

Surely *my* childhood was all right, Kathy thought, happy enough, absolutely unremarkable. She'd been dressed up and taken to concerts too, and she remembered looking forward to those nights — the fancy clothes, the buzz of people at intermission, getting to stay up later than usual. Adults always told her that she looked like Elizabeth Taylor in *National Velvet*. With a mother too busy to do it for her, she brushed her own hair, bought her own clothes, chose a black velvet party dress, wondering if it was right, real *national* velvet — having never seen the movie. Black hair and a white ribbon, black dress and white skin, black patent shoes and white socks — the colors of her father's chess pieces.

Camping in Vermont, firelight on her father's face, on his chessboard. He doesn't play with other people. He plays alone, out of books. Smell of burning wood, hots dogs and marshmallows. She cuddles into him. His arm wraps around her shoulders. She watches as he moves a chess piece. Mummy has always told her, "Your father was never the same after the war." Kathy has always thought it wasn't fair. She would never be able to know what he was like before the war.

"Did you drop bombs, Daddy?"

"Yes," he says, and she can hear something funny in his voice. "That's exactly what I did. I dropped bombs." Usually he won't talk about it, but now it seems he will. He and Mummy are drinking gin and tonic; he lets Kathy have a sip, and it's bitter.

Mummy isn't talking at all, stares into the fire. Overhead there are a trillion stars. "It's curious," he says, "how beautiful it is. If you can detach yourself from it, if you can stop thinking, they're trying to kill me." His exact words lost but the feeling of it remembered, the scattered fragments — beauty and fear, dangerous excitement — flying into Germany at night with no sound but the drone of the engine; white flak and the brilliant reaching searchlights on the ground.

And in England, when they're not flying, most of the men drink. "Why?" she asks him.

"So they won't have to think about all the good men who are dead."

But he doesn't drink. He plays the saxophone, plays with the swing band, or with a couple of other guys around a piano, or, if he has to, alone.

"Why don't you play it anymore?"

He smiles. "Because now I play chess."

Back home, she sneaks into the closet and takes it out of the case — battered, but shining and golden — more magical than anything in the world. The music teacher wants to start the kids on band instruments, asks each one, "What do *you* want to play?" Most of the kids shrug, don't know, but Kathy says without hesitating, "The alto saxophone." It's hers then, that ancient Conn. And surely she must have been happy; she couldn't remember anything that would make her think that she hadn't been.

"I really don't understand," Wendy said. "All I ever wanted to do was to play with the Pro Musica. And now I've done it. And I don't know why, but I'm going to be doing it again.

"I'm going to walk out onto the stage at the Queen Elizabeth Playhouse and sit down and play a solo piece. A *very hard* solo piece, and not just *technically* hard, but musically demanding. It'll be my chance to show everybody that I *am* mature enough to have that undefinable thing called 'musicality'... That's what they're all saying now, you know. 'Oh, she has technique coming out her ears, but it'll be a few years yet before she really has the nuance.' So I'm going to show them, damn it. I know I'm going to be scared to death, and I know I'm going to do it anyway, and it just doesn't make any sense."

"Do you like the music?"

"Of course I like the music. I *love* the music."

"Isn't that reason enough?"

"One would think so, wouldn't one?"

Wendy selected two slices of bread from the middle of the loaf,

dropped them into the toaster; her motions had both a vague-
ness and a precision about them, an abstracted quality. *Out to
lunch*, Kathy thought, amused, but then, catching it unexpectedly like a glint of light, a picture — Wendy lying on her bed, a
seductive, golden princess. Oh, so it's that old number is it, that
dangerous myth — the sleeping beauty. Was I like that? Inward,
sullen, floaty, weird, detached, *sleepwalking*? Sure as hell was.

Fifteen. All the chaos still locked inside, hidden. She already
spent most of her time alone in her room playing along with jazz
records, but her surface was perfect and gave away nothing. She
continued to dress in the schoolgirl costumes appropriate to the
only daughter of an Old Brahman family — blazers and pleated
skirts, knee socks and loafers — as she got tossed out of one
prestigious girls' school after another. She hated the kids who
could wear the styles in *Seventeen*, but she had no breasts or
hips, was five feet ten and wore size ten triple-A shoes at a time
when you were supposed to look like Sandra Dee. She made a
show of despising the girls who wore heels and crinolines, who
went out with boys. She had better things to do. Standing for
hours, blowing notes into the corner of two walls.

"Look," she said to Wendy, "you say that you were just doing
what you were doing, that you didn't question it. But it had to
be ah... I don't know, something more than just going along with
everything. At least the *music* had to be. Christ, Wendy, you're
a fanatic about it."

"Yes, I know I am. If I'm going to do it, I want to be good."
Kathy had to laugh at the firm and proper voice so much like
Paul's.

Wendy looked up, smiled. "Oh, I know it's arrogant of me, but
it's even worse than that. I don't just want to be good. I want to
be the *best*."

The toast popped up. Wendy began buttering it. "And I'd
damn well better be good, because if I'm not, there doesn't seem
to be anything else."

"Maybe not at fifteen, but there will be at twenty."

Wendy looked straight into Kathy's eyes. She was fully
present as she hadn't been before. "People usually mean sex
when they say that, don't they?"

"Not necessarily."

"I'm fully grown. I'm menstruating. Everything's supposed to
be working by now, but I don't feel a thing. I can't even imagine
it... Oh, I know what one *does*, but I can't imagine why one would
want to. I keep thinking about it with Perry. Isn't that ridiculous? But he's always flirting with me, and sometimes I think I

should say, 'All right, instead of a lesson today, let's go to bed.'
I *would* too, if I thought we could just do it like that and not have
it mean anything. But he'd probably be horrified. And then I
keep wondering what I'd do. I'm afraid I'd just lie there and
laugh because it'd all seem so silly."

Kathy was surprised to find that she was actually shocked.
"Do you find him attractive?" she said.

"No, I don't suppose I do."

"Wendy, you dopey kid, you don't sleep with somebody who
isn't attractive to you just because you're curious. You'll run into
somebody eventually, and you'll want to, and then it'll make
sense."

"Maybe. But what then? Should I do it?"

"Are you asking my advice?" Kathy said, her astonishment
growing.

"Yes, I am. A lot of girls my age are already having sex."

"Oh, I know *that*. I work at Van Free. But... I don't know what
to say." Would it do any good to tell her, "Don't do what I did"?
*Don't piss away years fucking every man who wants you and
hating all of them.*

"Don't be in a hurry," Kathy said. "You do know you have to
be careful, eh?"

"I know how not to get pregnant, if that's what you mean.
Please stop staring at me. You're embarrassing me."

Wendy threw two forks onto the table; they rang dully. "I
don't like boys my own age," she said. "They seem so... banal. I
wouldn't want them touching me. I wouldn't want to touch
them. But a grown man maybe..."

"You're asking for trouble."

"I suppose so. But don't worry, it's all just fantasy. I'm not
going to seduce Perry... or anybody else." Wendy was staring at
her plate.

Kathy watched the girl's jaws moving, chewing, and then
those frosty eyes were on hers, suddenly, without any warning
— one of Wendy's darting social motions; when you think she's
a million miles away, she's suddenly right there and wants
something. "For my solo, I, ah... don't want to look like a little
kid. I want to look... grown up. Even sexy."

"Yeah," Kathy said. *Now what*?

"Help me pick something?"

"What? You're asking me to go shopping with you? Come on,
Wendy, when have you ever seen me in anything but blue jeans?
Ask your mother. She's the expert."

"I'm not asking Mother, I'm asking you."

"What is this, a test?"

Wendy laughed, but she didn't answer.

"This is not a musical problem?" Hanna said.

"No," Paul said, "it is not a musical problem."

The old woman shrugged, palms up; Paul saw it as a proto-typically Jewish gesture — wry, jocular, ironic. But her dark eyes, studying him, were grave. He felt profoundly uncomfortable. "I really don't know why I want to talk to you about it," he said, trying to anticipate her.

He waited, but she didn't say anything. "I don't know who else to talk to," he said.

"No," Hanna said, "it is not just that you do not know some other who will listen. You choose me because you know me now. There is something you want from me, so?"

"That's probably right, but I'm not sure what it is."

"Ya. We will see. Now I will give you tea or coffee?"

"Yes, a pot of tea would be lovely." She stood, helping herself up with hands pressing down on the arms of the chair, walked into the kitchen.

When they'd been exchanging letters about her coming to Canada, she'd written: "In regard to matters of housing, my requirements are modest. This is my whim only, and not important, but it would be good if my room were to have windows so that when I looked from them I might see trees." He smiled, remembering it. He had done his best for her, and she kept the broad windows that looked out over the tree-lined drive spotlessly clean. The afternoon light from behind a silvery curtain of clouds was even and brilliant. He walked to the windows.

He was feeling a tension, an uncategorizable restlessness. He was feeling it in his stomach — almost like stage fright. He paced back and forth across Hanna's room several times before he realized that it might seem rude to her. He stopped in front of the only picture — an old photograph in a frame resting on the coffee table.

It was a family portrait. A bearded patriarch leaned on a cane; he was surrounded by sombre, moustached men, buxom ladies squeezed into hour-glass corsets — and children. The solemn little girl with braids and a white dress, intense eyes looking directly into the camera, was surely Hanna herself. He bent closer. There was writing at the bottom of the picture — Yiddish.

"Ya, that is me," Hanna said, returning with a tea tray. "So young I was. Five or six. That man there is my father, and behind him his father. The old man in the centre is my great-grandfather. So long we had to wait for that picture. I stood like a statue. Yet I am standing, so. It is not a good... what do you say?"

"Likeness?"

"Ya, it is is not a good likeness. I was... I do not know it in English. *Burschikos*. I was always running then... So, now you must tell me what is in your mind."

"Van der Geest," Paul said. He wasn't sure where to begin. Then he gave up, took the letter out of his briefcase, handed it to her. He sat down on the couch with her so he could read it again over her shoulder.


Dear Professor Crane:

Forgive me for having taken so long to answer, but I have only now completed my study of your analysis of the van Dorestad motet. I agree with you that your analysis and mine differ only upon trivial points. I hope that you have forgiven my little joke with you. When you were kind enough to visit me last summer, I wished not to prejudice you, so I did not tell you then my own conclusions. My hope was that you would arrive independently at conclusions similar to mine, and you have done so, and I am delighted. I will certainly cite your work when I publish mine. May I consider you an ally in the upcoming battle? We must expect that many of our colleagues will attack us with vigour and vehemence.

As to your speculations about van Dorestad the man, I find them quite interesting, but I must caution you that it is too early to say in print any of the things we write to each other in private, and I ask you to respect my wishes on this matter. If we must defend ourselves, as indeed we must, I suggest that we do so exclusively on musicological grounds. But I too am fascinated with the enigma of van Dorestad. I am amused that you so many thousands of miles away should find such an obvious point that I, here "at the scene of the crime," have missed. Given the most likely dates we can establish for the two men, given that they both lived and worked in 'sHertogenbosch, given that they were both members of the Brotherhood of Our Lady there, I believe that you are absolutely correct in assuming that Hieronymus Bosch and Jan van Dorestad must have known each other. The painter, of course, would have been considerably older than the composer. So much, and no more, can we guess with some certainty.

Yes, it is possible, as you suggest, that Bosch was a mentor for van Dorestad, but how could this be proven with no documentation? I must admit that I cannot look at a painting and study a piece of music and find similarities between these two such different art forms. You say that you "feel" a similarity in approach between these two men. Forgive me if I suggest that you keep such feelings within the privacy of your study where they are amusing to entertain and not present them to the world where they will be impossible to defend. Yes, if Bosch were a member of the Adamite sect, it is possible that he initiated van Dorestad into that sect, but here we have no more than one groundless speculation resting upon another.

This was, as you have pointed out, an extremely troubled time when every manner of heresy flourished in the Low Countries. Have you considered, however, that during the period when Hieronymus Bosch was an old man and Jan van Dorestad a young one, it was possible to hold what would now be considered extremely radical opinions and still be within the orthodox bounds of the Christian community? Yes, I am familiar with the arguments claiming that Bosch was involved in a heretical movement, perhaps Adamite, perhaps some other. But I have also read well-reasoned and researched arguments to the effect that there is nothing in the imagery of Bosch to suggest that he was anything other than the most orthodox of Catholics. Yes, it is true that Bosch attacks the clergy in his paintings, but that proves nothing. Some members of the clergy were then so notoriously corrupt that an attack upon them could come from the most orthodox sources as well as from the most radical.

I would suggest that if you were to pursue this groundless notion that van Dorestad was a member of, or influenced by, the Adamite heresy, you would be "on a wild goose chase." If we are to speculate, I would suggest that we look elsewhere. Between 1534 and 1535, a large number of Anabaptists came to Antwerp fleeing persecution in Liege and Maastricht. Their first martyr was beheaded in Antwerp in 1535. We know from the records of the Cathedral of Antwerp that van Dorestad was living there by 1544, that he was employed there at least until 1546. By the 1550s, Antwerp had become the major centre for Netherlandish Anabaptism, and the Inquisition was persecuting the Anabaptists with increasing ferocity, but nothing seemed to stop the spread of heresies. In 1561, the inquisitor, fearing a revolution, appealed to the regent to put the armed forces in a state of alert. If we must hazard a guess as to the exact nature of van Dorestad's heretical opinions, I believe that he would have been much more likely to have been Anabaptist than an Adamite.

I have here resources that you have not. What I write, I ask you again to retain as private between us. I have discovered, between 1545 and 1558, records of payments made by secular employers (including the city of Antwerp) to a musician who is called variously "Michael de Bois-le-duc," "Michael son of Gennin de Bois-le-duc," "Michael son of Jennine the Dutchman," and even (one entry) "Michael van Dorestad." He is described as a virtuoso performer on "all manner of instruments," including lute, recorder, shawn, crumhorn, fiddle, etc., and is praised for his ability to play "*discantus supra librum*" and "*contrappunto alla menta,*" that is, as you know, for his improvisational ability. The word applied to him is "ménestrel," a minstrel, a professional musician outside the employment of the church. In the last record I have found, he appears with his father ("the old man") and several other musicians who "delighted the multitudes by their wonderfully skilful singing and playing upon many instruments." When asked of his origins, Michael replies that he is only a "*pauvre compagnon chanteur*", a "poor minstrel singer."

It is difficult to avoid the conclusion that this Michael is the son of Jan van Dorestad. I have only just now made these discoveries, and I do not yet know if there is further record of Michael van Dorestad. If there is, we will be upon ground more safe. I am approaching further research by asking these questions: Why should a church composer like Jan van Dorestad stop composing for the church? Why should his son, who would have had the benefit of the best musical training of his time, not follow Jan into church employment? Why should this Michael descend to the bottom of the social ladder to be found playing secular dance music? Why should he claim to be only a "poor minstrel singer"? Why should his father, a man in his sixties or seventies by then, also be playing secular dance music? Why should we have so little record left behind of Jan van Dorestad, and why, given the stature of Jan van Dorestad (and yes, I agree with you, his motet is an absolutely splendid work), do we find only this one motet of his?

Paul couldn't stand it any longer. "Why is he playing it so cagey?" he said. Hanna looked up from the letter.

Paul couldn't sit still. He stood and began to pace. "All right, Hanna, now isn't it quite clear? Why's van der Geest avoiding the... Okay. Why have we found only one motet of van Dorestad's, he asks. Blandly, innocently, as though there's no reasonable answer in sight. Well, I know why. Because the Inquisition got their hands on every bit of Jan van Dorestad's music they could find and burnt it, that's why... And I have no real evidence of that, just a total conviction that... And then I stop myself and say, 'Hey, wait a minute, Paul. You're a musicologist. Stick to the notes.'"

"Just so."

"But I can't let it alone. Why should van Dorestad when he's an old man end up playing with his son in the sixteenth-century equivalent of a rock and roll band? Van der Geest even supplies the answer to that. They're heretics. They're in disguise. They're hiding from the Inquisition. *Hanna, it all fits together.* Why is that bloody man in Amsterdam, with all the resources he has available to him, being so cautious? He can get in his car and drive to 'sHertogenbosch, to Antwerp. He has the best..."

She raised a finger, cutting him off. "Stop, please. Why does it matter to you so much?"

"I don't know. The motet's an incredible piece of music, one of the finest works I've seen from that period. Somehow that puts me on van Dorestad's side."

"And his heresy?"

Paul shrugged. "I don't know what his heresy was, exactly. Van der Geest says Anabaptist. I don't know a damned thing about the Anabaptists."

"I know now why you talk to me," Hanna said. "It is you want me to say to you, 'Forget this historical work, perform the motet, and be done with it.'"

That stopped him. He laughed. "Yes, that's probably right. I've said it often enough to myself. I should schedule an evening in the auditorium, invite my colleagues, talk a bit about the secret chromaticism, and then perform the damned thing and let it be. Everyone would be impressed. I could write a paper on it, jump into the fray on the side of van der Geest. It would do wonders for my reputation. But it's just that..."

"Ya, you must say it."

"Damn it, they burnt his music."

She gave him a grave stare. "This is what I have thought you will say. But listen to me, Paul. Who is burning *your* music?"

It was such a good question he had no answer for it at all.

"I am old," she said, "so you must listen. That is a joke, ya? But there is also truth in it. Now it is more than scholarship you want, but you must not look for it in the past. If you do, it will be bad scholarship. Your friend in Amsterdam is right to caution you. I am sorry that my English is so bad and cannot say what is in my mind, but for this *geistegeschichtliche* work, ya?... For that, you must take time. It must season. It is like wood to make a fiddle. In the shop it must sit for years waiting. If you make a fiddle from it now, it is not a good fiddle. Do you understand?"

"Yes, I believe I do."

"Now let me see the rest of what he writes." She looked down at the letter.

My work on the van Dorestad motet will be published in the spring, and it is enough for me now to defend my musicological analysis. I regard with pleasure your suggestion that you might return to Amsterdam next summer, and, should you do so, I look forward to long and productive conversations. Your letter has certainly given me "food for thought." But forgive me if I sound like a cautious old man. Let us for the moment, my dear Professor Crane, concentrate upon problems of *musica ficta* for which we have been trained and leave theology to the theologians.

Should you return to Amsterdam, please consider staying with me. I have room enough. Greet for me your lovely daughter whom I enjoyed so much meeting, and I send greetings also to you and your daughter from Klaas Achterberg. Klaas has his own reasons for wishing you to return, and it is perhaps indiscreet of me to mention them. He is a reticent man, and perhaps you did not understand how impressed he was with the considerable talent of your daughter.

> Sincerely yours,
> Willem van der Geest

"This man is a good friend to you," Hanna said. "Do you not understand what he is saying to you... what is the English?... between the lines."

Paul didn't know what she was talking about. He sat on the couch with her. "All right, Hanna. What?"

"Your friend thinks what I think also. You must make time for your daughter now. I think this is better."

Hanna had just done it again: stopped him cold. "Wendy? What about Wendy? Everybody seems to think she's going great guns."

"Ya, she learns fast. Very, very fast. And always she tries too much. It will be her way."

"You were the one who said she should perform as much as possible."

"That is true, but also I did not know her then. Now I know her a little."

"I've tried not to push her."

"It does not matter what you try or do not try. You do not know yet how good she is. *You do not want to know*. But already she is too big for Mark Perry to teach. He is like a... *Wasserflige*. What is that? The little bug who walks on water?"

"A water skipper."

"Just so. He walks on the surface. He is light. He is charming. But nothing is serious. He does not know what he does with her."

"You don't think she should play this concert?"

"I did not say that. It is not so much this one concert. She needs other things. She is like a plaster saint. Still a child, but where is the play? Where is the boyfriend? Where is the lightness in the heart?

"Listen. We will play this concert. I am seventy-one years old, but I can still play very well, and people will listen and say, 'Ya, this is Hanna Rossenmüller, she is deep and rich.' That is my hope, and that is why I still play. But Wendy, she has no sixty years of playing. She has only a few, and she can do nothing but put everything back into the music, again and again... And she will feel empty. Whatever she can give, it will never be enough. And so she will give more and more. And then in a year or two she will put away her gamba, and she will never play it again."

"Oh, Christ," Paul said. "You sound like the voice of my conscience. I don't know what to do with her. I keep thinking, why the hell can't she bring some boy home? Any boy would do. But all she does is practice."

Hanna had put nothing on the white walls, and the light in the room was perfect in its clarity. Paul looked out at the day; the lines of rain were crystalline. Paul felt a sudden, puzzling exhilaration. He rose, walked to the windows, turned. The light glowing back from the bare walls was — there was no word for it. Except perhaps "perfect." Yes. Indeed it was perfect. And for one moment he felt completely in his life, balanced at the very centre of it.

Then the moment was over. He was disoriented. But he also (and he had no idea how) understood something about Hanna. "That happened to you, didn't it?" he said. "Didn't you quit playing for a while when you were a girl?"

"It is true. For two years I did not play the violin. I was younger than Wendy. Nine I was when for the first time in public I played. When I was twelve, they were saying many lies about me. How good I was. Ya, I was good, but I was not... seasoned.

"When I was seventeen, I stopped. I... Ach, I could say it to you better in German. But with the emptiness inside me I could not... Already too much from me they wanted, and I could no more give. When I came back to music, the Baroque fiddle I played."

She shrugged. "I look at Wendy, and in her too much I see myself."


"The people who write about us, they are very stupid," Hanna Rossenmüller was saying just as Kathy walked into the living room with her armload of firewood. The timing was perfect; Wendy had already lit the kindling. Kathy wanted to hear more, a context, but no one said anything; she knelt and laid wood onto the fire.

"When I am a child, they say I am a genius." Hanna smiled and looked directly at Wendy. "They say that I play better than Joachim, better than Hubermann."

The girl looked back a long, uncomfortable moment, her face expressionless, then got up from the edge of the fireplace, settled into a chair.

"It is not true. I am not a genius, and I do not play better than these men. But that is what they say, these people who write about music. Then, when I am a young woman, I do not play for a time. I come back to music, and I try to play it *im echten Stil.*" Hanna glanced at Paul for help.

"Authentically," he said.

"Ya. Just so. It is the beginning of the early music in Germany. They do not like it. They say it is ugly. They say, 'What has happened to Hanna Rossenmüller? She plays so well before, but now she plays this ugly music.' But I am only trying to play the sound that Bach would have heard in his own time."

Kathy was watching Wendy — the *wunderkind* as everybody seemed to be calling her now — taking it all in. Then Wendy caught her at it, sent her a tiny grin; Kathy grinned back.

"Then later, after the war, they have changed. They say that Hanna Rossenmüller is a great pioneer. 'She has taught us to hear again.' But I have taught them nothing. I have only been playing music. Now they say that Hanna is old-fashioned, romantic. She comes from the old school. It is all very pretty what Hanna Rossenmüller plays, but the new young people, they are the ones who play it right. In a few years I will be dead, and then they will say more lies about me. God knows what they will say, but it will be all wonderful. 'What a loss to music!'

Perhaps they will say that. But the music will go on without me, that I know. And all the time, it is the same person who plays, ya? I get better. Now I am old and I get worse. But it is the same person. I think they should not write about music, ya? They should only listen."

"But Hanna," Perry said, "you're not getting worse." He'd unbuttoned his vest, was sprawled on the couch with his feet to the fire. He'd drunk just enough to begin to slur.

"Ah," Hanna said lightly, "now you are lying to me too, Mark Perry. I still play very well, that I know. But fifteen years ago, that was my time. Now each year there is more stiffness in the hands. They say, 'Hanna what are you trying to make us do? We are too old for this.' I think, ya, I think so, I will go back to Switzerland this summer, and I will close up the fiddle in its case, and I will put it away upon the shelf. Then I will teach only. And I will walk up into the mountains very high to where the little flowers are. Up into the meadows. But I will not be an old fool who plays when she cannot play. Too many old fools like that have I seen."

"Oh, but you have years and years yet. And who but you could do justice to that glorious Stainer of yours?"

"It is beautiful, is it not? Fifty years now have I had it. Is that right?... Ya, that is right. Fifty years. It seems so short, but that is the truth. It has grown so valuable that I cannot pay the..." she glanced at Paul again, "*Die Versicherung*."

"The insurance."

"Ya, so it flies around with me on airplanes with no insurance. I have one student. He is ready, but he does not believe it. On the day when he believes it, I will take that fiddle from the shelf and give it to him. It will be his then. It is like the music, ya? We are here a short time, but the music is here forever."

"What a beautiful thing to say," Perry said.

"Ach, but this is too much old woman's talk," Hanna said.

"No, not at all, " Perry said. "Who will we have to tell us after you go, Hanna?"

She laughed. "Who will sit by the fire and talk on and on and on? Not Hanna. Now one of you must talk."

No one took her up on it. Kathy listened to the crackle of the fire. She was tired, slightly drunk, but she felt fine. She'd had a good day, as a matter of fact, she'd had an excellent day. She could hardly believe it. She'd spent the whole day with Wendy.

They'd gone shopping, to Kathy's amazement had turned into a couple of giggling girlfriends running from store to store as she'd helped Wendy put together a new, sexy image — patent leather pumps and all. By mid-afternoon, worn down by shoppers' fatigue and feeling a bubbly elation she hadn't bothered to examine, Kathy had suddenly decided that she couldn't possibly wear blue jeans to this dinner party. So she'd bought a skirt — the first one in years — and a sweater, and, to avoid facing the question of whether she was ready to shave her legs, dress boots. And then had chickened out, hadn't been able to wear any of it. Now she was wondering why, what she could possibly have been afraid of. And suddenly, not ready for it, not having really thought about it, she felt the full weight of what she could do, what she *might want to do* — move into this life and bust her ass to make it work.

Kathy felt a tightening in her stomach. She had to move. She got up to offer Hanna more brandy. The old woman nodded, held up her glass. Their eyes met. "When I was young," Hanna said to her, "I did not touch a drop. I was fierce. Nothing must stop my playing. When I was in America, I was like a nun. I studied and played, that was all. Now I drink each night a little to warm myself."

"You were at Columbia, weren't you?" Paul asked her.

"Ya, ya."

"You must have studied with Friedrich Bamberger then?"

"Oh, ya. Bamberger. For him I wrote my PhD."

Kathy sat down next to Paul, took his hand. "People were still telling stories about Bamberger when I was at Michigan," he said. "What was he like?"

"You would not know, would you? I forget these things. He was dead when you were still young. He was a very formal, old-fashioned German gentleman. He was terrible, terrible. I mean he was good, an excellent teacher, but he was *terrible*. I work for weeks transcribing the notes, and I bring them in, and he says, 'But where is the work, Miss Rossenmüller?' And I say, 'But look at the transcription, Doctor Bamberger.' And he says, 'That is not work. That is only *busy* work. Where is the *analysis*, Miss Rossenmüller?'"

Paul laughed. "That's good. I'll try it on *my* students."

Hanna laughed too. "Ach, ya, so correct he was... I could speak then English much better. So much I have forgotten it is as though I have never learned. It is better now than when I came in September, is it not?"

"Oh, absolutely, Hanna," Perry said. "Now you're totally fluent."

"So easy with the flattery, Mark Perry." She shook a finger at him. "One day it will bring you trouble. You must sometimes

speak the truth... But ya, he was a very hard man, Bamberger.
So stiff. So correct. It is strange when I think of it now. He tries
very hard to be American, ya? But he can be nothing but a
German gentleman. All that is happening in Europe he does not
mention. It is as though nothing is happening in Europe. He
speaks only of the music. And he speaks only in English. He
knows that I am German. He knows that I know that *he* is
German. But not once does he speak to me in German. Except
one time."

No one spoke for a moment. "When was that?" Paul asked her.
She hesitated. "It is a sad story."

"Oh, we don't mind a little sadness, do we?" Perry said.

Hanna had turned away from him to face the fire. She sipped
from her brandy glass. "All right, then. I will tell you. You know
that I am a Jew. You know what they have done to us in
Germany. I am here to tell you because I was in America then.
I was in America because I was... ach, damn this English... the
*Lieblingskind.*"

"The beloved child," Paul said.

"Just so. The darling daughter, is that not what you say? My
family had much money. They send me first to Holland, then to
America. Hanna must not stay in Europe. Hanna is delicate.
Hanna is an artist. And now it is Hanna who is alive, and they
are gone.

"But I am studying with Bamberger. I am working on my
PhD. I do nothing else. I have no gentleman friend. I play music
and I study. And for a year I do not hear from my family. I believe
that they are dead. Then I hear that it is true, ya. We know
before the rest of the world what is happening in Europe, in
Germany. But then they begin to tell of it in the papers, on the
radio, so that everyone will know. Doctor Bamberger, he knows
that I am German and that I am a Jew. He has not to me one
word in German spoken.

"It is late in the afternoon. It is a weekend. There is no one in
the music building. I walk down the hall, and he is in the
doorway to his office. 'Good afternoon, Miss Rossenmüller,' he
says to me. Something tells me that he wishes to say more, so I
say, 'Good afternoon, Doctor Bamberger,' and I stop. And then
he speaks to me in German. '*Stimmt das alles?*' he says. 'Is it
true?' I do not have to ask what he means.

"'*Ja, Herr Professor, das stimmt,*' I say. 'Yes, it's true.' We do
not say anything more. We only look upon each other. Then he
says to me in German, 'Please come in,' and I come in. And he
says to me, 'If it is true, then we must play Bach.'

"He is an old man, you must understand. His hands they are stiff. As stiff as mine now are. And he is not a performer, he is a musicologist. And the piano is out of tune. We do not light the light, but we play there until it is too dark to see the notes. Many times before and many times after I play Bach, but never again will I play Bach like that."

In the emptiness left after Hanna stopped speaking, there was no sound but the crackle of the fire, and then Kathy heard a brittle noise like a twig snapping. She'd lost track of Wendy, turned quickly and saw that the girl was sitting still as a stone with tears streaming down her face. Her fists were clenched until her knuckles stood out whitely. Her tears in the firelight made her face glow eerily as though she were looking out from behind a sheet of water. And Hanna must have turned to look at Wendy at the same time that Kathy had; she said, "Ach, such stupid things I have been saying."

Wendy cried out in a strangled voice, "Everybody stop looking at me."

Kathy turned to the fire. Time passed. And Hanna was the only one of them who could possibly speak. "It is what I have tried to say to you today, Paul, but before I have no words. I live now in Switzerland because I will not in Germany ever again live. But Bach, he had many children. He was not a simple man, but his life was simple. He was a professional, ya? He lived and wrote music and he died. He did not try to change the world, to bring down heaven to the earth. But in Germany we will never see his like again."

# VI

"Is it any better?" Kathy said. "Can you talk yet?"

"Yes, I think I can," Wendy said. Her voice sounded fragile, untrustworthy.

Even though it had been raining steadily all day, it wasn't particularly cold, but Wendy, bundled up in an enormous furry parka, was suffering a chill that had nothing to do with the weather. She hadn't moved a muscle since Kathy had buckled her into the passenger's seat. With her hood up, her face was the only part of her that showed — skin shiny with sweat, color like lard. Kathy heard bursts of chattering from the girl's teeth as though an intermittent dice game were going on inside her head.

"It probably helps to talk," Kathy said. "At least it passes the time."

"Oh, Kathy, I'm sorry. I feel like such a basket case. We've got both gambas, don't we?"

"Yes."

"Extra strings? Spare bow? The music?"

"Yes to all those things. Paul made a list, and I checked it off."

"I hate it for people to see me like this. One would think that one might be better able to cope with it by now."

"Jesus, kid, cut it out."

They were two hours early for show time, and Kathy found a parking space on a lower level. "Where are the gambas?" Wendy said, her voice too loud, "I mean exactly where? I'll need them to warm up."

"I know that." Kathy took Wendy's hand and led her away from the car.

"Oh God, this is awful. Maybe I'm not ready. Maybe I should have waited a couple years before I did it."

"Maybe. But don't say that until afterward."

There was no one in the Green Room backstage, but Paul had been there ahead of them. Wendy's music was set up on a stand; the Tielke and the French gamba were waiting in their cases leaning against the wall.

"See, it's all ready for you," Kathy said.

"Oh, I'm so *cold*."

"It must be seventy degrees in here. Give yourself a chance."

Wendy sat down on the very edge of the couch and wrapped her arms around herself. "Sometimes I look at the notes, and they don't make any sense."

"Do you have to read the notes?"

"No. I've memorized everything."

"All right then."

"But if I get lost, I'll have to read the notes." The dice game had started again.

"Goddamn it, don't just sit there and tell yourself horror stories. Get up. Do something. Go through the motions."

Wendy rose obediently like a hypnotist's subject, unwound her scarf, unzipped her parka and let it fall. Then she sat down again — plunk — and stared at Kathy. "I'm cold. Why did I think I wanted to solo? Wasn't it enough just to... But a *solo*."

"Shut up, Wendy. Take your boots off and put your shoes on." That's what you've got to do, Kathy told herself. Keep it simple, one step at a time. Just like the good old days with Steve, you tell them exactly what to do, and they do it.

Kathy took the patent leather pumps out of the bag and handed them over. Wendy slipped her feet into them. "Do I look all right?"

"Well, come here and look." Kathy caught the girl by the hand and dragged her to the full-length mirror.

"See, you look fine." It was a lie. The dress and shoes looked fine, but Wendy was a disaster. She huddled forward into herself, her shoulders hunched, standing splay-footed in a painfully awkward posture as though she were carrying a sharpened stake up her womb. It was a stance Kathy had seen once before — on an adolescent girl at Van Free who'd lasted only a month and later been diagnosed as psychotic.

"I wish I had my old clothes." Wendy was wailing like a six-year-old.

"Well, you don't, and it's too late now, so if you're going to wear the clothes, move like you mean it." Kathy pressed the flat of her hand into Wendy's stomach and pushed. "Straighten up. If you don't believe it, nobody else will either."

Wendy straightened up, brought her feet together, looked fixedly at her reflection in the mirror. For a moment she nearly made it, but then her face collapsed. She probably would have been better off doing her demure schoolgirl act, Kathy thought. At least that would have been familiar.

"Oh, fuck," Wendy said to the mirror and turned away. Found a blanket on the couch, wrapped herself up in it, lay down, closed her eyes.

Now Kathy was left in front of the mirror, seeing herself in a skirt for the first time in years, seeing the makeup on her face. But she couldn't put any energy into worrying about herself; she was too worried about Wendy. She withdrew to the far side of the room. Lit a cigarette. She was so angry she felt like breaking something. I missed my calling, she thought. I should have been a psychiatric nurse.

In the spring of their last year in Boston, Steve had left her quietly. He'd refused to fight about it, refused even to talk about it, which should have tipped her off that he was serious, but she hadn't wanted to pay attention to the clues. She kept waiting for him to come back; he'd always come back before. After a few weeks, she finally got it — he wasn't going to come back.

She was bored out of her mind by then, and broke. She'd always done their laundry and shopping and cooking, cleaned up their various ratty apartments, kept track of their money, made sure he showed up for rehearsals and gigs. She was sure he couldn't function without her, so she'd never felt kept. But the truth of it was that she had been; he'd always brought in the money. Stuck on her own now, she couldn't imagine anybody in his right mind hiring her to do anything. She'd endured an education of sorts at four private girls' schools, had been expelled from three of them and graduated from the fourth at the bottom of her class. She hadn't stayed at BU long enough to get a degree.

She'd taken a course or two at Berklee, had picked up lots of experience playing jazz in smoky clubs at four in the morning, but she'd never made a cent playing music. She hadn't held a paying job since she'd worked as a waitress at Arturo's. One night she went back there and sat for hours listening to a lethargic trio read through old bop charts, telling herself that it was simple. All she had to do was stand up, walk across the room, and talk to the owner. But the acid of those days had smeared her memory into total unreliability, and she couldn't remember if she'd quit or been fired; all she was sure of was that she'd spent a vast amount of time screwing Steve in his enormous balloon chair. She felt paralyzed. People go out and get jobs all the time, she told herself. There's nothing humiliating about serving coffee in a jazz club. But the waitresses were still leggy teenagers; they still wore miniskirts and flirted with the customers. All right, she thought, it *is* humiliating. Do it anyway. You've got to take care of yourself, and a little humiliation isn't going to hurt you. But now the slow-fingered clowns on the stage were trying to read a Monk chart, and she just couldn't stand it. I'm damned near thirty, she thought, and I can't do this again. I'll go on welfare first.

But she didn't go on welfare; she hit up her father for a few hundred bucks—which paid the rent but didn't solve anything. She kept waking up at five or six in the morning from a recurring nightmare. Steve was trying to get through to her on the telephone. He was sick or hurt. Or he'd been so badly brain damaged that when he tried to talk, all that came out was a monotonous gibber. Once, asleep, she even picked up the phone and was shocked instantly awake by the nasty buzz of the dial tone.

When the FBI showed up, it was almost a relief. Kathy walked into her apartment in the middle of the afternoon and found a large man in a gray suit sitting at her kitchen table calmly going through her address book. With a quick, involuntary motion, she spun around, looking for a way out. "Don't do that," said another man. He was in her bedroom.

"Don't make trouble," said the man in the kitchen. He pulled out his wallet and showed her something. She was horribly close to peeing her pants (a reaction she never would have predicted), and getting herself firmly under control took so much concentration she couldn't pay any attention to whatever it was he was showing her. (Later she realized that it could have been a driver's license, a credit card, anything at all.)

"How did you get in here?" she said and was surprised to hear her mother's snootiest Mrs. Astor voice coming out of her mouth. "Do you have a warrant?"

"The building super let us in," one man said.

"A warrant?" the other man said. "You've been watching too much TV, sweetheart."

"Change the channel," the one in the kitchen said. "So where's your boyfriend these days?"

"Boyfriend?"

"Steven Beuhl. You only lived with him for five years. Where is he now?"

"I don't know. What do you want him for?"

"You don't ask the questions, right? We ask the questions. So where is he?"

"He left me, damn it. What's this about? Draft evasion?"

"When did he leave you?"

Suddenly Kathy saw the beauty of what he'd done, and she stopped being afraid. He had left her with absolutely nothing to tell them.

"March," she said. "If I look at my calendar, I can give you the exact date."

Then it took her days to find him. She was sure he was still in Boston; she could feel his presence in the city, but no one had seen him. Peter was dead by then, the rest of the band had vanished as completely as Steve, and everywhere she went, she kept seeing agents. Was the fat woman in the parked car across the street an agent? How about the vague kid with the beard sitting on the steps of her apartment building or the emaciated man with a bad cold who followed her around Harvard Square? She tried to imagine what Steve would have said and could do it easily enough — "Come on, Kath, agents cost money. You think they can afford to put a tail on you twenty-four hours a day? Shit, not a chance." But it didn't help. She'd find herself stuck on street corners, her mouth dry, her heart racing, unable to think of anything, unable even to walk across the street when the light changed.

She finally ran into Jerry in a bar in the Combat Zone. She'd followed the music; his bass line had given him away. He was playing what Steve called "meat market music" — flat-footed rock hammered out for drunken singles. The drummer was so bad he sounded as though he were building a shed on the stage. The singer-guitarist wasn't much better, but Jerry was so good he almost pulled their sound together. He'd had his long hair cut off, was wearing a powder-blue leisure suit, and even though Kathy stood directly in front of him, he wouldn't meet her eyes. At the break she followed him into the back room.

"I've always liked you, Kate," he said. "Now just leave me alone, all right?"

"What the fuck's the matter with you? I just want to find Steve."

"You and a few other folks."

"What's that mean?"

"Anything you want it to mean."

"Fuck the head games, asshole."

She saw that he was just as angry with her as she was with him. She couldn't understand why. "Jerry, I'm so scared," she said before she could stop herself.

"Jesus, Kate. Why don't you get out of town?"

"Where is he, man?"

She watched him think about it. "Promise you'll never come in here again?"

"All right."

"I'm pretty sure I saw his van parked by the Cambridge dump."

It's like approaching the sea — gulls circling, screaming — but then the smell of decay destroys the illusion. Kathy circles the dump, slowly, looking up side streets. No van. All right, she'll have to go up every street. It might take hours, but that's all right, she's got hours. In the muggy overcast of July, she's sweating in her jeans, stops to rest at a corner where a high-rise is going up. Fifty feet in the air men are pouring concrete. She sees them outlined against a sky smeared poisonous white by air pollution. She walks.

She hears the music first, follows Jim Morrison's voice. She almost doesn't see the van; it's pulled in tight at the end of an alley. The music is blasting from an open window on a second-floor corner apartment in a building that should have been condemned. She walks into the stench of cooked cabbage, climbs the stairs. The door's unlocked. Steve's lying on a bare mattress on a single bed by the window, stereo speakers at his feet, turntable at his right hand. He hasn't shaved in a while. He's wearing nothing but stained jockey shorts. His forearms and thighs are marked with small, circular, weeping blisters. His huge eyes tilt slowly to meet hers, but nothing registers on his face. The song ends. He lifts the tone arm, moves it back, lets it drop. His placement is so accurate he must have been doing it for hours.

Kathy sits on the edge of the bed, presses the reject button. The tone arm lifts. She stops his hand. "You're looking good, Steven," she says.

He doesn't answer. Wipes the reject button with his thumb. Lights a cigarette. When he speaks, it's in the casual, conversational tone he might use in passing the time of day at a bus stop. "Don't touch anything, Kath. Don't leave prints."

Then she sees the gun lying next to him on the bed.

Wendy lay unmoving on the couch, and Kathy was down to the end of her cigarette. She dropped it onto the rug and ground it out under the sole of one of her shiny new dress boots. Even if it was a cheap shot, it gave her something to do with her anger. The problem with following her memories back to Steve was that they always led to disaster. And what was it they'd had together, after all? (Time should have given her enough perspective to answer that question.) *All right,* she thought, *don't lie to yourself. The main thing you had was sex that was as compulsive as a drug addiction.*

Then she heard firm, stolid footsteps approaching down the hall — Hanna Rossenmüller wrapped in a long, black coat and wearing an old-fashioned hat like something out of a Garbo movie. "Good evening, Katherine." Hanna looked at Wendy, turned back to Kathy with a trace of a smile. "What is the problem?"

"Looks like the worst case of stage fright in the history of Western music," Kathy said.

The black eyebrows went up. Hanna unhurriedly walked to the couch. "So, Gwendolyn, you are not enjoying yourself tonight?"

Mutely, Wendy shook her head. Damn, Kathy thought, it's no joke. Under the white-hot lights she'll look like we dug her up.

Hanna gave Kathy a nod and said only one word, not unfriendly, but definitive — "Out."

With an image of Wendy's sickly face floating in front of her like a spectral balloon, Kathy wandered into the theater lobby. It was still early; no one was arriving yet, and she continued on into the ladies' room. It felt odd to be walking in heels, but not as odd as she had expected. They weren't that high, and she even rather liked the feeling, the sense of being balanced on them. But how was Wendy going to do in *her* new heels? Fall down on the stage?

Kathy came to rest in front of the full-length mirror. She wondered what she would have thought of the clothes on somebody else — the sweater in soft tones of mother-of-pearl, the beige skirt, the dress boots. And she knew exactly what she would have thought — oh, well, *she's* certainly a lady. Why had she done it? She'd even put on makeup, borrowed a purse from Wendy to match the boots. Reaching back into herself for the *National Velvet* girl who'd dressed up for the sheer pleasure of it, she could find her easily enough, but the pleasure was no longer innocent, and she couldn't lose a small, whispering voice — probably Steve's, damn him — that was saying, "Sellout." So what was she doing, trying to look like a proper mate for Doctor Paul Crane?

But she had to admit it — the woman in the mirror looked all right, was even beautiful in the austere way that had always been her style. She'd expected to find it unpleasant to wear a skirt again, but she didn't; the cut and length were so much like what she'd worn as a teenager that it felt perfectly natural. She was almost comfortable. And the last time she'd been so thoroughly dressed up had been when they'd first come to Vancouver and she'd worked as a secretary; Steve had called her "Miss Perma-Press." That was it. She was still saying fuck you to Steve.

She'd come home from work every day to meet the wall of his silent disapproval. He'd never say a word; all she'd ever get out of him would be his standard-issue Zen disclaimer — "Whatever you're doing, Kath, *do it*." But that was bullshit. For special occasions he liked her in costumes, the more extreme, the better. But most of the time she was supposed to look like a beautiful boy — tough and dangerous. But no, that still wasn't right. The truth of it was that she never could figure out exactly what he wanted.

"I want my mind to stop," Steve says. He's naked, slouched, smoking, wet hair falling over his forehead. He snaps his head angrily to one side to clear his eyes, drags smoke, mouth tense, pinched. His body seems all angles, hard edges; one hand unconsciously twitches, shoulders jerking. He's drumming to a beat she can't hear.

It must have been the summer of sixty-eight. Yeah, that was right because only a week before Ned had gotten himself busted in that bloody mess on the Boston Common, and she and Steve had bailed him out. Ned had emerged from jail with a white patch over his scalp wound and his eyes set into a low-banked, murderous rage that would only get worse right up to the night when he'd disappear. Before that, when anyone had mentioned politics, Ned's reaction had always been, "Me? I play in a rock and roll band." But now he had a mission. Talking nonstop — crazy, snarling, and amplified as one of his own solos. "Jesus, man, we've got to show them. *We're going to show them*. The goddamned Neanderthals. The bastards with their pea-sized brains. Shit, they don't even know their time's run out. Evolutionary dead end. Well, we can't let them get away with it, all right? *All right!* This means war."

It was nearly four in the morning. She and Steve had just come home from the first battle of Ned's campaign. He'd whipped the band into a frenzy, and the band had passed the frenzy on to the audience, by the last set more of an orgiastic cult ritual lifting off toward riot then a rock concert. The rent-a-cops had panicked and fled to call the real cops. The real cops had arrived but had been so intimidated by the size and temper of the crowd that they'd done nothing but stand around at the edges watching as a dozen laws had been violated — too many people for the hall, the aisles blocked, the line between performer and spectator gone completely as Ned, still attached to his band by a long, blue umbilical cord, fingers caterwauling electric scream from the fret board, had jerked and howled his way deep into the massed people, as at least a hundred kids had pushed their way onto the stage in spasmodic abandon on a razor's edge between mania and hysterical tears, as several teenage girls had stripped off their shirts to gyrate bare-chested. Next week the band would find itself charged on every count anybody had been able to dream up — from contravention of the fire ordinances to the violation of an ancient Boston bylaw against "public anarchy" which had been passed originally to stop Emma Goldman from speaking. "Shit," Steve said with his Alfred E. Newman grin, "and we thought it was just music."

Steve was naked, pacing up and down the bedroom. He'd taken a shower to wash off the rank, worked-horse stink of playing. Strangely enough, he'd also shaved. Kathy could smell pungent lime. She was exhausted and wanted to go to bed, but Steve was jerking about like a marionette dangled from the claws of an invisible speed demon. "Jesus," he said, awe in his voice as though the discovery were too much for him to take in, "I can't come down."

Not just the concert, it had been going on for weeks, every day a little worse. He seemed to have forgotten how to sleep; no matter what he ate, he kept losing weight. If she'd wanted to, she could have counted every one of his ribs. He was beginning to look like a male Twiggy — shoulder blades like ax heads, hipbones like spear points. *Her* jeans fit him — that's how thin he was. The skin under his eyes looked bruised and tender, grayish blue semicircles that made his large eyes seem even larger, enormous black pools fringed with thick lashes. She didn't understand it. The unhealthier he looked, the sexier she found him. She liked his hair long ("Grow it as long as mine," she told him, only half joking), liked his body when it was harried, lean, driven with mad energy, worn down to the core. But she was also afraid of him. It was the farthest out she'd seen him.

"Did you like old Nedward?" he said, "that fucking berserker, old blue-eyed Viking. His guitar was a battle-ax tonight, and no bullshit. Didn't know how he was going to end it. Thought sure they were going to tear that goddamned place apart. Then when he pulled it off, I thought, fuck, it's right. It's working."

Ned had dug his draft card out of his wallet, held it up, yelled through the PA, "This is my fucking draft card, all right? The fuckers think they own me, all right? Well, we're going to build a new world, *all right?*" And he'd shoved the card into a candle flame and held it up like a torch. "Anybody else want to light a candle up here?" Kathy had counted twenty-six young men who'd climbed onto the stage and torched their draft cards.

"Amazing," Steve said. "It was fucking *religious*. Every time another card went into the flame, there'd be a dead silence like a drawn-in breath and then an explosion. Screaming, yelling. Jesus, it was wonderful. What a release. Made me wish I had mine back again just to get into the act." He'd sent his own draft card to heaven on the steps of the Arlington Street church back in April and, probably because of his wild mane of hair, had got his picture in the *Wretched American*. The FBI had turned up within the week.

He was leaning against the wall in a model's slouch, angular hips canted, scowling. "I can't come down," he said again. He sounded genuinely puzzled. "It's kind of scary, Kath. I don't know what to do with it." He stared at her with desolate eyes.

For the first time she understood that he was badly frightened. Well, why shouldn't he be? Unless he left the country, he was facing a minimum two-year jail term for draft evasion. The Cambridge narc squad, who'd taken to following the band around, could bust any of them at any moment. But, looking at him, she realized that he was afraid of something more serious than cops or jails, and she felt the kick of her own fear. Was it possible? Was he crumbling? The most nerveless, fuck-it-all freak she'd ever known? *What was she supposed to do with him?*

"Want to go for a run?" he said, meaning the bike — propelled missile rocketing out of town for the open highway where he could wind it out, search for that elusive top end he claimed he'd never found, something close to a hundred and fifty miles an hour.

She was terrified of the bike by now but knew she couldn't let him see her fear; he was having enough trouble with his own. "Sure," she said.

Even after all the men she'd fucked in the old days, she'd

never got entirely used to male bodies — the funny tail in front.
Steve's long prick bent slightly to one side, an oddly pale joke
hanging down with fuzzy tomcat balls underneath. He saw her
look and smiled just enough so she could see it. There was
something in his eyes, but she didn't know what. "You sure you
want to do your running *on the road*, Steven?" she said and got
an edge more smile out of him.

She waited, but he wasn't giving away a thing. It looked as
though she was going to have to do it again — draw her nerves
into a steel knot and endure another ride on what he called "that
thin, cold edge," his race against time and death. All she could
do to prepare for it was cover up as much of her vulnerable
surface as possible. She stripped off halter top and shorts, didn't
bother with underwear but pulled on her tight leather pants
directly over bare skin. He still hadn't moved. Naked, smoking.
He was getting an erection — not a full-blown one but just the
first teasing of blood. She tried to read his face. "Stop," he said,
"don't put anything else on."

"We'll get arrested, Steven," she said in the flat, ironic tone
she knew amused him.

He laughed. "No, maybe we won't go for a run." He looked
away, eyes narrowing. "Sometimes I hate you for being a
woman."

It was incredible how quickly he could make her angry.
"What the fuck does that mean?"

"Shit, it's not fair, the kind of orgasms you can have. Jesus,
the intensity. And I'm just a poor, sorry old male and go squirt
squirt and it's over."

It was funny. Her anger slid away. "I think you're romanti-
cizing the female orgasm a bit, Steven."

"Yeah, maybe. But I've seen you when you're really *gone*.
Eyes rolled up showing whites, screaming, your whole body
jerking. Kath, I've seen you when you've passed right out."

"But that's rare, man. That's not your ordinary run-of-the-
mill night. That's a once-in-a-blue-moon."

"Yeah, but at least it's possible for you sometimes, and with
me it's never possible." Although he was smiling, his eyes were
dead. "And the surrender, the total abandonment. Jesus, what
a relief that must be."

She knew — unpleasant connection like an acid flashback —
that he'd just made an admission of immense proportions. Oh,
so his habit of wearing her things — jeans and sweaters and
sometimes even underwear — hadn't been, as she'd thought, a
stoned-out casualness but something else. She'd known it all

along, of course. If there was anything to feel guilty about, she was as guilty as he was. She didn't want to know any more about it. "But you get to do something that I can't do, Steven. You get to fuck the audience."

"Sure, but you could do it too if you wanted. You could do it even better. And anyway, it may be an incredible high, but it's never enough. Just leaves me up with no way to get down again."

"What's happening? Be straight with me for once. What's the matter?"

"I don't know. That's no bullshit, Kath, I really don't. I'd tell you if I knew. It's just that... I'm all strung out, babe. It's getting worse. It's scaring the piss out of me. And this time it doesn't seem to want to let up. I don't know where it's going to end."

"The kind of shit you're into, I'd be scared too."

He spread his hands, throwing all that away — the show, the cops, the burnt draft cards, the narc squad, the FBI, the constant paranoia. "It's not *out there*. It's in here." He tapped his forehead.

No matter how much she might want to, it looked as though she couldn't avoid it. She chose her words carefully. "Anything to do with me?"

He didn't answer but instead gathered up his jeans from the floor, drew the wide garrison belt out of the loops, folded it in half, and handed it to her. The leather felt cold and unfriendly under her fingers. There'd been hints of this before, but always so discreet she'd been able to ignore them. "No," she said.

He shrugged. "All right. Maybe we will go for a run."

"What do you want, Steven?"

"I want my mind to stop."

When he spoke again, his voice was so low she could barely hear him. "I want to give myself to you without any reservations. Might be kind of crude, but it's the only thing I can think of."

She was astonished; mad Steve was genuinely embarrassed. "Yeah, it *is* kind of crude. I thought you were more complex than that."

"Me? Fuck, I'm simple as dog shit. What can I do, Kath? I could pour gasoline all over myself, I suppose, and just at the moment of orgasm light a match. I could rip my chest open and hand you my heart."

She wanted to touch him, reassure him. And she also wanted to understand. "Is it really that bad?"

"Yeah."

His erection had fallen down. He lowered himself to the floor, folded his legs up like a fakir, stuffed the pipe with dope, added small nuggets of hash, lit it, offered it to her. She squatted on her heels, took the pipe and inhaled — immediate lift, change in the light values, fizz at the back of her neck. "Let's forget it," he said. "Let's just get stoned, do something *you* want to."

She didn't know how he'd done it, but she knew she was hooked. "I'm not sure I want the power," she said. "I'm afraid of it."

"Yeah, I know. Having the power's the hard part. Giving up's easy. Shit, this is the wrong time for me. I could have been a saint, you know that? I would have been as crazy as any of them."

They finished the pipe. "You really want it to hurt, don't you?" she said.

He wasn't able to look at her. "If I can't trust you, Kathy, who the hell can I trust?" he said in a voice she believed. "You're damned right I want it to hurt."

"All right. At least *this once* it's all right. How do you want it? Across my lap like a little kid?" He said nothing. "Oh, it's for me to decide, is it?"

The night was hot, but he had begun to shake; even his teeth were chattering. The damnable thing about his games was that she always understood them perfectly. "Kneel on the bed," she said.

The first couple of swings were light, experimental. She didn't feel any emotion at all, not even the fear or disgust she'd expected. And then the physical movement itself, the cracking sound of the belt landing on his narrow ass, triggered a genuine anger in her. The bastard, she thought, with his obscurities and complexities. "Simple" he calls himself. Jesus, what a joke. His maddening Zen poses, his outright lies. She knew perfectly well he'd screwed Lyons' girls, not to mention all the other little dollies he picked up after the shows. And all the nights he hadn't come home and hadn't bothered to call. And even that she was doing *this* and didn't want to. It was all focusing into a single, hot point in her mind, and then she wasn't thinking at all — smeary red haze blotting out the room.

She stopped, panting for breath, and threw the belt away. She'd laid a crosshatching of red lines on his ass, blood just beginning at the intersections.

He hadn't made a sound, but he was shaking. She caught him by the waist and turned him over. His face was shining with tears. She felt cold and distant, a dry snakeskin sheath drawn over her heart, but he was turned on — fully stiff erection staring at her, small bend of moisture at the tip. Even with the prick poking at her, he felt like a pit she could fall into, a huge, black, empty hunger wanting more. What? But she knew what, stripped off her leather pants.

She was dry, used the foam to make herself wet enough, forced herself onto him, slammed him down with all her weight, thinking, want me to hurt you? Well, here I am, you bastard, all five-feet-ten of me. "I love you," he said.

She slapped him in the face with the open palm of her hand, and some part of her that had been only a nagging whine until then suddenly protested loudly. *Stop it. This is sick.* But she said, "Do you still love me, Steven?"

"Oh Jesus, yes. I love you, Kathy." A fervor in his voice. She believed him. He did love her. She felt a melting in him, an openness, felt herself open to it. As though what had gone before had been only a way in, that *this* was what mattered — the flowing together, as he'd said it, giving up. She let herself give up, wanting him. But he was too far ahead of her.

She arched up, drew herself off him, propped his head up with two pillows, and gave him her pussy full in the mouth. *All right, baby, you want it, then do it.* His tongue was wonderful; he'd never been so eager to please. And she still had enough control left to stop in time and mount him again. Thinking of him now as her docile pony, she rode first herself and then him to orgasm. Slipped off to collapse onto his bony shoulder, her heart like one of his drums — deep, rapid floor tom. "Hurt enough, you bastard?" she said. She was appallingly pleased with herself. But he didn't answer and in a few moments had fallen into a sleep that seemed deep as a coma.

She couldn't sleep at all, eventually got up. She threw the leather pants at the wall, hoping to wake him, but he didn't stir. She sat naked in the chair and watched him while he slept. She smoked one cigarette after another until the dawn began to turn the room blue-gray and she couldn't stand it any longer. "Steve," she said. He woke at once. She saw his open eyes like two shining opaque pools of oil; they didn't seem human. "Listen," she said, "you may have got your relief, but I'm strung out like a wire."

"Do you want a turn?"

"No thanks, man. I'll pass... Steven, listen to me. What if they're right and we're wrong? What if we're just fucked-up, spoiled, middle-class kids working out our neuroses?"

"Do you believe that?" His voice was fully awake.

"Sometimes."

"Hey, Kath, don't feel bad about me. I got exactly what I wanted."

"Oh, well, that's just fine, man," she yelled at him, "that's just dandy. But what about *me*?"

"We've been brainwashed, Kath... from day one. None of us escaped. Not one. Of course we've got weird stuff in our heads. Everybody does. But we've got to look at it. That's the only way."

"Fuck it, man. I've just had a look, and I didn't like it one bit. Jesus, some part of me enjoyed it, and I hate that. I don't ever want to do it again."

"That's fine. We won't ever do it again."

"Listen. What if we're just sick?"

"What's sick?"

"Don't give me that R. D. Laing crap. Sick is sick. Steve, you've got to listen to me. I can't tell any more if you're finding parts of me that were there all along. Parts of me that I just didn't want to look at. Or if you're ramming your trip down my throat."

He didn't say anything. She waited and then began to realize that he wasn't going to say anything. She got into bed with him, turned her mind away from the experience, folded it up and put it away. Eventually she was able to sleep. And in the next two years they'd play other strange sex games but never again that one. He would never mention it, but after he'd left her, he'd write from Toronto: "Remember how you used to say, 'But what if they're right? What if they are and we're just fucked-up kids?' And I could never admit that possibility. I think you were the stronger of us to admit that possibility. I think maybe you can save yourself with it."

Kathy had been so absorbed in her own memory that she'd lost track of where she was. She'd walked into the lobby. Now she looked outward and saw that the lobby was filled with people. With their jerky dignity they looked like so many birds strutting around the Stanley Park Zoo. Were any of them conscious, aware? Possibly, but there was no way she could be sure; in an innocuous, conventional way, they were all masked. She felt wholly detached from them — a secret alien — and she was as well-disguised that night as anyone. "Steve, you son of a bitch," she said to the ghost in her mind, "you knew, didn't you?"

An inevitable motion propelled events; part of the common delusion was that things happened randomly and by accident, but they didn't happen that way at all. She'd had an appointment here; she'd arrived on time, dressed for the occasion. She was standing out of the way, in a far corner, *in the lobby of a theater*. Soon a performance would begin, a show made possible by the conventions of artifice that everyone understood and accepted, but out here dozens of performances were already going on. The only difference was that the performers in the lobby weren't aware that they were performing. A twist in her mind, elusive, just beyond formulation. What the hell was it? Something to do with deceit, trickery. A psychic numbness, a self-imposed stupidity, was falling away from her, and she felt fully alert and awake.

She stubbed out her cigarette and began to walk slowly across the lobby — head up, stomach in. "If you don't believe it," she'd told Wendy, "nobody else will either." She saw men watch her, assess her, and she didn't mind; she looked them straight in the eye and saw them withdraw. She projected a force field around herself; it felt as effective as a glass wall. Amazingly enough, she liked this disguise, liked it as well as the boys' clothes she'd worn in her twenties, prowling through nights that always sounded like fifties jazz.

She reached the far side of the lobby, turned and walked back — aloof, controlled, aware — giving the performance her full attention. There's only a handful of people in your life who count, she thought, and to hell with everybody else. Nobody gives a damn anyway, and it's *all* a performance. That's what you were trying to tell me, wasn't it, Steven?

She'd returned to the exact spot where she'd begun, saw, across the length of the lobby, Evelyn Crane standing with her entire household gathered around her. Evelyn was looking directly at her, must have been doing it for quite some time; from the smile on the woman's face, Kathy knew that Evelyn must have followed her passage back and forth across the lobby. Kathy met the eyes — opaque blue like Wendy's — across thirty feet and felt an exchange, an obscure communication.

Evelyn waved; Kathy waved back. And then Evelyn was walking toward her — in faded jeans, a man's blue shirt with the sleeves rolled up, yellow work boots laced with rawhide. She was wearing no makeup at all.

"How's Gwendolyn bearing up?"

Evelyn was studying Kathy just as much as Kathy was studying Evelyn. "She's a mess," Kathy said to the question, but knew that neither of them was thinking about Wendy at the moment.

"You're quite stunning, you know that?" Evelyn said.

"Yeah, I suppose I do know that."

"Are you enjoying yourself?"

Enjoying? Kathy thought. Not the right word. "I don't know," she said. "It's been years since I've been this dressed up, and I'm not used to it. It's kind of..." She hesitated, not sure whether to tell the truth. If she wanted to stay in character, the proper ending to the sentence would be, "fun."

"It feels like a good disguise for me," Kathy said.

"Oh? Well, I did it so much it turned into a bore." Kathy was surprised that she saw no hostility in Evelyn's smile. "That's my purse, you know."

"Is it? I thought it was Wendy's."

"I suppose it is Wendy's now. I bought it for myself but never liked it. I gave it to her." And Evelyn began to giggle. She covered her mouth with one hand but couldn't stop it.

Suddenly both Evelyn and Kathy were laughing so hard that a middle-aged couple turned to stare. Evelyn squeezed her arms around her stomach as though caught with cramps, bent forward, shaking with laughter. "Oh, my God," she said, "isn't life ridiculous?"

She held out a hand; Kathy took it. "Let's be friends, Ev," Kathy said.

"Yes, let's be."

Kathy found her seat — orchestra center, four rows back. With an automatic gesture that went back twenty years, she swept the skirt smooth beneath her and sat down.

She was holding the purse on her lap — Evelyn's, then Wendy's. How strange. When she'd dropped her own wallet in, she'd noticed, almost subliminally, things of Wendy's at the bottom; now, with a cool and guiltless voyeur's curiosity, she opened it to see what they might be, found a pair of kid gloves, probably left there because they were the same colour as the purse. The perfect thing of hers to find, Kathy thought, smiling. She held one up to her own hand; it was so tiny she couldn't have begun to get it on. And there was also a tube of hand lotion, with a label in French, a wadded-up piece of flannel with a lump of rosin buried at its center, a coiled gut string, and a stenographer's notebook with a thin gold pen clipped to it.

She flipped open the cover of the notebook, read the heading. CLASS WITH KLAAS ACHTERBERG, AMSTERDAM, SUMMER, 1977. The fastidious handwriting was so minute she had to bring the page to within a few inches of her eyes to make it out.

"1)," Wendy had written, "Light upbeat. Very important." Wendy had underlined the word "very" four times. "2) Phrasing totally different from classical cello." Kathy ran her eyes down the rest of the entries; it was all technical stuff. But no, here at the bottom Wendy had written, "He's such a funny man, his eyes pop out when he plays and he snorts like a horse. He says I have to come to Europe. He doesn't speak very good English, so talks very slowly. You must come soon, he said. You must not put it off too long... Should I? Would Daddy let me?"

She's such a little kid sometimes, Kathy thought and continued to flip through the notebook, saw only blank pages. She was about to put it back in the purse when she found, hidden in the very center, a long entry. It had nothing to do with music. She began to read, then stopped, astonished. Wendy? Yes, the tiny handwriting was Wendy's. She began again, read all of it slowly.

"The land outside Amsterdam is flat and blazing with flowers, the sky overhead enormous. No one could possibly understand the paintings in the Rijksmuseum without walking here. I like van Goyen better than Rembrandt, my childish bad taste, Mother says, that I will outgrow, but the land itself says more to me than human faces. I float like a feather in a timeless suspension, not sure any longer who I am. The mood and feeling... the light of these nether lands... unbearable. Stupid tears alone in the hotel room. I want to stay here forever. Try to remember what Van Gogh wrote to his brother near the end of his life. Something like... I see everything now with a terrible intensity. His burning trees. Klaas Achterberg burns like that when he plays, it's in his eyes, and I felt like a stupid little jerk trying to play for him. He listened and then played it back to me and I heard it for the first time in my life. It's too much, I can't take it all in, walk with Dad in this flat beautiful land, and he talks on and on without looking at me. It's as though I've gone away. All about Anita his first girlfriend and how he met Mother and how he lost his way, turned into a professor of music when all he wanted to do was play the music. It's very sad and I don't know what to say to him. I play the music, but I don't know what I want. I float like a feather. I'm afraid of becoming lost. Inside me it's like a string that won't quite come into tune. No one understands, and I burn and burn. I don't belong in this family, all these stupid details of traveling, Mother and Cindy are driving me crazy. I want to be here alone. Can't anybody understand me? Oh, God, it hurts inside me. *Mon âme éternelle, Observe ton voeu, Malgré la nuit seule, Et le jour en feu.*"

Kathy closed the notebook, set the purse at her feet. She felt chilled. Her own diaries, her painful girlish outpourings written in the middle of the night, had been abandoned along the way — lost with her music. She had burned like that at fifteen, but time had taken it away from her, and she was seeing in memory, repeated with a maddening obstinacy, the same scene. The blackboard is struck once, from behind, by an invisible sledge-hammer and begins to topple down. Then Wendy is in her arms; she can feel the girl's heartbeat, and her own, and the black-board is struck again. Kathy was vibrating like the string inside Wendy that wouldn't come into tune. The girl she'd been ached with life at the center of her; the thirty-six-year-old woman sitting in the theater was an empty shell. To orient herself, try to grasp at some normal reality, she swiveled in her seat to look at the audience. It was a full house, but these people were all asleep — "the walking dead" Steve would have called them — polite theater-goers in their evening clothes. How could any of them possibly hear the music? There seemed to be a sickness everywhere in life now, a numbness wrapping away individuals into isolated cocoons. They all want something to tear through it, she thought. Anything will do as long as it makes them feel, gives them an illusion of life. Even blood.

The audience had begun to applaud politely. Paul was walk-ing out onto the stage in his tuxedo, disguised. The leader of the band, she thought. How did he appear to other people? A tall, distinguished man with a beard, an expert, the musical director, an authority? But she knew him and could see the strain on his face like erosion, and he looked to her, strangely, like a sad clown in a minstrel show. Hanna Rossenmüller in a shapeless dress followed behind him, disguised, then the other musicians. The last person to appear on stage was Wendy.

She crossed to her music stand — head up, stomach in, walking as though she meant it. More than merely in control of herself, she was moving with a remote snow-queen authority. The black dress was magnificent in its simplicity; tightly fitted at the waist, then falling straight to the floor, it made Wendy seem far taller than she actually was. Her bare shoulders gleamed whitely, and her long sweep of blond hair caught the theater lights and burned around her head like a nimbus. But her face was painted like a doll's. Someone must have seen her sickly complexion and decided to make her up, had overdone it. Behind the mask, every memory of Wendy as a person had vanished. Was that the kid so afraid of her own sexuality that she usually dressed like a twelve-year-old?

Wendy was carrying something. It was only the Tielke, of course. She sat down at her music stand, took the instrument between her legs, and Kathy saw that the girl's every movement was planned, aware, sent out a signal. A tremendous tension was building up in the audience. Wendy had achieved not something as simple as sexiness; she was charged with some fundamental energy — like white light. Exactly what Steve always had wanted me to do on stage, Kathy thought. What I was always afraid of doing.

Ever since she'd been a child, Kathy had been visited by moments of panic at other people's performances, fear that she would be forced by some power outside herself to do something outrageous and unforgivable, leap up in the middle of a quiet section of music and scream or suddenly begin to throw coins onto the stage. Now it was this: she was supposed to be playing. Soon she would rise like a sleepwalker, wander down the aisle, and take her place behind one of the instruments — the violone perhaps, big as a string bass — and try to join the music. And the show has begun.

Kathy looks up and sees, thousands of feet in the air, a set of parallel bars suspended from the ceiling; the performer is high above the audience, risking death. Wendy is walking out on a tiny catwalk. She's an exquisite girl with a hard, lean, trained body; that's why she's here, because she's totally different from the people in the audience. But her face is painted like a doll's, and she's carrying something in her arms that *looks like a life-size doll*. And then, as the asthma strikes her, Kathy bends forward in her seat, not a single mouthful of air left in the world.

Head between her knees, Kathy fights for breath. She can hear the musicians tuning up. She knows where she's arrived — dressed for the appointment and right on time — and the little tune that has been jiggling in her mind has found words. "I thought I heard Buddy Bolden say, 'You nasty buncha dirty, take it away. You're awful. You're terrible. Take it away. And let Mister Bolden play.'" *I can't escape it. I've got to look at it.* She straightens up. If she keeps her shoulders down, draws in the air slowly, she can breathe, but her ears are ringing as though conch shells have been pressed over them. The music in her mind is overpowering the music on the stage (they seem to be playing; she knows what it must be — an entire Vivaldi concerto — but she can't hear it, can only watch the fluid motions of the bows on the strings), and the corpse in the corner is Steve. He has lain for days on the bed, his eyes empty. He's brought the turntable close enough so he can move the needle back to the beginning to play the same song over and over until she has to flee the apartment to walk for hours in the hot summer night thinking, *He's right. I've got to leave. But not the way he's saying. It's crazy what he's saying, it's sick. If I stay with him any longer, I'll be as sick as he is.* And it's Jim Morrison's voice that's repeating the same ancient story in Steve's ears. *No, I will not do that for you, Steven.*

People are applauding, so the Vivaldi must be over. Kathy applauds too, automatically, although she hasn't heard a note. She stares at the program, reading the words again although she knows perfectly well what they say. *"Les Folies' Couplets* (Final movement of the Suite in D minor for the second book of viola pieces of 1701) — Marin Marais (1656 - 1728) — viola de gamba and continuo." All the musicians have left the stage.

Paul is walking back on; his face is inward, closed, but she knows, even without being able to see it, that he's sweating and sick. Then there's Perry with a horribly fixed smile. And last, Wendy. It's impossible to see a human expression on her painted face. She seats herself at the front of the stage, takes the seven-stringed French gamba between her legs, and Kathy can see the gray rain light of a thousand dawns of practice ringing her like a rosary — can see each detail clearly; it's as though she has been lifted up to the same level as the performers so she won't miss a thing. It's true — Wendy is a gymnast, and soon she will be dancing, thousands of feet in the air, with a corpse. If she makes one slip, she'll fall and die. But now she and Perry are tuning their instruments to the harpsichord. Buddy Bolden had blown his brains out through his trumpet. Jelly Roll Morton had died bitter and poor, crazy, writing to Roosevelt mad schemes for regenerating the world through music. And Steve? There's no way that Kathy can stop the voice in her mind from singing. It's Buddy Bolden's voice, it's Jelly Roll Morton's voice, it's Steve's voice. "I thought I heard Buddy Bolden say, 'You nasty buncha dirty, take it away. You're awful. You're terrible. Take it away. And let Miss Wendy play.'"

The shells over her ears are suddenly gone; Kathy is aware of every sound — the coughing behind her, the rustle of programs on people's laps, the last of the tuning from the stage. Wendy inhales — deep rise and fall of the rib cage under the fitted bodice of the black dress — takes the neck of the gamba in her left hand, raises the bow in her right, and closes her eyes. Time passes, so much time that the audience begins to stir. Kathy has drawn her body rigid, iron wedge in the seat. Sweat is pouring down her sides. She's clenched her fists until her nails are biting into the palms of her hands. And still Wendy has not begun to play. The girl opens her eyes. The audience hums — mounting tension, wasps's nest — but Wendy looks out and smiles, with that one tiny communication cuts off sound. Silence. Then, without any warning at all, she begins. Her father and Perry, riding on electric nerve, barely manage to come in with her. The first notes drawn out of the French gamba are deep, profound, and totally assured.

Wendy plays. And, as the music gathers, begins to roll with a tremendous force, Kathy can see that the girl is gradually leaving the stage. She breathes with her bow strokes; the muscles of her bare shoulders ripple under her smooth skin. A power that's murderous is emerging, but absolutely controlled; at the end of a phrase she drives the bow home to the bass strings, the instrument in her other hand whipping forward to meet it; the air is torn from her lungs with the motion, chest falling — great ringing chord. Sound of response in the audience — soft, collective sigh. Like hearing Coltrane or Dolphy or Parker, and Kathy knows now why bop musicians sometimes turned their backs on the audience. Bit by bit, Wendy has gone away. This is virtuoso music — Kathy's heard that said of it often enough — some of the most difficult ever written for the instrument, but there's nothing of strain or effort in the girl's playing, not even in this fantastic run she's just made, notes thrown out in a lavish handful — because Wendy has ceased to exist. The stage is empty. There's nothing left but the music.

To dance to such an emptiness — this music is old, melancholy and old, comes from an impossibly distant kingdom, lost not in the past but in the heart. It's pure grace. No one in this audience could have done anything profound enough to deserve the privilege of hearing it. Marin Marais. The dead live again. How beautifully Wendy dances with death.

Time returned. Wendy must have been playing for more than ten minutes. The last of the sound was still resonating in the air, then silence. Christ, wasn't anybody going to applaud? But Kathy couldn't applaud; she couldn't even move. A few hands came together, beating, then a few more; it was building up on all sides. People were standing up. Someone in the back shouted, "Bravo!" Then someone else. Half a dozen people were calling it out now, and then the entire audience was on its feet. Wendy had just awakened from a deep sleep; she rose unsteadily, couldn't manage to smile, stood listening to the applause beating around her. Finally she bowed deeply from the waist and walked off into the wings.

They called her back seven times. Each time she returned to bow — still unable to smile — there was more of her on the stage. She was gradually returning. Behind the painted mask, there seemed to be growing an enormous surprise. Kathy turned to look at the audience; she had to try to take it in, understand what had happened. She saw that Evelyn Crane was still seated, her face open and stunned, stripped naked. She finally rose to her feet, clapped automatically, but her eyes — frozen into wide blue shock — were like a mirror reflection of her daughter's on the stage. Kathy couldn't look at the woman any longer, turned away, embarrassed. And then, at last, she allowed herself to look for Paul. Ignoring protocol, he'd never left the stage, was standing by the side of his harpsichord, out of the way, several feet behind his daughter. He seemed to know that no one was looking at him. That fierce strain had left him now; his face was relieved — but vastly tired and somehow very old. What could he be waiting for with such patience? He stood, stooped, as though carrying a weight on his shoulders and neck. Endurance. And light poured down to reflect back from the gray of his large, drooping head.

Could the man called "Jan the Dutchman" (also known as "Magister Johannes") who was martyred with two companions at Wesel in 1561 be Jan van Dorestad? How ludicrous, Paul thought, to be ruminating over the possible ramifications of a footnote, particularly tonight. He opened his eyes; the first thing he saw, directly in front of him, was the enormous bouquet of roses arranged in a Dresden vase on the coffee table — Perry's tribute to Wendy. Trust Mark to overdo it. The living-room smelled like a bloody funeral parlour. "It must be late," he said. Neither Wendy nor Kathy answered him. The party was over, no one left now but the three of them, the ones who lived here. How profoundly odd, he thought — who goes and who stays.

Kathy was half reclining at the end of the couch, her head, in a tangle of long, black hair, thrown back onto a pillow, her body so abandoned that she could have been asleep — except that her eyes were open. *My lover,* he thought, and then, turning to see Wendy where she was sitting with one long, bare arm resting on the harpsichord as gracefully as a philodendron, her head inclined forward so that her blonde hair completely covered her face, *my daughter*. Those words, usually so safe, seemed difficult now, not meaningless, but obscure. Two women, two people. Strangers actually. But, my God, if they were strangers, then whom did one ever know?

He was exhausted, had passed from simple tiredness into a state so drained that it had ceased to matter whether he got to sleep that night or not. He was left suspended, his mind so clear and vacant that he was noticing oddities of alignment that ordinarily would have seemed either unremarkable or merely fortuitous. He and his lover and his daughter had arrived at the far corners of the living room to form a triangle with sides ten feet long. "How are you feeling, Gwendolyn?" he said, using her formal name, as he knew she'd understand, to make a statement of affection.

"I'm not sure," She drew herself upright. Her painted face had been a shock when he'd first seen it, had continued to be a shock ever since. There was no internal adjustment he could make to accustom himself to it. Frightening actually, that resemblance. Ev had always worn too much make-up. One hoped that Wendy would not make a habit of it.

"Paul," she said, a message in her use of his Christian name; he must listen carefully, "what did he want with me? That bloody reporter?"

Something was coming undone in Wendy's speech. He had counted the three glasses of champagne that had passed down her throat; she was now sipping on the fourth. This was her night, after all, her triumph, but nonetheless one's teen-age daughter should not be getting plastered. He answered lightly. "What did he want? I would imagine he wanted about ten column inches."

"Oh, Daddy, you know what I mean."

Something in the air — one felt it growing — unresolved dissonance. "Impossible to know what he's going to say," he told her. "Although I'm sure it'll be a rave of some sort. He wouldn't have bothered with the pictures if it weren't going to be a rave."

She looked at him, waiting for more.

"That man's an idiot," he said. "A musical cretin. A few years back we had a disastrous night. We were under-rehearsed. We couldn't stay in tune. Perry kept getting lost, and then, when he did come in, it'd be in the wrong place. Good God, you never heard such cacophony in your life. We awaited the review with a nearly Kierkegaardian dread, and that idiot wrote, 'Pro Musica up to its usual high standards.'

"And then there was the Gesualdo concert. Damnably difficult because the music is so profoundly mad, but we brought it off. And that ridiculous man wrote, 'So ugly and unmusical that one has difficulty in comprehending why these pieces should be performed in public at all.'"

"But what is he going to say about the Marais?"

"About the Marais? God knows. He'll probably be writing about you."

"That's what I was afraid of."

"Oh, come on," Kathy said. "You'll love it."

"Kathy," one's daughter, a chilly edge to her voice, said to one's lover, "I'm not that simple."

"I'd never accuse you of being *simple*, for Christ's sake."

Wendy yawned and rubbed her eyes. When her hands came away, she'd destroyed that uncannily artificial face, had turned herself into a clown — mascara smeared into black rings around each eye. "Paul? Dad?" Oh, he thought, both options? "Tell me honestly. How did I play?"

"Haven't you had roses thrown at your feet all night?"

"Don't throw me any more roses. Just tell me how I played."

He chose his words carefully. "It's difficult for me to assess you, Wendy. I think everything you do is wonderful. But I've never been so impressed with a student performance in my life." Was that too lavish? Perhaps, but her playing had moved him to tears.

"Thank you," Wendy said primly like the Stafford House schoolgirl she was. "I have to know how I'm doing. I don't want to be only... I want to be as good as Hanna, as good as Klaas Achterberg. If I can't, I don't want to do it. It's just too bloody much work and... Well, I'm missing out on a lot of things."

"Yes," he said. Unfortunately, my dear daughter, I know exactly what you mean. "If you put in the time, you could be as good as Hanna or Klaas. It'd take years."

"And I'd have to go to Europe."

"I know that."

"I don't want to go alone."

"Of course you don't."

"Oh, the two of you," Kathy said, laughing. "You sound like a couple of aldermen discussing the rezoning of Kerrisdale."

"It's only our manner," Wendy said giggling.

My darling daughter is drunk, he thought, closed his eyes, let his muscles sag into the support of the reclining chair. Hadn't Kathy learned by now that if he and Wendy didn't maintain this well-rehearsed style of interchange, they might not be able to talk at all?

That damnable footnote. He'd read it, then gone back to the text, then returned to the footnote, reading it over repeatedly until the words had turned to a meaningless babel. "Because of the paucity of documentation which survives," the text had read, "it is difficult to draw a coherent picture of the doctrines of the Netherlandish Spiritualizers (called by their opponents Libertines). It is possible to discern many influences at work: the tolerant humanism of Erasmus, the antinomianism of the Rhineland mystics, and even, in their more libertarian positions, the persistence of the mediaeval heresy of the Brethren of the Free Spirit." Footnote. His eyes had dropped to the bottom of the page. "In the teachings of the obscure Netherlandish mystic known as Magister Johannes or Jan the Dutchman, martyred with two companions at Wesel in 1561, it is possible to discern a direct doctrinal link to the late mediaeval Adamite tradition."

He'd written to Van der Geest, who had original sources available to him at 'sHertogenbosch, Antwerp, and Wesel. Until he received a reply, there was nothing more to be done.

And then Paul found words in his mind, knew them as a quote. *"If I could have two things in one..."* It was a poem, a very familiar poem, but he couldn't place it. What was the next line? It seemed important to remember. "I've advised the department," he said without opening his eyes, "that I'm taking my sabbatical next year." Damn, he couldn't remember how it went.

"What are you saying?" Kathy asked him.

"He's saying that we're going to Amsterdam," Wendy said.

"Is that right?"

"I'm offering it as a possibility."

Kathy sat straight up. "Thanks for telling me about it."

"It's still quite tentative."

"What about your mistress? What were you planning to do with her?"

How tactless, he thought. "Haven't you ever wanted to see Amsterdam?" he said, trying for lightness.

"Amsterdam," she said, pronouncing the word slowly as though it were a magical formula. "All I know about Amsterdam is that Eric Dolphy died there... okay. And so what would it say about me on the visa? Your *secretary?*"

"Why don't the two of you get married?" Wendy said. He felt the shock of her words throughout his entire body.

Kathy jumped to her feet. "It's a fucking conspiracy. You're ganging up on me." She began pacing up and down. "Wendy, you're outrageous. You act like the entire universe revolves around you."

"Why *don't* you get married? You're already living as though you were, and it'd make everything simpler, wouldn't it?"

"Paul, I'm being proposed to. *By your daughter.*"

He saw that Kathy could laugh at any moment, and so, for that matter, could he. Wendy *was* outrageous, but she had just saved him months of worrying. "It's an idea worth considering," he said.

"I have a husband."

"Do you?"

Kathy sank down next to Wendy on the couch. The shock that had hit him must have finally caught up with her. "There is some kind of law, isn't there?" she said slowly, "that if your old man takes off, and you haven't seen a trace of him in so many years, you can divorce him *in absentia?*"

"I believe there is. I can ask Bill easily enough."

"Bill who? Oh, he's your lawyer, isn't he? Doing your divorce from Evelyn. Jesus, it's all just a bit too incestuous for me."

"The divorce is only a formality now. Ev and I have worked it out between us. We're going to sign a separation agreement later this month."

"I suppose it *is* an idea worth considering." Kathy's dry tone was a mockery of his.

"Where would I go to school?" Wendy said.

"I suppose we could get a tutor for you. Or perhaps there are schools for British or Canadian embassy kids. If there are, your uncle could arrange it."

"The royal treatment," Kathy said.

"Please fuck off," Wendy said.

"Gwendolyn."

"Daddy, I'm sick of it. I'm sick of having people say things like that to me. Kathy, do you think it's *easy?*"

"I know it's not easy. Can't you take a joke?"

"Not yet I can't." Her eyes were intense with anger, a dramatic effect made ludicrous by the smeared make-up.

Kathy extended a hand, then withdrew it. "I don't know what to say, Wendy. I think you're magnificent."

Wendy bounced along the couch — an explosive motion, clumsy and graceful at once — to catch Kathy in an awkward embrace, gesture cut off before Kathy could respond. Wendy was on her feet then, backed away unsteadily; she seemed to be feeling, finally, the full effect of the champagne. "The prodigy," she said. "The child genius, the *Wunderkind.* The spoiled brat, the little fraud. Oh hell, hell, hell." She walked out.

"The artistic temperment," he said under his breath.

"No," Kathy said. "It's not that simple. Let's go to bed. I can't take any more tonight."

As they passed his daughter's door, he saw that it was closed. A crack of light shone out at the bottom. "Talk to her," Kathy said.

"I'm afraid, my dear, that I don't know what to say."

"Oh, Jesus, you give me a pain in the ass sometimes."

In their bedroom she said in an expressionless voice, "Should we get married?"

"I think we very well might. What do you think?"

"Oh, yeah, I think we very well might."

The tap was delicate and discreet, but he felt an inexplicable surge of adrenaline. "Just a minute," he called, "we're not dressed."

But Wendy didn't wait a minute, pushed the door open. She was wearing nothing but her slip and stockings, stood in the doorway supporting herself with one hand on the jamb. The hall light lit her from behind — brilliant areole with a dark centre. Her small body hung slackly, dejected. The blurred make-up, the posture, the simplicity of the white slip: she seemed, uncannily, like a child saltimabanque, and he saw her for a short, uncategorizable moment leaning against the side of a cart or wagon, exhausted, her head hanging down, bare feet in the dirt. Horses stamped, and he was suddenly dizzy and sick.

"Dad," she said.

"Yes."

"Do you always feel empty afterward?"

There was no use in pretending that he didn't know what she meant. "No. When you get older, that goes away. Then you either feel satisfied or relieved depending on how you did."

"I'm glad. I couldn't stand it if it were like this every time." Without saying good-night, she turned and walked away into the light.

Oh, it was always sweet to lie with Kathy, to feel the long lines of her body under the covers. He heard rain falling, and he was asleep already, but then perhaps it was a dream. He could hear music; he was sure of it. No, it wasn't a dream at all; he was awake, if only for a moment, and could hear clearly through the walls, wandering unsteadily in a thin, unspiralling line, the sound of bowed notes from Wendy's gamba.


Kathy walked into the kitchen and saw Wendy, already fully dressed, sitting at the table. "Jesus, you startled me." An odd remark, Kathy thought as soon as she'd made it. Wendy hadn't moved a muscle.

The girl was wearing baggy jeans, a sweater of her father's, and blue mary janes scuffed to the color of sand at the toes. Her hair hung in a thick, knotty tangle, hiding her white face.

"What's the matter?" Kathy said.

Wendy didn't answer. All right, try another direction. "Where's Paul?"

"At the university," Wendy said in a dull monotone. "He said he was going to the theology school."

"The theology school?"

"That's what he said."

Wendy looked up, and Kathy saw from the extraordinary stillness of the girl that whatever was going on was serious. The morning newspaper was spread open on the kitchen table. "What?"

Without speaking, Wendy offered her the entertainment page. If Kathy hadn't been at the concert, she never would have been able to connect the sophisticated young woman in the picture with the scruffy child sitting here in the morning sunlight.

"They really did it," Kathy said.

"They really did it. *I* really did it."

Wendy was posed with the gamba, not at the angle she played it, but with the neck tilted away from her like a prop. The instrument formed a diagonal line, framed her face, set off her long throat and bare shoulders; her head was turned away, semiprofile. Her madeup eyes were looking into the distance, her chin lifted to emphasize the slight upward curve of her nose and the modeling of her mouth — an angle that gave her a fragile balance, flower on a stem. Her lips were parted as though she were waiting to be kissed. "Jesus," Kathy said, "it's a fashion photograph."

"That's right. An Eaton's ad. I obviously have never played that odd thing I'm holding... It happened so fast I didn't even know what was going on. That goddamned photographer tilted the gamba away from me, said, 'Look over there,' so I looked over there. He said, 'Say ooh,' and I said 'ooh,' and he took half a dozen pictures."

"Who put all that makeup on you?"

"That graduate student of Dad's. I just sat there and let her do it."

"How's the review?"

"Oh, hell, it's a rave. Authority, sensitivity, power, and all that rot. Stunning virtuoso performance. Sixteen-year-old Gwendolyn Crane dazzled the audience, etcetera. The idiot called the Vivaldi 'pleasant,' passed over Hanna's Bach in a sentence. *The fucking thing's all about me.*"

"Isn't that what you wanted?" The girl didn't answer. "Come on, Wendy, isn't that *exactly* what you wanted?"

"Of course it's what I wanted." She snatched the paper from Kathy's hand, read from the article in a bitter, self-mocking voice. "Wendy, as she is known to her family and friends, has been allowed to develop at her own pace. Her father laughingly dismissed the suggestion that the Pro Musica has been hiding its brightest light under a bushel. 'Wendy could have soloed at any time she felt ready. We've tried not to push her.'

"And listen to this. Perry says, 'All I did was show her how to hold the bow and where to put her fingers down, and I've been running like a greyhound ever since to try to keep up.' Jesus! And the damned man didn't write a thing about the music. It's all lies. The review's a lie. The picture's a lie. The only thing that isn't a lie *is* the music. I played better than I ever have, but that's not what got me into the paper. That's not why they were applauding. Perhaps there were ten people in that theater who understood what the music was supposed to sound like, *and most of them were on the stage.*"

Kathy was trying to get her bearings. "Come on, I can't believe that you just sat there passively and let it happen to you."

Wendy's cheeks flushed with blood. Kathy braced herself for the explosion. She watched Wendy stop herself.

Wendy looked away, through the window at the sunlight. "No," she said, "it didn't just happen. I asked for the makeup. I knew exactly what that photographer wanted, and I gave it to him. Now I feel absolutely vile, and you're the only person I know who'd understand it."

"*Me?*"

"Yes, you. Don't you think I'm listening when you tell me things? I did exactly what *you'd* never do. Now I know why you'd never play with your husband's band."

Kathy was stopped. "Let's talk about that some other time... What did Paul say?"

"He thinks it's funny. He thinks it's all a marvelous joke. He wants to take us out to dinner tonight to celebrate."

Kathy had to laugh. "Don't take it so seriously. You conned them. It worked."

"Yes, it worked. And I debased the music to do it."

"Oh, hell, you didn't debase the music. The music was wonderful."

"Sure. *But who noticed?*"

"You're being too hard on yourself. You didn't debase anything. You just hung some good, old fashioned show biz on it."

"It shouldn't have any show biz hung on it. We should play it like the orphan girls Vivaldi wrote for. Hidden away behind a screen so nobody could see us... I'm glad I'm going to Amsterdam to study with Klaas. He scares me to death, and I'm glad he scares me to death."

"He'll cut you down to size pretty fast, won't he?"

"Yes, he certainly will. I'm looking forward to it." Wendy stood up. "I'm going to *practice*," she said, spitting out the word.

"Hey. Don't tie yourself into such a knot that you stop playing."

The girl spun around in the doorway. "You mean the way *you* did. Play your saxophone again, and I'll believe you when you tell me things like that."

Something immensely satisfying about this, Kathy thought. And long overdue. Evelyn's clothes hung on the bar in roughly chronological order so that taking them down was like moving backward in time. Kathy was into the sixties by now — mini dresses. They seemed sad and nostalgic and more than a little ridiculous. She threw them into the carton. When she was finished, there would be nothing left but an enormous bare closet.

The front doorbell rang. She paused, listening. Wendy stopped playing, banged downstairs. A man's voice. Must be a friend of Paul's. She heard Wendy returning, taking the stairs two at a time.

"There's a man here. He says he knows you."

Something in the girl's tone made Kathy turn around quickly. Wendy was hugging herself, standing in that stiff psychotic's pose Kathy had seen before.

"Who is it?"

"He says his name's Steve."

Kathy continued the motion she had begun, folded the dresses and laid them aside. Her ears began to ring. "That's not your husband, is it?"

"No, of course not."

Some part of Kathy had detached itself and floated away, was now watching the empty person who remained as she sat down on the edge of the bed. "Where are my cigarettes?"

Wendy pointed to her mother's vanity table. Kathy couldn't

move. Wendy picked up the pack and lighter and handed them over.

"What does he look like?" Her voice sounded dry, mildly curious — perfectly normal.

"He's very tall and thin and has black hair. He looks exhausted."

"Shit."

"He said the strangest thing to me."

"What?"

"I don't remember." Kathy looked into the girl's face. Head tilted to one side, blood in her cheeks. "That's not true. I do remember. Exactly. He said, 'What a fucking trip.' I thought he meant where he'd just come from, but he said, 'No, finding you at the end of the road. That's the trip.' Kathy, I've never seen that man before in my life."

Somehow the ceiling was where the wall ought to have been. Kathy heard a steady roar, pulse like sea surf. The detached part of her said, it's your own blood in your ears, stupid. "Kathy!" Wendy said.

But Kathy couldn't move; she was lying on the floor next to the foot of the bed. Wendy was holding a lit cigarette awkwardly in her hand. Kathy fought down a swimmy nausea and forced herself upright. She couldn't breathe.

"Help." Wonderful. A great thing to say. What do you expect *her* to do?

Wendy laid the cigarette into the ashtray and knelt on the floor. Kathy caught the girl in her arms and clung to her. She heard her lungs wheezing like old leather bellows.

"What is it? What's the matter?"

Kathy couldn't answer, but she wanted some of Wendy's strength and seemed to be getting it. The choking was letting up; she could feel air rushing in again. "Give me that damned cigarette," she said. She dragged, coughed on the smoke, dragged again. *Damn it all to hell*, she thought, *I'll show them. The bastards*. But she didn't know what she was going to show or who the bastards might be. "What happened? Did I faint?"

"I think so."

"Did he really say his name was Steve?"

"Yes. He said his name was Steve Beuhl. He asked for you."

"Jesus Christ, it *is* my husband."

"What's going to happen now?"

"Goddamn it, I don't know. Let me think." But what was there to think about? No amount of thinking would make him go away. "Jesus Christ, it's been seven fucking years."

She couldn't stand up. The room was rocking like a boat in heavy weather. She held out a hand and Wendy took it. And then Kathy followed the line of the dream downstairs and into the living room.

He'd fallen asleep, his head askew on the back of the couch. She should have known that he would have aged, but it was still a shock; her memories of him were so clear and fixed in time that seeing him like that, suddenly there, sleeping, shattered them in a single, sharp blow. His hair that had once been as thick as hers was now receding in two points on either side of his forehead; two deeply bitter lines had embedded themselves at either corner of his mouth. He was as thin as he'd ever been, his high cheekbones protruding like stones, but he'd outgrown his prettiness, his disquieting ambiguity. He looked worked and damaged. The blue-gray circles under his eyes weren't sexy anymore, had become loose pouches of skin that said — late nights, smoke, dark bars, running. The long fingers of his right hand, lying slackly open on the couch, were stained brown with nicotine; the heels of his cracked cowboy boots were worn down all the way into the leather. He'd finally aged enough to match his broken nose. "Christ," Kathy said and began to cry. Wendy, still holding her hand, led her into the kitchen.

"Oh, God, Wendy, he looks so old."

"He doesn't look that old. He doesn't look as old as Daddy."

"But you should have seen him when he was a boy. How beautiful he was." Kathy pressed her knuckles into her mouth and bit down on them; the tears blurred everything so that she couldn't see at all. "Oh, God. Oh, God. Steven. He was so beautiful."

Wendy pressed Kleenex into her hand. "I'll be all right in a minute," Kathy said. "Just give me a minute."

"Do you want something to drink?"

"Yeah. Give me a shot of Scotch."

Wendy must have poured more than a shot, but Kathy put it down at a gulp. "I guess I've got to say something to him, don't I? Could I look as old to him as he looks to me? Wendy? Don't go away, all right?"

"I'm not going to go away."

Kathy approached him gingerly. "Steve," she said.

His eyes opened, and she knew he must have retained that knack of being able to wake up instantly and totally. The dark eyes, at the center, hadn't changed at all.

"Hi, babe." His voice sounded infinitely tired. He didn't move his body, continued to lie sprawled backward, head to one side drooping like a cut plant, but he was staring at her. Finally he smiled. "Damn," he said, "but you still look so fine."

She had to turn away. The afternoon sunlight was streaming in at an angle from the west windows; the harpsichord glowed with it. "Jesus, what can I say?"

"That's my line." He sat up. "Not back two minutes and you're stealing my lines." He drew a pack of Player's out of his shirt and lit one. "You folks wouldn't have something like a beer in the house, would you?"

"Of course we do," Wendy said in her most formal tone.

His eyes followed the girl out of the room. "Who's your little honey?"

"She's the daughter of the man I'm living with."

He smiled, slightly, ran his finger across the break in his nose. That old, familiar gesture made her eyes sting. She looked away at the sunlight so he wouldn't see. "Kath, I haven't come back here to spoil anything, all right?"

"What the hell *did* you come back for?"

"It's as far west as the road runs."

"The hell it is, man. It keeps on going to Tofino."

He laughed at that. "Yeah, that's right. Shit, I don't know. I'll be on my way in a minute. Don't worry about a thing, all right? There's no problem but the rent, and the rent's paid."

"*You fucking asshole.*" She'd tried not to, but she was yelling. "Do you have any idea how much of a shock it is for me to see you like that? No warning. No warning at all."

"Yeah, I should have called. But I didn't know where to call. I spent the night in Hope. Jesus, Kath, almost ran out of hope in Hope."

"Where are you coming from?"

"Toronto."

"Been there all the time?"

"Yeah, no bullshit. Georgia boy lost in the snows... Jesus, but that looks good," he said to the glass of beer in Wendy's hand. A shaft of sunlight was passing through the glass so the liquid glowed amber. Wendy's hair glowed. Steve took the glass, toasted both of them, drank.

"Crossing Canada in the dead of winter," he said. "No fucking joke. Froze up on the prairies. Not the water, but the *oil*, for fuck's sake. And then coming down out of the mountains, what a trip. On one side Siberia, on the other the Elysian Fields. Shit, it ain't even raining."

He was studying Wendy with that assessing look Kathy knew too damned well, and Wendy saw him doing it. The girl didn't seem frightened any longer, was standing with her legs apart, feet planted firmly on the floor, her arms crossed in front of her breasts. She seemed almost angry. "What did you mean?" she said. "What you said to me?"

"Oh, well, honey, what *did* I say to you?" His Georgia accent was suddenly thick as corn syrup, and Kathy felt a tension that was so terrible and obscure she had to move away from it. She walked to the far side of the room directly into the shaft of sunlight. Her mouth had gone dry.

"You said, 'What a trip, finding you at the end of the road.' " Kathy had come to rest against the side of the harpsichord; she steadied herself on it.

"Can't hold a man accountable for what comes out of his mouth after three thousand miles on the road, can you? Nonstop and drunk half the way, Siberia on all sides and the sky coming down like iron? Jesus, kid, give me a break." He laughed.

"Tell me what you meant," Wendy said — chilly, persistent.

Steve looked away, answered in a slow and barely audible drawl. "Hell, I didn't mean anything. It's just that... I don't know... Hey, maybe I should put my act on the road. What do you think, Kath? I'll get a motel room somewhere and give you a call later on, how's that?"

Kathy couldn't speak.

"Know any good motels?" he said. "Couldn't hack the Cecil again. Hey, don't cry."

"Damn it," Kathy yelled at him, "I'm not crying." But she was.

"Aw shit," he said, standing up, "I'll call you later, OK?"

"Go on back in the guest room and get some sleep," Wendy said flatly. "You look terrible."

"Yeah, I suppose I do, don't I?"

Wendy took the empty glass from his hand. "You were going to drop it," she said.

"Yeah, I guess I was."

# VII

"I'll be damned if I'll let you toast me with ginger ale," she said. "Not today."

For a moment he was unaccountably angry. But then something in him came to a stop. Yes, he thought, one must let go now. One must find a new way to do all this. And he saw her point: for ritual occasions, one should use genuine spirits. "Right," he said, "a brandy."

He looked away, across the dining room where young people (most of them appeared to be single and courting) were being served by waitresses dressed like the maids in *Upstairs Downstairs*; he looked through the sweeping walls of plate glass to see his city in its most typical aspect: blue-grey haze, blurred amber lights reflected from wet pavement in the afternoon rain. (And with the view came the old betrayer: nostalgia.) And how many of these — yes, children is what he thought of them, actually — how many of them were founding a new family here this afternoon, and how many of them would end up, years later, in a lawyer's office taking it all apart? He and Evelyn hadn't courted in the restaurant of a posh hotel, however; they'd courted in the student union cafeteria.

Paul couldn't quite believe it: the months of wrangling were over. And when he had stepped out of the elevator in the bloody awful downtown high-rise that held the offices of her lawyer, had looked down a long hallway like something out of an angst-ridden modern painting and seen a slender figure silhouetted against a window — in jeans, with long hair swinging, striding toward him — he had, for one wildly disorienting moment, taken her for Cindy. He looked at Evelyn closely now; her public image might have changed remarkably, but the centre of her eyes had not, and would he ever know another woman as well as he knew this one? My God, they had done it; they had signed the papers; they were legally separated.

"Do you want a divorce?" he asked her.

"Doesn't matter a damn to me. How about you?"

"Yes, I do. I want to marry Kathy."

"Kind of hard with her husband camped in your guest room, isn't it?"

"Well, at least she knows where he is."

She laughed. "I find the situation totally bizarre. But then, it's none of my business, is it?"

"No, my dear, it isn't."

That seemed to have poisoned the conversation. He saw that she'd been watching him. "I haven't been in here in years," she said. "Used to come in a lot with Joan and Valerie and... oh, you know, what's-her-name from up the street. Back when I was playing the Kerrisdale matron. We'd sit and drink and complain."

"Sounds dreadful."

"No, it was actually quite pleasant in a bleak sort of way. We were all in the same boat... So has Kathy said she'll marry you, or are you just assuming in your usual baronial fashion?"

She'd taken him by surprise, manoeuvred him into laughing with her. "Yes, she's said yes."

"Much to my amazement, I like her. I think she's good for you."

"I'm glad you approve."

"The hell you are. So when are you going to bounce her husband out of your house?... She asks despite the fact that it's none of her business."

"It's a... well, a complex situation."

"Jesus, Crane, you drove me nuts for years with that."

"With what?"

"Don't give me that. You know what I mean."

"Yes, of course I know what you mean."

My God, he was tired. His doctor kept telling him that he should be getting some regular exercise, a bit of swimming or jogging or the like, but, damn it all, when was one supposed to fit that in? He hadn't had a minute to himself in weeks. It wasn't going to get any better. And what was the point of hashing over one's present absurd situation with Evelyn? He tried to think of something safe to say, and then, luckily, their waitress came back, bringing the brandies. He lifted his glass to his wife. "The very best to you, Evelyn."

She toasted him with a sombre face, surprising him: "The very best to you, too, Paul."

"So what are you going to do," he asked her, "now that you're a woman of independent means?"

"Exactly what I've been doing. And independent means? Isn't that a bit strong?"

"If you're careful with it..."

"Hey. Don't give me any lectures."

For an instant he felt that old, familiar frustration, but then he let that go, too. "You're right, Ev. No lectures."

She gave him a look he knew quite well, the one that said: is this a trick? Then he saw something change on her face. She drank the rest of her brandy. "You're right," she said. "I *do* have to be careful... You know, Crane, I'm sick of being the only person in that house bringing in any money."

"Oh."

"I think maybe Cindy and I will find ourselves a nice little apartment."

"Good heavens. I don't know what to say."

"You don't have to say anything. I'm just telling you."

They looked at each other. And then the words came out of him before he had a chance to assess them: "Evelyn, I'm in a bit of a bind. I just... I'm not quite sure what to do. I know you'll find this hard to believe, but it's true. I have tried to learn from what's happened between us. I want Kathy to know that... well, that she can make her own decisions."

She didn't say a thing. My God, *that* was totally unlike her. "And if I start behaving as though it's *my* bloody house..." he said.

"Hey. Crane. It *is* your bloody house. Her husband has no business there. Not for a single night. Let alone for... How long has it been? A couple weeks? Listen to me for once, okay? I like Kathy, and I've also got her number. Make the decision for her. Get him out of there. I'll give you ten to one that's what she wants."

"You know the strangest thing. I actually rather like the man," he said.

"That's beside the point."

"Yes, it is, isn't it?"

"Be yourself and you'll be fine. At least on this one you will be... And now I really do have to get back."

"Yes, so do I." He reached for the bill, but her hand was there ahead of his. "After all, I *am* a woman of independent means."

He heard Kathy's voice in his mind and said what he heard: "Smart ass."

Evelyn looked as though he'd slapped her, then began laughing so hard he was afraid, for a moment, she wasn't going to stop. Just as quickly, they were staring at each from the centre of a painful silence. He felt a hard, cold constriction in his chest. She put it into words for both of them: "Good Christ, it's legal."

"Yes, indeed."

"Paul? Take care of Wendy." And then she laughed again: a tense, unhappy sound. "God, what a thing to say. It's not like we're never going to see each other again."

"I will. I'll take care of her."

"Jesus, I know you will. Look, Crane, it's not simple, you know. A lot of our years together were really good. It's just that..."

He did something he'd never done before. He gently pressed his fingertips against her lips to silence her.

Paul stepped carefully through his own front door. It was light enough and warm enough. There was music playing. But he also felt the tension like a warning: the quietness in the house that allowed the music to come forward, to be so entirely what one heard. He was beginning to be able to tell the various saxophone players apart, and tonight it was Eric Dolphy, one of Kathy's gods. Then, passing the living room, he was startled to see Wendy, still wearing her entire Stafford House uniform, even the blazer, arranging kindling in the fireplace. He must have surprised her; she dropped a sliver of wood and looked at him without speaking. She'd put on old gloves to handle the wood, and his first impulse was to tease her, but he thought better of it. "How nice of you."

She shrugged. "Cindy's not around to do it. So how'd it go with Mom?"

"Fine. Couldn't be better. Give me a chance to settle, and I'll tell you."

Kathy had not come out to meet him in the hallway. He hung his raincoat in the closet and paused, trying again to sense the ambience of the house. The kitchen speakers were on; the living-room speakers were not. Dolphy was pulling away from the clearly stated tonal centre beneath him, but, just as one was beginning to think that the saxophone had departed completely into polytonality, a perfectly placed quarter note reestablished the link with the bass line. A virtuoso performance, Paul thought, and, of course, made up on the spot, "contrappunto alla menta" they would have said in the sixteenth century about the playing of such a ménestrel, a man like Michael van Dorestad, son of Jan the Dutchman.

Kathy was sitting at the kitchen table; she appeared to be doing nothing at all. She didn't look at him immediately; then she did, met his eyes. He felt caught at once in some indefinable tangle. The smell in the kitchen was like nothing he was used to: yes, Evelyn's French and Italian herbs were most emphatically gone now. He turned to the counter by the stove, picked up a jar, read the label: *whole chillies*. Then he found himself standing there and compulsively reading the label on every jar: *stick cinnamon, coriander, whole cloves, cumin, fenugreek, turmeric.* "Oh," he said, "so that's how you achieve your exquisite flavours."

She said nothing. He sat down at the table opposite her. In the last few days indentations had appeared at the front of her temples — small, circular pockets just beyond the outer corners of her eyes, an effect as though she were being pinched by an invisible vice. "So how was it?" she said.

"Excellent. It's signed. Everything's going to work out fine. How's everything here?"

"We're all fed. I guess that's the main thing." Her voice was low, dim, as though the words were sticking in her throat. "Vegetable curry. Wendy won't eat meat anymore, and he doesn't give a shit what he eats, and I... can't eat."

He waited. "Paul?" she said. "You know what I want to do? I want to take him back to my apartment... where the stereo speakers are still hanging up exactly where he put them. I want to sit him down at the fucking table *he* bought at the Sally Ann. And I want to say to him, 'All right, you son of a bitch, why did you leave me?'"

"Why don't you do that?"

"Because I don't seem to be able to do *anything.* I haven't said ten words to him since he showed up. Jesus, I feel paralyzed."

"Katherine," he said in the gentlest voice he could muster, "isn't it about time he left?"

"Oh, absolutely."

"Where is he, incidentally?"

She jerked her head toward the guest room. "He naps. Only sleeps a few hours at night, and then he naps, like a... yeah, exactly... like a wolf. God, I want him out of here. But Paul, please... This is a horrible thing to ask. Let *me* do it. Okay?"

Why, dear God, Paul thought, have I been surrounded my

entire life by difficult women? "When?" he said.

"Now you're angry. Please don't be angry. I just can't take it right now. Soon, all right? Now go deal with the princess."

That's right, Paul thought, one down, one to go. And was annoyed with himself. One's future wife and one's daughter were not, after all, chess pieces. And Wendy had the fire burning beautifully; she had not moved from in front of it. She rested on one hip with her skirt drawn carefully down to her knees. She has something of her mother's prissiness, he thought. Or at least the prissiness Evelyn *used* to have. "It's all settled," he said. "Everything worked out splendidly."

She was studying him. "We've got the house," he said, "and she's got damned near everything else. About custody, there's really no question. You and Cindy aren't children, and..."

"I don't care about any of that. I don't care who gets what. All I want to know is whether we can go to Amsterdam."

"Yes, of course we can."

"Kathy, too?"

"If she wants to. Your mother's accepted the situation."

She looked at the fire. "And you've accepted hers?"

He was surprised. "Yes, I suppose I have."

"Good. I don't want to worry about it any more."

"I didn't know you had been."

"Oh, Dad, what do you think?"

He didn't know what he thought. Her hair in the firelight looked positively splendid; she had finer bones than her mother. "Do you have time to hear the new Marais tonight?" she said.

"Of course I do."

"Don't say, 'Of course I do,' like that. Lots of times you haven't had time."

"I'm sorry."

"I'm not blaming you. I know how busy you've been."

"Gwendolyn? Things will calm down now, you know."

"I know they will."

He wanted to say, "Don't go yet. Let's have a chat," but he didn't. Wendy called down the hall, "Can I turn the stereo off?"; "Sure," Kathy answered, and he was left alone in his denuded living room.

He'd sold the wind instruments to the university; the walls looked skinned. But it's done, Paul told himself. Things are falling into place. Next is the performance. He settled into the easy chair by the fire and took van der Geest's letter out of his briefcase to read again.

Dear Doctor Crane:

I am sorry it has taken me so long to reply to your letter. To be absolutely frank, I expected that your reference to a "Magister Johannes or Jan the Dutchman, martyred with two companions at Wesel in 1561," would lead nowhere. "Jan the Dutchman" is as imprecise a label as, for instance, "John the Englishman" would be, and we need, of course, an identification more firm, so I must admit to you that I did not take your clue seriously and, therefore, did nothing about it until this afternoon.

I have just returned from the library where I, in a matter of only a few hours, traced the way back to a primary source: the Anabaptist *Book of Martyrs* written late in the sixteenth century. In it there is a brief account of the martyrdom of the three at Wesel. They are referred to as a "family in God." The *Book of Martyrs* concentrates upon a young woman known as "Katrei" who appears to have distinguished herself by her ability to remain silent throughout a particularly savage ordeal at the hands of the Inquisition. The other two were her husband and her husband's father, and these are called "Michael and Jan van Dorestad."

You may imagine my excitement upon reading this account. Here, in all likelihood, is our man. Tomorrow I will attempt to ascertain if the trial record at Wesel has survived. You may rest assured that I am "hot on the trail," and that I will write again as soon as I have discovered anything further.

My very best wishes,<br>
Willem van der Geest

P.S. Forgive me if I tell you that I am pleased to have my suspicion that van Dorestad was an Anabaptist even tentatively confirmed.

Jan van Dorestad was an Anabaptist? Paul looked into the fire and thought about that. He didn't believe it for a minute. He didn't have any solid evidence, and he didn't care if the Anabaptists in their *Book of Martyrs* had claimed van Dorestad along with his son and daughter-in-law as their own; it just wasn't right.

And Paul knew who it was he would have liked to turn over to the tender care of the Inquisition: the damnable and anonymous acquisitions librarian who had bought the microfilm of the *Book of Martyrs* that Paul had found easily enough in the library at the theology school. The work had been translated into both German and French, languages that Paul could handle, but the version he had available to him was a facsimile of the original which had been written in old Dutch. He had stared at it on the screen, feeling a rising frustration and rage. It wasn't close enough to German for him to be able to get even a remote notion of what it said. The bizarre language didn't look close enough to anything the least bit familiar; it might as well have been Urdu. Then the Union Catalogue had told him which universities in North America held the French and German translations. He could order any of them and expect delivery in a month to six weeks. Ah, the joys of scholarship in western Canada, he thought. The perfect place to be doing research into the history of the Low Countries in the sixteenth century.

But there was a certain advantage to not having a myriad of primary sources to drown oneself in; one could try to see things writ large. All right then, let us imagine (Paul thought, as though lecturing to his students) what the Anabaptists would have been like. They were serious and industrious people, dedicated to plain speaking and plain dress, radical Protestants who thought of the Pope at Rome as the Antichrist himself, who hated all the elaborate trappings of the Church — the ceremony and pomp, the system of indulgences, the complex theology that interposed priests and saints between man and God. In waves of uprisings, the Anabaptists smashed Church icons. They tried to live like the early Christians. They were eager for martyrdom.

Now let us consider what we know of Jan van Dorestad. We do not know when he was born, but we do know that he was admitted to the Brotherhood of Our Lady in 'sHertogenbosch in 1506, so let us arbitrarily guess his age then at sixteen and see if it works. Paul rummaged in his briefcase for a note pad, looked up and saw that Wendy had come in silently and was sitting on the harpsichord stool. "I just want to finish up something here," he said.

"It's okay, Dad."

The fire had burned down; Wendy put her old gloves back on and carefully laid two more logs onto it. In the kitchen the dishwasher was going, filling the house with a flat background of white noise. Where was Kathy? Upstairs? Where was her husband? Sleeping, presumably. And Wendy appeared happy enough to sit in front of the fire. Nothing was required of one for the moment. Good God, a free half hour. Paul looked down at his notes.

Nowhere. Then Steve slammed hands to catch himself. But it wasn't an elevator shaft that had swung open under him, only a narrow bed, and his arching body, ready to run, was poised to no good purpose. A wasp-yellow bulb burning in the corner, ache of blue at the window, the steady curtain of rain outside, and sleep still pressing him down like a promise. How many more times would he get to do it like that, put the world back together like stringing beads? Each bead is a moment, then it's gone into memory. That's right, *time*'s the label for it, you're still the drummer, and you're still counting. Come on, man, you can do it again. *Make it make sense.*

Kathy led you back to this room at the end of the hall, and you were so crapped out you almost fell over before you got there. "Kathy?" you said, meaning: Hey, contact? OK? Anything?

"Later," she said, "I can't take it in."

Jesus, sleeping and waking in a strange place, that's when it all comes unglued, lying in the dark with the blankets pulled up, shaking and sweating, your teeth going in your head like maracas, and nothing you can do to *make* it make sense, alone, deserted by all your voices, just a movie playing on the ceiling, flash clips. It's Arturo's for the last set. You're launched, you're flying, you're motherfucking gone — port wine and smoke and sweet acid — and she's Astarte, Cybele, Artemis, no bullshit, Diana the Huntress in a leather miniskirt, boots to the knee and long hair swinging, five feet ten of hard muscle over clean white bone. "Say, baby, you got a whip at home?"

"Up yours, asshole," but with a hint of a smile. "Want something to drink or you just come in to look?"

The drummer's dropping bombs — ka-blam, spang, splat — the bass man, standup, is walking it away with that old four-four like time itself, and horns, bebop, a-rebop. "Have a double nectar with a dash of ambrosia, peach pit on the side," but she brings you a beer, saying, "Out of ambrosia, will this do?"

"Sure. And will *this* do?" holding out your hand with the day-glo cap on it. The current surges her eyes wide, big green pools, and you've outcooled her.

"What's that?" You can hear the hesitation like gears stripping.

"Courtesy Mr. Stanley Owsley."

"No," she says, but you wait her out to closing time, sweeping it up under yellow lights fat as grubs. She sits down with you. There's something happening, later you'll know what it is. Her old man didn't show up again. He's back there in Roxbury out to lunch again, lying on a tabletop with a snoot full of doogie *again*, and you're sliding into home right on time. "You got anywhere to go?" she says.

"River Styx," you say, but the Charles will have to do, whipping by on Bike Number Two, making the lights streak out, her breasts pressed against your back, bare thighs straddling your black iron horse, thunder like apocalypse. Stop to watch how the water shimmers, hot night, couples strolling. Dope's no problem for her, doing up a J, but it'll take her months to get around to admitting how scared she was of that other thing, that little earthshaker from California. She aint going to show it though, nothing but hard and bouncing back like a load-bearing spring, kiss in the summer dark until you're panting for her like a starved yellow hound. "You going to tease me to death, baby shake?"

For an answer she slips off her panties, nothing fancy, just your standard-issue white cotton, and throws them at you. "Not here," she says. "I'm not much of a nature girl."

Behind the acid your apartment building is an exotic Medici palace, balcony around a courtyard where the sky could fall down. Peter's door next to yours is open, spilling tungsten light, seems perfectly normal for him to be at home to the world, his living room opening out into the night itself, and every breeze scented with dope and incense, dreamy black ooze of opium from a left-hand corner shadow, warm pulse of safety, children's hive, Eden where no Boston cop would come, not tonight, and no CIA, FBI, intergalactic mind police either. You look up and see all the other open doors, half a dozen. It's a conspiracy. Everybody's tuned into the same radio station and all the radios are giving us sweet Grace and the Airplane.

Kathy loves it, you can see it, and looking up three floors you see Jerry, your bass player, and his blond lady, hair hanging down like Rapunzel. He throws you a star, lump of hash big as a marble right into your perfect palms. Peter and his Lolita, little mod girl with hair cut off like a boy's, have wrapped you up in a smoky embrace and kisses all around. You even kissed him, a silly smooch, while Kathy and the girl kissed for real, open-mouthed. Kathy whispered in your ear, "Come *on*, man!" Drifted into separate couples, separate apartments, closed doors, and you offered her again that glowing orange owl. She knelt and licked it off your fingers, tongue like a wisp of fire. Under the soft leather skirt she was wet like the round blue earth.

Naked, you lay back on the balloon chair, and dressed, she straddled you just like she'd straddled the bike, sank down, her mouth saying, "Ah" without a sound. "You've got more hair than any boy I've ever seen," taking it between her hands, winding it around your face, and then no more words. Jesus, how the hell could you follow an act like that?

She lost her gig, of course, and the long intertwining nights began when you'd stand side by side in front of the mirror, staring. "Jesus, we look alike." White skin, black hair, the same long angular bodies, and turning away from the mirror found we'd taken the glass with us, still searching for ourselves in each other. And when we were screwing, we'd forget for hours who had the prick and who had the cunt.

But you woke to the strange night and she was a black silhouette in the doorway. "Steven, are you hungry?" Has it been thirteen years? Is it possible? Thirteen fucking years since you met her? You remember those bodies in the mirror clear as you remember anything, how unmarked they were, how white. "Steven, are you awake?" Her voice was dead as rock.

"Yeah, I'm awake. Give me a minute. My mind's kind of scattered." The silence went on. The black shape of a woman didn't move. "Light a light," you said, and immediately, like she'd been waiting, poised, for just that cue, the overhead light bit the room into focus. She'd changed her clothes, taken off the jeans she'd been wearing, put on a sweater and a skirt. It was a message. She'd brushed her hair. Thin, beautifully intricate spiderwebs of lines sprayed away from her eyes on either side; her mouth was dented. Her face was dead as rock. "Kath?" She turned away.

"This is Paul." An enormous man in a gray suit. Stiff, careful, embarrassed. Took your hand a moment and then *he* turned away. The air was heavy, weighted at the corners, an impossible pressure. Nothing to do for it but run — the apologies, explanations, jokes, silly tumble of words already building up back of your tongue — but you were cut off at the pass by a child with unmarked white skin. She moved easily through that dead space, walked to your side and stood with you like she'd protect you if it came to that. "Did you sleep all right? Do you feel better?"

"Yeah, thanks. I was coming apart at the seams."

All of you sat down around the table. There was no sound at all but the clinking of silverware until Wendy said, "How long did it take you?"

"About thirty-six years." And Wendy was the only one who smiled.

And later you looked at Kathy to see if she was ready yet, and the next day, and the day after, but all she could say to you was, "Give me time."

Until you woke again to the strange night and there was a black silhouette in the doorway. "Sorry. I thought you were awake." And who the hell was this? Shadow at the center where the face ought to be but golden haze at the edge.

"Yeah, I am awake." Although you hadn't been.

"The door was open."

"Yeah, I sleep with the door open sometimes. Light a light."

You saw her without any labels, not even "girl." And swear to God she was so close, you were looking at her so hard, you could see the pupils in her eyes slowly contract. And then she said in a voice like that of the young Hayley Mills, "Do you often sleep with all your clothes on too?"

"If I think I've got to run. And do you often walk in on strange men in the middle of the night?"

She had no answer to that one, so you just looked at each other a while longer.

"I can't sleep," she said. "It happens to me a lot."

"Yeah, I know that one. It's a bitch."

"I did wake you, didn't I? I'm sorry."

"No, you're not. What time is it anyway?"

"It's around five. I've got to go to school in a couple hours."

"Terrific."

"I usually walk until I get sleepy again."

Don't ask why, but there you are trotting along with her through the streets of Kerrisdale. She's talking to you like you're a goofy old uncle who used to bounce her on his knee. "I started getting insomnia the summer I was thirteen," she says. "Before that I wouldn't have been able to imagine what it might have been like... to go to bed and not fall right to sleep. I suppose there's a very simple explanation for it. My period started that fall, and so my body must have been changing. It didn't make any difference how tired I was. Sometimes when I was most tired, that's when it'd be the worst, three or four nights in a row."

Moving fast against the chill drift of rain, blocks without seeing anybody. "Thank you for walking with me," she says. "It's better than staying in bed and worrying. I'll feel awful tomorrow, but tomorrow night I'll be asleep by nine or ten."

You keep on going until the houses run out, until you're on a road on into the middle of nowhere, and she says with no lead in, "Why wouldn't Kathy play with your band?"

"Oh, she told you about that, did she? Shit, I never knew why she wouldn't."

"She said that she always thought you wanted her for the flash and not the music."

You look over at her, little blond kid in her yellow raincoat. You've seen her for years, always somewhere at the back of the crowd, silent and motionless and golden and impossible, and she's the one you've been playing for since you first picked up a set of drumsticks. Yeah, you've seen her a million times, thought, I know why you're here, baby, sweet baby, and before the night's over, you're going to move to *my* beat. But this one's too close for comfort. She knows something and she wants something.

"How do you separate the flash from the music? I suppose we could have prerecorded her and played the tape, but put her on the stage and there's no way she could have been anything but beautiful."

"I've used it," Wendy says. "It made me feel... I don't know. It felt as though I were debasing the music."

"Don't know about your music, but with rock and roll, it comes with the territory."

And where you've got to amazingly fast could be another country, another time. No streetlights anymore, broad country roads, can even hear horses off somewhere, snorting, and the iron sky hanging over it all like misfortune. "Where the hell are we?"

"This is called the Southlands," she says, and, "I've got to go back now. I've got to practice."

But neither of you made a move, and the light started to spread out at the edge, that running slit of blue that's called dawn, and swear to God you saw her then, light to light, like she was ready to slip away through the crack and set up her home in paradise.


Steve needed a smoke, sat up, lit one. Paced for the millionth time the length of the small room, and back — doing hard time. Sat down again to look through the note cards that'd been waiting there so patiently for him to get around to them. Who got burnt for saying that the Jews were Christians already, who got hung up to starve in an iron cage for saying that the Trinity didn't exist or that everybody was going to get saved, even Satan. Notes about a bunch of crazy fuckers meeting naked in a cave until the Inquisition grabbed their asses. The Greater Question and the Lessor, and sweet Jesus, it's unbelievable what they did to people with their wheels and red-hot pincers and molten lead and just simple things like water and rags. And yeah, of course, fire. And how the hell could a human being do

any of that to another human being? But you know the answer
to that one, don't you? Bobby Lyons' voice: "You should have
spent the night with the question boys, Stevo. It was a real riot."
Safe and sane Kerrisdale? You bet. Sure he's sane, a real
professor, every note card's got its footnote. Yeah, candy man,
so isn't it about time you put your show on the road?

Steve pulled his boots on, walked out of the guest room and
on down the hall. Planned to pause at the living-room door,
planned to say, "See you folks later," planned to get in the van,
drive it away, keep on going. Where? Don't ask. What do you
want, man, a future? But at the living-room door saw the fire,
saw Wendy in front of it knee socks and all, and she gave him a
grin, saw her old man in his chair with his books, making more
note cards. Sorry, folks, I changed my mind. Please let me in,
just for a while, just one more time. Swear to God, I won't make
a mess. Let me sit by the fire and get warm, just for a while, just
one more time. Swear to God, you won't be able to tell the
difference between me and a houseguest.


All right, Paul thought, where were we? If van Dorestad entered
the Brotherhood at sixteen, he would have been born in 1490,
right at the time when the *Maleus Maleficarum* was being
promulgated. That would mean he'd been married at twenty-
four, martyred at Wesel at seventy-one. That was all plausible
enough. And he would have been twenty-six when Hieronymus
Bosch died.

Van Dorestad must certainly have known Bosch, who would
have been a venerable figure in that small, lively town. He must
certainly have been influenced by Bosch's obscure, strangely
pornographic images. Like Bosch, he may have been acquainted
with alchemy, occult lore, the Adamite heresy. Van Dorestad
was married in his twenties, in his forties was paid for singing,
choir leading, and composing. He probably had been a musician
his entire life, trained in the Church. By his early fifties, he was
in Antwerp, still working as a composer. It was then, in all
likelihood, that he wrote the superb motet, *Tunc Jesus Ductus
Est*, that ranks him in skill with the best of the Netherlandish
composers.

And Paul heard a faint movement, looked up, was startled to
see that Kathy's husband had walked in so quietly he hadn't
heard him, was standing tentatively a few feet back from the
fire. Paul smiled automatically. The man gave him a nod, an
expression that was what? apologetic? and settled into a chair,

carefully placed his run-down cowboy boots on the hassock and picked up the newspaper. Paul saw the man and his daughter exchange a look, a greeting. Well, he's certainly made a hit with her, he thought.

But back to van Dorestad. Right. Not only did he excel in traditional counterpoint, but he experimented with chromaticism, invented an ingenious and elaborate system to hide the innovative quality of his work. He was a man expert in ambiguity, secrecy, double meaning. He must have written a huge body of material, but only this one motet survives; the rest must have been seized and burnt by the Inquisition. So van Dorestad must have been branded a heretic. And did he publicly proclaim his faith, take up his cross in imitation of Christ, court martyrdom — like the Anabaptists? Most emphatically not. By his late fifties, he was appearing with his son, playing secular dance music, a social shift comparable to that of Murray Schafer ending his career by playing in the Canadian Legion. When they were finally caught, they must have been hiding out; van Dorestad's son claimed that they were only "poor minstrel singers," but it obviously didn't wash. At seventy-one, van Dorestad was tried, and executed. Was this the career of an Anabaptist? Not bloody likely.

Let us now, Paul thought, ask some basic questions. Why did van Dorestad move from 'sHertogenbosch to Antwerp? Well, if one wished to be at the centre of things, Antwerp was the place — but dangerous. The first victims of the Inquisition had died at Antwerp. When? Paul began searching through his note cards. But heard the rustle of the newspaper, was caught, then pulled back into the present, glanced up, saw that the man's face was hidden by the *Vancouver Sun* — Kathy's husband: how very odd. And Wendy was yawning. "Sleepy?" he said.

She shrugged. Poor kid, he thought, waiting so patiently. But he continued to look for the date.

"What's in the paper?" Wendy asked Kathy's husband.

"Cloudy with showers," the man answered her.

"That's news?"

"Guess not, huh? The bus strike's still on."

Wendy giggled. "You don't have to tell me *that*."

It's curious, Paul thought, how easily the two of them talk to each other. He gave up on the Lutheran. "You could get your driver's license," he said.

She came back at him immediately. "I'd be delighted to get my license. Do you have time to give me driving lessons?"

Yes, he thought, it's long past time to close up the books for the night. "Don't they have a driver's training course at your school?"

"Stafford House? Daddy, you must be joking."

He gave her the smile that would tell her that he had been, and her expression said something like, "Oh, you're hopeless." She stood, stretched, poked at the fire.

"Bunch of terrorists snatched some dude in Italy," Kathy's husband said from behind the paper. "Blew away all five of his bodyguards."

"Why?" Wendy asked.

"Beats me. I've kind of let my firm grasp of Italian politics slip a bit in the last few years. But here's one I really like. Seems like the lead pollution in Vancouver is higher than it is in Trail where they've got one of the world's biggest lead smelters. But health officials say there's no need to worry. Don't you just love the way they always take care of everything for us?"

There's no point in going over everything one knows about Antwerp, Paul thought. A much more interesting question is what was van Dorestad doing in Wesel when he was captured, tried, and executed? It was 1561; what was happening then? Paul sorted through his notes, found an entry. "Netherlands, 1561. The Inquisitor appealed to the Regent to put the armed forces in a state of alert. Fear of a general uprising." And a few years later that uprising would occur: the Dutch would go to war and throw out the Spanish — along with their Church and their hated Inquisition.

But where was Wesel? Paul found it on a map on the flyleaf in one of the books at his feet: a dot that appeared to be on the river Rhine. A good, healthy distance from Antwerp, but obviously not far enough to keep van Dorestad out of trouble.

"Some of the headlines are a real riot," Kathy's husband said. "U.S. Science Hunting for Death Beam. Boy Spattered with Blood Standing behind Victim."

"You have a morbid sense of humour," Wendy said, but she was laughing.

"Yeah? And here's the best one of all. You ready for it? It's perfect. You remember William Calley, the My Lai massacre dude? Well, he's residing down in Columbus, Georgia, these days, and he says his main ambition in life is to sink into anonymity."

"Why is that funny?"

"Guess it helps if you've actually been to Columbus, Georgia."

Paul saw Wendy looking at him with puzzlement in her eyes. She wants some help, he thought. "You're from Georgia, aren't you?" he said to the strange man, not knowing what else to say.

"Sure. Atlanta."

"Do you ever go back?"

"Last time was, I guess... sixty-six or sixty-seven."

"Do you miss it?" Wendy asked.

"Miss it? No. You don't miss a place if you've never left it."

From what Kathy had told him, Paul had been expecting her husband to be a wild, demonic madman, but Steven Beuhl wasn't like that at all; rather he seemed vague, misplaced, apologetic. A helpful man who made his own bed, never left a dirty dish in the sink. A cleanly man who washed his entire threadbare wardrobe every few nights, who showered every day and wore an aftershave as sweet as a woman's perfume. And this man's compelling, dark, somewhat red-rimmed eyes were now focused precisely on his; Paul was the first to look away.

Wendy was yawning enormously. "Why don't you go warm up?" he said to her. "I'll be along in a moment."

And then Paul saw his daughter and Kathy's husband exchange a look that was affectionate, even tender. "Good night," she said. Paul heard Wendy's footsteps as she climbed the stairs, walked on down the hall and into her room.

Paul closed up his books and notes, packed them away in his briefcase. "Thanks for putting up with me," Steve Beuhl said.

Profoundly surprised, Paul looked up. The man's eyes were gleaming with a moist intensity. There was a curious mixture of hardness and softness in that face: sharply aquiline nose with a Z-shaped bump at the bridge (had it been broken?); tight, thin lips, badly chapped, and high, hard cheekbones, but the chin had a gentle cleft in it, and the smile changed everything. It was the engaging smile of a sad, difficult little boy who knows how to be charming. The man's forehead was high, white, and lined. His skin had a yellowish cast, looked unhealthy, but his hands were beautiful — slender and long-fingered, with high, standing veins like blue wires. There was no doubt about it: despite a considerable seediness, there was also a peculiar and compelling dignity to this man.

"The standard response," Paul said, "is, 'Oh, it's been no trouble.' But I can't honestly say that. I have enjoyed meeting you, getting some sense of you."

"Yeah, same for me. But it's long past time for me to put it on the road, huh? We both know that. And believe it or not, I am going to do it. Next couple days probably. And I did want to say thanks."

And Paul knew that *he* should say something more now. But

what? The silence was growing increasingly uncomfortable.

"What are you working on?" Steve Beuhl asked him.

"Oh. A sixteenth-century motet. Obscurity of obscurities, actually."

"Odd that we're both musicians. Or maybe not so odd. Kathy always got off on musicians."

Paul most emphatically did not want to discuss Kathy. "I'm not sure I'd describe myself as a musician," he said.

"You must play something."

Paul pointed at the harpsichord. "I've been told that I'm a good continuo player."

"You work from a figured bass?" The man must have seen the startled expression on Paul's face; he grinned, said, "Ha! Fooled you. You took me for a cretin."

Paul felt an irrational blur of emotion; the conversation could spin away from him, out of his control. Of the possible progressions, he chose the safest. "Yes, of course I work from a figured bass. It's the only way to do it."

"I knew you'd say that. If that ain't a musician, I don't know what is."

"Oh, I don't know. As long as you remember never to allow both hands to move in the same direction at the same time, you stay out of trouble."

"Come on, professor, give yourself a break."

"All right, it's *not* that simple. Yes, you do have to have the theory absolutely down in your bones to do it. And I do. But I don't practice enough to be first rate."

"Yeah? Me, neither. I just play. On my good nights, they say you can't tell the difference between me and a drummer."

Upstairs Wendy was playing the Marais. Steve smiled. "She's good."

"Oh, indeed."

"You've got a good life here."

"I think so."

"Look, man, I'll... Ah, shit, let me get it just as simple as I can. Kathy and I have been split up for years, and it's all just a formality now. If she ever wants to start the paperwork, I'll make sure she always knows where I am. You following me?"

"Of course. Thank you."

And, once again, it was an ideal time to end the conversation, but Paul couldn't quite do it. "What kind of music do you play?" he asked.

"Anything with a pay cheque attached."

"What do you love, then?"

He saw something change in the man's face. "Good question. Straight down the highway kick-ass rock and roll. Played every other damn thing under the sun, but I keep coming back to that. And no matter where it's going, I seem to be able to go with it... No, that's not right. Now *I'm* bullshitting *you*. The truth is I can still keep them scrambling to match me, even if they are kids... Just keep wondering how much longer. Hard to grow old in the rock business, you know... But what do I love? Looking out on the dance floor and seeing the honeys moving to my beat."

The man spoke with his voice pitched high in his head; it was a nasal, eloquent, carrying orator's voice — both American and southern — neither of which qualities Paul usually heard as attractive, but from this man speech was attractive. It was true: as unlikely as it should have been, Paul liked this man. "Functional music?" he said.

"You got it."

"I've played Renaissance dance music, but no one was dancing. I wished they had been. I've often thought about what it must have been like in a small town when the whole community danced, when they played all night long. Certainly not a *performance*, not a decorous evening with an audience sitting politely, listening, applauding after each piece. It was the... to use your words... the straight down the highway kick-ass music of its time. And I've often thought... If I were not constantly circumscribed by the university, if I could do exactly what I wanted, I'd try to play it the way it should be played."

"Maybe you will yet."

"Maybe I will."

Steve Beuhl looked away; he appeared to be thinking. "It's not just that it's functional," he said. "It's something else. Something... ah, shit." He turned and looked directly at Paul. "It's in the heart."

Paul met the man's gaze and held it, not comfortably; he felt a profound, wordless exchange. And this, certainly, was the time to stop. But Paul wanted a sense of resolution. And he saw, suddenly, the Renaissance image of the turning wheel: *fortuna*. Knowing full well that the modern phrase would not carry the weight of that image, he said it anyway: "Good luck."

# VIII

Sure, you can make it all make sense. Sure you can, Stevo. Now you can hear a deep sad, melody played so assured, so fluid it could be a record, but it's not, it's Wendy, and you've memorized every inch of the ceiling. Even in a professor's house they've got cobwebs. Inhale the smoke that'll kill you if something else doesn't do it first and run by a few more flash clips. Pick any night when she scratched at your door, when you got up, dressed, because you were waiting for her and found her ready with her raincoat on.

Got to know every twist and turn of those Southlands, feeling them out in the dark. And what is it she wants to know? Shit, she wants to know everything.

Nothing sleazier than a night-town club in the middle of the afternoon, warehouse off Queen Street with the windows boarded up, bunch of old tables and folding chairs, and some damn fool painter with a high-heel fetish has slapped up gigantic canvases all over the place, paint thick and ragged, women from the waist down, walking up stairs, walking down stairs, or just standing still in the middle of some dumb fuck's back. Outside it's snowing like Siberia, but you'd never know it, might as well be an air-raid shelter. Nobody there but the band and the old gimpster, the dude who sweeps up last night's flotsam. Spider-web light from bare bulbs and nothing to hear but the hum of the amps and his broom going swish swish swish.

But in a few hours you'll be playing again for real, and the kids will be dancing and the energy will run free and then you'll feel good, but it's smoke break now, and your dreams are lying low for the moment (that death you'd been thinking about like a parenthesis) but you know you can reach down and grab it any time you need it, for the kick, like riding seat of the pants an inch above a railroad spike.

"What's that mean?"

"What's what mean?"

"Death like a railroad spike."

"Ah, shit, kid, you know what it means. Death, right? I mean for real, no bullshit, when you remember you're going to die. Really, really, really. And you can't let yourself remember all the time or you'd go nuts on the terror of it, so you keep it around for the kick. So when you're alive, you can live, you know, boot it on home. Which is why I can play with a bunch of teenagers, and they're scrambling to match my beat. You got it?"

"Yes. I understand."

Want to run, want to run, want to run, Jesus, energy driving you howling nuts down to your fingernails. And slamming down on the beat, you see Alison's evil eyes looking straight at you. "Harder." You dig for it, murder under your sticks. "Harder." Jesus fuck. Sweat jumping down your sides. "Harder." You want it, you got it, babe, and it's there, finally, riding the edge of catastrophe. This hard enough for you, bitch?

But listen. It's not then, it's before, it's in the pause. Maybe it's in the afternoon when you're rehearsing or maybe it's at night just before you start your first set, but there's a moment big and blank as a goose egg, and that's what counts. Sometimes you can hold it for just a second or two, other times it can last whole minutes. If you think, *my God, this is weird*, you've already lost it, but while you're in it, *there's no time*. (It's like when you walked into my room that first night, but I'm not going to tell you that.) And when you've been there, it comes through in your sound. A lot of people try to fake it, but there's no way you can fake it. Listen, do you know what I'm talking about? *It's when there's no time*.

Listen, Wendy, you've got to believe me.

Wait a minute, candy man, who're you talking to? She's not around to hear you. He sat up, lit a new cigarette from the butt of the old one. Lay back again to stare at the ceiling.

*Moment* and *memory* should be from the same root, he thought, too bad they're not, and glad you still keep the Harvard boy around to come up with shit like that. But anyhow, they're not connected, one's about *motion*, the other's about *mind*. *Moment*: momentum, movement, a minute portion of time. *Memory*: memorial, mindful, musing, brooding; the Greek root means trouble, and it's a service for the dead. Perfect, huh? It's all right there. And no matter what you do, moments turn into memories and then they're not real anymore. Or else they're too real. Like the blood that's everywhere.

Blood splashed on the floor. Walls smeared with blood. Like somebody was painting with blood. You're floating easily around your apartment without a care in the world. It's evening. Was morning when Kathy left, sun high and harsh and yellow. The time's gone, that's it. It's so simple you've got to laugh at it. Right, it's happened before, the time kind of fell away, and that's all there is to it. Was after she took off the black vinyl raincoat, threw it at you, took off the mini dress, the boots, threw them at you, said, "They're your turn-on, Steven, you wear them." After she took a shower. After she got dressed again, in jeans and a T-shirt. After she said, "You and Lyons should fuck each other and cut out the middleman." Yeah, it was right after that.

But wonder how everything got broken, how the chairs got smashed, the stereo got kicked in, every plate and saucer reduced to a million fragments on the floor. Odd, you're thinking, like somebody went through with a hammer, almost funny. Somebody must have been really pissed off. And then you look at the big full-length mirror and see that it's completely smashed, brilliant shining needles of glass exploded in all directions, and the wood backing doesn't reflect a damned thing. The wood backing is smeared with blood.

You step outside onto the porch, into the lovely icy air — October, twilight, the crack between the worlds, and Don Juan's never around when you need him. But who needs him because the moment's big and blank as a goose egg and there's no time. You light a smoke and the white paper immediately soaks up blood. It's all over your fingers. Trying to smoke, you get it on your mouth. Sticky, warm, a little salty, kind of fun. And somebody's banging on the door. How odd that there's people, separate, walking around with their separate minds thinking to themselves. How odd that *anything* is. Everything that is could be some other way. And Peter's yelling, "Steven, are you in here? Jesus, fuck! What the hell's happened?"

Then he's on the porch with you, big puppy-dog eyes, and he believes in it all so much you've got to laugh. If you're a person with a separate mind thinking to itself, you're *supposed* to believe in it, you're not supposed to notice that it just is and you can't possibly make it make sense. "Steven," he says. "Jesus fucking Christ, man, you're bleeding to death."

"No problem. Just some of that good old-fashioned high melodrama we've all heard so much about."

"What the hell happened?"

*Happened? If the moment's over, it's memory, and memory isn't real.* "Beats the hell out of me."

"Where's Kathy?"

Annoying how he's forcing you to pretend it's real. "Shit. I don't know. She's off somewhere. Don't worry man, none of this blood's hers."

And that hooks you. Because, if she hadn't walked out, *some of this blood would have been hers.*

"She went out last night and fucked Lyons," you say just like it matters.

"Why?"

"Isn't that what they do when they want to get your ass? Go fuck somebody else? *Isn't that what they always do?*"

He's staring at you. "For Christ's sake, we've got to get an ambulance."

"For what?"

*"Steven, you're bleeding to death!"*

He drags you inside, makes you lie down on the floor. Naturally you've ripped the phone out by the roots, "Shit, shit, shit," he's yelling. "I'm going across the hall. Don't move, man. I mean it."

Flat on the floor, stare at the ceiling, and you know you're back because the fear's so big if you didn't grind your teeth together, you'd be screaming.

And then you know where you've been. You'd already checked out. Oh God, how absolutely tacky human life is.

They let him ride in the ambulance with you, and you're drifting, getting goofy, but you remember him saying, "He's evil. He doesn't deserve to live."

"Aw, come on, Peter, who can say that about anybody?"

"I mean it. I'm going to get him."

And you sure got him, didn't you, old buddy? Yep. And I've always wondered what you were thinking that last moment when you were running down that alley in Roxbury and you felt that first forty-four magnum slug catch you in the small of your back. Know by the third or the fourth one, you weren't thinking anything at all, and now you're a dead man's voice in my mind, and so's Lyons.

Hey, fellows. Where did you go?

"I loved the year I was twelve," Wendy said. "I really wanted to stay there."

What does she want from you? Steve thought. Don't cop out and say "everything." There's something specific she wants, something rock solid, down home, good old nuts-and-bolts kind of want. "What was so great about being twelve?" he asked her.

"I'm not sure. I really hated being little... No, that's not right. I didn't hate it. I didn't know enough to hate it. When you're little, things are just the way they are. It's only when I looked back on it I realized I hated it. Dad always thought I was wonderful, but Mom... You haven't met her, have you? I look like her. I'm small and blond like her. But I have Dad's eyes. I suppose I think like him too. But what was I saying? Am I boring you?"

"One thing you aint doing, kid, is boring me."

"Anyhow, the only thing Mom liked doing with me was taking me out so her friends would see us together and say, 'Oh, Ev, she's so beautiful. *She looks just like you.*' So she'd dress me up like a... well, like an icy-sticky sweet little girl. Don't laugh. You should have seen me. And off we'd go to the ballet or the opera or the symphony, and... This must all have a point. What was I talking about?"

"What a hot shit year it was being twelve."

"That's right. It was a perfect year somehow. Mom started leaving me alone, and... Oh! She must have started having her affair with Davey then. I just now thought of it. That makes sense. Yes, she must have. And I didn't see much of her, and Cindy and I were getting along OK, and I made a big jump with the gamba.

"I've made two big jumps. That was the first one. All of a sudden it stopped fighting me, or I stopped fighting it, or something. That was the year it stopped being notes and started to be music, I mean really fast, almost overnight. The second big jump was after I had a lesson with Klaas Achterberg in Amsterdam last summer. But anyhow, the year I was twelve, all of a sudden everything was right. That was it, Steven, it just felt right." And suddenly she was giggling like a ten-year-old. "It was before I got my period. See, I'm a textbook case."

She reached out and took his hand just like it was the most natural thing in the world, and they walked along like that, hand in hand, on back into the Southlands where there wasn't a single streetlight, and it was the goddamned middle of the night. Don't ask, candy man, just do it.

"My gamba teacher would like to make love to me," she said,

and she was holding Steve's hand. "I can tell by the way he looks at me."

"Do you like that?"

"Yes and no. It's flattering and it's scary. Oh, he'd never do anything about it. Dad would kill him... You know, some men get turned on by girls in school uniforms. I can see the way they look at me on the bus. Why is that?" And she was holding his hand.

"A sexy body in a little-kid outfit, right? Like a girl and a woman, both things at once. It's a mind game. Men get off on mind games."

"I know that. I don't know how I know it, but I do. Sometimes I think I know too much. Maybe that's what I liked about being twelve. I was still *asleep*. Does that make any sense?"

"Sure."

"I hope you don't mind me telling you all this, Steven. I don't really have anybody to talk to. I can talk to Kathy, but... well, not lately I can't. Ever since you came back, she's been... Well, you know how she's been. But I hope you don't mind me telling you all this.

"You know, I have a real talent for getting what I want. The problem is that I don't *know* what I want. To play the gamba as well as Klaas, I do know I want that. It sounds arrogant, but I don't mean it that way. I feel really humble about it too, but if... I don't know. What was I saying? Oh, I know I'm afraid of sex. There are girls in my class... even at Stafford House, can you believe it? And they're already having sex. But it's not simple. It's not just that I'm afraid of it. I'm afraid I'd like it too much. Am I embarrassing you?" And she was holding his hand.

So what could he say to that? "Sex can be anything at all."

"Oh, come on, Steven, don't do that to me."

He had to laugh at that one. "All right, damn it, it *can* be anything at all. It can be fun like a couple kids playing, or it can be boring, or it can be a drug, you know, like you've got to get it or you'll die. Or it can be a real bummer, like maybe the ugliest time you've ever had in your life. And it can be... well, shit, the closest you ever get to God. Something like that."

"What's that like? When it's the closest you ever get to God?"

She stopped walking so he stopped too. She was still holding his hand. And even in that muddy dark, he could still see how blond she was. "No words for that one. You go to church ever?"

"Of course. When I was little."

"OK, then, it's like grace. The grace of the Holy Spirit."

Dawn was at the edge. He waited. He knew he had to wait for

her. "I know that too," she said. "I don't know how, but I know that too."


Stuck in his goddamned little white cell, fly to flypaper, Steve felt himself flattening out a little more every day, getting more useless and goofy. He lay on the same goddamned narrow little bed, smoking cigarettes, watching the reruns on the ceiling, thinking — go out, asshole, go anywhere, drive around in circles, sit on the beach in the rain, do any fucking thing, but don't stay here. Or maybe even talk to Kathy. How's that for stimulating, award-winning, absolutely novel idea? Yeah, just go and have a little heart to heart after all these years. That'll fix up everything, won't it? But then it took him hours to get around to it — to lever himself up, put himself in motion, one foot after the other. He found her sitting at the kitchen table. She had on a sweater and a green wool skirt, and she looked up at him when he walked in and then looked away and she didn't move a muscle when he sat down.

"Well, how you doing, old buddy?"

She said nothing.

"Gee, Kath, you sure are making things difficult with all that cheery bright chatter pouring out of your mouth. Hard for a man to get a word in edgewise, if you know what I mean."

And the front doorbell rang. "Your timing's impeccable, asshole," she said in a dead flat voice, got up and walked away with her skirt snapping.

Steve stood up. Don't pay any attention to me, folks, just the friendly neighborhood idiot. Saw the professor arrive at the door at the same time Kathy did, saw an old lady in a black dress, people coming up behind her. Fled back to his cell and closed himself in. Heard the hum and bustle out there. Oh yeah, they'd been talking about it. Some kind of rehearsal.

Then, *ring*, the telephone. Then Wendy was tapping at the door. "Steven, it's for you."

For me? he thought. Jesus, you've got to be kidding. I don't exist, I'm anonymous, I'm a black hole, for Christ's sake. He walked into the kitchen, grabbed up the phone, and it was good old Annie Epoxy. "Alison?"

"Who the fuck do you think it is, your fairy godmother?"

"Where, ah... Where you calling from?"

"Toronto, asshole. It's where I live, remember?"

Through the door to the living room Steve could see Paul chatting with the old lady. And Wendy hadn't moved. Wendy had curiosity oozing out every pore. Wendy was standing three feet away from him. Sometimes she looked to him like a cat at a window — a fixed round-eyed stare — and she looked like that now, her eyes aimed right into his, and she was playing wonder child for her daddy, so what he was seeing was an impeccable picture of Little Miss Innocence in a jumper and knee socks and what he was hearing was an evil pissed-off voice yelling at him across three thousand miles. "You're fucked, you know that? You old, burnt-out, fucked-up shit. You're *old*, asshole. You're dead. You're a walking corpse, man. You're a fucking disaster."

"Hey, Ali, lay off. I told you the night I met you. Find a kid your own age."

"Lots of drummers in town, man, but none like you. That's when you're alive. The only time. No, that's not right. In bed. You're alive there too. The rest of the time it's voodoo city. Jesus, I'm so fucking pissed off at you. You gone back to your old woman or what? Who's your toy now, Steven?"

"Well Christ, Ali, it's a little difficult to carry on this sort of, ah... conversation at the moment. If you follow me. It's, ah... kind of out of the question, as a matter of fact."

"Out of the question my fucking ass. You're fucked, you *old man*."

And Wendy was looking straight into his eyes. He covered the mouthpiece, said, "Get the hell out of here, will you? Jesus Christ, kid."

She looked like he'd slapped her. Then was gone in a flash. And all of a sudden it had kicked in — that good old killer's juice. If Alison had been standing in front of him, he could have beat her to death with a chair. "Hey, bitch. Shut up a minute. Who the hell are you to be doing what you're doing? You knew why I came up to your place that night. Goddamn right you knew. Didn't you?"

"Yeah, I knew."

"Sure you did. So why the hell don't you go back to wherever the hell you come from... Where the hell is it you come from, anyway? Rosedale? *Who the hell are you?* Don't give me that old-man shit. You're a goddamned suicide case. Ten lines of toot up your nose every fucking set and catering to the sicko trade. Great stuff."

"I stopped that when I was with you. I never saw another man when I was with you." Jesus, and now she was crying.

"Oh, my God, Alison, cut it out. You're better off without me. Yeah, it's fucked, it's all fucked, you said it, but do you have to go out that way? Who you want to be? Janis? Morrison?

Hendrix? You want to kiss the sky and get out? You know who the hell I am if anybody does. What the hell were you doing playing around with *me*?"

And so, of course, she told him. He stood in the bright, friendly kitchen, listened to her voice over the phone line, and thought, Jesus, when you hang up, it'll be gone, the moment will be memory, and then it'll be just another one of the voices in your head going on and on.

"I thought we could make it," she said. "You're the only man I ever... You were so fucking careful, man. And it's so easy to slip with that shit. You think I'm dumb, or what? *You know what it's like, Steven.* And we trusted each other. And I never slipped either, not once. Did I? Did I ever slip?

"You know how good that was? We're a perfect fit. You think you're going to find somebody else like me? I've got another drummer. He's not as good as you, but nobody's as good as you. But I don't care about any of that. I don't want a drummer, I want you. Why'd you leave me, Steven?"

Good question. Why'd you leave Georgia? Why'd you leave Harvard? Why'd you leave the United States of America? Why'd you leave Kathy? And, same as always, Lyons' voice was there to whisper the answer in his ear.

Now he was crying too, but he held it in, his chest filling up with the bitter sea and the ceiling coming down like iron. In the next room they were singing, in *Latin*, for Christ's sake, and Wendy's voice was just as pure and fine as he'd known it would be. So what could he say to that other voice so far away? *I love you too?*

"How'd you find me, Ali?"

"If you're not planning on paying the phone bill, you can find anybody. Look, man, I'm coming out there. I got a seat sale. Do you want to meet me at the airport, or are you going to make me look for you? I'll find you, you know."

"Oh, goddamn it, Alison." So far down he'd try any lame thing. "You can't afford that. Where the hell did you get the money?"

"From my dear old dad. He owes me, and he knows it. You didn't even guess close... Rosedale? Jesus! Caledon Hills. And I was just a fucked up little kid playing an electric guitar up in her room, playing it through a headset so I wouldn't disturb anybody, so I wouldn't be any trouble to anybody. I was nothing. I didn't exist.

"Nice respectable family, eh? Nice quiet girl, doesn't give anybody any shit. Hardly opens her mouth. Some days you can't see her at all. Sits in school and prays, dear God, don't let them be drunk again. Then an hour later, she's praying, dear God, I changed my mind. Let them be drunk. Let *him* be so drunk he won't come into my room again tonight. Oh, you better believe he owes me. All right, Steven, you got it? Now someday you're going to have to tell me how *you* got so fucked up. Are you going to meet me at the airport or what?"


Back in his cell, Steve heard them singing a cappella, church music, that old stuff the professor was into, with Wendy on top like the angel on the Christmas tree. And he waited, old crooked drummer, counting out the time. At a quarter of three in the morning, she turned up with her pajamas still on. "I'm too tired to walk tonight. Can we just stay here?"

He closed the door. She sat on the edge of the bed. She was shivering. "I'm scared, Steven."

"What are you scared of?"

"I don't know. We're not doing anything wrong, are we?"

Anything wrong? Good God, kid, whatever made you think a thing like that? But he said, "What? Talking to each other?"

"Oh, I know we're not doing anything wrong, but I know what it'd look like if somebody caught us. It's strange, isn't it? Hold my hand, Steven. I'm really scared."

He took her hand and she was cold and wet. "Jesus, kid, you're freezing."

They were whispering because upstairs Wendy's father and Steve's wife were sleeping. At least he hoped they were sleeping. And she was holding onto his hand like a lifeline. "I don't know how to tell you," she said. "It isn't that I know what to say and I can't bring myself to say it. It's that I don't quite know how to... All right. When I played my first solo with the Pro Musica, what I said to myself was, I'll show them. They don't think I have it, but I do. Not just technique. Not even musicality. A lot more than that. What it takes to *feel* the music. Something in the heart."

"Did you?"

"As it turned out, I had more than that, and... Steven? Is it all right for me to tell you this? What are you thinking? You're the only person I've ever met who can... I know you can understand me."

He really didn't want to hear that one. What the fuck do they take you for, he thought, a rehabilitation center for damaged girls? But he said, "Go ahead. Give me more of it."

"I hear the way the music *should* be. Not all the time but

sometimes. And Dad thinks I've been studying, reading Thurston Dart or somebody, but I haven't been. He says, 'You've really been doing your homework, Gwendolyn.' He's really proud of me. And I feel like such a fraud, because I haven't been doing any homework. I just *heard it right*. Do you understand? It's almost like a radio. This is specific, Steven. Every period of music has its own ornamentation, its own conventions, and... You said about your music, 'You can't fake it.' Well, this is nothing you can fake. You've either got it or you don't, and *I can hear it*, and it really scares me. What is it? It feels... I don't know."

"Dangerous."

"Yes. Exactly."

"Shit, you're talking about a power position, an energy position, right? There are lines that hold the world together, but sometimes they fall away, and then you're out there in the middle of a big black nowhere, and *anything* could be coming through you, right? It *is* dangerous. You're right to be afraid of it."

And *you'd* better start being afraid of it too, candy man, because all those warning lights are blinking, those blood-red signs saying: *Stop*. And what *you're* hearing is a high pitched wail, a keening like the muezzin in the tower, that sound that's always been there in rock, black dudes had it first and then it came sneaking into top-forty mainstream through Maurice Williams and the Four Seasons and a dozen other groups, and it's the sound that says you're dealing with a condition that's got no relief. "What else you afraid of?" But you already know the answer to that one.

"I'm not sure if I can... All right, it started in Amsterdam."

"Hey. Wendy. We're not talking about Amsterdam. Right? We're talking about right now."

She hasn't learned yet to have a face that won't give her away. No accident that Alison was yelling at you from Toronto and now the same damned night you've got this one sitting on your bed. She's so furious she could start screaming and blow the whole show. Except that she won't, you know she won't. But she's going to get you. Yeah, you can see it coming.

In her pajama top she's got a pocket, and out of the pocket she pulls a piece of paper, hands it to you. It's the piece of paper underneath the one on the pad by the phone in the kitchen, and she's rubbed over it with a soft pencil so you can read it clear as what Moses brought back from God — the flight number, the day, the time. "Who's this?" she says.

"Jesus, kid, who the hell are you, my parole officer?"

"I'm sorry. I don't know what I'm doing."

"You sure as hell don't."

This is it. The knife's in the pocket of your jacket right where it's been since you picked it up on your way out of town. Why? Don't ask why. You hand it to her.

"What's this? I don't understand."

"Just take it, all right? Yeah, that's the way to hold it. Now press the button."

The soft murderous click and the blade's out. Scared her half to death and that's exactly what you want.

"*That's* who's coming in on that plane, all right? First night I met her, she threatened to cut my balls off with that thing, all right? She's a singer, and I was her drummer, all right? We fucked each other, all right? That's who she is. *Now what the hell is it to you?*"

"How do you close this?"

"Push on the button and then push on the blade."

She folds that cutting edge away, then drops the knife into her pocket. She takes the piece of paper and pushes *that* into her pocket. Now her face isn't giving her away, and you don't know who she is anymore. "No, Steven. That's not the right question. *Who am I to you?* That's the right question."

Score one. Don't underestimate this kid.

"You ever read Blake?" you ask her.

"Yes."

"Really, or are you just bullshitting me?"

"Yes, really."

"You know the one about the worm in the rose?"

"Yes."

"OK, you got it then."

"No, Steven. That's not right. You're not the invisible worm, and I'm no sick rose. I'm really not a sick rose. Believe me."

"Suppose I believe you, then what?"

"Then you'd stop patronizing me."

"Jesus. All right, kid, you want it, you've got it. The years between us don't count. That I've got a prick and you've got a cunt don't count. We're eyeball to eyeball. Now tell me what you want from me."

"I want to learn from you."

"Suppose what I've got's real ugly."

"Learning's never what you expect."

"Oh, so you've read *that* too, huh?"

"I read a lot."

"Yeah, and your mind probably never turns off, does it?"

"Never."

"You're good, you know that? You're really good."

"I've been told that before."

And then, with the knife still in her pocket — Alison's knife — she was gone. He lay on the bed and listened to her gamba. She didn't start with scales this time, kicked right into the melody, la da dum, tee da da dum. It was Bach. Usually she played it fast, but now she was taking it slow as fireweed honey, and moments turn into memories, so how the hell can anything be real?


"I'm sorry about the other night," Wendy said. "I was being impossible, wasn't I?"

"Impossible? Shit."

Just like Alison, just like Kathy when you first met her, they want so much. Jesus, Steven, why don't they let you alone? Haven't you got anything better to do with your time than play midwife to crazy mutant children floating in from another galaxy? So hold her hand that's probably like a wet cold fish under her glove — you've felt her hands like that before — lean into the rain, and walk. Leave the safe and sane houses of Kerrisdale behind, walk on out into that black patch that's like another time, another country, where you can feel horses everywhere even if you can't see them. The sky's nothing but falling water so what's essential is invisible to the eye, and who the hell said that? Oh, my God, Steven, aren't you glad that your twenty years of schooling come in handy for something? No matter how weird the occasion, you can always come up with some perfectly obscure quote for it.

"I think I keep coming back here because it's like the Netherlands," Wendy said. "Like the Low Countries. You know, we drove from Amsterdam down to Antwerp."

"What the hell you talking about?"

"Listen. Can you hear the horses?"

"Hear them? What do you think, I'm deaf?"

"I don't know what it is about the horses, but... Before you came, I'd do this all alone. I'd just stand and listen. I don't know what it is I expected to hear. I used to think I had to keep coming back here because it reminded me of the Low Countries. I knew I had to remember. But then I thought, no. It's that the Low Countries reminded me of something else, and *that* reminds me to remember. Does that make any sense?"

"Oh, hell, kid, you can't always make it make sense."

"Steven? I don't seem to be able to sleep much at all anymore."

"Yeah? Well, I'm not exactly getting in my peaceful eight hours either."

"I really am sorry about the other night. Here's your damned knife back."

He felt the cold, thin, smooth shape of it being pressed into his hand. He dropped the knife into the pocket of his jacket.

"You really scared me," she said.

"Yeah? Well, that's exactly what I was trying to do."

"Then you succeeded. But why?"

Take her hands and make her look at you. Even as dark as it is, if you stand close, you can still make out each other's faces. "Listen. You don't need me in your life, OK? You think you do, but you don't. I'm trouble. I'm real bad news. And I can't say it any clearer than that. OK? That's why I wanted to scare you, OK?"

Long silence, but you know what's coming. Like a couple conspirators working their way around to that inevitable discussion of how to do it — whether by knife or poison or a quick sniper's bullet. "I know how we'd be able to sleep," she says.

The cards are on the table. So the only way to play it is like you don't quite see it. "Gwendolyn Crane, are you making a pass at me?"

"I didn't think you were ever going to notice."

"What the hell you expect me to do about it? Right there in your daddy's house? Are you out of your goddamned mind?"

Her smile's as wicked as fox grin. Teeth. "I'm beginning to think," she says slowly, drawing it out, "that you haven't got the jam."

Nothing you can do with that but laugh your ass off. "That how they teach you to talk in that goddamned girls' school?"

"I said it so you'd laugh. At least that's half the reason."

"I can take the joke, but, baby, can you?"

"What do I have to do, walk into your room naked?"

"You're serious, aren't you?"

"Yes."

Four million schemes, plans, possibilities, endless crooked paths going around in spirals, a circular labyrinth, but always winds back down to the same zero bare as a white plate. "Where'd you get *your* jam, baby shake?"

"I don't know what you mean."

"Boy next door? Your girlfriend Carla? Your music teacher? Where?"

"Nowhere. No jam, Steven. Empty."

You take her into your arms and give her a hug and try your damnedest to make it feel like goofy old Uncle Steven, some friendly old fart who hasn't got it up in years. "Oh, baby, let's just leave it alone, OK?"

And then back in the little white room, Steve kept on talking to her for hours even though she wasn't around to hear him. You've got to believe me, Wendy. I never wanted to be an evil dude. All I wanted was to open the doors of the saucer, wide as love, and take you all on board — men, women, children, dogs, cats, and mice — and sweep out to the stars across a glittering night that's called eternity.

# IX

Rain. And out of the darkness a single note held for eight beats of the clicking metronome. Still half asleep, Kathy knew something was wrong. Then she was wide awake, looked at the alarm clock — four twenty-eight in the morning. Practicing is sacred, she thought, but this is insane. And then Kathy remembered that Steve was downstairs.

She felt a tightening in her lungs. The goddamned crazy ruined son of a bitch, she thought. It wasn't any wonder Wendy couldn't sleep; the whole house was tense as a wasp's nest. I've got to get him out of here, she thought, but right now the important thing is for *me* to get some sleep or I'll be a zombie the whole goddamned day tomorrow. And Wendy was ascending the scale; Kathy let herself go with the sound of the gamba, every note predictable. Maybe she could use it; she'd done it before. And felt herself unwinding, drifting. Lines were coming loose, shifting — images in her mind that were nearly physical, motion down corridors, past doors.

And she's done this before. Another man's body in another bed. *No, don't do that.* Do what? *Just don't,* she told herself, but it was too late; she was already doing it. And Kathy awoke with a crash, her body rigid. She knew immediately where she was, opened her eyes, and the room came swimming up out of a poisonous murk just before dawn. The man was breathing in a slow, deep rhythm; with every exhalation, his mustache flared. If she didn't hate him so much, it'd be funny.

Kathy was still wearing exactly what she'd walked in wearing — the black vinyl mini dress with nothing on underneath it. She was sweating. She pushed back the quilt, slipped quietly out of bed. Lyons didn't stir. The windows were pushed wide, a strong wind was blowing, and the room was cold. And she'd almost forgotten Lyons' silent girlfriend, Susie. If that was her name. The naked girl was awake too, her hands pressed between her thighs, her childish body contracted into a tight, fetal knot on the floor at the foot of the bed.

Kathy gestured. *Come on. Get up. Let's get out of here.* The girl shook her head no. Kathy felt a fury so intense that for a moment she was sure she could actually do it, pick up the gun — the Colt thirty-eight police special, as Lyons had told her at least a dozen times — load it from the box of bullets waiting on the top of the orange crate, fire it into his sleeping body, keep on firing until the gun was empty.

"Get up," Kathy whispered. The girl was only tied symbolically. Her hands were free. To get loose, all she'd have to do would be unknot the clothesline wrapped around her neck. But again she shook her head no.

Kathy stood a moment looking at the shivering girl. Then she gathered up her things. Out on the street the lights were still shining — nasty, inhuman green. No cars. Kathy sat on the curb to lace up her boots. The icy air bit at her bare thighs. She stood up, tugged down the goddamn little skirt, and walked. The plastic boot heels pinged hard on the pavement, and the October wind was hammering at her in mad, freezing gusts, a hint of snow in it. She couldn't remember when the subway started running.

She was wide awake now, and she needed a smoke. She didn't want to remember any more of this. She needed to get up, go downstairs and yell at him, "Get out of my life, Steven." But she continued to lie there, listening to Wendy's gamba, listening to Paul's breathing.

The sound of the gamba stopped. Kathy heard herself wheezing. Then felt it again — the dangerous, anguished tightening. Shot immediately out of bed, hurried down the dark hallway, locked herself in the bathroom. Dizzy, hating herself, fumbled in the medicine cabinet, hating *him* for doing this to her. She blasted her lungs with Ventolin, leaned against the wall, her eyes shut, and waited until she could feel it working. Blasted her lungs again. She'd got it in time — clear and easy. She pushed the window up so she could get the fresh air, feel the rain. Directly below her, yellow light was spilling out onto the lawn from the guest room.

She lit a cigarette, felt the smoke burn in her soft lungs. Felt the tightening on the back of her neck, felt her heart rate quicken. She didn't want to know, but she already knew. She must have known all along. Steve and his goddamned Blake quotes — "If the doors of perception were cleansed..." and that other one, "Sooner murder an infant in its cradle than nurse unacted desires." *What a fucking bad joke,* she thought. *And we believed it? Good God, we were so stupid. So young and vulnerable and goddamned stupid.* And she watched as Steve and Wendy walked out of the house, into the rain, and vanished at the corner of the street, hand in hand.

Just as though there was nothing going on the least bit unusual, Kathy got up at the same time she always did. She drove Wendy to Stafford House just the way she'd been doing ever since the bus strike started. She made small talk with the girl just the way she always did. Then she drove back to Kerrisdale, called Van Free from the deli and told them she was sick. Right, asthma again, the ready-at-hand, all-purpose excuse. She drank four cups of coffee, smoked a cigarette with each of them. Memories were coming back now. She was practically drowning in them. Whole scenes that had been hazy or vague or even nonexistent were now vivid as hallucinations.

It's Roxbury, and everywhere she goes there are black faces, black men. "Say, baby, you looking for somebody? Well hey there, white woman, pretty woman, there's just you and me, and you the one."

She doesn't give a shit about the men. They come close, reach for her, peer into her face, see her eyes and then draw back. "Sorry, lady, thought you was somebody else."

It's funny, it's a fucking riot. All she has to do is let them get a good look at her.

Snow piled in the gutters, white with dirty tops, the sidewalks slick with ice, and she's just at the edge of a nod. Doesn't matter how cold it is; she can't feel it anyway. Doesn't matter how many tiny steps she has to take; if she just keeps on going, she'll get to the subway station. But then she's down — bang! — sliding on the ice. Sees blood on her left knee but can't feel it. Rolls onto her belly, pushes herself up. Makes herself walk. A single block feels ten miles long.

She falls again. Lies on the sidewalk wondering what to do next. Can't make it like this. Just can't. Maybe take off the slingback heels and walk in her stocking feet. What, on a night that's twenty below zero? Yeah, why not? But her fingers won't work. She can't unfasten the straps on her shoes. OK, then, just keep on going. She's back on her feet, and the blood running down her leg is just something to look at.

OK, pretend each step is an eighth note, moderate swing time, thirty-two bars. She makes it through the tune four times before she gets to the station. Then, thank God, she can phase out. Comes off the nod just in time to change cars. Oh God, God, God, she's beginning to *feel* again. And she's passing from one world into another — black to white. She's coming down. The subway rattles her teeth.

Hunched up in the corner of the car in her fake-fur coat, collar up to her chin. White men don't look at her at all. White men pretend she's not there. She's in Cambridge. Remembers enough to know it'll be terrible after she comes down. Moment of all-out panic — she can't possibly survive the night without a little something. Not much, just a taste, just a little more doogie would do it. But there's no choice; it's too late.

She's kept the key, lets herself in. But Steve's not home. At first she isn't sure he lives there anymore — it's so strangely bare. Some of the furniture's gone. It'd be really weird if he'd moved out and somebody else came in, a stranger, and found her like this. But then she sees that he's piled up all her clothes neatly for her in a corner.

There's the outline on the wall where the full-length mirror used to be. Why is the mirror gone? It's like one of Steve's mind-breaking puzzles — is the mirror gone so she won't have to see what she looks like? She's so ashamed she can't think of anything but dying. She should take a shower, wash off the caked layers of makeup, get out of this sweaty, trashy dress, but she can't even stand up. Now that she's inside a warm building, she's burning up. She falls onto the bed.

She doesn't know how much time's passed, but he's bending over her. "Jesus, Kathy, you sure are looking good."

"Fuck you, asshole."

He bends closer, stares into her face, into her eyes. He whistles between his teeth. "You've really done it up right this time, babe. What the hell is it? Serum hep?"

For an answer she draws her left arm out of her coat and shows him the underside of it. She wants to tell him, wants to hurt him with it. "Mainly smack, but anything, Steven. Even water." She hears herself laugh. "You fall in love with the point after a while, Steven. You'll even do water."

He grins — wolf teeth. "So how are the folks in Roxbury these days?"

"Last time I saw them, they were passed out on the tabletop."

"Always liked your friends, Kath. Quiet, you might say. Well, come on, get your act together. We're going down to Cambridge City."

"I can't go in there with tracks all over my arm."

"The hell you can't. We're going if I have to carry you."

She won't let herself cry. "Hey, bring me some jeans, OK? I can't go in there in these fucking clothes."

"I love you, Kath. You're crazier than I am." He washes her face, helps her into jeans and a sweater. Down at the emergency ward he's such a sweet talker that they let him take her home.

Puts her to bed in a flannelette nightgown. Wipes the sweat off her face with a cold cloth and feeds her lemon juice squeezed into water. "Well, you won," she tells him.

He stares at her. "Won? Shit."

She begins to understand; he doesn't know what she's talking about. How could he? There wasn't any way he could have known that she'd wanted him to come after her, stop her. Couldn't have known that all she'd wanted had been a good, screaming fight and some honesty out of him for a change, something real instead of that con-man mask he was always wearing, and maybe a chance to do what she'd never been able to do — cry in front of him — to say, "I'm sorry about Lyons. It was really horrible. And I just did it to hurt you." A chance to say, "Hold me, Steven, I'm so fucking scared."

But damn it, she still has to try to get him. "I've always been a sucker for points," she says, light throwaway effect. "It's the rush, man, that's so beautiful."

"Kathy, if I ever catch you anywhere near a needle again, I'm going to beat the piss out of you. And I mean it."

From his flat, even voice she knows how thoroughly enraged he is. She has to turn her face away so he won't see her smiling.

She's finally done it. She's finally won.


Kathy drove back to the house. She didn't even take her coat off, walked straight into the guest room, banging the door open in front of her. "Wake up, you son of a bitch."

Her eyes adjusted to the murk of the room. She saw that he was already looking at her. His eyes were still that alien, metallic nothingness she'd never been able to read. "Get up," she said.

"What's happening?"

"I want to ask you some questions, that's what's happening. Now get the hell up."

He threw back the blankets. He still slept in nothing but a T-shirt, and his prick looked exactly the way she remembered it—that long, skinny dangle of pink eel. Staring at her, he pulled on jockey shorts and jeans. She swept back the curtains, and the room was filled with cool, gray light that let her see him with a terrible, raw clarity.

"You want to make some coffee?" he said. His voice didn't give away anything more than his eyes did.

"Fuck your coffee."

"Jesus, Kath, you sure know how to make a man feel good first thing in the morning. Loved and welcome. Right at home, you might say."

"Cut the crap, OK? I don't want to hear it. After all these goddamned years I'm finally ready to stand up to you. All right, now why don't you tell me what the hell you think you're doing with Wendy?"

He still smoked Player's. He lit one, inhaled smoke, coughed. "Shit," he said.

"Come on, asshole. Straight answers. What's going on with Wendy?"

"Been telling her stories about the rock-and-roll business. That's it. That's all. She's a curious kid... Mind if *I* make some coffee? My caffeine level's a little..."

"I don't give a fuck what kind of stories you've been telling her. You're not telling her any more of them. And you're not taking her for any more little strolls at five in the morning either. Steven!"

He'd pushed her out of the way, was already halfway down the hall. "Where the hell you going?"

"I'm going to take a pee," he yelled back at her. "And I'm going to make coffee. Now just lay the fuck off for a minute, all right?"

Good, she thought, I'm getting to him. Now just keep pushing. Don't leave him any room to maneuver or he'll slip off the hook.

She followed him into the bathroom. "Oh, for Christ's sake," he said.

"Straight answers, man. And then you're going to pack up your shit and get out of this house. And you're not going to see Wendy again. Have you got that, Steven?"

"She's a big kid."

"You want me to haul her ass out of school, have a chat with her? You want me to tell Paul what's been going on? Oh, man, if you want a real bloody mess, you can have one. *Have you got that, Steven?*"

"Yeah, I've got it."

He zipped his fly, stepped forward. She braced herself in the doorway so he couldn't get out. He stopped in front of the sink, looked into her face. Again those blanked-out eyes. "Come on, Kath," he said. "You're being ridiculous."

"If you don't start talking, you're going to see just how ridiculous I can be. All right, who killed Peter?"

"Oh, shit. You know perfectly well who killed Peter."

"Yeah, but I want to hear you say it."

"Bobby Lyons killed him."

"Why?"

"Because Peter set him up."

"Set him up how?"

"Jesus, Kath, all this is shit that's over and done with years ago. Get on with your fucking life, all right? I'll clear my ass out of here, and you can file for a divorce and marry the fucking professor. For Christ's sake, let me out of the bathroom."

"How did he set him up?"

Steve threw his cigarette into the toilet, stepped toward her. She forced herself to hold her ground, not moving a muscle. She forced herself to stare directly into his eyes. He stopped, then retreated, crossed his arms over his chest and let himself fall back against the far wall in that model's slouch she remembered so well because it used to turn her on. Time was folded up like an old theater program. The beautiful boy with the mane of glossy black hair blowing in the bright eastern light was this shabby man, this pathetic man. But she had to be careful, had to hold onto the anger, even though tears were filling up her throat. "How did he set him up?" she said.

"Oh, fuck. Well, old Peter was running a lab, all right? Running it for Lyons. So Peter cleaned out about twenty thou worth of shit, stashed it somewhere, did a deal with the cops, and flew to Philadelphia to say hi to Mom and Dad. Sat there waiting for the roof to cave in on Lyons. Fine and dandy. Except that Lyons had the best law money could buy, and that was lots of law. They'd got him flat-footed, so they couldn't just throw it away, right? But he was out on bail. Had a dozen bright boys looking for technicalities, right? And given the money that was flowing, they probably would have found a few, who knows? But anyhow, puppy-dog Peter, he can't just sit it out in Philadelphia. He's got to come back to Boston, the dumb shit, which is why he's dead. And you knew all that, damn it."

"Sort of knew it. Or knew most of it. But it's nice to hear it so clearly put."

"Give me a smoke."

She threw Steve one of her cigarettes, lit one for herself. "Now you listen to this story for a minute," she said. "Let's pretend it's something we saw on TV, OK? Here's this Vietnam vet named Bobby Lyons, and he's really crazy. He's dealing drugs in a very big way, and he's doing so much methamphetamine, he glows in the dark. Unstable? Well, that's putting it mildly. And *you* know Peter set him up. And *you* know he's capable of killing Peter. And so, when Peter doesn't show up for a gig, a really heavy gig, the first one you guys have had in months, what do you do about it? You hand your girlfriend the keys to Lyons' apartment... God knows why you've got the keys to his apartment, but we'll let that one pass for the moment. So anyhow, you send your girlfriend over there. And you don't even tell her what's going on. Now if you saw that show on the telly, what would you say about yourself?"

"I wasn't thinking too clearly."

"Terrific, Steven. I love it. Want to try it another way?"

Something was happening in him; she could see it by the contraction of the muscles around his eyes, but she didn't know what it was. She tried not to let herself even begin to feel how afraid she was.

"How the fuck do you smoke these things?" he said. "Nothing to them. Rhetorical question, right? Shit, Kath, you're a big, strong, tough woman. I know that. But even though I've been declining and falling at a great rate, I ain't no pushover, if you follow me. So if you force me to move you out of the doorway, all we're going to do is hurt each other, and frankly, I don't see the point to it."

Was he bluffing? No, she didn't think he was. She stepped out of his way. He walked quickly past her into the kitchen, began banging open cupboard doors, taking out his anger on them.

"Cut it out," she said. "Sit down. I'll do it." She took the coffee beans out of the freezer.

"The professor likes his coffee fresh ground, huh?"

"Don't call him that. His name's Paul."

"Sorry. I think he's OK, you know."

"Fuck that, Steven. Let's just get on with it. So what is it you weren't thinking very clearly?"

He slumped into a chair facing the window, let his body go slack. "Ah, shit, Kath, I don't know... Well, Lyons had fucked you, OK? And he wanted to fuck you again. It was something he could use against me. And... Shit, you probably never knew this, but he was afraid of you, kind of in awe of you. The thing you've got to remember about him was that down at rock bottom he was just a jerk-off loser kid from Watertown, Massachusetts, and people like your old man were... You might as well have been one of the Kennedys, the way he thought of you. Which, of course, gave him one hell of a big thrill when he was shoving his cock in you. Sorry. I guess I'm still pretty bitter about that. Anyway, if I went over there and found him with Peter, he probably would have killed both of us, and if I was going to do that, I had to be ready to... Well, anyhow, I figured if it was you that turned up, some kind of Looney-Toons scene would go down, but nobody would get killed. Chances are, both you and Peter could have walked. That's the way I was thinking anyway."

"Jesus, you could have told me that. If I'd known, maybe I could have... *except that it'd already happened by then.* But damn it, Steven, why didn't you tell me?"

He made that familiar shrugging gesture, hands out, shoulders slumping; she must have seen it a million times, and she knew now that she'd always misread it before. It didn't say, like Alfred E. Newman, "What? Me worry?" but something else, something like, "It's too much for me, babe, it really is."

He looked away from her. He said, "I didn't want you to see how far I'd sunk."

Don't cry, she told herself. If you cry, you'll lose it.

"Lyons gave everybody what they wanted," he said. "Ned was so strung out on acid he was chasing his tail through the galaxies. And Peter got the biggest chemistry set he'd ever seen. And Jerry and Dave... well, a million lines of toot and all the doogie in the world. The whole band was... And me? Well, don't suppose there was a single one of those little space girls of his I didn't screw. You knew that, didn't you? And for what? You know, Kath, the biggest fucking lie? Yeah, I could blame it all on the times, and I have, and I will again, but shit, that doesn't let me off the hook... but we all believed that goddamned lie... *do what you feel like.*"

She was standing with the can of coffee beans in her hands. She forced herself into motion, ground the beans, filled the coffee maker, turned it on. Something was shifting in her. If she let herself feel, she'd feel too much, and then what? On some level, lost down in herself somewhere, she *had* known most of it. And she could have got him to Canada sooner, maybe even before it was too late. But why should she have been responsible for him? Because in his own screwy, fucked-up way he'd been responsible for her. And there was something even more than that.

Steve smiled at her — the old shit-eating grin he called it —

and, for a moment, he was himself, exactly the way she remembered him. I'll always love him, she thought. And I'm finished with him now.

She poured them both a cup of coffee, sat down at the table. She took his left hand, turned it over, ran her fingertips over the ragged scars. "When did you do this?"

"When you left me."

"That's what I thought, but I could never stand to ask you. I felt too guilty. Oh, Steven."

Damn it, now she *was* crying. "That was awful. I've gone over it in my mind a million times. I walked in. I said, 'I've been with Lyons.' I took off that goddamned kinky outfit I'd been wearing, and..." She couldn't get the words to keep coming out.

"You said, 'You and Lyons should...' "

"Shut up. Don't tell me what I said. I remember what I said. Jesus, Steven, it wasn't just you that fucked it. We both fucked it."

"Oh, babe, it's so many years ago. Let it alone. I mean... shit, who's to blame? Like I should have known you would have headed straight back to those scag heads in Roxbury. I could have gone down there and found you."

"Except that I didn't. I sat in Mr. Bartley's and waited for you."

His face wasn't blank now. "Mr. Bartley's? How the hell was I supposed to know that?"

"You always had lunch there. Every fucking day."

He was staring at her. She'd lost control of the words; they just kept tumbling out of her mouth. A part of her had pulled back, was listening, was thinking, *Oh, so that's what was happening, was it?*

"I thought you'd come in," the woman said. "I thought we'd have a big, screaming fight and get it over with, get it clear. You want to talk about the lies we believed in, how fucked up we were, how stupid? Shit, I didn't know that there were things you couldn't do, things you couldn't say. I thought you could do *anything*. It was all part of the show. Fucking Lyons, walking out on you. I was just trying to get your ass. I didn't want to leave you. I didn't want us to split up. I just wanted a... I just wanted to know that you loved me."

Oh, God, he was crying, had tears in his eyes. She couldn't stand it. But his voice was flat. "Oh, shit, Kath, it's so fucking intertwined. It was Peter who found me bleeding all over the fucking place. It was Peter who dragged my ass down to Cambridge City. And it was after that he started saying, 'I'm going to get the son of a bitch.' He told me he was going to set

Lyons up, and I told him not to, but he did it anyway. And he called me from Philadelphia, the city of brotherly love, right? And I said, 'Look, man, if you come back to Boston, you've got to be prepared to kill him,' but he came back anyway. And Lyons took him down to Roxbury and chopped him in half with a forty-four magnum, and it's mostly my fault."

Kathy felt as though there had been a pane of glass in her mind and it had suddenly shattered. "Wait," she said. "Stop." Her hand was shaking so badly she was sloshing coffee everywhere. She let the cup drop to the table. "A forty-four magnum?" she heard herself saying.

"Yeah. Why? What? What's happening?"

"I thought it was that Colt thirty-eight... that police special."

"Oh, Jesus, you mean the other..."

"Yeah. Lyons had it the night I was with him. He kept playing with it. That little girl... Oh, fuck, I'd forgotten this. I mean like... really... nothing. He kept shoving that goddamn gun in her mouth. Oh, Jesus!"

She was wheezing. She had to stand up. She couldn't breathe. But she had to breathe. "I know what kind of gun it was. He kept telling me over and over what kind of gun it was." It was somebody else talking, some other woman.

"I thought that was the gun he'd used to kill Peter," the woman said. "You mean there were *two guns*? I don't understand. Steven? *I don't understand.* Then I found you in that shit hole by the Cambridge dump and... You had that gun, that thirty-eight. *Why did you have his gun, Steven?*"

She could barely make him out. He was a dim, blurry figure still sitting at the kitchen table. "So when you dumped it in the concrete..." he said.

"Shut up. I can't think. I can't breathe. Just shut the fuck up."

Slow. Breathe slow. Come on, you can do it. And there was a woman somewhere, in some other place very far away, who was saying, "Why were there two guns?"

"Because if you're going to have a duel, each of you's got to have a weapon, right? That's why. Don't you understand what he was like?"

"Those men from the FBI," the woman said. "Looking for you. Is that what they were? From the FBI?"

"I don't know."

"What the fuck you mean you don't know?"

"Did they show you ID?"

"They showed me something, but it could have been anything."

"Did they leave you a phone number?"

"No."

"Did they get in touch with you again?"

"No."

"Shit, Kath, that was the Maf. Oh, my God, I'm so fucking sorry."

Kathy made a fist of her right hand, pressed it into her mouth, bit down on it. *Hey*, the distant voice in her said, *that isn't going to help you breathe*. But she kept on doing it. She tasted blood. Now it's just cold, she thought. It's cold. It's fucking cold.

"Kathy?" the man said.

She made a gesture, pushing him away. It was ridiculous. He was nowhere near her. She'd fled to the far side of the kitchen. "Lyons," the woman said. "Then who...?"

Suddenly she was through it. She could breathe. She could see him. She could see everything. Everything in the kitchen was bright, clearly defined. "Oh, shit, Steven," she said. "You killed him, didn't you?"

"Of course I killed him."

What do you say now? she asked herself. Was there anything more to say? She sat down at the table. There was still a little coffee at the bottom on her cup. It was cold.

"When you leaving?" she said.

"Right now."


When things got tough, Kathy thought, you could always have an asthma attack so you wouldn't have to think about it, but you're not having an asthma attack, are you now, baby? No, you're breathing clear and easy as you please, not a wheeze left anywhere to help you, and you can remember it all.

Spring at the cusp of summer, the first day when the shift is palpable, heat shimmering up from the sidewalk. High, blazing sun and people crowding Harvard Square, bicycles, walkers. She's just bought two oranges at the corner newsstand, turns back to the street, and Steven is waiting for her, leaning against the wall by the rack of foreign newspapers, his hips canted, a mysterious smile on his face. She hasn't seen him since March, but slips easily into the circle made by his guiding arm; he leads her into the sunlight.

"You're looking good, babe," he says.

She hands him an orange.

They begin walking toward Central Square, slowly, at a leisurely stroll. Remembering — when she's with him, she's aware of what he's aware of. Before, she'd not particularly noticed all the girls in miniskirts; now, in the electrical field of his attention, they are everywhere.

He knows that she knows he's watching. "They say minis are going out. Sure as hell don't look like it."

"You bastard," she says without heat, "we were together too long for it to end like this."

His long thumbnail bites into the skin of the orange — smell of volatile oils. He's smiling, the breeze blowing back his long hair. He must have just washed it, sweeping around his head in a billowing mane, and there's a brightness to him, beautiful and detached; he seems almost joyous.

"Just a hand or two to play out," he says, and they're walking, arm in arm, as though he'd never left her. "Look at that little number." A coltish kid in a skirt that just covers her ass. "Hey, I love it," he says in an oddly crooning voice she doesn't quite know.

"Got yourself a little honey, Steven?"

"Oh hell no. Running it off by hand. Keeps things simpler. How about you?"

"Taking a break from men. You can all go fuck yourselves." She says it lightly, and he laughs. "You playing anywhere?"

"Naw. Strangest thing. My band keeps vanishing on me."

At Bow Street, passing the bicycle shop. He's humming a little tune, a country sound; she can hear the fiddle in it. And suddenly she freezes, stops to stare at him. He's somewhere else. He's genuinely crazy. He looks back at her, smiling, a silken sheen in his eyes. "I've missed you, Kath," he says in the gentlest voice she's ever heard from him.

Her eyes sting. It's all right; she's wearing sunglasses. The day is changeable — passing through compressed spaces where the sun beats down, alternating with chill shadows that goosebump her arms. Those short skirts look obscene to her now. When she first wore them, she was was in love with the image — sassy and free like some sprightly English bird winging through a mod romp with the Beatles on the sound track — but eventually they just made her feel vulnerable, exposed, up for grabs. And then, after the night with Lyons, she knew she would never wear a miniskirt again. Into the long silence she says, "I'm too old for that shit, Steven."

"The hell you are. You're just afraid of the zing." He draws his own sunglasses out of his shirt and puts them on.

"Yeah, probably. Well, have you forgiven me yet?"

"Me forgive you? That's a laugh." His hand falls onto the small of her back and he guides her on down the street.

They move into high summer. In a few weeks her jeans and boots will be too hot, but she'll go on wearing them anyway.

"Our mythology comes out of Pepsi ads," she says, sure he'll know what she means.

He does. "Buy us a sports car to go with your shades, babe. Tear off a quick one on the perfect clipped green of the nineteenth hole. Hey, will you do something for me?"

"What's that?"

"Just a little joke." That strange country tune's now a thin whistle between his teeth. She recognizes it finally; she's heard him sing it a hundred times. "Bound to lose, riverboat gambler's bound to lose."

"What kind of a joke, Steven?"

"Little joke on old Bobby Lyons."

"Leave me out of it, man."

"Yeah, that's probably the thing to do." He guides her into an about-face, and they start strolling back toward the gray-green shadows of Harvard Yard.

"Central Square's a drag," he says. Whistling. "Shit, maybe we ought to go down to Georgia, open up a little club, right? Few card games in the back. Could you get behind it?"

"I've about run out of Boston."

"You and me both, babe."

"All right, you've sucked me in. What joke?"

"Oh, I just want you to give old Bobby a call."

"Saying what?"

"Saying this. *Bob Lyons? There's a bust on its way. You've got about ten minutes.*" He delivers the words as though he'd rehearsed and polished them, with a vivid crackle that's totally different from the honey-soft drawl he'd been using only a moment before.

"And what's going to happen then?"

"He's going to hop in his Alfa and drive all over hell and gone getting rid of a bunch of shit, and I'm going to be laughing."

"He'll know my voice."

"Doesn't matter whether he knows it or not. If you live in paranoia city, anything could mean anything."

She doesn't speak. "Anything could mean anything," he says again. "Shit, you could have been on the payroll of the Cambridge narc squad all along for all he knows. You could be working for the Maf. Or it could be a *test*, right? But he'll have to move. No way he can do anything else."

"What for, Steven?"

"For the yuck."

"Why don't you try getting your laughs somewhere else, man? Haven't you just about run it out?"

"Oh yeah, just about run it out." Bound to lose. Bound to lose.

They're both wearing sunglasses now, looking at each other with blank mirror eyes. At the corner of Harvard Square again. Girls crowd the street, and he's aware of every one of them. She's aware of just how much he *is* aware. Jesus, the incredible energy of him, high tension lines of it. In a clear, swooping insight she sees how they could go with it, move with it; what's always stopped her is something like pride. She's never known whether she should throw that pride away or hang onto it as the essential core of herself. He's always pretended that his own ego was dispensable, that he'd be hers in any way at all if she came on with enough force, but it was a lie. His pride was brighter, sharper, harder than hers. If he'd truly wanted to give himself to her, he would have told her what the hell was going on.

She takes off her sunglasses, squints at him with bare eyes. He smiles, removes his shades too. His eyes are gleaming like satin. "You con man," she says.

"Yeah. Right." He shrugs. "You want to live in a Pepsi ad, babe? Come to Georgia with me. We'll leave today."

"The South scares the shit out of me."

"How do you know? You've never been there. It ain't all *Easy Rider*." She doesn't answer. "Scares the shit out of me too," he says. "Ain't that reason enough?"

"And do what?"

"Borrow some money off the old man, open a little club, start a band. I don't know."

"You're serious, aren't you?"

"I could jump any way at all. Why don't you try one?"

"California?"

"Sure. Want to leave right now?"

"What about the FBI?"

A slow, bitter smile spreads across his face. "Right. What about the FBI?"

She puts her sunglasses back on. Grinning, he puts his on too. "Safe," he says, "they'll never get us now."

She laughs in spite of herself. "Canada?"

"Fine. You tell me, and we'll do it."

"Damn it, Steven, I don't want to *tell* you. That's what's been wrong the whole goddamned time, you know that? Either you're running the show, and I'm your party doll, or all of a sudden you give up and I'm supposed to run it. Why the hell couldn't we ever..."

She doesn't know how to finish the sentence; he does it for her. "Yeah. Partners. Fifty-fifty. Sure. OK."

"I don't believe you."

"Oh, babe, I don't know. I'm in a kind of strange space." Bound to lose. Bound to lose.

"I noticed."

He tilts his head away toward the sunlight, twin yellow balls of fire blazing back from the green mirrors over his eyes. Like a plant tipping, she thinks. What a beautiful man he is, all that lovely hair flowing around his shoulders.

"So you call Lyons," he says. Hard, biting edge. "It's got to be timed, right on time. Twelve minutes of twelve. How's that for a magic number?"

"I'm not going to do it."

"Kath," he says, *"You mean to tell me you don't owe him?"*

The day has become enormous around them; the people on the street are wind-up toys. She could go anywhere, do anything. The United States of America has recently paid a little visit to Cambodia, and down at Kent State innocent children have been shot dead; now the sun is shining like two hot, bitter lemons in blind, green eyes, and the girls are still wearing miniskirts.

"All right," she says, "tell me again what I'm supposed to say."

Good morning, little schoolgirl — Pigpen's opening line, old hippy joke that Steve had been singing to himself for the last hour as he'd floated the van in a random search pattern through this tree-lined genteel neighborhood, giggling like a bona fide cretin getting off on the same dumb twist long after everybody else has given up on it and gone home. He rolled down the window and stuck his head out to catch the drift of the hazy rain, saw his own grin like the Chessy cat's fading away behind the gauze scrim of this nostalgic Chinese landscape painting, everything flat and featureless, the mountains nothing but paper cutouts, broad streets of mildew and missed connections, stucco boxy dollhouses arranged neatly in a swamp, city of fanatical gardeners, six-inch slugs, and dripping conifers smelling of gin — Vancouver.

Yeah, you come cheap these days, he thought, amusing yourself in the Taoist rice-paper void. Can't look it up in the phone book, no, that'd be too easy for you — got to take off instead without even knowing for sure the part of town it's in and sniff it out on telepathy. But now he couldn't help grinning because after all those days and nights stuck in that weird little cell he was loose in the world again, because his manic genius had come back like a million volts, because he'd done it, pulled up to the curb just a half block up from the discreet sign, white letters on a natural wood ground — STAFFORD HOUSE SCHOOL FOR GIRLS — carefully placing the van between the entrance and the bus stop. Light a smoke now to help the twitch along, no problem, folks, just your friendly neighborhood child molester.

And you've made it right on time — procession of kidlets up the sidewalk past the van — ghosts of children distanced and muted like memory in the mists of spring. So what is it, Steven? Twenty years of getting older and playing to girls who just keep getting younger so now you've got nothing left for it but to fabricate appointments at the schoolyard gate? Or are you just here because Kathy told you not to?

The bigger girls were on their way out now and up the sidewalk, and damn, he'd almost missed her. Yellow plastic raincoat and matching sou'wester hat tied under her chin, made her look about ten, blending in with the other children, but the first giveaway was the gamba case in her gloved hand, and then, of course, she turned her head and cast out a sweep of that impossible blond hair. Traitor's heart skipped a beat just like fourteen again, catching sight of some beloved Sally or Susie across the school yard — Romeo forever — and suddenly he wanted to take his hangdog face and rancid fantasies of redemption and sneak away with them on the wet shame of his own predicament, put the van in gear and ooze past the water running in the gutters and keep right on going out into the middle of English Bay. Steven, you flaming asshole, why don't you just give it up?

"Hey, little schoolgirl, can I come home with you?"

Flash of blue eyes, flushed bird going up — scatter of wings — so far out to lunch she hadn't even seen the van. "Steven!"

"Ten years I've been waiting to deliver that line for real."

"Are you waiting for *me*?" said like she couldn't believe it, little pop of a sentence she didn't catch quick enough.

I'm so waiting for you that the rest of the world's just stopped like Don Juan's trump card. "Sure. I'll take you home."

"Come on, Carla, he'll give us a ride," to her little buddy — a child, an absolute baby, no lie, not a curve in sight and black hair in pigtails for Christ's sake, and big suspicious eyes that were saying, *I* know all about men in vans. "It's all right, Carla, I know him." But Carla wasn't having any, not about to climb into any old rapist's wagon, had stopped dead with books clutched to her flat chest and total panic written all over her, probably memorizing the details for the cops later, already telling herself the whole repulsive story — Wendy's messed-over white corpse dug up out of a shallow grave with dirt in the open eyes. And seeing the fear on that little-girl face, Steve saw himself. *Old. Burnt-out. Hippy.*

But Wendy shrugged, walked around to the other side, and climbed in, laid her books and gamba case in the back. "She going to run straight home and call your daddy?" Steve said under his breath.

Wendy gave him a quickly narrowing stare. "Yes, she just might do that," leaned across him to try it again. "Carla, it's all right. *I know him.* He's a friend of my father's... Do you want a ride?"

*No!* mute Carla said with her head, but seemed slightly reassured, waved half-heartedly, lowered her pigtails and walked against the rain, stiff as a little mule. Steve put the van in gear and pulled away, careful and easy, drifting down the wet street, slow motion getaway. "*Are* you going home?" he said.

"I *was* going home."

"What the hell you doing giving me your past tense, Gwendolyn?" That's it, man — light and easy, slow and breezy.

Pause. "I'm giving you anything you want with my past tense, Steven." Said in her best British deb voice.

Goose-bumped sweating pig, Steven Beuhl, stopped for a red light and lit a new smoke on the butt of the old. "Tell me how to get there."

"I'm serious, Steven."

"Wonderful. Delightful. Fantastic. Terrific. Tremendous."

"I don't want to go home. Seeing you is more important." Light changed, he pulled away, smoke in his throat and not a good word in his head. "Why didn't you call me?" she said.

"I know you well enough to call you?"

"You know me too well not to... I wasn't sure I was ever going to see you again."

"I wasn't sure you were either."

"I knew that's what you were thinking. I knew you wouldn't call. You could have at least called *Kathy.*"

"Yeah, I could've, couldn't I? Where are we going?"

"I don't care. Anywhere you want."

"I don't know this damned city." And added, after a moment of sticky indecision, "Kathy knew where I was. I *did* call her."

"Well, she didn't tell me. You didn't expect her to, did you?"

"No."

"Why didn't you call me? I couldn't very well ask her about you."

"I'm glad you understand."

Stopped for another red light, he turned to look at her. Goddamn that child's rain gear, goddamn that hat tied under her chin and those mary janes and knee socks. Steve took it out on the van, kicked it down, tires squealing, fishtail and slam. "Steven!"

"Sorry. I'm a bit frazzed."

But you *can* hold it together, he told himself, wind it through the rain easy as a feather. "Where are you living now?" she said.

"Basement room in the east end."

"What are you doing?"

"What the fuck you think I'm doing? I'm playing in a fucking rock band that's what I'm doing. Jesus fucking Christ. Three young punks from Nanaimo come down to the big city to make their fame and fortune. So fucking green they can't tell the difference between yours truly and a sane man. So glad to get a wizard like me on drums that they pitched right in and cleaned out the root cellar to make me a bedroom. Wonderful little space. Used to be full of jam jars, you know, right next to the octopus furnace, conveniently located right off the backed-up sump in case I should decide to drown myself in the night. But it aint a bad life. Beats the hell out of Bangladesh."

Long silence in the fuzzy rain. She wasn't laughing. Alison would have been laughing. Even Kathy would have been laughing. And he sneaked a glance at her, at that perfect milk-white profile. She was looking straight ahead at the road. "Where the hell we going?" he said.

"The Endowment Lands."

"Tell me how to get there. It's your city."

"You're going the right way. Just keep going west. It doesn't matter how you go."

"Shit, kid, that's practically a koan."

"Steven...? What's the matter with you? Are you going to vanish again?"

"Just keep on going west, isn't that what you said? It doesn't matter how you go."

"Yes, it does matter. It matters to me."

"Who the hell are you to take it on, schoolgirl? Jesus!"

"Why the hell were you waiting for me then?" And that was such a damn good question there was no answer for it at all.

Moments turn into memories and then they're not real anymore. So why does it still hurt so much?

You never really knew what they meant by cops' eyes until you tried to stare down that pair. Pale blue, a little watery, and it wasn't that they were threatening, or suspicious, or hard, or anything like that. It was that they were nothing. "Why do you think you know him?" So you had to go through it again, how Peter hadn't made the gig, how he'd been running with some heavy dudes, and the cop finally says, all right, and then what got to you wasn't that Peter was chopped in half, it was the expression on his face.

The cop wants to know just what heavy dudes he'd been running with. You give him your best dumb-ass answer. "Jesus, man, I don't know. Maf probably. I stay away from shit like that." And you ask him what did it.

"Forty-four magnum," he says, flat, like there's no question.

"Bet my money by the gambling rules," that old song says. Yeah, and you were betting more than your money. The first thing you did was leave Kathy. "Why, Steven?" she said.

"Any day now the FBI's going to come knocking at the door, and I don't want to involve you."

"Jesus, that's bullshit. They haven't started hassling draft dodgers' girlfriends yet." She sat there staring at you, trying to read your mind from that bluffer's dead-pan you were giving her. "It's because I slept with Lyons, isn't it?"

"Oh fuck, Kath, that's over and done with. That's past history."

"It's because I couldn't play the night Peter died. I let you down. That's what you think, isn't it? If I'd played, you'd still have a band. Is that it?"

That one was pretty good, so to make sure she went on thinking it, you turned away, saying, "Well, Kath, I don't know," and you lay down on the bed and waited. Eventually she got up and went out and while she was gone, you packed up and left. Rented a furnished room, and you kept everything in the van because you knew you might have to move fast.

The gambling rules. Right, you were starting to run, Steven, stringing out flat, and you let yourself go with it, every day a little more. "Going from town — town to town," is what that song says, "come and lay your dollar down." The towns are in the mind, the stakes are getting higher. He has a girl or two in his place all the time now, those bright little space kids, and he keeps them in shiny plastic. "Sweet Peggy-Sue, Mary-Lou, Susie-Q," he calls them, and you dress them up in one thing or another and ball them on that big bed of his, and afterward you lie there next to him, your shoulders touching, and he passes you a smoke, lights it for you. "How are you doing, Steven, old buddy?"

"I'm doing just fine, Bob."

"Now isn't this little Cindy-Sue a hell of a juicy piece of ass?" and he pats her between the legs. "Don't you just love the way she loves it?"

"Yeah, it's wonderful, Bob." And you lie there and smoke cigarettes, and sometimes he grins and says, "Now wasn't that a shame what happened to poor old Peter?" Your mind's singing, "Bound to lose. Bound to lose. Riverboat gambler's bound to lose." And that other old Southern fiddle tune, "Oh me, oh lordy my, goinna start me a graveyard of my own."

"Yeah, really a shame, Bob," you say. "Wonder who did it?"

"Shit, must have been the Maf. Don't you think so, Steven?" and he laughs.

"Yeah, and you better watch your own ass, man, or it'll happen to you."

"Oh, they can't get me, Stevo, I'm too quick."

Oh me, oh lordy my. "The old cat was quick too, Bob."

The space girl's walking around in boots and a miniskirt, no top and no panties underneath, and Lyons decides to tell her war stories about the question boys in Vietnam. "You know the cutest one I ever heard, this really is a cute one, takes the cake if you know what I mean. Some peasants supposed to be helping out the Cong, you know, but they wouldn't admit to shit. So what they do is, they get this couple, right? The woman's pregnant, right? So they take a gun and stick it in her husband's ear, tell her she's got to do what they say or his brains are going to go splat. And then they give her a whole bunch of ice and make her hold it against her belly. Can you dig it? And she's got to hold it there until the baby dies inside of her. Now isn't that one cute? Here, Cindy-Sue, have another toke for the head."

But she's gone, can hear her sobbing in the bathroom because it's dawned on her that she's got nowhere left to go, and you say to him just like you're talking to a good old buddy, "You know, Bob, you are just about the most evil son of a bitch I ever met, and that's no bullshit."

"Well, Susie-Q's a big girl. About time she stops believing in Santa Claus, don't you think?" with a wink, "and maybe I just made it up."

"Yeah, maybe you did. But that doesn't matter, does it?"

He laughs, passes over the joint. "You know what I learned in Vietnam, Stevo? Learned that good little blue-eyed American boys will do anything if you scare them bad enough. And we know, don't we, what a fucking shit hole it all is."

It's the only time he ever shows you something that makes you think he might have been just like anybody else once, God knows how long ago. He isn't grinning, he isn't bobbing or winking. "I was green as grass when they sent me to Vietnam," he says. Soft. "Green as grass. Well, you can be a sucker and die or you can be a bastard and live, and that's the only act that's playing," and then it's back, the song and dance — "now isn't this some wonderful shit, man? Aren't we having such a good time? We're tight like a nut on a bolt, you and me, Stevo, and we're looking good."

"But maybe tomorrow, Robert, it's us behind the ice cubes, right?"

"You right, man. You got the joke. You absolutely right." He laughs till the tears run down his mustache.

Then he gets that nasty little thirty-eight. It's clean and oiled and ready to go. "Present for you," he says.

"What for?"

"Well, man, I've got me that sweet-talking forty-four magnum, and who needs two guns, right? It's a dangerous world we live in, Stevo, and I'll sleep a little better nights knowing you have it if you need it."

All the time in the world goes by while you hold it in your hand and he watches you. Bound to lose, bound to lose. "It's not loaded," he says. "You'll have to do that one for yourself. But don't worry about it being traced. It's cold." He starts giggling. "Yeah, man, it's ice."

And later you're screwing the space girl, tasting the salt in her mouth while she hangs onto you, her eyes stretched out, her nails digging into your back. She stares at the ceiling with her dead doll's face and you're lying on her with your prick still inside, Lyons right next to you on the bed, can feel his mustache brushing your shoulder. He lights you another smoke. You take it and stay inside her.

Old Steven had a wreck and he broke his fucking neck, now he can't read a letter from his home. Oh me, oh lordy my, goinna start me a graveyard of my own. "You could save the Maf the trouble," Lyons says, "couldn't you, Steven?"

"Well, shit, I don't know, Bob. Do you think I'm quick enough?" You're still inside her and you're smoking your cigarette.

"Well, I don't know either, Stevo. And if you don't know and I don't know, then who the fuck knows? Hey, Susie-Q, do you know?" She doesn't say a word of course. "Shit, you see. She don't know." Start me a graveyard of my own. "But maybe you are," he says and smiles, "quick enough."

No way to get away from that one, is there, Steven? And now he was driving the getaway van through the haze, driving it slower and slower, almost down to a crawl, driving west, carrying the golden girl. He looked over at her. She was looking straight ahead. "Hey, Wendy, you sure you don't want to go home?"

"No," she said.

"There aint nothing here," he said. The Endowment Lands.

"That's right." Looked at her. Blue eyes like incoming flash across a million empty black miles. "Drive on back through there," she said pointing. "Get out of view of the road."

"Nothing but trees... Shit, Wendy, that's a sea of mud back there."

"Go on."

"Hey, I don't think it's a good idea." You're a fucking master of understatement, aren't you, candy man? Not a good idea? That goddamned warning note's ringing like somebody's kicking the gong around from one side of your skull to the other. Gong around, gong around, got to stop kicking that gong around. *Stop it, man, all right? Just stop it.* "Jesus, Wendy, it's raining like a son of a bitch. There's not going to be anybody out in those woods. Nobody for miles. I'm going to take you home."

"You're not going to take me home." And she dropped one gloved hand over Steve's on the steering wheel.

Her kid gloves. Black ones today. "Shit, you run across some man with a glove fetish, you'd drive him bananas."

"My hands get cold very easily. I never thought of gloves as sexy, but I guess they are, aren't they? I'm glad that at least *something* I do is sexy... Go on, Steven, get us off the road."

Gong around, gong around, got to stop kicking that gong around. Steve eased the ticking van back through the tall green trees, turned off the ignition: ca-bang, ca-bang, ca-bang from the engine, a drummer that couldn't quit. Got to run, got to move. And he felt the treacherous seat begin to move under him, very gently, like a ripple in a water bed. The pressure on his head was enormous. He lit a cigarette. His hands were shaking. Gong around, rain rain, gong around, rain rain.

The pressure was a huge hand, was the roof of the van, but there wasn't any escape from it; outside it'd be in the rain, in the sky itself. Steve bent and pressed his forehead into the steering wheel. Talking to the dashboard, talking to his bony knees. "I know you're a weird kid, that you're not what people think you are. But Jesus, can't you tell the difference between me and a human being? Jesus, kid, you take chances."

"I'm not taking any chances. *I know what I'm doing.*"

"If that's what you think, then I'm going to take you home."

He reached for the key in the ignition, but she caught his hand. He jerked back.

"You're shaking," she said.

He couldn't look at her. He was cold, clenched his teeth against it. Words pinched out through rigid jaws. "You're in over your head, baby. You don't know who you're dealing with."

She held out a hand to him. Break.

The girl was wearing black kid gloves. The man didn't take the hand, but drew farther back into himself, impacted. The man watched himself squeeze his arms tightly around his chest so the shaking couldn't rip him apart. The man needed to press his back into the seat. The cold rain-colored daylight hurt the man's eyeballs just under the ridge of skull, thumb on bruise. The pressure on the man's head was enormous.

"Shit, you just don't know," the man heard himself saying.

He turned to look at her, his neck floating around on ball bearings, rotating world. The girl was white and shining. The green west blurred, but the girl in focus, shining. The man felt the seat under him moving deeply now, a tide of motion. He squeezed his elbows into his chest until he was compressed, compacted, a pinched black iron pipe. Then he exploded. Smashed open door, metal slam at the wind, jumped into rain. He was running through the alien green trees.


You're out of the van, slapdash down the trail, green smear, that nothing of sky, hemmed in, claustrophobic green bent toward the middle, curving, coming down, bent around your ears. "Steven!" she's yelling, a skimming owl behind you, a long float through the slashing rain. Run, feet tangled in mud, leaf mulch. Bang into trees, turn, make her human again. See a little kid in a yellow plastic raincoat, her socks coming down, her legs splashed with mud all the way to her knees. She stops ten feet away, and you stare at each other. She's panting and you're panting, see no way out at all, just more trees, enormously, going on forever. She could run you down with no trouble, too many years of smoke in your lungs, and she's young and light as a cat. But she doesn't try to come close, stops on the other side of the trail. You're lined up like two chess pieces. "Steven, listen, you've got to listen."

"No." But you can listen. The thing that comes and runs you has gone away — *for now*.

"I don't care whether you want to or not, you've got to." If you tilt straight back and let the rain pound you full in the face, it makes the sockets of your eyes fill up with water, you blink, the water burns, and there's a patch of sky up there, rolling ink gray, between treetops. "Let me alone, Wendy. Go away."

"No. Listen. I was asleep. I didn't know that I was asleep. Do you hear me?... I woke up and it had all been sleep, fifteen years of sleep. I woke up in Amsterdam. I didn't know it was going to happen. We got off the plane, and the airport just looked like any other airport. And then I knew I'd been expecting something to change. It felt like something very fragile I was carrying in my hands. I had to balance it very carefully, walk very carefully, but I knew I was expecting something. And I thought, oh, is this all? It's just another airport. It could be Toronto or Vancouver."

"I don't want to hear it."

"I don't care. You've got to hear it... And then I thought, yes, it's here after all. It *is* going to happen. It was when I saw the canals, the old parts of the city, the cobblestones. Daddy and I went to a hidden church. You go in through somebody's ordinary house and then up a narrow flight of stairs and there's a whole little cathedral in there. It's a hidden church. They had to do that because of the persecution. And I thought, it's happening."

Hammering in your ears like an endless press roll. "What's it got to do with me? Why the fuck you want to tell it to me?"

"Shut up, Steven... We went to the house where Anne Frank stayed, and I felt it... inside my chest. It began to hurt inside my chest, and I knew it wasn't something I was carrying in my hands, it was inside me, that very fragile thing. It was going to open up, and I thought, I've been asleep. I've been asleep for fifteen years."

"I don't want to hear it."

"Shut up... Daddy took me out to Klaas Achterberg's. He lives outside the city. The land is unbelievably flat, and every inch of it is cultivated, and the sky... My god, Steven, the sky is everywhere. It's huge. It was raining that day, not raining hard like this, but overcast and drizzling, a kind of gray drift of rain. It was like the paintings in the Rijksmuseum. And everything was hurting me then. Everything I looked at hurt me. The sky hurt. The flat countryside hurt. And I had a lesson with Klaas. We read some Marais. I played it and then he played it, and I *heard* it for the first time. I knew what it was supposed to sound like for the first time. He's such a funny round little man. He doesn't look like anything. He could be a farmer. But then he plays, and the music just comes pouring out... as though it were coming up out of a deep fountain. And I knew how stupid I was, how I couldn't really make *music*. I knew that all I'd been doing had been playing the notes. And then Dad and I walked for hours afterward and it was still raining."

You're hooked, you're a shining silver fish jumping on a tense wire, and now you've got to know. She's shaking with cold. She sees you look and takes a step forward. "Stay where you are, all right? Just stay right there."

She stops, draws back. "Dad talked to me in a different way than he ever had before. He talked to me as though... It's hard to describe. For a while I wasn't his daughter, I was... not just a friend. More than a friend. I was his colleague, something like that. He told me all kinds of things I never knew about him. He told me about the first woman he ever slept with. He told me about studying with Thurston Dart in London. He told me about how he'd wanted to play early music, bring it to life again... and I couldn't say anything to him. I just walked. I felt like the sky... big and flat and gray. I couldn't say anything at all because it was opening up inside me, and I knew I'd been asleep. I kept thinking about when I was a little kid and Mummy used to dress me up and take me to concerts, and I was asleep. I used to play my cello, and I was asleep. I got up every day and went to school, and I was asleep. And I kept thinking, I've got to remember. If I don't remember, it'll slip away again. It was the most horrible thing I could think of... for it to slip away again... but I couldn't stand the pain inside me. Mummy and Cindy would be out on the canals or something, and I'd tell Daddy, 'I've got to take a nap. I'm really tired,' and I'd go into my room and cry. It hurt so badly that I had to cry, but I didn't want it to stop hurting. Because if it stopped hurting, I'd just be asleep again. I thought, I've got to keep the pain... as though it were something sharp to press myself up against whenever I had to. Because if I lost it... do you understand? You've got to understand."

"Goddamn it, of course I understand."

"I wanted to stay in the Netherlands. I wanted to spend the whole vacation there. I wanted Mummy and Cindy to go on to Italy and Daddy and I to stay in Amsterdam, but I couldn't even say it. There wasn't any way to say it. All the plans had been made. We were going to rent a car and drive to Paris. But then everything got changed, and I knew something terrible was going to happen. I couldn't say anything. I just watched, and everything started going wrong. Cindy and I were picking at each other all the time as though we were both five years old again, and Mummy and Daddy were fighting, and everything was going sour, and I couldn't do anything about it. Part of me was just *watching*, and I'd act like a spoiled little bitch, and Cindy would act worse, and we'd be yelling at each other, and

Mummy would be yelling at us, 'My God, will you girls stop it!
You're driving me crazy.' And I'd watch and think, Wendy, why
are you doing this? But I couldn't stop it. And then we decided
to go to Antwerp..." She stops talking. "I don't know any other
way to tell it, Steven. Just like this. All the trivial details one
right after the other. It feels as though I have to tell you all the
silly trivial details."

"Yeah, you've got to do that."

"Daddy wanted to follow the route of the Netherlandish
composers down into Italy, but he didn't tell Mummy that, he
just said, 'I think we can pass on Paris this time,' but she really
wanted to go to Paris and so did Cindy. Cindy had the idea that
she was going to get her hair cut in Paris, you know, *styled in
Paris,* and she wanted to buy some French clothes, but Daddy
had decided that he wanted to go to Antwerp, and then over into
Germany, down through Switzerland, and into Italy. He told
Mummy, 'Well, we've never been to Antwerp and we have been
to Paris. We've never been to Bonn either,' and he told her about
the Rubens paintings in Antwerp, so she gave in. I didn't want
to go to Antwerp. I didn't know why. I just didn't want to, but I
couldn't say a thing.

"I kept thinking how modern the highway was. We drove
straight to Antwerp, and everybody was fighting all the way.
When we came into the city, my heart sank because it was so big
and modern and dirty-looking, and I thought, It's ruined.
They've ruined it. And Daddy just wanted to stop at a motel...
they have motels, you know, just as in North America... but
Mummy said, 'No, we'll go to a good hotel,' and she was allowed
to win that one because she hadn't wanted to go to Antwerp in
the first place. So we stayed in a big hotel that was right on the
river... the Schelde... and we looked at the Rubens paintings. I
hate Rubens."

You've got to laugh at that one. "Oh, you do, huh?"

"Yes. He's too flamboyant. Too showy. But we had to look at
all of his paintings we could find. And we went to the cathedral.
It's really huge inside, but you don't realize it at first. We walked
around. There were two more damned Rubens paintings in
there, and we had to look at them, and by then the pain was so
bad that I didn't think I could stand it... It started down in my...
started right between my legs and went right up to the top of my
head. It felt as though I were being ripped apart, and I had to
fight it all the time. It gave me a headache to fight it like that,
and Mummy said, 'Oh, she's got one of her migraines,' and they
sent me to bed. And I lay there and I was thinking, Yes, that's

what she thinks of me. To her I'm just a spoiled, pampered little bitch of a kid. I cry for no reason. I have migraines. I get sick at my stomach and throw up. I'm like the princess who can feel the pea under all the mattresses... That's exactly what she thinks of me, and she hates me for it because that's what she was like when she was a girl. But I thought, I'm not really like that. I'm not like that at all. That's just what I *look* like. It comes from being asleep for fifteen years.

"They brought me something to eat, but I couldn't eat it, and I saw Mummy looking at me with that expression she gets, and I knew she was thinking, 'Oh, you little bitch, I'd like to strangle you,' and then they all went to bed. They were in one room and Cindy and I were in another, and I kept twisting around in the bed because the pain kept getting worse. I couldn't cry because Cindy was there. It was the worst pain I've ever felt in my life. And then, all of a sudden, it stopped. It was just gone, and I felt this huge open space. I wasn't frightened at all. I thought, this is what I've been waiting for. And a voice said to me, 'You have to go out by the river.' So I got up and got dressed. Cindy woke up and looked at me and said, 'What are you doing? I'll tell Mummy,' and I said to her, 'Cindy, if you tell Mummy, I'll make your life so miserable you won't be able to believe it,' and I looked at her so she knew I meant it. She said, 'All right. I won't.'

"It was just dawn, and I walked along the Schelde. I knew it was dangerous for me to be alone, but I didn't care. I stopped to look at the water, and the big open space got even bigger. It was like a vacuum. And then it started filling up. It was like liquid flowing down from the sky, a thick liquid coming down. It started with a single drop, and then it kept on coming until it filled everything. It was blood.

"It all filled up with blood, and I stood and waited, and the voice said, 'See how Christ's blood streams in the firmament,' and I said, 'I see.'"

"Shut up, Wendy. I don't want to hear any more of it."

"You've got to hear it. You don't have any choice... And then the blood parted like a curtain, and behind it was whiteness the color of milk. And the voice said, 'This is how it was in the beginning of all things,' and I said, 'I see.'"

"And then a form began to take shape very high. It was like a swirl in the milk, and then it took a shape and a form. It was like a feather. It came floating down very slowly, and it was a piece of paper all rolled up. It glowed like the sun. And the voice said, 'Read what is written,' and it fell at my feet. I picked it up and opened it, and it said, 'You will speak to the peoples,' and then the paper burst into flames and turned to ash in my hands, and everything turned dark around me, and then I was frightened for the first time. I was terrified. And I knew I could die. And I thought, I don't want this. I don't want this to be happening to me. I want to be just an ordinary little girl. I felt very little. I started to cry. I thought, I'm only fifteen. I haven't had a chance. I don't want this to happen. And then I was standing by the River Schelde in Antwerp. It was just dawn, and the birds were singing everywhere, and I was frightened and ran back to the hotel, and I thought, I'll never tell anyone. I can't tell anyone. I want to go home. I want to go back to Vancouver, because it's my home, and I just want to be invisible. I just want to go to school and play my gamba and grow up and go off to college or get married or something and be safe. I just want to go home and be safe."

# XI

Dear Doctor Crane:

Yes, I did indeed receive your short letter. I am sorry that it has taken me so long to reply, but I have been uncertain precisely where to begin. Before we had not enough information. Now we have too much, or, to put it in a way more accurate, we have too much information of the wrong kind. I have just this morning entered into a tangled thicket of primary sources which appear to contradict each other so consistently and on so many points that it is impossible for me yet to clarify them, so I must leave these sources for later study. I will now lead you along the path I have taken so that you may see for yourself how I have arrived in my present straits.

Soon after writing to you my previous letter, I quickly discovered various accounts of the trial at Wesel summarized by modern scholars. In the interpretation of the events, these scholars differ among each other vehemently, but the main events are documented and simply enough stated.

In the winter of 1561, a band of approximately thirty people, including families with small children, were camped in a caravan hidden in the woods near Wesel not far from what is now the border between The Netherlands and Germany. In the early morning just before dawn of February the third, they were surprised by local authorities, arrested, taken to Wesel, and imprisoned there. Immediately ensued a long wrangle among both secular and church authorities about what should be done with the prisoners, some arguing that they should be sent to Cologne, others that they should not. The Duke himself apparently wished to release the prisoners, arguing that they had broken no laws, but his opinion did not prevail. The political issues involved were obviously quite complex, and I make no claim to understanding them.

The upshot of this, however, is that the prisoners were tried at Wesel in the spring of that year. The trial was conducted by a personage called Albrecht Böhm, referred to by some modern writers as "the magistrate" and by others as "the inquisitor." It appears that he was brought in from Cologne for the purpose of conducting the trial, but it is yet unclear to me exactly who he was, a priest, certainly an expert on heresy, but no modern scholar bothers to identify his precise origin.

The leader of the group tried at Wesel was a young woman calling herself "Sister Katrei." Two others were tried with her: an old man known as "Magister Johannes," also called "Jan the Dutchman," and a younger man called "Brother Michael." Katrei was accused of being the notorious heretic known as "Margaret, the prophetess of Antwerp," who had been tried for heresy and condemned to death *in absentia* in Antwerp in 1558. During the trial, Katrei apparently admitted to being Margaret of Antwerp, and some scholars argue that she was, indeed, Margaret, whereas others argue that she was not. And here, Doctor Crane, allow me finally to reply to your letter. I have conferred with several colleagues from the School of Theology who have helped through this thicket to guide me so far as I have come, and not one of them believes that those tried at Wesel were Anabaptists. So I must admit that your arguments, "purely speculative" as you called them, are supported by the evidence. I congratulate you on your speculations. I believe that they are, at least in their broad outline, correct.

Albrecht Böhm appears to have been initially convinced that those who had fallen into his hands were Anabaptists, but, during the course of the trial, apparently changed his mind. The three were tortured and asked a series of doctrinal questions. Katrei spoke not a single word during her entire time of imprisonment. Michael and Magister Johannes (Jan van Dorestad as we know him to be) did answer. Michael denied any knowledge of religious matters, but van Dorestad spoke at great length, and it is at this point at which the modern scholars begin to wrangle among themselves as fiercely as did the authorities at Wesel. What appears to emerge from van Dorestad's testimony is a picture of a radical antinomian conventicle preaching a mystical communalism similar to that of the Netherlandish spiritualizers. So far all scholars agree, but no farther. How one proceeds to interpret the beliefs of those tried at Wesel depends upon whether one does or does not believe that Katrei was Margaret of Antwerp.

The evidence that Katrei was Margaret of Antwerp is strong. We know already that "Michael son of Jennine the Dutchman" was married to a Margaret Baker at Antwerp, so, having established magister Johannes as our old friend van Dorestad, to establish the Michael tried at Wesel as his son agrees with what we already know from the records at Antwerp. It does not appear implausible that Margaret Baker and Margaret the Prophetess of Antwerp are one and the same. Second, even though Katrei remained silent during her imprisonment and trial, many testified against her, and the doctrines attributed to her are similar to those promulgated by Margaret of Antwerp. The doctrines emerging from van Dorestad's testimony are also similar to those of Margaret of Antwerp. Finally, there is her admission. Some scholars argue that it should be taken at face value, others that it was wrung from her by torture and so should be discounted. My inclination is to believe it.

About Margaret of Antwerp we know much. She could have been little more than a child when she began her career as a mystic and chiliastic preacher in Antwerp in 1549. Lutherans in Antwerp described her as "a young slip of a girl" who "spoke with incredible subtlety for one of her years" and "convinced many of her damnable heresy." By the early 1550s she had acquired a following and was being called the Prophetess of Antwerp. The Lutherans accused her of preaching not only the doctrine of the nonexistence of sin but also that of universal redemption and also accused her of "licentious, unclean, and unnatural practices." It is possible that these last charges laid against her had little substance outside the overheated rhetoric of her Lutheran opponents, particularly if she were indeed Margaret Baker, for, surely, one engaged in "unnatural practices" would not have been permitted the sacrament of marriage.

Modern scholars are astonished that Margaret escaped the attention of the Inquisition as long as she did. She must have fled the city by 1558; that was the year she was tried *in absentia* and condemned to death for heresy. The views for which she was condemned, as stated in great detail in her trial, include the following: that every man and every woman has the Holy Spirit but "some see and some do not see," that for those "born again" there is no sin, that hell is not eternal but "only for a time," that all will be saved "even the Antichrist himself," and that all will live again in the flesh, not once, but many times. This last doctrine, I am told, is an astonishing one for the period and is, in fact, so anomalous that it is difficult to explain how Margaret might have arrived at it. To attribute to her, as at least one writer has done, a knowledge of the Albigensian heresy three hundred years after it had been suppressed seems dubious to say the least, as does the suggestion that she was acquainted with the Jewish Cabala. Those who condemned her of heresy saw her as continuing in the tradition of the radical libertarian, Loy Pruystinck, who had been executed in 1544, and her teachings do seem similar enough for there to have been a direct influence. But, whereas Pruystinck appeared to have held the Averroist view that flesh and spirit are totally independent from and have no influence upon each other, Margaret claimed something quite different, and, from the point of view of the Inquisition, far more radical. This is the enigmatic statement attributed to her: "We come to the spirit through the flesh as we come to the flesh through the spirit."

Let us now return from Antwerp to our trial at Wesel. Katrei (and I must admit that I believe she was Margaret of Antwerp), Michael, and Johannes (van Dorestad) were condemned of heresy and executed. By the end of the trial, Albrecht Böhm (the inquisitor or magistrate or whoever he might have been) appears to have undergone a profound inner transformation. He released all the remaining prisoners without even placing them under sentence of public ecclesiastical penance, and, within the year, left the church and renounced the Catholic faith. In 1564, he wrote a strange book titled *Rebirth in the Bitter Christ*, and he was later, in 1580, himself executed for heresy.

The primary sources, then, are these: the Anabaptist *Book of Martyrs*, the trial record at Wesel, and Böhm's book. I must admit that I allowed myself considerable amusement at your description of discovering in your library the *Book of Martyrs* in its original language. I have read through that work, and I do not trust it. My thoughts upon the *Book of Martyrs* I must save for a later time after I have studied the other works. The trial record, you will be pleased to know, is in Latin. I am just now beginning to read it. Albrecht Böhm apparently wished to direct his work to the common people, and he wrote in the vernacular German of his time, so I am having some difficulty with his book. In it he also gives an account of the trial at Wesel. All I can say at this point in my research is to repeat that the three sources contradict each other.

Forgive me please, Doctor Crane, if I must close here. I will be writing to you again as quickly as I can. I am looking forward with great pleasure to your arrival in Amsterdam this summer.

By performing van Dorestad's *Tunc Jesus Ductus Est* you will have "beaten me to the punch," but for your effort to do so I can feel only admiration. Would it be possible for you to record the performance? I would most enjoy hearing it. And also, once again, give, from both myself and from our colleague, Klaas Achterberg, the warmest regards to your lovely and talented daughter.

Yours most faithfully,
Willem van der Geest

No use asking why you can't sleep, Steve thought, and no use pretending that you've never asked the question before, but every time around the cycle it's a little bit worse, so you're stringing out now, man, like a single silk stripe against the sky. Not in the night, not in the afternoon, not in the morning — will that vile mind of yours stop rattling away, and it's all right when you've got something simple to do like drive three thousand miles across Canada in the dead of winter, but the minute you try to come down and rest, forget it.

Only so many times a man can jerk off and then right back at ground zero, frozen center where nothing moves except that voice that drones on and on and it always turns out to be one of your own. Oh God, dreaming the temple where you scratch at the door, the priestess who opens for you is young and slender as the Ace of Wands, ice-flow eyes, and you tell her, "I've run the course, babe, and run it west clean out of road, what the fuck you expect, I should always be in motion?" and she takes one cold white hand and closes down your eyes. Nothing left for you but to be the gimpster sweeping up after all the hard nights, your broom going swish swish swish in the corner and your balls hung up on the wall with a red ribbon, dried leather walnuts like something in a Chinatown window, and Jesus, Steven, you must be crazy to jerk off to a story like *that*. But not in the night, not in the afternoon, not in the morning, and not ever, rocky road to Dublin, Van Morrison's Belfast city too, Bruce Cockburn's Toronto, Georgia boy grinding to a halt in a narrow basement room, east end of Vancouver, city of mist and chill, April, 1978, dated like a news release.

How the fuck do you grow old and venerable in the rock business, Steven? The answer is, same as always, *no way*, you kiss the sky and get out.

Steve threw back the sleeping bag, pulled on jockey shorts and jeans, smelled his own stink, sweating it out again, insane diet of beers and grease burgers. Pulled on his boots, shirt, jacket. Hammered at the catch holding the window, banging it with his fist until it gave, rammed the window out into the night and his head after it, for the rain. He was looking at ground level through dead scrub and bushes, looking at nothing but soggy earth and square black shapes, and then overhead drawn ink wires. Noisy street in front, cars whishing by, sad tires on wet pavement, everything laid back and hazy, but out there somewhere it was starting to rock, energy starting to move, in dozens of bars there were dozens of bands, and teenage kids in tight disco jeans, secretaries on the town in stockings and heels, poor crapped-out old Indian ladies in baggy sweaters, drunken women falling down, hookers on the corners — oh yeah, you've played the Hastings Streets of the mind and doubtless will play them again before the show's over. Hookers and hustlers follow him down, follow him around, come and lay your dollar down.

What the hell you want with me, Gwendolyn Crane? Didn't I run far enough for you, and fast enough? Didn't I jump high enough, roll over quick enough, bang them drums hard enough? I asked for light and you give me this? Hey baby, sweet baby, watched you once when you'd been playing that gamba of yours. You stood up, pressed your fists into your lower back and pushed, stretched the muscles, and all of a sudden I saw who you were — the dancer who lives forever, not yet a woman and no longer a girl, caught at the divide and stuck in time, legs apart. and the deep bow curve of your back, arching, hardly any breasts at all to push out at the front, bending backward, span cast into the darkness, aiming. *You're* the one who answers the scratch at the door, so close my eyes down if you want, but tell me please, sweet angel, didn't Charlie Manson have some love in him too? Sure he did, it was just that he listened to the wrong voices, that's all. So let me hear the voices again and let me choose again. That's not too much to ask, is it?

Fuckers dropping off to sleep on all sides and I'm stuck here trying a little plea-bargaining, not any dignity left, rain-in-the-face like a cigar store Indian, saying, "Hey, can't I sit this one out?" Yeah, but know the answer to that one already, so why bother to ask? All right then, I'll play the hand that's down on the table, but how about this one, "Can it mean something?" Yeah, I've begged a million times, "Please don't tell them that you know me," pretending I've never heard of you, but can't I be that rough useless stone the builders forgot? I know who I played against, and he was a little too quick for me, but — Shit, what the hell am I asking? And who am I to ask for anything?

My God, delusions of grandeur, you fucking asshole, any old
way you choose it? Shit, offered simple human flesh, you
reached for sun instead, going to redeem it all, and so redeemed
nothing. What the hell you doing, Steven, but what you've
always done? Talking to yourself. It's never meant nothing, it
don't mean nothing now, and it's never going to mean nothing.
Dignity? What a fucking joke. A goddamned slug run over on the
road has more dignity than you do.


Kathy was stuck in the bathtub. She didn't know how long she'd
been laid out there, but certainly for over an hour; she'd had time
to smoke three cigarettes, and she still didn't want to move. She
turned on the hot water tap; she wanted the heat to penetrate her
muscles, sink into her body all the way down to the very center
of her bones. She wasn't used to being alone in the house in the
afternoon, and it felt too quiet; she could hear rain pounding the
windows, the furnace blowing, the creak of wood settling, clocks
ticking. She could sense the space outside the bathroom — the
rooms and hallway with no one in them. She was feeling that old
familiar bleakness, detachment, as though nothing mattered a
damn and she'd forgotten how to care that nothing mattered a
damn.

The phone began to ring. No one knew where she was; if she'd
gone to work, she wouldn't be getting home for another hour. "To
hell with you," she said to the world at large and stayed in the
tub. She counted to twelve, and then the ringing stopped. She'd
called in sick that morning for no other reason than she hadn't
felt like going in; she'd been in slow motion ever since, and she
didn't care. The mood she was in, she'd do anything that might
make her feel better.

She lifted a leg out of the water to look at it again. Her skin
had gone bright pink from the heat, gleamed wetly — a
standard-issue feminine image, hairless for the first time in
years. She'd had to change the blade twice, but now, having
done it, she couldn't quite remember why she'd ever thought it
mattered if she shaved her legs or not. She smoked another
cigarette. Then she pulled the plug, lay in the tub till the water
drained away. She got out, dried herself. In Evelyn's dopey
mirrors she saw a woman who was pretty damned impressive
for thirty-six years old. Right, two packs a day and no interest
in food whatsoever; stress does wonders for the figure. And
looking at all the reflections of herself, thought, OK, the mirrors
can stay, but the goddamned Egyptian plates have got to go. And

the black and gold has got to go. One of these days, if I can ever work up the enthusiasm for it, I'm going to paint it white, every speck of it.

The phone was ringing again. She wrapped a towel around herself and walked quickly into the bedroom. It was Wendy saying, "Hi, Kathy. Is Dad home yet?"

"You know perfectly well he's not coming home. You're having dinner with me, remember?"

"Yes, that's right. That's what I'm calling about. I'm not going to come home. I'm going to work on my socials project with Carla."

"Sure," Kathy said automatically. "Just get to the university on time." One of these days, she thought, the bedroom's going to be white too, and those horrible heavy drapes are going to go.

"Tell Dad I might be a few minutes late, OK?" Wendy was saying. "But I'll certainly be there."

"You damn well better be. You're performing tonight."

"Of course I will. And, ah… it's not really a performance. Just something in the music school. And besides, I'm *singing*. And besides, why should I sit around the house for a couple hours and jitter? This socials project is due on…"

"Hold it a minute," Kathy said. She hadn't been paying attention before, but now she focused on Wendy, what the girl had been saying. Something was wrong here. "Where you going to have dinner? Carla's?"

The pause went on so long that Kathy could hear whole snatches of conversation from girls chattering in the backround, and then, behind those voices, other voices, distant and unintelligible — electronic gremlins talking to each other somewhere in the web of the phone system. "Well, probably," Wendy said. "Or we'll just stop somewhere. Or something."

"Where are you?"

In the tone of "what a dumb question" — "I'm still at school. Look, Kathy, I'm in the office, and people are waiting, and I can't really…"

And Kathy finally got it. "Hey. Have you called your father? You know he's in his office."

"The line's busy."

"Well, try it again. Look, kid, I don't know what you're up to, but tonight's not the night, OK? You know how important this is to Paul. Don't blow it."

"Kathy, I *know* it's important. As difficult as you may find it to believe, I *am* a responsible person. I know how to ride buses around Vancouver."

I am sick to death of teenagers, Kathy thought. "Paul's not going to be exactly delighted with you."

"If he's undelighted, it's between us, isn't it?"

"Yeah, except that you've put me in the middle. I'm supposed to deliver your message."

Kathy waited. Wendy certainly was calling from school — the giggling girls were still at it in the background. And Wendy *was* perfectly capable of getting to the university on her own. So who am I to be playing cop? Kathy thought. I'm not her mother.

"All right," Kathy said. "I'll tell him. But where can he call you?"

Again there was no answer. "Wendy, sweetheart, you may be the best gamba player in Canada, but you're also sixteen years old, and you damn well better give me a phone number where your father can call you."

"Look, I'll call him back. Or I'll call Mother. How's that? So you're off the hook. Is that what you want?"

"No, that's not what I want. Just tell me where you're going to be, princess. The school? Carla's? Where?"

Kathy heard the line go dead. "Fuck," she said.

She hung up, stood there a moment, confused. Then she understood that she wasn't sure of anything.

Kathy started coughing. It was that tight, dry, painful cough she'd developed in the last few weeks. She bent forward, pressed her hands into her breastbone. There was a pain in her stomach too — a small, cold bundle of it — and more pain spreading out under her rib cage. When she could straighten up, she walked into the bathroom, got her cigarettes, lit one, came back and sat down on the edge of the bed in front of the phone. Without planning to do it, she dialed the number she'd memorized.

A belligerent male teenage voice answered immediately, saying only, "Yeah?"

"Is Steven Beuhl there?"

"Yeah, hang on."

Top-forty rock was hammering away from a radio on the other end of the line. She heard footsteps approaching. Then, far too quickly, there he was. "Yeah?"

Kathy had been conning herself; she was not detached at all. Her heartbeat accelerated; her mouth went dry. She heard him say, "Hey, old buddy, whoever you are... are you there?" She couldn't speak.

"Kath, is that you?" he said.

She was almost ready to say something. She took a deep breath so she could do it. "Wendy?" he said. She hung up.

Kathy didn't know how much time had passed, but she was already getting dressed, doing everything automatically. She opened the packages, put on the panty hose and bra. Now she was putting on the new gray suit. She opened the box, took out the matching pumps, slipped her feet into them. They'd felt surprisingly comfortable in the store, and they still felt comfortable now. She'd never in her life owned a pair of shoes like that.

The woman in the mirror looked all right. She looked ordinary, normal. She could even be married to a university professor.

Kathy was glad it was still raining. She parked in the Student Union lot, opened the umbrella she'd borrowed from Wendy's room; it was probably Evelyn's, but she didn't care. She didn't walk directly to the music school but took off on a circular route through the campus. She hadn't bothered with dinner; the thought of eating made her sick. She needed to walk a bit. She needed to smoke. Maybe that would help to clear her mind — if she could figure out what needed to be cleared.

The sky was thick and dark and in motion, and she liked it like that. She could walk in the pumps perfectly well, and anybody who thought she shouldn't be wearing them could go fuck himself. She felt as though she were acting in some old, crummy melodrama, but one that was hers, had been hers long before she'd ever met Steve — walking down the cobbled streets of Beacon Hill, headed for downtown Boston, for some dingy club where she could play it out to the bitter end. But by the time she got to the music school, the sense of herself in a starring role had dropped away, and, once again, she didn't know why she was doing anything she was doing. She was early, and there was no one around. She took the elevator marked FACULTY ONLY, rode it up to Paul's floor.

He wasn't in his office. She walked down the long, straight hall until she heard voices coming from 507. She stopped outside the closed door, heard Paul and Hanna Rossenmüller. They were arguing about something.

Hanna was practically yelling; her words came out in a rush. "Erasmus, you have mentioned him. He is good *Christian* man. Him you must read. In Latin, ya? No, do not smile. I am not with you joking. You read Latin, and some Christian men are good men, and he is one... But I forget myself, Paul. I am sorry."

Paul said something. His tone was conciliatory, but Kathy couldn't make out the words.

Hanna's voice burst out again — "Hölderlin and Nietzsche you must also read. Do you know how it ended for them?... Ya, but you must these things know. I am a Jew, and this I know. Always when the Christians quarrel, it is the Jews who die. That is what this Christian heresy means for us. For the plague we are blamed, and we die... Ach, Paul, *Ich kann nicht...* The Rhineland prophets, do you them know? The Drummer of Niklashausen? The children's crusades? Münster? All these you must know. And who is this little man with his moustache, this little Charlie Chaplin man who struts and yells? A heretic also he is, a Christian heretic. The old gods back will he bring. The heresy of blood, so? *Das Tausendjährige Reich...* How do you that in English say? The millennium, is it not so? The heresy says always the same thing. Down to the earth the heavens we will bring, but first the blood must flow."

Kathy didn't know how she knew it, but she suddenly understood that Paul was in trouble. She opened the door as quietly as she could. Hanna was still talking. Kathy stopped just inside. They were so intent on each other that neither of them noticed her. "This little man in Germany, it is religion he brings," Hanna was saying. Her voice was quiet now. "It is heresy. It is very old. You must read of it. But this I know. He brings the millennium, this heaven on earth, and we die. Oh, it was written that we should be a light to the nations, and such a bright light we have made."

Kathy stepped forward. Paul saw her, looked shocked. He sent her a message with his eyes, but she didn't know what it meant. And Hanna obviously hadn't seen her yet.

"Please, Paul, I am sorry," Hanna said. "It is just I think so much now it comes again. It is much on my mind. We are *organishe...* a people of the family, but I have no family now. In Amsterdam there are beautiful synagogues, but there are few people left to worship in them. For *Das Tausendjährige Reich* there are few people left. When I go to Amsterdam, always I visit there the synagogues, and always I speak English when I am in the Netherlands. I have all my Dutch forgotten, and you know how bad my English is, but in Holland, I speak English... *because I do not ever speak in German there.*"

Then Hanna saw Kathy. It felt to Kathy like a four-bar break; the three of them were frozen, caught, counting the beats. It was Hanna who saved them. "Ach, too much old woman's talk," she said. She walked out of the room.

"What the hell was that all about?" Kathy said.

Paul's face looked damaged. He stared at her; for a moment

she was afraid he'd forgotten who she was. Then he tried to laugh, said, "Oh, God, I don't know. Hanna and I seem to have developed a difference of opinion. Has Wendy got here yet?"

"I haven't seen her. Did you talk to her?"

"No, but Evelyn called me. Good old Ev." Kathy heard how tense and controlled his voice was. "We may have our differences, but when it comes to the children, we're a united front. Upon that we're in total agreement. Back each other all the way. So what does dear Evelyn do? She tells Wendy, 'I don't see any problem. Meet them at the university at a quarter to eight.' Wasn't that delightful of her?"

"Terrific," Kathy said. "Very helpful. Damn it, I told Wendy to call you. You mean she didn't?"

"She certainly did not. I've been in my office all afternoon, and the phone was never busy."

"Shit. She's up to something."

"I know she's up to something. But what? Oh, damn it, we're running out of time." His voice was rising. What was happening to him? She'd never seen him like this before.

He paced to the far side of the rehearsal room and back. When he looked at her, she could see that a tiny muscle in his left eyelid was twitching. He reached into his pocket, took out the keys to his car, pressed them into her hand.

The keys felt cold. "I'm parked just outside the building in the little faculty lot," he said.

"Paul, what are you asking me to do?"

"For God's sake, bring her back here, will you?"


In Paul's office, Kathy dials the house, lets the phone ring twenty times. As it's ringing, she finally allows herself to know that she knows where Wendy is.

Dry mouth, heart pounding, Kathy runs every red light leaving the campus. On the straight stretch through the Endowment Lands, she's got Paul's car over a hundred, runs another red light, hears horns behind her, screaming brakes, wailing, receding, thinks, *Jesus! Cool it.* Lets the speed drop to fifty. *Watch it, watch it, watch it* — she's repeating the words like a mantra. She stops for red lights now, but every time she does, her heart races. The terrible lethargy that has been holding her down for days is gone; it's painful not to be moving. And checking her watch, she sees that she'd made the university to Main Street in twelve minutes.

Now she has to look for it, search it out, wandering around in a part of town she doesn't know, somewhere off Victoria, but Steve's angels are with her for once, and there's no problem. She's pulling up in front of the ramshackle house. Yeah, that's the right number. The front windows are dark. No answer to her knock. She stands on the porch thinking that this doesn't make any sense at all. Tries the door. It's not locked. She hesitates. At the end of a hall, in a room that's probably the kitchen, she can see a light. But the house is silent. Hating herself for the triviality of it, she's thinking, why do I have to be dressed like *this*? "Hey," she yells. "Anybody home?"

She listens, holding her breath. The house feels abandoned. Fear has focused her down to a tiny point of brilliant consciousness; she feels so tightly strung that if a feather fell, she'd jump ten feet. Balancing her weight carefully, she steps inside, slips off the pumps, pads silently on down the hall and into the kitchen. People have been drinking beer and cocoa. Then in a mirror in one of the bedrooms sees herself — a lean, tall woman in a conservative gray suit, frightened eyes, hair swinging, turns away at once. In the living room, she stands in front of the stereo. She doesn't know what she's supposed to be looking for. The place smells like the sixties — dope.

She doesn't know how she knows where to go, but she does. Down the narrow stairs to the basement. Steve's clothes are thrown everywhere. The bed looks like a rat's nest. Lying on the tangled sheets is a small piece of white notepaper. And of course she's seen paper exactly like that before. She picks it up. And of course she's seen that small, precise handwriting before.

"Dear Steven," she reads, "I'm sorry I missed you. We're performing the motet tonight at eight o'clock in the music school, and I really want you to hear it." Then Wendy had drawn a tiny, accurate map of the campus, showing Steve where to park, marking out the exact route he would have to walk to the music building.

"Please call me. If you don't want to call me at home, call me at Stafford House any school day between noon and one o'clock and tell them you're my father. I know that everything is all right and worry about you because I don't think you understand that yet. I'd write more, but I've got to rush. If I'm late for the performance, Dad will kill me. Please come to it. And even if you can't, please call me. Love, Wendy."

By the time she'd driven back to the university, Kathy had achieved a state of murderous calm based, she supposed, upon an anger so enormous she simply didn't give a good fuck any longer what might happen to herself or anybody else. She parked Paul's car in the faculty lot, lit a cigarette, and, taking her own sweet time about it, walked toward the music school. The rain had changed from the steady downpour of an hour before to a hazy mist; the angular buildings of the campus looked out of focus. When she stepped into the faculty elevator, she looked at her watch and saw that it was ten minutes to eight.

In 507 everything seemed perfectly normal, and Kathy knew that's exactly what she'd expected to find. Paul — looking like himself again — was standing just inside the open door talking to his little bitch of a daughter. He saw Kathy, caught her eye, smiled. She smiled back, an automatic reflex. And of course Wendy had made it on time; there she was in her full Stafford House uniform, telling her father more lies. And there were clusters of people — all of Paul's colleagues, his graduate students, Hanna talking to Mark Perry, and, walking toward her, Evelyn, who must have left her boyfriend at home.

"Another opening, another show," Evelyn said.

Kathy heard herself laughing. "How are you, Evelyn?"

"Never been better, actually."

And then, suddenly, Wendy arrived directly in front of them, obviously dying to say something.

"Made it, I see," Kathy said.

"Of course I made it. Everything's fine."

"Is it?" Kathy said. "Why don't you just tell me about it."

Wendy inhaled to speak, then, looking up into Kathy's face, stopped herself.

"One of these days, princess," Kathy said, "you and I are going to have a little chat."

"Fuck right off," Wendy said from between her teeth.

"Hey, girls," Evelyn said, "no fighting, no biting." She gathered Kathy and her daughter each by an elbow and lead them away toward the auditorium.

"You guys are the worst fucking band I ever heard, eh?"

"Really?" Steve said. "Shit, could have sworn we was even worse than that." He was stopped just outside the door to the can because this little jerk-off of a man had put himself in the way. "Hey, come on. I've got to crap."

Steven, impersonating friendly, dropped a hand onto the black leather shoulder, but the little fart swatted back clumsily, recoiled, fists up. "I'll crap *you*, turkey."

` Problem with him, Steve thought, is he's too short. Amazing the owner of that insanely loud voice that's been braying from across the bar all night should turn out to be this minuscule little prick. Image like the sixties gone to rack and ruin, long dirty hair, bald on top, jacket hanging open to show a pot gut and a yellow tee shirt with what was probably his life motto stenciled on it in red block letters: BOOGIE TILL YOU PUKE. Great to see a perfect example of how far we've come in ten years, right there before our eyes, live and three dimensional — an old, burnt-out, hippy. "Oh, for Christ's sake," Steve said. The goof was so drunk he could hardly stand up.

But the rest of the boogie boys were arriving to pull their buddy out of the way. "Come on, man... Come *on*... Let's not have any trouble, eh? Have another beer, eh?"

"Fucking turkey." The man spat on the floor. He'd been aiming at Steve's boots but had missed by a mile. Steve saw an opening and slipped through it into the can. "Jesus," he said out loud.

Single yellow bulb in the middle of the ceiling, so old and dim and feeble Steve couldn't tell whether the inch of liquid all over the floor was water or piss. Bowels churning, he jumped into the crapper and locked himself in. Well, drummer, you're really down to the pits again, aren't you? Nice little gig, play from eight at night till three or four in the morning, make forty bucks a head. Terrific. And your audience is the seedy and infirm, the halt and the lame, the drunken Indians, teenage hookers of all sexes, and these pathetic, burnt-out, middle-aged assholes who still wear their hair halfway down their backs. Ah, how sweet it is.

Should have passed on the suey at the Chinaman's up the alley, or maybe it was the sweet and sour pussycat, but now it was coming on like a case of turista, liquid pouring out like a trapdoor jerked open. I LOVE TO SUCK BIG HARD COCKS, a magic marker scrawl on the door to the can informed him. And the boogie boys had followed him in, were paddling around in the slop out there. He smelled dope. "A fucking Paki, eh?" one of them was saying. "So I goes, let's stomp on his rag for him, eh? Shit, fucking turkey. So scared he practically turned *white*."

That's it, fellas, yuck it up, you're stuck in time and you don't even know it. Of course the tragic trio from Nanaimo, B.C. (with yours truly on drums) must sound like a boiler factory to you, it aint your music, and God knows how the kids even *heard* punk rock in Nanaimo, let alone learned to play it, but they did, and they aint half bad, and I may be the same age as you burnt-out assholes, but at least I'm still in motion.

Shit, it was actually kind of funny. The kids from Nanaimo sure weren't ready for *this* slice of the big time, ready to run off the stage when the burn-out boys started banging on the tabletops with their beer glasses, started chanting "Boogie, boogie, boogie," like a goddamned aboriginal tribe, started throwing beer at the band. "You don't walk off a job," you had to yell — although who the hell did you think you were kidding, candy man? You've walked off plenty — and yelled, "Turn up, turn up, turn up. Dominate the fuckers with the sound," and so you turned up everything there was to turn, and after that it hadn't mattered a damn what you were playing, you were giving that lobotomized crowd exactly what they'd come for — the good old walking talking rock-and-roll avalanche. But a damned bad night when you've got to do your own singing. Jerked the boom stand over to your drums, tilted the mike down, yelled through it, "One chord, all right? A C chord." And then bawled out an old Southern country tune that didn't work half bad with a punk beat under it, rammed it right down the throat of drunken Hastings Street — "I wish to the Lord I never been born, or died when I was young."

A penciled note on the crapper door said CASTRATE FAG-GOTS. Blue smoke curling up to the ceiling like an eyeful of flies, and a voice somewhere intoning, "Tell me about it, man. Why don't you just tell me about it?" Steve leaned back against the cold wet porcelain. His guts were finally empty. He wiped his ass, pulled up shorts and jeans. Here you are, man, once again playing among your own people — the good plain ordinary folk.

Stepped out of the can and, damn it, they were waiting for him. "Now you fellas aren't planning to pick a fight with *me*, are you?"

The little fart was the vanguard. Of course. "You want to fight, turkey?"

Steve was sick of it. Sidestepped the windmilling fist, snagged the little man, flipped him around as a shield against the others, levered him up into a hammerlock. Free left hand dipped into jacket pocket, whipped it on out, and *click*.

"Switchblades preferred, asshole," Steve said and pressed the point against the naked throat, right on target for the carotid artery.

"Talk to me, sweetheart," Steve said, crooning. "Let me hear the whole sad story of your life. Let us weep together like brothers."

The little man in his arms stank worse than any polecat.

Steve pushed the point in until he could see the first tiny bead of free blood. For the first time in months he felt something like joy. That he could feel anything at all was something like joy. "Shit, you aint much of a conversationalist," he said. "Not a good word, huh?"

The little man's eyes were bulging. Spittle was dripping from the corners of his mouth. "Well, fellas, what do you say? Should I carve him or not?"

Five frozen faces stared back at him. Nobody was moving a muscle. "All right, fellas," Steve said, "now you listen up real good. When I turn this here motherfucker loose, there's only one thing I want to see. And that's the backsides of you all, stepping right along out of here. If I see anything other than that, then somebody's going to get cut. You got that?"

Steve jerked the knife away, shoved the man away, helped him along with a boot up the ass that sent him sprawling. Steve transferred the knife from his left hand to his right. "How you assholes die is of no concern to me," he said.

Filing out, they looked like the seven dwarves going by Snow White's coffin. The little fucker was last, yelled back over his shoulder, "We'll be back."

"You do that, asshole."

Steve let himself sag back against the wall, laughed out loud. "Ah shit," he said. "How sweet it is."

Kathy had to fight to stay awake. It was too warm in the recital hall; Paul had already been talking for half an hour, and she hadn't been able to follow much of it. Now he was going on about someone called Guillaume de Machaut, was writing out yet another example of music on the blackboard. "Most well known example of this sort of thing," he was saying. "*Ma fin est mon commencement, et mon commencement ma fin...* My beginning is my end, and my end my beginning. And the music, as you can see, does exactly that. Identical lines running from the beginning and end simultaneously."

Kathy hid a yawn behind her hand. Evelyn caught her at it, leaned over to whisper, "Better get used to it. You'll be hearing it for years."

Kathy suppressed a giggle, then felt guilty about it. She stared straight ahead and tried to pay attention.

"Ockeghem," Paul was saying, "built into his works all manner of devices that reflected the cosmic order but that were not *able to be heard*. He uses, for example, the number 999 associated with the Virgin Mary, but no listener, not even the most erudite, could have been expected to hear the devices based upon this number. Such things used to puzzle me when I was a graduate student. Just as all of us have, I grew up in the pragmatic modern tradition, and I thought, if no one can hear it, then what is the point of it? A similar question might be asked of the entire fourteenth century with its isorhythmic writing. But then, attempting to think the way Ockeghem himself might have done, I thought, oh, but the Virgin Mary herself will hear it, and so will God."

The specialized audience laughed at Paul's little joke, and he smiled faintly back at them. "The music exists, then," he said, "on the ladder of natural law, the great chain of being that stretches from the plowman in the field who will hear nothing but pretty sounds, all the way up to God in heaven who will notice, and approve, of Ockeghem's complex devices."

Paul's voice was still going on and on, and, once again, Kathy lost the thread of it. Give it half a chance, she thought, and maybe it will all settle back into routine — the shopping, the cooking, the dishes, the evening paper. Maybe after enough time it will be just as though Steve had never come back at all. And then she was drifting. Almost asleep.

Kathy jerked herself back to consciousness, tried to force herself to concentrate. Arranged in a row of straight-backed chairs on the stage were Wendy and the others who were waiting to stand up and sing the van Dorestad motet with Paul — if he was ever going to get around to it. Christ, he seemed to be running down the entire history of western music. But she thought she could hear the beginning of a summing up, the rounding off toward a close.

"Lowinsky was quite right in asking himself how we could possibly account for such a strange procedure. When we speak of truth today, we usually mean the truth of empirical science, and that truth is generally thought to be something that can be stated formally and clearly, something with only one meaning. But in working through the van Dorestad material, it has begun to occur to me that there is another truth, one that cannot be communicated directly and clearly but that requires a tension, a double-faced ambiguity, to be communicated at all." He paused, frowning, and looked down at his notes.

Kathy was drifting; for a moment she saw Steve, not what he was now but what he had been. "It'd be a favor," he was saying in a softly crooning voice. "It'd be a kind of tenderness." They're in that slum apartment by the Cambridge dump. The summer heat is appalling. "We could make love, then just talk quietly," he says. "We could say goodbye. Then when the fireworks started, you could do it. Then just throw it there on the floor and walk out. Remember what was good. Remember how much we loved each other. All right, Kath? Will you do it, Kath?"

Kathy woke with a hard contraction of her muscles against the back of the seat. She caught herself. She'd been falling.

She could see the people on the stage so vividly it was painful; she could hear every sound in the recital hall — the coughing behind her, the rustle of programs on people's laps, the swish of paper. Behind the lecturn, Paul was looking down, turning through pages and pages of notes. He appeared to be lost in thought.

Kathy felt the rising tension in the audience. Her heart began to race. What had happened to him? Had he lost his place completely? Was he ever going to say anything? Then Paul raised his head—it was a slow, deliberate motion—and looked directly at Hanna Rossenmüller. His eyes and the old woman's were locked together for several seconds. Then, just as deliberately, he turned the last of his notes face down. He finally looked out at the audience.

"The research into the historical background of this motet," he said, "is in its preliminary stages. About van Dorestad the man we know nothing at all."


You remember it all, don't you, crooked drummer? Sure you do. You counted off beats of rest, ticked them off from the downbeat, everything timed to perfection just like the Atlanta Symphony.

They're all packed into that place of his that night just the way you knew they were going to be, the GIs and ex-GIs, the stoned freaks, and the little plastic space girls — the Mary-Lous and Susie-Qs — the pipe going around, the Stones on the stereo, crystal meth in the can, and you're honkered right down next to him, shoulder to shoulder. "You my man, Stevo, right?"

"Just you and me, Robert, and you the one."

Feel the soapstone pressed into your hand, take it and drag. The hash tastes like candy. You can't be looking at your watch too often or he'll catch you at it. Timeless is the number, so what are you doing with time? Keeping time, that's what you're doing. Aint that your job, drummer? He's talking to a Susie, so you slip back the cuff of your jacket just a hair, see that, yeah, it's time. Hurry up, please, gentlemen, it's time. "Got to crap," you say under your breath to nobody in particular.

Lock the bathroom door behind you — fat chance of anybody hearing the click over four million decibels of Mick Jagger — and fast, you jerk up the window and snake out onto the fire escape. You're hung up there in the night, and with the hash in you, can't resist a look. Above, stars through Boston haze, powdered sugar over milky ink. Below it's the black alley, the buildings lined up, city rectangles. Stretch on your wrists, muscles pulled tight, hanging arc with the moon rising on your left. But can't go on looking, you're about out of time.

Scramble on down the fire escape and a tiny demon's hand reaches out to stop you, snags your jacket, but it's just a nail. Tear free and keep on going. Hang drop to the ground, take the fall with bending knees easy as a creamed cat, and then you're running across the moist dirt of the backyard. Got a key to his garage because you've done him some favors. You had it copied before you gave it back, of course you did, and of course he knows that. Just part of the game, right?

He probably expects it in his apartment, but you know better than that, know how he sleeps with that forty-four magnum so close he can grab it in a second, and sure he'd blow you away in his own apartment, not a doubt in the world. You've learned his ways by now, know him a hell of a lot better than Peter did, and that's what you're betting on, that you can second guess him the whole way down the pike.

You're in the garage now, the door shut behind you. Can smell oil and gasoline. You know what he keeps besides his Alfa, know about his tools, and it's waiting just the way you remember it — the tire iron. Hold it in your hand, feel the hard rough metal, the weight of it, test it with a light tap or two on your other hand, on your open palm. Oh yeah, it'll do the job. It'll do just fine. And you know just where to wait because he's right-handed. He'll take the gun into his left hand, open the trunk with his right. Never seen a man yet who could open a trunk with his left hand if he was right-handed. And you know what's in the trunk. Suitcases full of clothes, ordinary clothes like an insurance salesman might wear, except the shoes have hollow heels filled with uncut smack. So pick your shadow, check the time, drummer, and wait. In a few seconds Kathy's going to call him. And if she doesn't? Well, then the show's over.

But if she does call, he's going to smile and say to himself, "Oh no you don't, Stevo, not tonight." He's going to say, "Sure, maybe a bust coming and maybe not, but crazy Steven's got the keys to the car, to the trunk." So you're betting he's not going to jump right in the Alfa. No, he's going to have to check the trunk first, have a little look. Something like a quarter of a million in there. And you know he doesn't care about the money by now, but he has to act like he cares because that's part of the game.

So wait, not moving a muscle, and you count. Eight and a half minutes, until the tension is singing like one of Ned's solos, until the whole fucking world is singing with it. No relief, man, just wait. And he's a little late, but he's there. Garage door goes up, rattle, *bang*. He leaves it up. He's walking fast, coat draped over his right arm. Seen him do that before, and you know that magnum's in his hand just as sure as you know he's got the hammer drawn back and ready to fire. The night's strung out like a bat whistle. You've already done this a million times, you've dreamed it, it's a fucking acid trip. It's as real as the gas smell in your nose. Shit, it's too easy. You're running him like a robot.

He shifts the gun into his left hand, hauls the key out of his jeans with his right, shoves the trunk key in, and he's bent forward. You're wearing sneakers and the floor's concrete and you're there, right on time. But then you miss the count. You goddamned fool. *Because you've got to make sure he knows.* "Lyons," you say.

Too fast. Coat's falling and the magnum is pointed straight at your belly, hammer back just as you knew it would be. Anybody ever say a man can't fire a gun with his left hand? He grins, makes a little clicking sound with his tongue on the roof of his mouth — "Tsk, tsk" — stands looking at you.

"Oh well, Steven," he says in that voice you know like a brother's, "you weren't quick enough."

You're a dead man.

Then he does the strangest thing in the world. He pretends you're not there. He sweeps the aim of the gun away from your belly, turns back to the trunk, bends down, and starts to unlock it. You hit him. You lose time.

When you come back, the inside of your right hand's full of blood, burning like it's been torched, and you've mashed his head good. It's true, brains are gray, and they're soft and squishy like Jell-O. You look at those slots you've beat into his head, and you think, a madman did that. You wipe your blood off the tire iron with a handkerchief, throw the tire iron down, stuff the handkerchief in your jeans. He's dead as a man can get. You look at him, at that ruined head, and you know he's beat you. You're running now, and you can never love again.

Paul nodded to the others; they inhaled together — timed perfectly together — and began to sing. And even though they had rehearsed it in the living room a dozen times, Kathy had never genuinely heard the music before. Paul had told the women, "Never forget that you're supposed to be boys," but Wendy was the only one who sounded like a boy. She was singing the highest part, and her voice was a clear, sweet treble. *"Tunc Jesus ductus est..."*

It was astonishing music; it overlapped and murmured, the words repeating. It was like a wash of water, surf. Kathy looked down at the English translation and read, "Then was Jesus led up of the Spirit into the wilderness to be tempted of the devil." They were singing the Latin words over and over. When she'd been a child, Kathy had tried to imagine angel choirs; this sound was what she had tried to imagine.

Suddenly it was changing, moving. Kathy heard the modulation clearly, the unexpected twist of it, a disquieting fall, a dizzying sweep. The hair prickled on the back of her neck. *"Iterum assumpsit eum diabolus..."*

She read: "Again the devil taketh him up into an exceeding high mountain and sheweth him all the kingdoms of the world, and the glory of them; and saith unto him, All these things will I give thee, if thou wilt fall down and worship me."

It was continuing to modulate just as Paul had said it would. It was restless, incomplete, always in motion, a shivering tumble of sound that never stopped or paused, continued to push on down a crooked road toward an unknown destination. Wendy's voice didn't blend with the others, soared above like rippling silver light. Kathy had never heard music like this before. She didn't know what to do with it.

*"Tunc dicit ei Jesus: Vade, Santana..."*

"Thus saith Jesus unto him, Get thee hence, Satan, for it is written, Thou shalt worship the Lord thy God, and him only shalt thou serve."

The women were dropping out one at a time, and the music that was left for the men had become winding and sinuous and enormously sad. It was getting darker. Then a moment of passage, a vast hollow sonority like a gate, and then center, rest. The modulation was completed, had come home on a rich sweetness built firmly on the bass.

Now only Paul was left, holding a long, profoundly deep note. He fell silent, waited with his head bowed.

After a moment, the recital hall began to fill with polite applause.

"You got any Southern Comfort?" Steve said, laughing privately at his own lame joke. But, amazingly, the Greek produced a dusty bottle of it from somewhere behind the bar, several shots left at the bottom, poured the whole works into a beer glass, and pushed it over — a gesture so unexpected and gracious that Steve's eyes filled with tears.

The Greek's eyes were small, watery, and black. "You boys going to play again?"

"Yeah. Sure. What do you think? Of course we're going to play again."

"Good. Then we go home."

Steve carried the glass out onto Hastings Street. For the moment everything was slowed down, suspended. Cars rolling by, a knot of goofy-looking people approaching along an askew and shifting tangent, the streetlights nostalgic and sweet, even beautiful. The wet pavement, some old-fashioned neon, yellow glow of the pawnshop window on the far corner, so many lost dreams piled up behind that glass and wire mesh — guitars and violins, amplifiers, saxophones, even a string bass — shed skin of musicians who'd moved on, back to the canning plant or the office or the road.

Shit, Steve thought, once it was a joy to rattle down city streets, drummer, pulse of the world, something just great waiting around every corner, just beyond reach. But you're stopped now, you've run it out and could drift away in this misty city, nothing left but a hapless shamble. Chase it all west and eventually you get stuck at the edge where the sun falls into the sea and dies with a hiss. And, like a premonition of spring, he saw how he could do it, walk out and keep on walking, glass in hand, not even bothering to go back for his jacket, let alone his drum set, yeah, without the van, without his night's pay, without a word to anybody, drift hazily up Hastings Street letting the falling water soak him to the skin. But to do what? A drifting shadow, Zero the Fool, back to the empty beach at Tofino where there's nothing but gray gulls, to lie down in the sand and sleep? He drank and tasted the South — his own private joke for the South — his own blood on his tongue.

The strange people were getting close enough by now to turn into discrete units, and aha, Steve thought, *here's* our audience, finally showing up right when you need them — the kids. And remembered how weird Alison had looked when he'd first seen her, and Jesus, how did they all learn to do it, get the image right all over the world at the same time, imported records, fanzines, generational mental telepathy, or what? Who the fuck knows, but here they are again with their orange and green hair, ripped raincoats, garbage-bag shirts, torn stockings and spike heels, old dirty rubber running shoes, makeup on everyone, the boys too, a sooty smear around the eyes like cut-rate vampires. And safety pins and razor blades and lengths of chain from the hardware store, and one girl having a little difficulty walking because her knees are tied together with a snot-coloured scarf. "Pretty vacant," Steve said to them, and one of the girls blew her robot identity to give him a grin for it. Shit, behind the bombed-out image they were just babies.

They were headed, just as he knew they had to be, for the bar, *his* bar. Love you all, he thought, toasted the empty space where they'd been, and drank off the last of the syrupy South from the beer glass.

He walked back inside, moving it easy. The punk kids had pushed up directly to the stage and were standing, lined up and rooted to the spot like department-store dummies. Despite the melodrama in the crapper, the boogie-till-you-puke crew had never left the bar, were still hanging out in the back like a bunch of sullen cavemen, and Steve saw that the little fucker had passed clean out, strings of greasy hair hanging down onto the table, bald as a monk on top, one hand still wrapped around his beer glass, black grime under his nails, his pals sitting around him, stunned and stupefied. Steve gently patted the little man as he passed, gave the rest of them the high sign.

Steve was almost happy now at the end of the night. A fat Indian woman had taken him by the shirt, hands tugging, doing two things at once — getting his attention and preventing herself from tipping slowly over onto her face. "Play me some song, eh? Play me some song. Want to dance."

"Sure, lady. I'll play and you dance. That's exactly how it's going to be." He gently disentangled her fingers from his shirt, aimed her broad buttocks at a chair and willed her into it. She sat down, slack-faced, and drank somebody else's beer. Steve climbed back up onto the stage. No matter how dead they were trying to look, the punk kids were cranked up and ready, but the regular clientel was crapped-out and flattened by now, lost in a catatonic stupor, mumbling, a few collapsed forms even snoring. "Here we are at the tag end, boys," Steve said to his band. "Can we still kick ass?"

ONE, TWO, THREE, FOUR. Heigh ho, heigh ho, it's off to work we go, the boiler factory kicking in, no warning, no problem, folks, just the end of the world, that's all, the first nuke that takes it out falling splat in front of the speakers. Heard it plenty from Alison, all her records, the Clash and the Sex Pistols and X-Ray Specs and the Banshees, and you can do it just fine, can't you, candy man? Shit, you stepping along so fast, double bouncing the bass peddle, sweat in your eyes, those teenagers from Nanaimo barely keeping up. Think you burnt *me* out? Think again, motherfuckers.

The kids are bounding up and down like kangaroos, rigid arms with fists stuck up in the air. Ah, sweethearts, I love you. Know you never heard of him, but it's Uncle John playing for you tonight, come to take his children home. And shit, even the Greek seems to like this howling chaos. Nodding, washing glasses, his moist eyes seem to be saying, "Go to it, boys."

But the explosion had wakened the little boogie-till-you-puke man. He sat up and shook his head, peered around obscurely with half-lidded eyes, saw the punks in front of him, wadded up an empty potato chip bag and threw it at them — absolutely pointless gesture that nobody seemed to notice. Let his head drop again, a moment, then jerked upright, fully awake, like he was seeing, for the first time, exactly how far he'd sunk.

Underneath the screaming wall of noise a single low-frequency vibration built up from the little fucker, detached itself and, slow as honey, uncoiled across the bar. Steve thought he could read that stunned mind — *What the hell you doing, man, drunk again, pissing away your life for nothing, going nowhere, hanging out with this same bunch of clowns in this dribbling asshole bar and listening to this shit?*

But, as usual, the voice turned out to be one of Steve's own. The worm that flies in the night and blights the rose, and the blight turns out to be nothing more than the same tune played over and over again until it's got no more sense to it than stale puke. Jesus, you flail around, reaching, grabbing, trying to *feel* something, even blood, pain, riot, disaster, murder — anything at all — but nothing's left, and then you're a drunken old Jim Morrison, no longer the beautiful boy, the leather queen, the lizard king and saint, but just a confused silly old wet fart on the stage who can't think of a goddamned thing to do but pull out his limp prick and wave it at the audience. Shit, can't go out that way, end up as some pointless asshole, vague and incomprehensible, stumbling around in the box at Nuremberg while a bunch of dumb fat mindless corn-fed farmers from Iowa stare at you and wonder how such a piddling little gray man could have been so goddamned evil.

But you wrote the script, candy man. Can see it coming, and it's all so fucking useless. The little fucker was up on his feet, stumbling across the treacherous floor, to try to pick a fight with the punk kids.

The tune, if you could call it a tune, had come crashing to a stop. Steve grabbed a live mike and said through it, southernly, "Hey, asshole, lay off. It's too late for this shit." His voice sounded hollow bouncing off the walls, like a bus station attendant announcing, "Now leaving for Gainesville, Athens, Augusta, Milledgeville, Macon, Griffin, and Atlanta."

The man looked up at the stage with a stupid smile. You know that sweating pig look, only seen it a million times before. It says, "Hey, you've got to understand. I don't particularly want to do this, aint going to make me happy to do this, shit, if I could get out of it, I would, but you see how it is, if I don't do it, my balls will drop off."

The man threw a glass of beer into the face of a little girl with orange hair.

She's too shocked to do anything but shake her head, but the rest of the punk kids are moving in to protect her, and so, naturally, here come the boogie boys from the back to gather around their man. The Greek aint no help. He's staring at the glass he's polishing.

"Hey," Steve says softly through the mike, "you don't have to prove nothing to us, buddy. We all know you're the meanest mother in the valley."

The kids from Nanaimo, too fast, like Keystone Kops, are packing up their guitars. Scared shitless. The Greek's turned the overhead light on, yelling, "Closing time, closing time." Anybody with any sense is jumping up, scurrying out, silly Groucho Marx explosion of activity while Steve, stopped finally, just sits behind his drum set. The little fart pushes up to the stage and stares him in the face. "Hey, turkey, I'm sick of your fucking shit. Need that fucking knife, eh? Why don't you fight like a fucking man?"

Abandoning mike, Steve speaks directly to the bleary eyes, to the terrified eyes. "Cash it in, buddy. I got nothing against you."

"I'll cash you in, turkey."

"Don't be ridiculous." Steve stands, stretches, lays down his sticks.

One of his buddies is tugging at the little man's arm, but he shakes off the restraint and jumps up onto the stage, so drunk he almost doesn't make it — flaccid, loose, strings cut, head drifting side to side, working hard to focus. Steve laughs, knowing how perfect it is. "Here," he says and offers the little man the knife. "You take it, OK? That make you feel any better?"

Steve turns away and begins to pack up his drum set. Behind him, he hears the click of the blade opening. He doesn't even look.

The shock blows it straight up like a pillar of fire, time torn away in an instant, lights burning bright again. On his knees where he's fallen, Steve hears voices yelling all around him. Twists up to his feet, feels a blazing in his back, hiss of air, adrenaline kick. The little man stands frozen, mouth hanging open, eyes wide and spilling over. Steve grins at him, gray southern wolf, crab-scrabbles arm behind back and finds the handle, grabs it and pulls.

"Jesus!" through his teeth, feels blade scrape bone coming out, scrape rib. "Jesus!" But then it's better. Blood fucking everywhere, maybe in his mouth too, salty taste. Hand's covered with blood. The switchblade's covered with blood.

The man's friends are pulling at him, trying to get him out, but he won't move, stands rooted, not able to believe he's done it, and waits for Steve to carve him. Steve folds up the blade, throws the knife away. "Get him out of here," he yells. "Hurry up. The cops will be here any minute. Go on. Move!"

Everybody's staring at him. Blood must be streaming down his back, can feel it on his jeans, shit, he's trailing blood, spurting it, a goddamned fountain of blood, and laughing, stumbles for the door. His motion has freed everyone. The man and his buddies are off and running, the punk kids are running. "Hey, hey, hey," the Greek's yelling, trying to hold him back. "Stay still. Don't move. I call the cops. Hey, *stay still.*"

"Shit, got to get outside. Can't stay in this fucking place, man."

Steve pushes the Greek's hands away, keeps on moving into the swimmy blackness, pain in his lung, on the right, incredible, fearsome. But he's made it outside into the rain where he wants to be. And he's not alone. There are children holding him, guiding him, as he lets himself sink slowly down onto the pavement. "Oh fuck," he says and lets his head fall back so the rain can wash him full in the face.

It's true, a big enough hit can still get you off, blown to hell and gone, mind racing at ten million miles to the minute, read-out in the blue circle, chrome-streaked and moving, lights a smear, the lights of Hastings Street along the Charles River, swear to God, Kath, one more massive onslaught and the stars will break, cut loose and pin out like firewheels.

Hears his own voice, "Oh Jesus!" weeping in fear and pain. It hurts, but shit, better than zero nothing, aint it, candy man? And you know what you've done, don't you? Crying now for every-body you've ever hurt, and already the sirens are wailing down the city. "Oh shit," Steve says out loud, "I'm so fucking sorry."

Then sees the children around him, bending over him, touching him. Weird painted little faces. The girl with orange hair has tears streaming down, turning her makeup to black streaks. She takes his hand. He squeezes it. "Oh baby," he says, "sweet angel. Don't cry for *me*."

Amazing how fast the cops can turn up sometimes. The punk kids cleared away. The shiny black shoes. "Just lay still, pal. Don't try to move. What was it, a knife?"

The Greek. "Stabbed him, stabbed him right in the back, eh? Just stabbed him."

"Shit," Steve yells, the panic hitting. "I'm coming unraveled. I'm getting simple."

"Don't worry about it, pal. Just don't move, OK?"

The sirens are singing for you like Saint Dylan's locusts, so many sirens, so much rain, so many lights in the city, so many voices. Here's a little brown-skinned man with a neat black jacket, some kind of symbol on the front pocket, bending down to take your pulse. "Keep him still, keep him still."

"Where'd it go in? On the right?"

"Got to get fluid into him. Hepatic artery."

"Just take it easy, my friend. No, don't try to sit up. We're going to take care of everything now."

"Jesus, I think it went through his liver."

Lift onto stretcher. "Hey," Steve says, giving them the old grin, "blow your sirens for me, man. Make them wail, all right?"

"Don't worry, you'll get lots of sirens." Cloth around his arm, blood pressure. "What happened, eh?"

"Shit, not important. Poor fucking asshole, too drunk to... Just stuck it to me, right? That's all. He didn't know what he was doing."

Wail it, wail it, wail it, city lights streaking by, wailing down the city. "Hey, his blood pressure's falling off. He's losing too much blood."

Yeah, and it's muddying up your mind, everything going thick and clotty on you. Damn, it's too fast, too fucking fast. Never thought it'd be this fast. Try to hold onto something, anything. If you can hold it clear to the end, then you're through your Bardo. OK, Kathy's long black hair hanging down, Sloopy, old rock and roll sweetheart. Alison's big almond eyes. Wendy in the rain. But it's going, washing away, can't keep any of it. Focus, man, it's important.

"Hey," Steve yells, "hey, hey." Alone and afraid.

"Yeah, buddy."

"Got to tell them something, OK?"

"Yeah, right. What?"

But you've lost it again, shit, for how long? Time's running out on you, drummer. But you can't lose time yet, have to hang onto it, have to remember. Jesus, focus, you've got to focus. "Tell them..."

But what the fuck can you say? Coming undone, coming apart, swimming upstream into black glue. It's a door, like fear, like iron. It's bare planes across which cold wind drives continually from a black center. And you'll be running forever, out there alone in it fucking forever. But shit, that's not it. You see it then, you've got to hang onto it. But you can't hang onto it. "Aw fuck," Steve says, laughing.

"Jesus, his pressure's falling off. We're going to lose him. Too much blood."

Black clots. Ink and cottage cheese. Can't hold it, all clotting up and washing away. But you've done it, and they're home free. So all right, Steven, give it up. It's not hideous, it's sweet. Saint Steven, you'll be their comfort when you're gone.

Steve lets go. The pain's gone. The tears are gone. The lights of the city are gone. He can no longer hear the sirens, the voices. No longer remembers their faces, remember his own face. He's pushing at the door now. Door is iron is fear. Door is immense and won't budge. And then with a slam he's through it. Last memory unwinding like trailing cloth, wisp of melody with a drumbeat under it. He thought he'd be running forever across a windy dark plane, but when he pushed through the door, the sun rose upon him.

# XII

Kathy looked out the open window at the glory of the spring day. It was cruel how beautiful it was — the brilliance of the sun, the flowers bursting into bloom. And Steve's ironic ghost was out there somewhere, a shit-eating grin on its face. "You couldn't do anything right, could you, asshole," Kathy said to it. "Did you mean it as a blessing or just another one of your warped jokes?"

"It's yours now, babe," the voice in her mind said, "so you run it."

"Oh, thanks a hell of a lot," Kathy told it. "But did you have to die to give me that?"

As usual, the ghost had nothing more to say. She set the horn case down on the table in front of the window, opened it. She looked out at the day. "If I could," she told him, "I'd say the Bardo for you." But she didn't know how. And whatever ritual they'd used to bury him in Georgia didn't count; she had to find her own ritual, and this was the only thing she knew.

She sighted down the barrel. Just as she should have known, the horn wasn't playable. The pads had shrunk and dried up. Many of her reeds had cracked. She selected the best of them, put it in her mouth, and sucked on it. The cork that should have held the mouthpiece firmly in place had shrunk. She greased it and heated it with her lighter. Eventually it swelled enough to do the job. And then she was at the window with the strap around her neck and the Selmer in her hands. Could she do it?

She inserted the reed, tightened the ligature. She closed her eyes, took the horn into her mouth. It didn't matter how many years had passed; she'd always remember what to do. Stiff lower lip drawn back across bottom teeth, mouthpiece held at the sides with the lips, top lip stiff, sealing off the mouthpiece. She blew, and nothing happened. My God, she thought, I haven't got a single chop left in the world. She blew again, and a terrible honk came out, a G. She played the notes of the upper stack — G, A, B, C. She tried for an F and couldn't find it. The horn felt impossibly stiff and dry. Kathy felt impossibly stiff and dry.

She kept pushing air through the instrument—G, G, G, then an A. Then G, A, B, C, D. She felt the horn giving a little back; her mind had remembered all along, but now her muscles were remembering too. She tried the lower notes — F, E, D. They came wheezing out. And, after only a few minutes, the muscles in her cheeks were beginning to hurt; the muscles in her throat were beginning to hurt. Saint Morrison, Saint Jimmy, Saint Janis he'd called them. "Hey, you guys out there," she said to them. "Give him a break, OK? Take him now and give him some rest."

Blowing, she felt a fierce pain knotting her stomach, her chest. It was coming in waves. There it was again, another spasm of it, a contraction. And she was remembering the changes for something, four or five notes of something. She was blowing part of a tune. And the pain struck her again; her entire body arched with it, jerking, contracting. It was terrible, frightening, but she wasn't going to let it stop her. She blew through the horn.

Suddenly she knew what it was, how simple it was — tears — and the moment she knew, she was torn apart by them. She hung on and cried through the saxophone. She couldn't believe how much was pouring out of her; it felt like a sea. Tears streamed down her face, wet the reed, wet the barrel. Tears wet her hands, wet her fingertips. The horn was wet, everything was wet. With a terrible difficulty, making a terrible fog-horn honking, she was playing "C Jam Blues."


Kathy held the car at an even forty miles an hour on Oak Street and caught every light green. The sun was everywhere; she felt the heat of it on the right side of her face, looked toward it, saw Wendy's hair as a spray of white gold. The girl was looking straight ahead through the windshield. "I didn't even know he had a girlfriend in Toronto," Kathy said.

"Well, he did."

"How are we going to recognize her?"

"I don't know. I just think we'll recognize her, that's all."

They didn't speak again until Kathy had parked. "Don't you

think we ought to tell your dad about it?" she said.

"No," Wendy said.

In the terminal Kathy read on the video monitor that the flight was early, had already landed. At the far end of the building passengers were already on their way out. "There," Wendy said — the distant, slender figure of a young woman with orange hair, in a leather jacket and gleaming pants that looked like plastic. Kathy couldn't help laughing. "You're probably right," she said.

"Of course I'm right."

Kathy stepped forward, but Wendy caught her hand. "Let me do it, OK?"

"Are you sure?"

"Yes, please. I'm sure."

Kathy lit a cigarette, watched Wendy walk fast across the length of the terminal, and then, without warning, felt a profound inner shift. She saw the two girls as enormously far away now, but brilliantly defined, like distant figures in a bright painting. The pleats in Wendy's uniform skirt snapped as she walked. The girl with orange hair had stopped, was looking around. Wendy walked up to her, spoke. The other girl stepped back awkwardly. Kathy inhaled smoke all the way down to the bottom of her lungs, held it, felt it there. Held it.

If the girl with orange hair took those ridiculous heels off, she and Wendy would probably be the same height. Kathy slowly let the smoke flow out of her nose and mouth. The girl with orange hair jerked one hand up to her face, pressed it hard into her mouth. Kathy blew out the last of the smoke, then, taking herself by surprise, dropped her cigarette onto the floor and stepped on it. Wendy extended a hand; the other girl hesitated, then took it. The two girls embraced. Kathy's mind felt empty as an eggshell. Then, moving with a powerful sense of inevitability, she took her cigarettes and lighter out of her pocket and dumped them in the first trash can she saw.


My Dear Doctor Crane:

Thank you for sending me the tape of your performance of the van Dorestad motet. Please do not feel the need to apologize for what you call "the amateur nature" of the performance. A more polished reading would have been possible with professionals, but we must remember that the root of the word "amateur" is "love," and the love of the music shines through every note. I am looking forward with deep pleasure to working with you during the coming year and hope that, together, we might attempt a number of public performances, not only of the van Dorestad motet but of other music of the period.

But I must now turn to the purpose of this letter, which is to bring you up to date on the van Dorestad research so far. I am in the process now of preparing a detailed chronology based upon primary sources, with particular interest in the points at which the primary sources contradict each other, and, I must warn you, these points are many.

The people seized near Wesel in 1561 were certainly musicians. All sources agree upon this point. The "inquisitor" or "magistrate," Albrecht Böhm (the reason that modern scholars are unclear as to his exact role is that the primary sources do not tell us), appears to have arrived from Cologne very quickly, but then the complicated wrangling which led up to the trial took nearly two months. Böhm appears to have played upon the fear, general to the time, of a popular uprising, and the Duke, against his better judgement, was eventually persuaded to proceed. Böhm obtained total authority for conducting the trial, and, in March, had the three leaders of the imprisoned group brought before him: Sister Katrei, Brother Michael, and magister Johannes (who is, as we know, Jan van Dorestad).

Michael spoke on their behalf, the other two remaining silent. He claimed that none of them had the slightest interest in religious matters whatsoever, and that they were only a band of itinerant musicians with their families seeking employment in Germany. It was true, he said, that they referred to each other as "brother" and "sister," but that was a custom only and had no religious significance. Böhm asked Michael a series of doctrinal questions concerning baptism and the sleep of souls after death, to which Michael replied consistently, "We do not know about such things." After several days of torture, he was still persisting in his denials, adding only, "I am but a poor minstrel singer," but when torture was first applied to Katrei, his wife, he suddenly burst forth with a ringing denunciation of his captors, calling them "disciples of Satan" and "followers of the Antichrist." Böhm asked Michael once again to admit his heresy, to which Michael replied, "Whatever you say we are, we are."

Their statement was taken to be an admission of guilt, and Michael was sentenced to death by drowning, "a second baptism" as Böhm ironically put it. At dawn Michael was bound to a wooden plank weighted with stones and dragged into the river. Asked for the last time to repent of his heresy, he refused and, when offered the crucifix to kiss, replied, "Cast your wooden god upon the waters. He will float better than I."

As the river closed over him, he cried out, in the words of Jesus: "*In manus tuos, Domine, commendo spiritum meum.*" His body was retrieved and hanged on display in iron chains for the instruction of the people.

Böhm now turned his attention to Katrei. Of all the actors in our drama, she is to me the most mysterious. I do believe that we will be able to demonstrate that Katrei is, under another name, the infamous Margaret of Antwerp, but even though we establish this identity, we are still left with a puzzling figure. When Böhm asked her if she were, indeed, Margaret of Antwerp, she replied with the only direct communications her captors would receive from her during her long imprisonment and ordeal. She made gestures indicating that writing material be brought to her and then wrote in Latin the one sentence: "I am she."

The *Book of Martyrs* (written, I must add, years after the events had taken place) claims her as an Anabaptist and portrays her as an unlettered girl, dutiful, obedient, and kind — even somewhat simple-minded — her primary virtue being Christlike patience and endurance in the face of her terrible suffering. It is impossible to reconcile this view with the young woman who was not only able to write at a period when literacy among women was marginal, but was able to write in Latin.

The trial record brands her as a witch and gives us the impression of a sinister figure, accused of blasphemy, unnatural acts, fornication with a number of men, including her father-in-law, and various works of black magic: causing cows to dry up, men to become impotent, chickens to lay stones, and the like. She was said to have been widely feared. But this view of her is contradicted by the fact that the local magistrates argued that she should be executed in secret out of a fear of causing an uprising because she was "loved widely for her many acts of charity, kindness, and healing among the people." (And, indeed, she does appear to have made an enormous impact upon the local peasantry; I gather that, for decades after her death, she was revered by the local populace as a saint, and, to this day, her memory persists in the regional saying, "as silent as Katrei.")

Finally, there is Böhm's own view of her, written three years later when he was deep in the throes of guilt over having caused her death. Not only does he call her a saint, but he claims her as his own personal redemptress, a statement that sheds more light upon the character of Böhm than it does upon that of Katrei. That Böhm was a deeply disturbed man whose recollections are not to be trusted is obvious both from the terrible ferocity with which he proceeded against Katrei and then from the intensity of his later conversion.

Let us return to the trial record. Since her arrest, Katrei had not uttered a single word, and even the most intensive and prolonged torture had done nothing to loosen her tongue. Several peasant women were brought forward who claimed that Katrei had performed acts of witchcraft and blasphemy. It is difficult to escape the conclusion that Böhm coached the witnesses, but, upon the basis of their testimony, she was convicted. Böhm was extremely vexed by her powers of remaining silent, which he said, quoting the *Maleus Mallificarum*, must have been given to her directly by Satan himself. To exorcise the demon in her, he ordered that her hands be broken; then he had her bound, gagged, and submersed in freezing water and afterwards taken into a heated room where spirits were poured over her and lighted. This strange procedure did not work, and she continued to remain silent.

Böhm then proceeded to have her tortured for several days. Throughout her ordeal, she uttered no sound, "not even a sigh." She was finally slowly executed with hot coals, pincers, irons and the like, a process that lasted from sunrise until shortly after sunset. Throughout, she "lay as one asleep neither moving nor uttering a sound." That she was conscious during the terrible last day is apparent from the statement that "from time to time she opened her eyes and looked about at the assembled crowd."

The old man, Master Johannes (van Dorestad), had not been as perfect in his silence as Katrei. Although he had not spoken since his capture, he had "groaned and cried aloud" under torture. While witnessing Katrei's ordeal, he offered to answer any question put to him if she were to be spared, an offer that was refused. After her death, he began to speak freely. He talked so much, in fact, that at one point Böhm exclaimed: "Only the flames will silence you."

In my previous letter I have already sketched out the beliefs of van Dorestad and their similarity to those promulgated by Margaret of Antwerp. Let me add here only some very interesting new points. Van Dorestad refused all religious categories, saying, "We are not Lutherans or Calvanists or Loyists or Catholics. We are brothers and sisters who recognize each other in the wilderness of the world." He also said that "the Turks and Saracens are more godly than Christians who murder their fellow Christians." He did not deny charges of performing acts of magic, saying only, "Those born in the spirit may act in the spirit." My colleagues in the School of Theology have pointed out to me that images of mediaeval alchemy appear frequently in van Dorestad's testimony.

Van Dorestad gave Albrecht Böhm grounds for condemning him of heresy ten times over. Most annoying to Böhm appeared to have been the doctrines of the non-existence of sin and of universal redemption. As van Dorestad was being burnt to death over a slow fire, Böhm asked him if he still persisted in his heretical claim that all would be saved. "Yes," van Dorestad said, "all will be saved. Even you."

This answer, Böhm was to write later in his own account of the trial, melted his heart, and he shortly returned to ask the dying man to forgive him. "I forgive you with all of my heart," van Dorestad is supposed to have said (but there is no mention of this exchange in the trial record). Böhm then tells us that van Dorestad died "with great courage, calling aloud to eternal God for mercy upon his soul," whereas the trial record states simply that van Dorestad "died, hardened in his heresy." Burnt with van Dorestad were a number of books and other writings seized with him, including works of music.

After the death of Johannes, Böhm released all the remaining prisoners, left the church, and renounced the Catholic faith. In 1564, he wrote his *Rebirth in the Bitter Christ*, prefacing his book with a quote from Thomas Müntzer: "He who does not wish to accept the bitter Christ will eat himself sick of honey."

Böhm writes that when he was presiding over the trial at Wesel, "Satan was speaking in my ears in a voice so sweet I took it to be that of the Holy Spirit." In his own account of the trial, he spares us no detail of the sufferings endured by Katrei and her companions, and the cataloguing of tortures, I must admit, makes difficult reading. His own recollection is so much more horrifying than that of the trial record itself (which is horrifying enough), that I suspect that Böhm, driven by his own guilt, embellished the facts with his own disturbed fantasies. Particularly disturbing to me, in the light of this context, are Böhm's frequent references to Katrei's "pure, youthful beauty."

"After all this had taken place," he writes, "the blood of these innocent lambs burnt so hot upon my heart that I could not stand it, nor find any peace in my soul."

He recounts how he renounced his reputation, his possessions, and willingly accepted "the poverty of the bitter cross of Christ," and began travelling "to and fro preaching true repentance." Peace finally came to him through a vision of Katrei who told him that his sins were forgiven and that she had washed him clean with her blood.

The closing pages of Böhm's book consist of a plea for peace amongst the warring Christian factions, and, indeed, Böhm appears to have dedicated the remainder of his life to the role of a peacemaker, preaching not only a toleration amongst Christians, but a general toleration that extended even to Jews and Turks. It was in the pursuit of his ironic mission that Böhm died when, in 1580, he visited the revolutionary messiah, Jan Willemsen, in an effort to persuade him towards pacifism only to find himself arrested as a follower of Willemsen's, which he had never been, and was taken to Cleves with him to be executed. Ironically enough, Böhm died in exactly the same way van Dorestad had, by being burnt to death over a slow fire.

Theologians, I gather, place Böhm in the context of the Netherlandish spiritualizers and claim that after his conversion he became one of the most libertarian and deeply mystical figures of his age. "The word of God," he writes, "is all dark and incomprehensible even as God himself is. And no one of us may know himself saved and another damned, but such things are known only to God himself. But alas! if we should draw the sword to slay our neighbour, in opposition to the Word of Christ who bade Peter to put up his sword in its sheath."


Paul stopped reading, turned off the light. For a moment everything was totally dark, and then, as his eyes adjusted, he saw that it was just dawn. Soon he would be taking his family to the Netherlands in search of further details of this lost man, Jan van Dorestad. The nether lands, Paul thought. The lands beneath, the low lands, but *all* of it was lying just beneath, waiting to be touched, brought to life again. They would cross measurable miles in an airplane to get there, but the genuine nether lands were in the heart. Slowly, feeling all his years, he climbed the stairs, returning to the bedroom. She still slept peacefully; he heard her measured breathing.

He pulled back the drapes and looked out to watch the silent streets fill with the clear light of the rising sun that was also the risen Christ. He'd felt the worst of the physical pain in his eyes. The heat and light had hurt his eyes long before the flames had reached them. He didn't know how he had stood the pain, but he had. A vain, proud, touchy man, he had felt the burning of his music worse than that of his own flesh. But finally, after all those lost years, it had been redeemed and sung again. He should have closed the motet with the old formula, however, sung on the reciting tone: *"Gloria Patri et Filio et Spiritui Sancto. Sicut erat in principio et nunc et semper, et in saecula saeculorum. Amen."*

*In saecula saeculorum*, Paul thought. It's usually translated "world without end," but it means, literally, "into worlds of worlds." The music continues forever, goes on into worlds of worlds.

He turned away from the window to face the sleeping figure on the bed. "Kathy," he said to wake her.